"Both powerful and sensitive, this is a wonderfully rich and rewarding book."

—Susan Wiggs

"A medieval of stunning intensity. Sprinkled with adventure, fantasy, and heart, *This Is All I Ask* reaches outside the boundaries of romance to embrace every thoughtful reader, every person of feeling."

—Christina Dodd, bestselling author of
A Knight to Remember

"Sizzling passion, a few surprises, and breathtaking romance . . . If you don't read but one book this summer, make this the one. You can be assured of a spectacular experience that you will want to savor time and time again."

—*Rendezvous*

"An exceptional read."—*The Atlanta Journal-Constitutuion*

A Dance Through Time

"One of the best . . . a must read." —*Rendezvous*

"Lynn Kurland's vastly entertaining time travel treats us to a delightful hero and heroine . . . a humorous novel of feisty fun, and adventure."

—*A Little Romance*

"Her heroes are delightful . . . A wonderful read!"
—*Heartland Critiques*

"An irresistibly fast and funny romp across time."
—Stella Cameron, bestselling author of *True Bliss*

If I Had You

Lynn Kurland

BERKLEY BOOKS, NEW YORK

THE BERKLEY PUBLISHING GROUP
Published by the Penguin Group
Penguin Group (USA) Inc.
375 Hudson Street, New York, New York 10014, USA

Penguin Group (Canada), 10 Alcorn Avenue, Toronto, Ontario M4V 3B2, Canada
(a division of Pearson Penguin Canada Inc.)
Penguin Books Ltd., 80 Strand, London WC2R 0RL, England
Penguin Group Ireland, 25 St. Stephen's Green, Dublin 2, Ireland (a division of Penguin Books Ltd.)
Penguin Group (Australia), 250 Camberwell Road, Camberwell, Victoria 3124, Australia
(a division of Pearson Australia Group Pty. Ltd.)
Penguin Books India Pvt. Ltd., 11 Community Centre, Panchsheel Park, New Delhi—110 017, India
Penguin Group (NZ), Cnr. Airborne and Rosedale Roads, Albany, Auckland 1310, New Zealand
(a division of Pearson New Zealand Ltd.)
Penguin Books (South Africa) (Pty.) Ltd., 24 Sturdee Avenue, Rosebank, Johannesburg 2196,
South Africa

Penguin Books Ltd., Registered Offices: 80 Strand, London WC2R 0RL, England

IF I HAD YOU

A Berkley Book / published by arrangement with the author

PRINTING HISTORY
Berkley edition / October 2000

Copyright © 2000 by Lynn Curland.
Cover illustration by Studio Hiriko.

ISBN: 0-425-20868-0

BERKLEY®
Berkley Books are published by The Berkley Publishing Group,
a division of Penguin Group (USA) Inc.,
375 Hudson Street, New York, New York 10014.
BERKLEY is a registered trademark of Penguin Group (USA) Inc.
The "B" design is a trademark belonging to Penguin Group (USA) Inc.

PRINTED IN THE UNITED STATES OF AMERICA

15 14 13 12 11 10 9 8 7 6 5

To Matthew, who is my comfort, my joy, and my forever home.

And to Elizabeth, who says the word home *with all the feeling in her baby heart.*

If I Had You

Prologue

England, 1215
Artane

The young girl stood at the door of the healer's quarters and looked out over the courtyard, eyeing the dirt and flat-laid stone that separated her from the great hall. Judging the distance to be not unmanageable, she released the doorframe she had been clinging to and eased herself down the three steps to the dirt. And then she grasped more firmly the stick she leaned upon and slowly and painfully began to make her way across the courtyard.

Sunlight glinted off her pale golden hair and off the gold embroidery on her heavy velvet gown. Though it was much too hot for such a garment, the child had insisted. It hid the unsightly splint that bound her leg from hip to foot.

She looked up and saw that the hall door was closer than it had been. No smile of relief crossed her strained features; she had yet far to go.

"Ugly Anne of Fenwyck!"

"Thorn in Artane's garden!"

The voices caught her off guard and she stumbled. She

caught herself heavily on her injured leg. Biting back a cry of pain, she put her head down and quickened her pace.

They surrounded her, not close enough to hurt her with anything but their words, though those were surely painful enough. Pages they were, for the most part, with one notable exception. A young man joined in the torment, a freshly-knighted soul who should have known better. They circled her as she hobbled across the smooth stone path leading to the great hall, taunting her mercilessly. The knight folded his arms and laughed as she struggled up the stairs.

"Why the haste, gimp?"

The maid had no time for tears. Safety was but four steps away. She ignored the laughter that followed her and forced herself to continue her climb.

The door opened and the lord of the hall caught her up in his arms and held her close. Her stick clattered down the stairs but she had no stomach for the fetching of it. She clung to her foster father and let his deep voice wash over her soothingly as she was pulled inside the hall. The lord reached out to close the door, paused, then frowned deeply before he pushed the wood to.

Had the girl looked out before the door was closed, she would have seen a dark-haired, gray-eyed lad of ten-and-four standing on the front step of the healer's house, having come to take his own exercise for the day. And she would have seen the rage on his face and the clenching of his hands at his sides; he had witnessed the last of the tortures she'd endured.

And had she been watching, she would have been privy to the events that followed. The lad shrugged off his brother's supporting arm and called to the young knight in angry tones. The knight sauntered over, his mocking snort turning into a hearty laugh when he heard the lad's challenge.

There was no equity in the fight. The boy still recovered from a fever that had kept him abed for half a year. The knight was five years his senior. And the knight had no qualms about humiliating the lord's son each and every chance he had.

It was over before it had begun. The dark-haired lad went facedown in the mud and muck. The last shreds of his strength deserted him, leaving him wallowing helplessly. His brother stepped forward to defend him and earned a pair of broken fingers for his trouble. The knight sneered at them both, then walked away, the older lads in his entourage snickering behind their hands as they followed him, and the younger ones slinking away full of shame and embarrassment for the lad who had no strength to rise to his feet.

The girl witnessed none of this. She was gently deposited inside the chamber she shared with her foster sisters, and had the luxury of shedding her tears of humiliation in private.

Her young champion shed his tears in the mud.

1

England, 1225

The young woman sat atop her mount and looked down the road that separated her from the castle. She had traversed its length many times over the course of her ten-and-nine years and felt reasonably acquainted with its dips and swellings. She was, however, eager to be free of its confines and, as a result, off her horse, so she viewed it with a keen eye. Judging the distance separating her from her goal to be not unmanageable, she took a firmer grip on her reins and urged her horse forward.

Her destination could not be reached quickly enough, to her mind. Behind her rode her matchmaking father, his head likely full of thoughts of the half dozen men he had left behind *him* at Fenwyck, men desperate enough for his wealth to take his daughter in the bargain. Before her lay her foster home, the home of her heart, the home she had left almost half a year earlier only because her father had dragged her bodily from it. She had despaired of ever seeing it again.

But now she was released from her father's hall, if only briefly, and Artane was but a short distance away. That was enough. It would have to be. It might be all she was allowed to have.

"By the saints, I'm eager to be out of this bloody rain," her sire complained as he pulled up alongside her. "How is it, mistress Anne, that I allowed you to enlist me in this fool's errand in this blighted weather? My business with you is at Fenwyck, not here!"

Anne looked at her sire. A weak shaft of autumn sunlight fell down upon his fair hair and glinted on the gold embroidery adorning his heavy surcoat.

"You look well, Father," she said, praying she might distract him and knowing a compliment could not go astray.

"As if it served me to look well, given the circumstances!"

"It was kind of you to bring me to Artane," she said, keeping to her course. "I very much wished to bid Sir Montgomery a final farewell."

"It will be too late for that, I should think," her sire muttered. "He'll be dead by the time we arrive."

But Anne could only assume by the way he began to straighten his clothing and comb his hair with his fingers that he was seeking to present the best appearance possible, even if such an appearance was only to be made at a burying.

She turned her mind back to more important matters, namely staying in the saddle until she could reach the castle. Her leg had not borne the rigors of traveling well. Though but four days' slow travel separated Fenwyck from Artane, she suspected she might have been better served to have walked the distance. She wondered if she would manage to stand once she was released from the tortures of her journey.

Despite that very real concern, Anne felt her heart lift with every jarring clomp of her horse's hooves. The stark stone of the castle rose up against the gray sky, a bulwark of safety and security. By the saints, she was glad of the sight. Though her sire continued to curse a variety of objects and souls, Anne let his words wash over her and continue on their way to more attentive ears. She was far too lost in her memories to pay him any heed.

She remembered the first time she had come to Artane. The castle had been little more than branches marking the place for the outer walls and twigs outlining the inner buildings. The construction had seemed to take but a short time, likely because she'd been passing her days so happily in the company of the family she'd come to foster with. There had been a sister for her, just her age, and brothers too, though she'd paid them little heed at the time. The lord and lady of the yet-to-be-finished keep had treated her as one of their own and for that she had been very grateful.

And then had come the time when she had first noticed the lord's eldest son.

He'd been hard to ignore.

He had announced his presence by putting a worm down her dress.

A particularly jarring misstep by her mount almost made her bite off her tongue. Anne gritted her teeth and forced herself to pay heed to her horse. Perhaps her memories did her more disservice than she cared to admit, especially when they went in that particular direction, for indeed there was no purpose in thinking on the lord's eldest son.

She looked up and realized she was almost in the inner courtyard. She had rarely been more grateful for a sight than she was for the view of the keep before her. She had the captain of Artane's guard to thank for the like, as the summons to Montgomery of Wyeth's deathbed had been the only thing which could have freed her from Fenwyck's suffocating walls.

Anne wended her way carefully through the crowded courtyard. Artane was a busy place with much commerce, many fosterlings, and numerous lordlings continually looking to curry Artane's favor. She supposed it was pleasing to Lord Rhys to find himself in such demand, but she herself would have been happier had the castle been a little less populated. It certainly would have made the negotiation of her way toward the great hall a good deal easier.

She suppressed a grimace when her horse finally came to a halt. The beast was well trained, thankfully, and spent no more energies moving about. Anne stared down at the ground below her mount's hooves and wondered how best to reach it without landing ungracefully on her nose. She took a deep breath, twisted herself around so as to keep hold of her saddle, then slid slowly to the ground.

"Anne!" Geoffrey exclaimed with an accompanying curse. "I told you I would aid you."

"I am well, Father," she said, forcing herself to remain upright instead of giving into the urge to lean her head against her horse's withers and weep. The pain in her leg was blinding, but she supposed she had no one to blame for that but herself. She had been the one to shun the cart her father had wished her to ride in. She had also been the one who had declined the numerous halts her father had tried to force upon her.

"I begin to wonder why I ever sent you here," Geoffrey said curtly. "I vow they bred a stubbornness in you that I surely do not possess. Mayhap you had been better off to remain at Fenwyck."

Anne had no acceptable answer for that, though her first thought was "the saints be praised you sent me away." She was too old at ten-and-nine for such childish responses, but there hadn't been a day she hadn't been grateful for her fostering at Rhys de Piaget's keep. She suspected, however, that she had best keep such observations to herself.

"We may as well go inside," her father said, sounding as if it were the very last thing he wanted to do. "He'll come to fetch us if we tarry here."

"The lady Gwennelyn will be glad to see you," Anne offered.

"Aye, but that objectionable husband of hers will be

there as well. What joy is there in that for me? It only serves to remind me that she chose him over me."

"As you say," Anne said, wincing at the protests her leg was making as she put weight on it.

"Gwen did want me," Geoffrey said. "And sorely indeed."

"Of course, Father," Anne agreed, but her mind was on other things—namely trying not to sprawl face-first into the dirt.

She looked at the great hall. The distance separating them was greater than she would have liked, but not unmanageable. She took a deep breath, then pushed away from her horse. She carefully crossed the flat stones she'd walked over for the greater part of her life and let the familiarity of them soothe her. By the saints, she had missed this place. How had she survived Fenwyck the previous half year? How would she have endured her childhood there? The saints be praised she had never been forced to have the answer to the latter. She suspected that 'twas only recently that she truly understood how fortunate she had been. Gwennelyn of Artane had lavished love and attention on her that she never would have had at her father's hall.

Of course, none of it would have come about had the lady Gwennelyn not had such a long acquaintance with Anne's sire. It had never become more than that, for there had been little love lost between them—despite Geoffrey's boasts to the contrary.

There had been even less affection between Geoffrey and Rhys de Piaget, though Anne knew the two men counted each other as staunch allies. Anne had heard tales enough of their early encounters to know how things were between them, though neither the lord or lady of Artane had disparaged her father. Her father, however, had certainly never been so polite in return. Fortunately, his relationship with Artane had continued to be amicable enough for Anne to have found herself deposited inside Artane's then-unfinished walls, and for that she was grateful.

"Come on then," Geoffrey said, taking her by the arm and starting toward the hall. "We may as well go inside."

Anne felt her leg tighten with each step she took and she came close to begging her sire to stop. But that would have led to a recounting of her childhood follies, Rhys's lack of attentiveness in allowing them to happen and a host of other things she knew she could not bear to listen to. She looked up the steps and cursed silently at the number of people coming and going. Well, she had no choice but to make her way through the press if she wanted to find herself a chair. So she gritted her teeth and counted the steps that remained her until she could enter the great hall and sit in peace.

And then a form blocked her path. She looked up and flinched before she could stop herself.

"Why the haste, lady?" the knight asked. "Surely your journey here has been arduous."

Anne suppressed a grimace. Of all the souls she could have encountered in this crowd, it had to be the lout before her.

"Well, here's a man with a goodly bit of chivalry," Geoffrey said, pushing Anne out of the way in his haste to clasp hands with the man. "I believe I should know you, shouldn't I?"

The knight bowed politely. "Baldwin of Sedgwick, my lord. I am well acquainted with your daughter."

Aye, there was truth in that. His acquaintance with her included naught but torment and she had no stomach for any more of it. Anne knew he wouldn't dare insult her before her sire, but that hardly made being in his presence any less unappealing.

Her sire turned to look at her pointedly and she could just imagine what he wished to say. *Look you here, you stubborn baggage. Yet another man who might be induced to wedding you for enough gold in his purse.* Anne looked past her father to Baldwin. She was unsurprised to see him wearing his customary look of disdain. Perhaps he would be bold enough to mock her within earshot of her father.

But when her sire turned again to face Baldwin, there was naught but a polite smile there to greet him.

"Are you wed?" Geoffrey asked bluntly. "You are heir to Sedgwick, are you not?"

"Nay, my lord," Baldwin said, shaking his head, "my brother is. And he has just recently been blessed with a son, William. So as you can see, I am well removed from any chance of inheriting."

Geoffrey grunted. "Well, there's much to be said for a little hunger for something better. My daughter's not wed, you know. She has her flaws—"

"A weak leg," Baldwin supplied.

"Aye, that," Geoffrey agreed.

Anne could hardly believe they were discussing her so openly, and she had no desire to hear more. The saints only knew how blunt her father had been with all the other men he had invited to his keep for a viewing of her and her dowry. And as far as Baldwin went, she knew he would only become nastier in his discourse regarding her, for she knew with exactness what he thought of her. Hadn't she heard the like for as long as she had known him?

She pushed past her father and walked away, though it cost her much to do so without limping overmuch.

The hall door opened before she reached it and Rhys himself stepped out into the crisp autumn air. Before Anne could say aught, Rhys had descended the handful of steps and pulled her into a sure embrace. The relief she felt was almost enough to make her knees give way beneath her. She was safely home. Perhaps beyond all hope she would manage to stay.

She heard her father's complaining long before he came to stand behind her.

"It was foolish to come," Geoffrey said, "but she insisted. She shouldn't be traveling about with that leg of hers."

Anne gritted her teeth. Rhys never would have continued to remind her of her frailty, nor would he have hourly warned her to have a care. Nay, he would have let her push herself to the limits of her pride, then merely picked her up and put her in a chair. Rhys was the only reason she had spent months learning to walk again after her accident; his approval was the reason she struggled each day past the limits of her endurance.

Or so she told herself. Her true reason for wanting to overcome her limp was something so painful she rarely allowed herself to think on it. The approval she sought was from someone who never looked at her twice when he could help it, who had earned his spurs early then gone off to war. Nay, his was approval she would never have.

A pity his was what mattered the most to her.

Anne felt Rhys give her a gentle squeeze before he pulled away. Anne suspected that she'd never been gladder to see a soul than she was to see the one man who might possibly be able to save her from her sire's ruthless marital schemes.

"A long journey, my girl," Rhys said. "But the sacrifice means much. It grieves me though, to give you the tidings I must."

"See?" Geoffrey said pointedly. "I told her 'twould be for naught." He snorted in disgust. "All this way for but a burying."

Anne felt the noose begin to tighten about her neck.

"And not even for that," Rhys said grimly. "We couldn't wait any longer."

"Then we surely won't be staying long," Geoffrey said. "I have plans for her at home, Rhys."

Anne closed her eyes and prayed with all her strength. Would that some saint would take pity on her and provide her with some means of staying at Artane. Her fondest wish was to be watching her father ride back to Fenwyck from the security of Artane's battlements. To be sure, she had packed an extra gown or two for just such a happening.

"Montgomery was very fond of Anne," Rhys said. "I've no doubt it would have comforted him to see her again."

"I don't think—" Geoffrey began.

"Aye, well, ofttimes you don't," Rhys said shortly. "Go inside, Geoffrey. Gwen will want to see you."

Anne watched her father hesitate, then consider. Apparently the lure of the lady Gwennelyn's beauty was still a powerful one, for he grumbled something else under his breath, but went inside the hall without further argument. Anne took a deep breath, then looked up at her foster father.

"Are you well, my lord?" she asked.

Rhys smiled gravely. "Well enough. Montgomery was a good friend and he will be missed. He would have been pleased you came home, though."

She was relieved to see he was bearing the loss well. Sir Montgomery was the last of Rhys's original guardsmen to have succumbed to death's grasp. He'd lost twins named Fitzgerald not two years earlier and that had been a grievous blow to him. To lose Montgomery as well had to have grieved him deeply.

"I am sorry to come so late," she said.

"You couldn't have known." He tucked her hand under his arm and turned toward the stairs. "Now, what foolishness did your sire press upon you to keep you so long from your true home?"

"Suitors," Anne said with a shudder.

"Poor girl. I can't imagine he presented you with much of a selection."

"He didn't."

"Leave him to me," he said. "I know how to redirect his thoughts."

Aye, to scores of bruises won during a wrestle, she thought, followed closely by *Ah, that you could.* But she said nothing aloud. She was but three steps from the warmth and comfort of the hall and that was task enough for her at present.

Once the last step was gained, the hall entered and the door closed behind her, Anne could only stand and shake. She looked at the distance separating her from the hearth with its cluster of comfortable chairs and stools and thought she just might weep. Her pride was the only thing keeping her from falling to her knees. Rhys didn't move from her side. She knew he would merely wait patiently by her side until she regained her will—and from that she drew strength.

But before she could muster up any more energy or courage, a whirlwind of skirts and dark hair descended into the great hall and ran across the rushes. Anne braced herself for the embrace she knew would likely knock her rather indelicately onto her backside.

"By the saints, *finally*," were the words that accompanied the clasp and kiss. "Anne, I vow I feared your sire would never let you from Fenwyck!"

Anne held on to her foster sister and sighed in relief. "To be sure, 'twas nothing short of a miracle that I am here," she agreed.

Amanda of Artane pulled back and rolled her eyes passionately. "What dotards did he have lined up for you to select from?" she demanded. "None worthy of you, I would imagine."

"And that sort of imagination," Geoffrey said from where he appeared suddenly behind Amanda, "was, and no doubt continues to be, your mother's undoing. You might be well to curb the impulse in yourself."

As Amanda turned to face him, Anne suppressed the urge to duck behind her, lest the inevitable argument come to include her. Amanda was painfully frank and had no sense of her own peril. Anne was torn between telling her to be silent, and urging her on. Perhaps Amanda could convince Geoffrey that Anne was of no mind to wed as yet—especially to any man of his choosing.

"My lord Fenwyck," Amanda said, inclining her head, " 'tis a pleasure to see you, as always."

"You've your mother's beauty," Geoffrey grumbled.

"Unfortunately, you've her loose tongue as well."

"Gifts, the both of them," Amanda conceded. "Now, about these suitors . . ."

"I have chosen several fine men—"

"Likely twice her age—"

"You know nothing of it," Geoffrey returned sharply. "And you, mistress, are well past the age when any sensible man would have taken you and tamed you."

"As if any could—"

Anne waited for blows to ensue, but she was spared the sight by Rhys stepping between his daughter and Anne's father.

"Enough," he said sternly. "Amanda, see Anne to the fire. Fenwyck, come with me. You've had a long journey and I've warm drink in my solar. You can take your ease there."

"He could better take his ease at Fenwyck," Amanda muttered.

Anne bit her lip to stifle her smile as she watched Rhys lead her father off, but she couldn't stop her a small laugh when Amanda turned and scowled at her.

"Oh, Amanda," she said with a gasp, "one day you will truly say too much and find yourself in deep waters indeed."

Amanda flicked away her words as she would have an annoying fly. "Did you but know all the things I think but do not say, you would find me to be restrained indeed. Now, come and sit by the fire. You'll tell me all your sorry tales and I'll weep with you. Then Mother will come, we'll tell them to her again and she'll speak to your sire. You know she can convince him he's a fool."

Anne suspected that such a thing was even beyond the lady Gwennelyn's powers, but a maid could still hope. At the moment, though, she sorely needed warmth and to sit, so she leaned on her companion, hobbled over to the fire and sat with deep gratitude on something that didn't move.

As Amanda had ordered, Anne's tale was first told for

her ears alone, then others joined to hear the horrors she had endured. The murmurs of displeasure, the cries of outrage and the threats directed at her father were sweet to her ears and she found herself smiling for the first time in weeks.

She was with those dearest to her and, for the moment, she was free from undesirable suitors. The morrow would see to itself. After all, she had been released from her father's hall and that was something she had been certain would only happen should she find herself leaving it thanks to an unwanted husband. Yet there she was, sitting comfortably by the fire in the company of those souls dearest to her heart.

It was as sweet as she'd known it would be.

The evening passed most uneventfully, with the family having moved to gather about the fire in Rhys's solar as was oft their custom. Anne went with them and counted that a privilege indeed. Though others fostered at Artane, Anne found herself the only one of those so drawn into Artane's intimate family circle. That was just another of the reasons Baldwin of Sedgwick loathed her, of that she was certain. He was Rhys's kin, yet he remained without the solar door. Baldwin was, however, not the soul that took it the hardest. His sister, Edith, also had come to live at Artane and Anne suspected that such denial into the lord's confidences and pleasures ate at her the most deeply.

But for now Anne need worry neither about Baldwin nor his sister, nor anyone else for that matter. She was home, for the moment, and that was enough. She sat in a chair next to Amanda and looked about her in pleasure.

Her foster parents sat close together, hands clasped, seemingly as content as they had been the first time Anne had seen them together. Their happiness was plain to the eye, as was their pride in their children. And why not? Between those they had laid claim to through adoption and those of their own flesh, they had a brood to be envied.

Anne looked at their eldest girl child, Amanda, and felt her customary flash of envy. But by now, it was a gentle sort of yearning that somehow she herself might have been born with the beauty Amanda possessed. And it wasn't only Amanda's beauty that Anne couldn't help but wish for herself; Amanda had a fire and spirit that Anne knew few women could hope to call their own. But long years of watching her foster sister had shown Anne that such spirit did not come without a price—namely Amanda's rather vigorous disagreements with Rhys about how her life should progress. It was not an easy path Amanda trod, but Anne loved her just the same and was grateful for her friendship.

Miles was next to Amanda not only in terms of age, but where he sat. He looked very much like his sire, which meant he was powerfully handsome indeed. Where they differed, though, was that where Rhys was generally cheery in his outlook, Miles was brooding. Anne, however, found Miles very much to her liking for though his moods might have been gloomy, his wit was fine. She was happy he was home now that he'd won his spurs. She suspected he wouldn't remain long, but she would enjoy him while she could.

Miles's younger sister, Isabelle, was Amanda's likeness in visage, but not in temperament. She was very sweet and as tractable as could be expected from having passed all her time in Amanda's company.

The youngest children were twins, male-children. Fortunately for the rest of Rhys and Gwen's children they had come last, else Anne suspected none of the other children would have been conceived. Their mischief was nothing short of breathtaking and she suspected that they had given Rhys most of the gray in his hair.

But even with the children there, the scene before her was incomplete. Missing were Artane's two eldest sons, but that was nothing unusual. Robin and Nicholas had squired at another keep, then come home briefly after earning their spurs at the tender age of ten-and-nine. Then had come the decision to join the crusade. Nicholas had never truly wished to, but Robin had convinced him 'twas their duty. The time spent had been fruitless as they had arrived just in time to find the defeated knights returning home. Robin's exact reasons for having wished to go were still a mystery. All Anne knew was that she hadn't seen Artane's heir in over five years.

Though that could change at any time. Anne knew Rhys had sent for his son three months earlier. The saints only knew what was keeping him away. Anne had heard the servants speculating that afternoon about the like; the reasons bandied about were everything from him being prisoner in some angry father's dungeon—for having despoiled his daughter, no less—to his having traveled to the Holy Land to collect himself a harem. Anne cared for none of the speculation, so she had quickly retreated from the kitchens.

All she knew was she probably wouldn't have one last sight of Robin before her father sold her to some man likely twice her age who cared nothing for her.

Anne shifted as her leg began to pain her. At least here no one gaped at her as she did the like. At Fenwyck, sharp eyes marked her slight limp, men stared at her, as if they couldn't believe her ugliness was so apparent, her father's wife and her daughter treated her as if she were helpless, far too helpless to do anything but sit in the solar and sew. Coming to Artane was a relief, even though it meant coming back to the site of former disgraces and back to stones that whispered childish taunts as she passed. She could ignore those well enough, especially if she managed to avoid Baldwin of Sedgwick. What was more difficult was not being able to go anywhere inside the walls without knowing that Robin had been there before her. His ghost haunted her, awake or dreaming.

She wanted it to stop.

Or did she?

At present, she wasn't sure what would be worse. But what she did know was that even if she were forced to spend the rest of her days with memories of Robin tormenting her, it would be a more tolerable fate than to find herself packed off with her trunks to some unknown lord.

But that would come later. For now it was enough to be home and to listen to the familiar sounds of the family with whom she had grown to womanhood. Far better to think on what was happening around her than to speculate on what might be happening in France. The saints only knew what mischief Robin was combining at present. It likely entailed some woman or another and the sounds that would result from that were ones Anne had no desire to hear.

She opened her eyes to find her father staring at her. He pursed his lips and shook his head meaningfully. Anne had no trouble understanding the unspoken message.

Do not accustom yourself to this, my girl.

Anne felt Amanda's hand on her arm. Her foster sister leaned over and whispered in her ear.

"I vow we'll see him thwarted before a fortnight is out."

Anne nodded, grateful for the distraction. She knew that not even Amanda could manage such a feat, but at least thinking on it allowed her to turn her thoughts away from Robin.

But she hoped in whatever bed he found himself at present, he loitered with several handfuls of happy, persistent bedbugs who would cause him to cry out with anything but pleasure.

2

Robin of Artane was not a man to take the enjoyment of his pleasure lightly.

So as he wallowed in the aftermath of a well-earned bit of the same, he savored it as fiercely as he had the first time he'd felt the like. He closed his eyes and relished the sweat pouring down his face, his limbs trembling, and his heart beating so hard in his chest, he thought it might burst free. The mighty sense of victory won, of challenge vanquished, of his considerable skill used to its fullest; truly, could there be anything more satisfying? Could he have but fallen asleep at that moment, he might have found a decent rest for a change.

A pity he found himself but standing in the middle of the lists with three layers of mud and dung on his boots, and not abed with a handsome wench.

Unfortunately, such a sorry state seemed to be the extent of his good fortune of late.

But Robin wasn't a man to shun what fortune came his way, so he kept his eyes closed and enjoyed the smell of sweat, leather and dung. Things could have been much worse.

The savoring, though, never lasted as long as he might

have liked, for there was always another conquest to be made and his pride would not let him rest idle. He dragged his sleeve across his eyes to wipe away the sweat, then looked at the cluster of men standing near him. At least he had a clutch of them where they couldn't scamper off across the fields. Such, he supposed, was the happy part of loitering at his brother's keep in France. The less-than-pleasing ingredient in that stew was that since Nicholas found himself comfortably ensconced in one of his own halls, he was reluctant to leave it to seek out the pleasures of warring. Robin had given that his best efforts cajoling, bullying and brandishing his sword—but to no avail. Nicholas had his feet up before the fire inside, several handsome wenches attending his every need and a soft chair beneath his backside. Robin suspected he might have more success prying an entire complement of nunnery inhabitants from their clothes than managing to separate his brother from his comforts.

Damn him anyway.

Robin knew he could have made his own way at any time, but Nicholas was, after all, his family and there was something to be said for having family about.

Even if it came at the price of a good battle or two.

He scowled. There was no sense in complaining, for it would serve him not at all. He turned his mind back to the matter at hand and hoped it might be enough to soothe his foul mood.

"Another," he said hoarsely. Perhaps he had spent too much of the afternoon shouting at the fools in his brother's garrison. His own men had been exhausted much earlier in the day. As a result, there were few men left to stand against him. It did not bode well for a successful evening. "Sir Guy, come face me and let us see if you are as womanly as your fallen comrade."

Sir Guy drew his sword and came at Robin with a curse. His skill was great, but Robin kept him at bay easily. Years of fighting, either for his king or for himself, had honed his instincts until he likely could have fought with his eyes closed and his mind numb from drink. He countered each of Guy's strokes without thinking, watching his opponent closely, waiting for the first show of weakness or hesitancy. He waited longer with Guy than he had with Guy's predecessor, but the moment came eventually and Robin took full advantage of it, knocking Guy's sword from his hand and putting the point of his own sword over Guy's heart.

"Peace," Guy said heavily.

Robin stepped back. "Another."

And so it went until there was no one left for Robin to fight. He looked about him and swore in frustration. It looked as if he might be finished for the day. But at least he had aught to hope for on the morrow. Despite his chafing at his confinement, he did enjoy the luxury of constant training more than the uncertain sport of war. Battles were never as consistent as he would have liked. There was too much time spent traveling from place to place, waiting for the sieges to flush the quarry out, listening to his men celebrate afterwards and not having the stomach to celebrate with them.

Robin resheathed his sword and turned his thoughts toward supper. Perhaps a quick meal would give at least one or two garrison knights time to recover. He might have a bit more sport yet before he sought his bed—alone, as seemed to be his lot.

It was truly a pathetic state of affairs.

He strode back to his brother's hall. He realized he'd flattened his squire only when he stepped on him by mistake.

"Mindless babe," Robin said, hauling the lad of ten-and-six to his feet. "Watch where you're going."

"Aye, my lord." His young cousin, Jason of Ayre, backed up a pace and bowed hastily. "Forgive me, my lord. Lord Nicholas waits within with a message from Artane. I believe 'tis from your mother and the tidings are evil—"

"Evil?" Robin echoed. He pushed Jason out of the way,

unwilling to wait for his squire to divulge more. He ran
to the hall, leaving Jason to follow or not, as he would.
His heart tightened within his chest painfully. The saints
only knew what sort of disaster had befallen his family.
He never should have stayed away so long. There was no
good reason for him to have remained in France.

Actually, there were two good reasons for the like, but
those were things he never thought on if he could avoid
it.

Robin slammed the hall door behind him and looked
for his brother. Nicholas stood near the fire with a piece
of parchment in his hands. Robin strode over to his fair-
haired sibling and took the letter away.

"I wasn't finished," Nicholas protested.

"You are now," Robin muttered.

He read the epistle only far enough to learn that Montgomery was grievously ill before Nicholas snatched it
back from his hands. Robin didn't fight his brother. Whatever else was to be read there was likely concerning the
family and those were tidings Robin had no stomach for
at present.

It was guilt, he knew, that pricked at him so fiercely so
as to keep him from reading about home. After all, it
would have behooved him to have made the occasional
appearance at Artane so that the villagers might recognize
him if something were to happen to his sire. Even worse
was that his father had been sending for him repeatedly
over the past few months. He should have gone back before now.

But return he hadn't and that left him with little heart
for tales of home. He preferred to let Nicholas pass on
what news he deemed important.

He had heard, through Nicholas's reading of their
mother's previous letters, that Montgomery had been
wounded. Robin had assumed the men would recover, but
apparently he'd been mistaken. Though his parents would
likely survive the loss well enough on their own, perhaps

it was time he returned home for a small visit. He would pass a bit of time with his father and see how his family's keep had withstood the wear of the past few years. He could also see to his own holdings. Aye, there were several things he could do whilst he tarried for a few days in England. Perhaps the sooner he went, the sooner he could leave.

"We should go," Robin said with a sigh. "And likely within the fortnight."

Nicholas didn't look up from his reading.

"Oh, make haste with the bloody thing, would you?" Robin demanded.

Nicholas ignored him.

Robin clasped his hands behind his back and stood with his backside to the fire. At least he might be warm for a moment or two whilst he contemplated the many mysteries of life and how he seemed to be caught up in a goodly portion of them.

There was, for instance, the mystery of his brother. Robin looked at his sibling and scowled. How sweet it must be to have so little weighing upon one's mind. Robin watched as his brother stretched his legs out and sprawled in his chair, looking as if he hadn't a care in the world. And just what cares could he possibly have? He wasn't the eldest son.

Nor did Nicholas's parentage seem to trouble him. If he fretted over the fact that his father was heaven-knew-who and his mother a servant girl, he never showed it. And why should he? He was the beloved adopted second son of one of the most powerful lords in England. He had his own keep in France and other holdings in England that had made him a very rich man indeed. Women panted after him by the score and Nicholas somehow managed to avoid leaving any bastards behind him. Robin couldn't understand it and couldn't help but be irritated by it.

Robin's worries were so many, he couldn't bring them all to mind in a single sitting. Even though he had been adopted by Rhys de Piaget just as Nicholas had been, he was heir to Artane and all that came with it. It was no secret that his sire was actually the late baron of Ayre. After Ayre's death, Robin's mother had married the captain of her guard, Rhys of Artane. For Robin there had been no question whether or not he would accept Rhys as his sire. From the time he could remember, he had wanted to belong to Rhys de Piaget in truth. Even so, with that claiming had come heavy responsibilities, responsibilities Robin hadn't shunned.

He was constantly being watched by his men, other nobles, whatever royalty happened to be about—all waiting for his first misstep, his first sign of weakness, his first failure in the lists. It had always been that way and would likely continue to be that way far into the future. Not only did his own honor rest upon his performance, his father's honor rested there too.

It was a burden Nicholas felt not at all. If Nicholas didn't show well in a tournament, which rarely happened, he shrugged it off and contented himself with a handsome wench. Robin could never be so casual about it. Every confrontation, every encounter meant the difference between success and shame. He couldn't fail. He wouldn't fail. He would die before he was laughed at again.

"Now," Nicholas drawled, "this is interesting."

"What?" Robin asked, wondering just what his empty-headed sibling might find to be noteworthy.

"Mother sent word to Fenwyck."

Robin frowned. "Fenwyck? Why? It isn't as if Fenwyck had any love for Montgomery."

"I doubt it was Fenwyck himself she was giving the tidings to."

"Who else there could possibly care?" In truth, Robin as well couldn't have possibly cared, but Nicholas seemed determined to pursue this course to its end.

"Why," Nicholas said, looking up at Robin and blinking, "Anne, of course."

"Anne? What about Anne?"

Nicholas continued to blink owlishly, as if he just couldn't muster up the wits to speak with any intelligence at all. "I'm sure Mother sent word to Anne at Fenwyck."

Robin felt his belly begin to clench of its own accord. Hunger, obviously. He should have eaten something before he began to listen to his brother's foolishness.

Anne at Fenwyck? She must have returned for her yearly fortnight. Odd, though, that she would have left if Montgomery had been failing. She was fond of the old man.

"Didn't I tell you?"

"Didn't you tell me what?" Robin asked. Odder still that his mother would have had to send word that Montgomery was failing. Anne would have been returning shortly just the same.

"Anne's been at Fenwyck since before spring."

Robin looked at Nicholas. It was all he could do to manage to smother his look of surprise. "Spring?"

"Didn't I tell you?"

It was an enormous effort to keep breathing as if the tidings were fair to putting him to sleep.

"Spring?" he repeated, cursing himself weakly for being able to say nothing else.

Nicholas nodded, then turned back to his letter. "Her father is seeking a husband for her. He's likely been showing her about like a mare at market, knowing him. Mother says that even if Anne is released to bid Montgomery a final *adieu*, she likely won't be allowed to stay long. Fenwyck fair forced her from Artane with a sword at her back before—"

Spring? Then Anne had been captive at Fenwyck for nigh onto half a year. 'Twas nothing short of a miracle that she hadn't been wed already.

And then another thought came at him with the force of a broadside.

Anne had been at Fenwyck for half a year and Nicholas had said nothing.

Robin tore the parchment from his brother's hands, flung it aside, then hauled the dolt up and shook him.

"When did you plan to tell me?" he shouted.

"Tell you what?" Nicholas asked calmly.

"I thought she was at home, you fool!"

"I suppose," Nicholas said slowly, "that I didn't think it mattered to you."

Robin suppressed the urge to slap himself. By the saints, what was he doing? The last thing he needed was to provide his lackwit brother with fodder for his romantic notions! He forced himself to unclench the fistfuls of his brother's tunic he'd grasped, then took great care to smooth the fabric back into something resembling the flat business it had been before it had been assaulted. Robin stepped back and took a deep breath.

"It doesn't," he said. "It doesn't matter at all."

"Doesn't it?" Nicholas asked.

"It doesn't matter to me where she is," Robin continued. "It merely angers me that you haven't told me all that Mother put in her letters."

There, that sounded more reasonable.

"Well," Nicholas said with a slight smile, "I suppose there is aught else I have neglected to tell you."

Robin braced himself for the worst. "Aye?"

"I haven't been as detailed as Mother has been in her demands to have us come home."

"No doubt," Robin muttered.

"She's threatened to come to France herself and prod you from the lists with her blade."

Robin shuddered at the thought. His mother could heft a blade, 'twas true, and at times she managed to get it pointing in the right direction, but inevitably she came close to dismembering anyone she so hoisted a blade against. But Robin knew his mother very well, and knew her threats were not idle. Perhaps 'twas time he returned home, lest he force her hand.

Indeed, there was no sense in not making every effort

to return to England as quickly as possible and see how things progressed at Artane. Aye, no sense in not doing that as quickly as possible. Who knew what sorts of adventures he might stop his mother from having? His sire would surely thank him for it. 'Twas yet another reason to leave with all haste.

Nicholas started to sit back down, but Robin snagged him by the tunic before he managed it.

"Pack your gear. We'll leave immediately."

"Why the hurry?"

"Mother will have need of us."

The corner of Nicholas's mouth began to twitch. "Thinking to rescue Anne from her unsavoury suitors, brother?"

"Father will likely have need of us as well," Robin continued, ignoring his brother's grin. "And I don't like to dawdle whilst I travel."

"We'll likely return home too late to see her, you know," Nicholas said. "Unless we make great haste. And look you what great haste you seem determined to make."

Robin would have thrown his brother to the rushes and stomped that bloody smirk from his face, but that would have only added fuel to Nicholas's pitiful blaze. "Hurry," Robin commanded, then he strode across the great hall, ignoring what he was certain was naught but more witless babbling.

Robin took hold of his squire on his way through the doorway.

"Bid the men ready themselves. We leave within the hour."

"Aye, my lord," Jason said, nodding with wide eyes. "As you will."

Robin went back to the lists. Jason would see to their gear and Robin suspected he might be better served to stay out of the way. He began to run. He liked the way his body burned as he loped along the outer bailey wall. The blood thundering in his ears pleased him as well, as it almost succeeded in drowning out all his troubling thoughts. The saints only knew he would have little luck finding any wench to aid him in the task; his temper seemed to drive them all into Nicholas's arms.

He ran until he couldn't catch his breath. Then he stopped and stood hunched over with his hands on his thighs, and sucked in great gulps of air. He didn't want to go home, but he knew he had to. His mother would have need of him, his father too. Montgomery had been dear to them both. He hadn't managed to get himself home to see anyone else buried in the past five years; perhaps it was time he made the effort now.

Besides, the sooner he arrived, the sooner he would be of service to them both. A ship could be convinced to deposit him and his brother as far north as possible. That would save them the time of trying to ride north from Dover. Aye, that was sensible enough. If he decided to stay longer in England, his gear could be sent for.

But he suspected he would only stay a fortnight or two, long enough to assure himself all was well, then hie himself off to court. Perhaps he would be exceptionally fortunate and avoid having to clap eyes on Baldwin of Sedgwick, who was no doubt still strutting about Artane with the same arrogance that had irritated Robin when Robin had been but a lad of ten-and-four. Aye, Baldwin would likely be wearing the same smile Robin had seen him wear when he'd reached out and broken two of Nicholas's fingers. Robin could remember the smile surprisingly well, given the fact that he'd seen it through the mud dripping down his face and into his eyes.

He consciously unclenched his fists, trying to ignore the fact that he'd tightened them in the first place. He could hardly help himself. He didn't think on that afternoon when he could help it, but at times it caught him unawares.

Unfortunately, his feud with Baldwin of Sedgwick had lasted much longer than a single afternoon, and he suspected that was why it pricked at him so. Baldwin had arrived at his father's gates almost at the very moment those gates had been finished. Baldwin's uncle had sent him along to foster, though at the time Robin couldn't understand why he'd bothered, as Baldwin had been nigh onto winning his spurs. But come he had, and he'd been as unhappy to arrive as Robin had been to see him at the gates.

There had been instant animosity between the two of them and in his more logical moments, Robin had realized that Baldwin hated him for his birthright. Robin would be, after all, Baldwin's liege-lord in time. Rhys had no use for Sedgwick, or its inhabitants, so their cousins had little need to worry about losing their beds at the moment. Robin had never seen the place, but he'd heard tales enough of its wretched condition to have wished to avoid it as well.

But even had he possessed the glibness to say as much, he suspected Baldwin wouldn't have heard it. The miserable brute had taken every opportunity to goad and annoy Robin until Robin had been relieved to escape his home and go off to squire with another lord. He'd gone off, glad to be free of torment and determined to acquire skill with the sword that would leave Baldwin stumbling in surprise the next time they met.

Robin straightened and sighed deeply. He'd trained himself well, he'd become a man and now perhaps 'twas time he put his childish memories to rest. Baldwin would not best him. He could avenge himself easily of any slight. Perhaps he would go home, walk the paths of his youth, and do his damndest not to think on memories that still afflicted him. He could avoid Baldwin easily enough.

And perhaps he could also avoid that other soul that continually haunted the edges of his thoughts.

He didn't want to think on her. He didn't want to see her in his mind's eye. And he surely didn't want his pulse to quicken at the thought of being in the same keep with her.

Anne.

By the saints, he'd never expected that her father would snatch her away so unexpectedly.

Though why it should have come as a surprise, he didn't know. She was ten-and-nine, surely old enough to have been wed a time or two already. He should have done something about that, but he hadn't. He couldn't have—for more reasons than he cared to admit.

He began to run again, forcing his legs to pump hard against the dirt. He shoved away his thoughts, praying the exercise would tire him enough to escape them until the business of travel could consume him. Home he would have to go, but the less he thought about it ahead of time, the easier it would be for him.

Or so he hoped.

3

Anne made her way carefully down Artane's passageway, doing her best to avoid her father. She hadn't seen him about that morning and for that she was grateful. Perhaps he would become distracted by other issues, forget about her and leave. Perhaps Rhys would persuade him that he would do better to spend his energies training his step-daughter's husband in how to look after Fenwyck's holdings than seeking an already-trained lord for Anne to wed. Perhaps a handsome nobleman would stumble through Artane's gates, look on her and profess undying love.

Perhaps she would grow a new leg and enough beauty to hold such a man.

She sighed and paused before Rhys's solar. With any luck Artane's lord was within and hoping for a bit of conversation. There wasn't a queue of souls waiting without to see him, so perhaps she might have her desire. There was much she could discuss with him. 'Twas possible he might have knowledge of a place in which she could hide herself until her sire forgot he had a daughter for sale.

But she hadn't put her hand up to knock before Rhys's

angry words cut through the wood as if it hadn't been
there.

"Why?" Rhys demanded. "Why do you persist in this,
Geoffrey?"

"Persist in what?" Geoffrey answered. "Finally finding
a husband for her?"

"Aye," Rhys said. "Her future is here!"

"With whom?" Geoffrey asked shortly. "Robin?"

"Aye, Robin—"

"Then where is he?" Geoffrey demanded. "Where was
he when she was twelve and of a marriageable age?
Where has he been the past seven years when he could
have made her his bride? Where is he today?"

"He is off—"

"Aye, off," Geoffrey snarled. "Off doing the saints only
know what whilst my daughter grows older by the hour."

"She belongs here," Rhys insisted.

"As what? Dowager aunt to Robin's score of children
sired on anyone but her? I will not give her to a second
son, Rhys, nor a third or fourth. The heir she will have,
and 'tis obvious yours is uninterested!"

"If you would but give the matter more time—"

"She must marry, Rhys, and the duty falls to me to find
someone who will have her."

"Many would take her, and gladly," Rhys said angrily.
"If you could just see past—"

"See past what? A crippled girl with little beauty and
a youth that fades with each passing day—"

Geoffrey's words were abruptly silenced. Anne suspected Rhys had just planted his fist in her father's mouth,
for there was a bit of garbled noise, then a great amount
of cursing from both parties. Furnishings made great
sounds of protest as they were apparently trodden asunder.
Anne knew that such unruly behavior would bring along
the lady of the house, and Anne could not bear to see
Gwen at present.

She turned and fled back down the passageway as
quickly as she could manage. What she wanted to do was

walk along the seashore until her hurt receded. Unfortunately such a journey was far beyond her capabilities after the rigors of travel, so she settled for the battlements. The climb there would be taxing enough.

No guard stopped her as she slowly mounted the steps, nor did anyone deny her access to the walls. She crept along the parapet, clinging to the stone. Her balance was less than perfect on the ground; being that far above the earth was greatly unnerving. But it was much less unnerving than being below and listening to others discuss her, so she suffered the unease.

She stopped at a likely spot and turned her face toward the sea. The wind blew her hair back over her shoulders and whipped itself against her cheeks. It was only then that she realized her face was wet. She hadn't meant to weep. Indeed, there was little to weep over. She knew her father hadn't meant to be cruel. She suspected that his concern for her warred with his desire to see his holdings pass to a suitable son-in-law. But it was never pleasant to have her flaws noted and considered so openly.

What hurt the most was knowing that he likely spoke the truth about Robin. She knew he did not love her, despite what his father might have wanted him to do. Fool that she was, she couldn't help but wish things were different. Perhaps if she had been beautiful. Perhaps if she had two straight, serviceable legs. Perhaps if she had looked more like Amanda than she did herself. The only thing she could say in her favor was that she didn't possess the gap in her front teeth that her father sported. But that was small comfort when faced with the truth of things.

Robin could have wed her years ago if he'd wanted to.

But he hadn't.

And that left her with a path before her that grew more intolerable by the footstep.

She drew her sleeve across her eyes and stared out over the water. The wind blew fiercely, but the chill was a welcome one, for it brought some semblance of calmness to her soul. Perhaps her sire had no choice but to look beyond Artane. 'Twas a certainty he had to find someone to manage his holdings. The man to whom his wife's daughter was wed could not manage his gear, much less any lands. She was the only hope of holding Fenwyck and perhaps her sire was only doing what he must.

Ah, but the foolish dreams of her heart. It was the letting go of those that pained her the most. Anne stared out over the sea, watching it wash in against the shore ceaselessly. She wondered if her heart's desire watched the same thing and what the thoughts were that consumed him. Was it possible he spared her even a brief thought now and then?

Nay, she decided grimly, it was not. His thoughts were of war, bloodshed and bedding as many women as possible. She'd heard more tales than she could stomach of the swaths he cut through not only England but Normandy and the whole of France. He likely spared her no thought unless it was one of relief that he must needs not endure her presence.

"The dreams of my heart," she whispered, "are too foolish even for me—"

"Anne!"

That shout almost sent her toppling. The curses that followed left her with no doubt that her father had found her.

"What do you here?" Geoffrey demanded. "And talking to yourself as if you were mad? Bloody hell, girl, think! Would you have that gossip preceding you to every hall in the north?"

"But—"

"Come below," Geoffrey said curtly, but his hand on her arm was gentle. "We've aught to discuss."

Anne waited until she'd reached the upper passageway before she put the only ruse into play she could.

"I feel faint," she lied. "Might I hie myself to Amanda and Isabelle's bedchamber for a time, Father? I will join you once I've recovered."

Her father looked momentarily confused, as if she had

upset his finely laid plans. Anne took advantage of it and put her hand to her forehead, hoping to affect a look of true suffering.

"Very well," Geoffrey said reluctantly. "We'll talk later." He walked her down the passageway, then deposited her in front of the bedchamber. "Come to me when you've recovered."

And that will require at least a fortnight, Anne thought to herself as she sought refuge behind a closed door. She put her ear to the wood and listened to her father's footsteps recede. Once she knew she was safely sequestered, at least for the moment, she rested her forehead against the door and sighed deeply.

Perhaps it was time she had a good look at her plight and resigned herself to the truth of it. The desires of her heart made little difference when she could no longer deny that Robin wasn't going to thunder up on his black steed and rescue her from a clutch of greedy suitors. Her choices seemed to be either to wed where her father willed it, or find a way to remain at Artane as something other than a daughter-in-law.

She pushed away from the door with a deep sigh and hobbled over to the bed. She sat, then lay back and stared up at the canopy. She would have to wed. There was no other choice. Her father's lands were too many and her dowry too rich a prize for her to escape her fate. The only thing she might possibly control was the timing of her journey to her matrimonial prison. Her father had had her at his mercy for nigh onto half a year with no success in finding her a mate, for she had done her best to discourage the lot of them. Perhaps she could barter with her sire for a remaining half year at Artane if in turn she gave him her most cooperative self when she returned to Fenwyck.

She suspected her sire could care less about her willingness to behave, or lack thereof.

But it was worth a try. And until she thought of a way to persuade him to her way of thinking, she would avoid him.

And she would pray for a miracle.

•   •   •

It was well past sunset before she forced herself to leave the chamber. She shunned supper and company below, and made her way to the lady of Artane's solar. She had passed innumerable hours there and the memories were warm and pleasant ones. Surely a new idea or two would occur to her there. Her sire likely wouldn't look for her there either and that added reward was too powerful a lure to resist. And with any luck, she would find that chamber empty as well. Unfortunately, Gwen had a number of ladies and foster daughters who lingered there, so the chances of it were slim.

Gwen's ladies Anne could have borne, as well any number of other maids, but she had to admit as she made her way upstairs that she would be less than pleased to see Edith of Sedgwick. It wasn't that Edith was particularly unpleasant. It was that Anne felt sure Edith envied her her place in Artane's family. As Anne wasn't certain how much longer she would enjoy that place, she couldn't bear the thought of having it frowned upon.

The passageway and stairwell were dark as Anne passed through them, but that was not so unusual. The keep was a drafty place at times with the winds from the sea assaulting the walls continually. Torches often went out. Anne made her way down the passageway from memory and stopped before the solar door. She frowned. It was usually kept closed yet it stood ajar.

And then she heard a faint jingling sound.

The hair on the back of her neck stood up and she stifled the urge to bolt. She quickly entered the solar. It was empty, but somehow that didn't please her as much as she'd thought it would. Then again, perhaps quiet was just what she needed. She turned to shut the door.

Then she paused, her hand on the latch. Best to leave it open, perhaps, while she brought the fire back to life. Then she would make certain the chamber and passageway were empty.

She took a deep breath and let it out slowly. She was home. No harm would come to her. She walked to the hearth where embers still burned weakly. Kneeling on the floor, she leaned over and blew, trying to bring the fire back to life. She sat back after a moment or two, looking about for a bit of wood or peat to toss on the flicker of fire she'd coaxed out.

The door slammed shut. Anne heaved herself to her feet, then spun around, wishing frantically she had a sword and the skill to use it. What had she been thinking to come here alone?

"Who's there?" she called, cursing the tremble in her voice.

No one answered. She let out her breath slowly. As if she should have expected an answer.

Then reason returned to her. The torches had been out, hadn't they? 'Twas naught but the breeze. Doors closing with vigor was a common thing in the keep.

She brushed her hands on her dress. Coming here had been a mistake. What she needed was to be abed, not wandering about the keep like a restless spirit. She took her courage in hand and crossed the chamber with as sedate a pace as she could manage. She left the solar and started down the passageway.

And she could have sworn she heard the same tinkling sound.

Perhaps 'twas nothing, but her imagination more than made up for it. She gasped, pulled up her skirts and limped for the stairway as quickly as she could. Voices coming up from below were like a light beckoning at the end of a tunnel. Anne stumbled down the stairs, wincing each time she had to put her weight on her leg. How she hated autumn with its chill!

She tripped over the last step and would have gone sprawling had strong arms not been there to catch her fall. Rhys set her back on her feet, then frowned as he saw her face.

"Anne," he said, "what ails you, daughter?"

"Nothing," she said weakly. "I think I'm overtired."

Rhys hesitated, then nodded and bent to kiss her forehead. "Off with you then, girl. A good night's sleep will serve you well."

She nodded and limped down the corridor to the chamber she had always shared with Amanda and Isabelle. She closed the door behind her, leaned back against it and sighed. What she wanted to do was lay abed for the next fortnight. Unfortunately, she knew that would only make matters worse. As unappealing a task as it seemed, she would have to rise each day. If she didn't, her leg would tighten and take her days to have it be useful again. She walked across the chamber and sat down carefully on the bed.

And all her troubles had come about because she, at the tender age of nine, had been dared to ride an unbroken stallion and she'd done it, just to silence Baldwin who had called her uncomely. The memory of being flung down in the lists was still very fresh in her mind. She could still see the horse stumbling and stepping on her leg, shattering the bone in her thigh. Ah, the agony of not being able to faint . . .

"Anne?"

The door opening startled her. Anne turned around to look at Amanda. "Aye?"

"Merciful saints, what befell you?"

"Nothing," Anne said. "I'm merely weary."

Amanda came and sat next to her. " 'Twas a hard day for you, Anne. Come, let me put you to bed."

Anne didn't protest. She allowed Amanda to help her into bed and tuck the blankets up to her chin as if she'd been a small child.

"I'm glad you're home," Amanda said with feeling. "These have been the longest months of my life."

Anne smiled dryly. "I'm sure they haven't been. The race for your hand is on, Amanda. Even the men my father has brought to inspect me can do nothing but babble about your beauty."

"Then they are fools," Amanda said. "They view me as naught but a necessary evil they must endure simply to have my dowry. Guy of York was here a month ago and I vow I thought him ready to check my teeth and ask Father how much feed I would require each day."

Anne laughed. "He did not."

"Aye, he did. I called him a horse's arse and bid him look for a mare in some other stable. They tell me they do not care about the lands and gold, but I can see them counting in their heads even as they cut my meat for me at the board. I'll not be considered a mere bargaining piece."

"At least you have the luxury of thinking thusly," Anne said with a sigh. "I daresay even the vastness of my father's holdings doesn't compensate for my ugliness—"

"Cease," Amanda exclaimed. "Anne, the last time you peeped into a polished mirror was when you were but ten-and-three. That was six years ago, sister. No one is fetching at ten-and-three."

"Oh, Amanda, you know that isn't true. You were as beautiful then as you are now. And look at Isabelle. The garrison knights can hardly breathe when she walks by them."

Amanda looked at her helplessly. "Anne . . ."

Anne blinked back tears of humiliation. "I beg you not to speak of this more."

"Foolishness," Amanda said, but her tone was gentle. "Anne, I grew up envying your pale hair and green eyes, thinking you the most lovely creature I ever saw. Time has only increased your fairness. Your features are nothing short of angelic, your humor is ever sweet and your goodness shines from you like a beacon. And if you'll know the reason men have not offered for you in the past, I'll tell you. Father has ever demanded the right of choosing your husband and your sire has always refused to grant it to him. Still they argue over this—"

"I am ten-and-nine," Anne exclaimed. "Old enough to be wed years already!"

Amanda leaned over and kissed Anne's cheek. "Sleep, sister, and think no more on it. Father had new stone laid in the garden this summer and 'tis smooth and fine. We'll walk there tomorrow."

Anne nodded as Amanda rose. Perhaps she had it aright and it was best not to think more on such matters. What sense was there in it? She had learned much at Gwen's hand and had at least a few bits of knowledge and skill to offer a husband. She still had not mastered her temper, but perhaps she would be lucky enough to find a man who would not provoke her and would not expect a woman who was beautiful.

It was unfortunate that the only man she had ever wanted did not fit that description at all.

She sighed and rolled over, tired of chewing on her troubling thoughts. Movement didn't help. Amanda and Isabelle making ready for bed didn't distract her either. There was something nagging at her and she could not seem to discover it nor ignore it.

When it came to her, her heart pounded in her chest so loudly and so rapidly, she was sure Amanda would wake up and bid her be silent. All hope of sleep fled. She was lucky to be alive. Bloody lucky. She was not so big a fool that she did not realize that a door would only slam shut when wind from an open window forced it shut.

There had been no open window in the solar that evening.

4

Edith of Sedgwick stood in the northeast tower chamber
at Artane and watched deepening twilight through the arrow loop. It took little time for the darkness to envelope
the sky over the sea, so she waited patiently until the
gloom had descended truly. Waiting was never a burden
for her, for patience, she had to admit modestly to herself,
was her second greatest virtue. Indeed, could anyone
doubt it, should they but examine her circumstances?
Hadn't patience been what had won her a place at all at
Rhys de Piaget's hall? She'd planted the seed in her father's mind that she really should be going north with her
brother. It had taken years until the seed had borne fruit,
but she had enjoyed the fruits of her waiting.

Of course, she hadn't been welcomed with particularly
open arms, for she was, after all, of Sedgwick and there
was no love lost between Artane and her kin. But even
that would change, of that she was certain. Weren't her
present straits a perfect example of the lengths she was
willing to go to in order to have her desire? Instead of
the comfort of Artane's solar, she conducted her business
in a drafty guard tower.

Patiently.

But did a body but know the truth, he would have to agree that while patience was something she possessed in abundance, her greatest virtue was her ability to plan an intrigue. Unfortunately, her plots of late stood to be ruined by the silly child standing before her. Edith looked at her and struggled to smother her annoyance. She was greatly tempted to slap the girl—and several times at that. Her fear, however, was that by so doing, she might dislodge whatever wits remained the wench. And Maude of Canfield had few enough as it was. Edith took a deep breath to regain her composure.

"Surely," she said calmly, "I heard you awrong. You did what?"

"I slammed the solar door. Scared the piss from her." She laughed gleefully. Her bracelet flashed in the candlelight as she flapped her hands animatedly. "She bolted like a rabbit. Or as well as a lame rabbit might manage."

Edith looked at the girl and wondered mightily if she might not have made a fatal mistake in choosing this one. But what other choice could she have made? Maude was perfect for her needs—assuming she could be controlled. Edith folded her hands sedately in front of her. It was better that way; at least she wouldn't be tempted to use them.

"In the future," Edith said, "you will restrict yourself to taking on the tasks I give you."

The mercurial change in Maude's mood was almost unsettling to watch.

"You'll tell me nothing," she snapped. "I've a stake in this as well."

"We've discussed this, Maude."

"And I'll not be told what to do by you! I am a baron's daughter!"

"Aye, the youngest of a large brood sired by a very minor and unimportant lord," Edith said.

"More important than yours," Maude returned hotly. "Sedgwick is a cesspit and I vow I wonder how you managed to crawl . . . ah, crawl from . . ."

Edith watched as Maude realized that she had said too much. Apparently Maude's pride warred with her fear; Edith watched the emotions cross her face in rapid succession. It was fascinating, truly, to see the progression. And then Maude seemed to gather her courage about her.

"I don't fear you," she blurted out.

Edith inclined her head. "Why would you?"

Maude looked passing unsure of herself. "Well, I don't."

"Of course not. But in the future, you will leave off with your own plans. The lady Anne is not the prey."

"I don't like her," Maude said with a scowl.

Edith smiled. "She hasn't harmed you—"

"And you weren't abed with him when he called out her name instead of mine!" Maude exclaimed.

The tower chamber door slammed shut and Edith looked to see her brother standing there. Baldwin glared at Maude.

"Begone, you silly twit. Hide yourself in the kitchens until you're needed."

Edith pursed her lips as Maude fled, then she looked on her brother with disfavor. "She's useful."

"She's addle-pated. Whence did you dredge her up?" he asked, drawing up a chair, producing his dagger and beginning to pick his teeth with it.

Edith allowed herself a moment of silent disgust over her brother's lack of manners, then gave him the shortest answer she could think of.

"A chance meeting in a solar full of ladies," she said. "Where else?"

"I thought as much," Baldwin said with a grunt.

Actually, nothing could have been further from the truth. Edith had learned various useful skills during her childhood and the most useful had been the ferreting out of information from whatever seedy source was handy. She smiled grimly to herself. At least her torturous youth at Sedgwick had not been completely wasted. It had taken Edith only a handful of months to unearth various items of interest that one soul in particular would have wished to remain buried.

And once she'd obtained a name or two, she'd taken up her journey south on the pretext of going on a pilgrimage. Her first halt at Berkhamshire had proved fruitless, but her destination of Canfield had yielded more than she could have hoped for. Maude had been spurned, seething and distinctly out of favor with her formerly adoring sire who could not understand her repeated refusal to wed with anyone of his choosing. Edith knew who Maude pined for, knew the last time they had lain together and marveled greatly at the girl's tenacity and patience.

It had reminded her, she thought a bit wistfully, of her own.

A shorn head, a covering of cloth for the remaining blond hair and Maude had become a servant looking desperately for a bit of charity. The few questions asked had been answered promptly and accepted for truth. For Edith, unlike her older brother, had found favor in Lord Artane's eyes from the moment she'd been deposited inside his gates like unwanted refuse. She knew very well how the game was played and she played it well. The favors she asked were few, and those were usually granted graciously.

But that graciousness never made up for what she was denied.

"Mindless twit," Baldwin groused. "She'll befoul the plans, sister. Mark my words."

Edith was much more concerned about Baldwin than she was Maude. Maude might have been stupid, but she was, after all, merely a woman. Baldwin was just as witless, but he possessed a cruelty she had seen only in men. Had she not been convinced she could control him as well, she might have feared him.

"Maude believes herself fated to have him, Baldwin," she said patiently. "A woman will do much for that kind of love."

"Poor sister," Baldwin sneered. "Jealous of her? Or are

you jealous of Anne? Will you have Robin for yourself?"

Edith only remained silent. There was no sense in allowing him to bait her. Her brother was ever ready to fight; she had better ways to spend her energy. Besides, he was a fool if he thought she concerned herself with either Maude or Anne of Fenwyck. They were merely obstacles to be removed in time.

"You need to control her," Baldwin grumbled. "I'll not have her ruining my scheme."

His scheme? Edith bit her lip to keep from pointing out to him that his thoughts couldn't possibly rise to the level of a scheme. Baldwin never thought further than the bottom of his cup or the end of his blade.

He had risen and was pacing. "He'll return home soon enough, I'll warrant. Damn him to hell anyway. I should have done him in years ago, while I had the chance . . ."

Edith leaned back against the wall and braced herself for the tirade. Her brother's shortsightedness would be his undoing someday. But for now at least his anger was steady and that would serve her well.

As long as his plans were in accord with hers, of course.

And that was something she could control for now. Robin of Artane would return soon enough and Baldwin could do with him what he willed.

To a certain point.

"I'll kill him this time," Baldwin growled, his pacing growing more agitated.

"If you're here."

Baldwin scowled at her. "Did you hear, then? Artane has sent me off to do his business at a handful of his bloody fiefs. Mayhap he knows I'll kill his son if I'm here."

Edith suspected Rhys had sent Baldwin away just to be free of his presence. What she did know for a certainty though, was that Baldwin was going along as the guard to one of Rhys's vassals, not as Rhys's agent. She suspected that was a fact her brother preferred to ignore.

"I would be afraid if I were him," Baldwin said darkly. "I'd be afraid for Robin's sorry neck."

Edith pushed away from the wall. "Brother," she said quietly, "how could killing him possibly avenge you?"

"He'll be dead!" Baldwin said, his chest heaving. "Have you no wits left you?"

Edith frowned, as if she truly had to struggle to concentrate. Baldwin thought her emptyheaded, as he did all women, and Edith never disappointed him. It was better that way.

"But," she said slowly, "if he's dead, you'll no longer have the sport of tormenting him."

"Ha," Baldwin said scornfully. "You want him for yourself and it grieves you to think of him lying rotting in the ground."

Edith smiled, and she made certain it was a tremulous, hopeful smile. "Aye, well that is part of it."

"I knew it," he said with disgust. He spat at her feet. "He has what should have been mine. I'll have Sedgwick and I'll have it without him as my overlord."

Edith struggled not to sigh. She'd been listening to the same litany for as long as she'd been at Artane and those were ten very long years. Baldwin raged about like a stuck boar, but his rages had been in vain. Robin had been gone much of that time, leaving Anne to bear the brunt of Baldwin's wrath. And even Edith had to admit that Anne had been a poor substitute. There had never been any equity in that fight.

Not that Edith cared overmuch for equity. She'd certainly never enjoyed the fruits of it.

"The bastard," Baldwin spat.

Well, that was something else to be discussed, but Edith decided that now was not the time. Baldwin was beginning to rant and that usually led to his descending to the ale kegs in cellars and that never produced anything besides staggering pains in his head the next day. Best distract him while she could.

"But kill Robin," she said, "and you're left with four other brothers."

"I'll kill them too."

There was a certain appeal to that, but that was something to be savored later. She hadn't dragged Maude away from Canfield only to stand idly by and watch Baldwin slay the entire de Piaget clan. The others could be seen to in time. Robin was her prey now and for other reasons than Baldwin could imagine up in his heart.

And she didn't want him dead before she could put him through a choice bit of agony.

And who better to start with than his love?

Never mind that he hadn't returned for her yet. He would. Edith had watched the pair of them carefully over the years. He would return and he would claim Anne for his own.

And then Edith's revenge would begin.

Baldwin stopped dead in the middle of the chamber. It was sudden enough that Edith looked at him. His expression was one of surprise. And then he broke out into a smile.

And the sight of that, his being her brother aside, was enough to send shivers down her spine.

"I'll kill all the lads, then marry Amanda," he said in wonder. "*That* would give me control of Sedgwick."

"But Amanda is not the daughter of Rhys's flesh," Edith pointed out. "Her sire was the baron of Ayre."

Baldwin looked momentarily perplexed.

"The lady Gwennelyn was wed to Alain of Ayre," Edith reminded him. "Amanda is not of de Piaget's flesh."

"But he's claimed her as his own," Baldwin argued.

"But is that claim enough?"

Baldwin shook his head, as if he shook aside an annoying fly. "I'll think on that later. First the others must be seen to."

He could think on Amanda's inheritance, or potential

lack thereof, all he liked, so long as he didn't kill anyone before their time. Edith wasn't about to have her brother foul her plans.

"Humiliate Robin first," she said gently. "You need your revenge."

Baldwin paused and considered, stroking his chin. Then apparently the thought of Amanda was more temptation than he could resist, for he smiled again and chortled.

"Aye, she's a beauty," he said.

"Revenge," Edith reminded him.

He frowned, then cursed. "I'll think on it more when I return. And don't you do anything while I'm away."

"Of course not," Edith agreed, but Baldwin was on his way out of the chamber. The door slammed shut behind him.

Edith sighed and retreated to the alcove. She put her candle on the opposite bench and sat. At least Baldwin would be distracted for a bit and that would leave her free to pursue her own plan.

Baldwin had seen at least some of her heart and that distressed her. That she should be that transparent about anything was unsettling.

For she did want Robin.

But she only wanted him after everything he loved had been methodically destroyed before his eyes. Baldwin could have the satisfaction of dispatching Robin's kin. Edith had the stomach for the doing of it, but there was no sense in denying her brother a bit of enjoyment as well. Aye, all Robin loved would be gone and he would be left alone to suffer.

And then once he was kneeling at her feet in agony, she would see the end of her scheme brought about and she would be avenged for the hurts done her.

She closed her eyes. Aye, she would be avenged, he would die in misery and then she would be at peace.

But she could wait for that. Now was the time to reconsider her plans and make certain she had forgotten nothing. Artane's heir would arrive within days, she was sure of that, and then it would begin. There were so many things she could do to afflict him, it was hard to choose.

There would be time for that decision later. For now, she would sit and think and enjoy the quiet.

A woman of great patience needed to do that now and then. It was good for her soul.

5

Robin stood at the prow of the ship, glad of the chill of the predawn wind. His thoughts had kept him awake for most of the night. Saints, he was in a sorry state. It had to be the confinement. The captain had forbidden him to pace above deck and the hold below had been completely inadequate for his pacing needs. But now the captain was abed and the first mate had been glared into submission. Unfortunately, even the full run of the ship seemed not to be enough. Robin dragged his hand through his hair, then leaned against the railing, conceding the battle. Let the thoughts come. Perhaps if he paid them heed, they would lose their power over him.

He could hardly believe Anne had been at Fenwyck for the past half year. By the saints, she must have been miserable. He was certain her journey there had indeed been against her will. Why would she go, when her home was at Artane? He sometimes wondered what she truly felt for her sire; she certainly didn't know him very well. In her youth, she had gone to her sire for a required fortnight each year, weeping as she left Artane and frantic to return once she'd reached Fenwyck.

Did not his parents treat her as just another daughter?

Did not his father scold her just as he would have any of the rest of his children? The times had been very few, though, as the crestfallen look on Anne's face had been enough to consign him to a hell of guilt for days afterwards.

One of the worst times, save the time her leg had been crushed, had been when Anne was ten-and-two. One of the pages had dared her to ride Rhys's mighty destrier. She had and ridden it well, until Baldwin had approached and sent the stallion into a frenzy. Robin had been home at the time and likely should have stopped her, but he'd been training like a madman and she had been up and riding before he'd come to his senses. He'd then watched, open-mouthed and horrified, as she'd clung to that bucking stallion with a tenacity any knight would have wished for his own. Before he'd found his wits to move, his father had plucked Anne from the saddle, then shaken her until her teeth rattled. After he'd shaken her, he'd given her a tongue-lashing that had raised the hackles on Robin's neck. Rhys had been especially furious at the deed in light of Anne's weak leg and what could have happened had it failed her. Anne had sobbed for hours, grief-stricken that she had disappointed the foster father she adored.

Robin had wanted to go to her, to explain that Rhys was angry because he loved her, because he had come so close to losing her. Somehow the words had never made it past his throat. He had wanted to be gentle with her, to be tender and kind. It had been impossible. How could he have comforted Anne when all he wanted to do was throttle her?

And for precisely the same reason his father had had?

"Can't sleep?"

Robin almost fell overboard in surprise. "By the saints, you startled me," he said weakly.

Nicholas leaned on the railing. "Mooning, Rob?"

"Feel like a swim, Nick?" Robin snapped.

Nicholas only smiled pleasantly, his gray eyes twinkling with amusement. Robin blinked his own gray eyes and wondered, not for the first time, just how it was he and Nicholas had come to look so much alike. Perhaps it was that they had spent so much time together. At least Nicholas wasn't repulsive to look at—or so Robin supposed, not being much of a judge in such matters. Robin suspected that if he'd had to look like someone, 'twas better to look like his brother than someone far uglier.

"Mayhap that swim would serve you better than me," Nicholas remarked. "You look positively bewildered."

"Damn you, Nick, leave me be," Robin grumbled. "I cannot stomach your foolish words. I've had almost a se'nnight of them already."

"Stop being so prickly, Robin."

"I am not being prickly!" Robin exclaimed, giving Nicholas a heated glare. "I just needed some fresh air. And some *peace*," he stressed.

Nicholas sighed and turned his face forward. "You've been in a foul mood for months," he said. "In fact, you've been impossible since we left England. I don't know if you'll remember this, but except for a miserable trip or two to court and that disastrous journey to Canfield for the fortnight which we won't discuss in detail, we haven't been back in almost five years. How is it possible you've been so testy for so long?"

Robin scowled. "I've had much weighing on my mind."

"Such as?"

"Hard to believe as it is, Nicholas, even I give myself over to the contemplation of life and its mysteries now and then."

Nicholas laughed. "Ah, Rob, I know you're not truly as shallow and uncaring as you seem to be."

"Do you *want* me to toss you overboard? Or do you take your life in your hands simply because you are destroyed that you could no longer satisfy your mistress and she pitched you?"

"That was not the reason she left," Nicholas growled.

Robin almost smiled. Ah, how sweet it was to know at

least one thing that could disturb his brother's enviable calm. It was difficult to ruffle Nicholas, but always immensely entertaining.

But before Nicholas could either retort or retaliate, Robin held up his hand in surrender. He had the feeling his brother's revenge would cause him a goodly amount of discomfort and he had no more stomach for that than he did for Nicholas's words.

"I know that wasn't the reason," he sighed. He turned again to stare out over the moonlit water. "I won't provoke you further."

"No doubt very wise," Nicholas agreed. "The saints only know what I would be tempted to do to your pretty visage otherwise."

Robin only grunted.

"Why don't we speak of your vats of troubles instead of mine?" Nicholas asked. "Surely that will entertain us for quite some time."

As tempting as it was to unbend far enough to speak his heart truly, Robin was too much in the habit of keeping that poor heart protected. He rarely admitted the truth of his feelings to himself in the stillest part of the night. How could he possibly admit anything aloud? He felt his brother's gaze boring into the side of his head, but he ignored it. The last thing he needed was to discuss his innermost secrets with his dreamy-eyed sibling and hear the laughter that was sure to follow.

"Very well," Nicholas said pleasantly. "If you've no mind to bring them up, I'll aid you. Let us speak of Anne."

Robin gritted his teeth, but said nothing.

"Why do you think she stayed away for so long?" Nicholas asked.

"I don't know and I couldn't care less."

"Don't you have any feelings for her at all?"

As if he would babble the like to his brother! "Anne of Fenwyck is feisty, opinionated and contrary," Robin said. That at least was truth. "When I do take a wife—

and the saints pity me when that unhappy day arrives—
I'll have a woman who'll obey me, not give me her opinion at every turn."

"I see," Nicholas said wisely. "Then you haven't the stomach for Anne's fire."

Robin could only grunt in answer.

"A meek, obedient woman is the one for you," Nicholas continued.

"Aye."

"Just like Mother."

"Aye."

Robin regretted the word the instant it left his lips. His mother was anything but obedient and his father loved her all the more for her spirit. But he'd be damned if he'd let Nicholas trap him so easily.

"You're nigh onto pushing me too far," Robin said, mustering up what irritation he could—and that was never difficult when it came to Nicholas poking and prodding him. "I don't need your opinions and I don't want your advice. When I feel the need of a legitimate heir, I'll saddle myself with a quiet woman who won't vex me when I take a mistress, nor trouble me when I ignore her for years on end, which I fully intend to do."

"And Anne is not lovely," Nicholas said, slowly. "I suppose that is something you also consider."

"Beauty does not matter to me."

"And, to be sure, Anne does not possess any of it—"

Robin glared at his brother. "There is naught amiss with her face and if you tell her differently, you'll answer to me."

"And her temper," Nicholas continued with a shudder. "Passing unpleasant."

"There is naught amiss with her temper either!"

Nicholas looked at him appraisingly. "Why, Robin, I think you love the girl."

Robin's lunge almost sent them both overboard. Nicholas laughed weakly as he lay on the deck with Robin sprawled over him, his hands at his throat.

"That was close," he said.

"And you are as giddy as a mindless milkmaid," Robin snapped.

"Am I?" Nicholas asked, still grinning like the idiot Robin knew him to be.

But it was a knowing grin and somehow just that much more terrifying for the knowledge behind it. That was all he bloody needed—to have Nicholas babbling what he supposed to be Robin's heart to anyone who would listen. Best disabuse the fool of his idiotic notions whilst he had the chance.

"I give Anne less thought than I do what color tunic to wear each day. She's as skinny as a boy and about that handsome," Robin growled. He was lying, of course, but it sounded convincing so he kept to his tack. "If I wanted a woman, I'd choose someone with a bit of meat on her and a face that I could look at without wincing."

A blinding pain in his face made him instantly release his loose grasp on Nicholas's throat. He was dumped onto his back and banged his head smartly against the deck. Before he could think to start cursing his brother, he was hauled to his feet.

"Don't say anything else," Nicholas bit out softly. "Think what you like about her, but don't say it out loud. And for pity's sake, don't say it to her. If you do, I'll make you regret it."

"I never would," Robin grumbled, shoving his brother away from him. He rubbed the back of his head in annoyance. "Go to bed, Nick. Mother will see those dark circles under your eyes, think my fist caused them, and take a switch to my behind for my trouble."

Nicholas paused. "And leave you here to stew alone?"

"Begone, dolt. I need not your aid."

Nicholas pursed his lips. "Don't pace all night. Anne will worry if you look too haggard."

"Just go, would you?" Robin ordered crossly. He heard his brother's retreating footsteps and leaned against the rail with a sigh.

Of course Anne wasn't uncomely. And Nicholas was a
fool if he thought Robin would ever say anything to hurt
her. He might have possessed but a little chivalry, but he
knew when to trot it out. Besides, he would never comment on Anne's appearance because he would never have
the chance. How could he when he never planned to be
in the same chamber with her, much less speak to her?

Aye, that was the wisest course of action. He bloody
didn't care for her. He never had. She was obstinate, and
disagreeable and she had a perverse fondness for doing
exactly the opposite of what he told her to do. How could
anyone expect him to endure that for the rest of his life?

Anne wasn't the cause of his problems, but she certainly wasn't the solution either. It was best he stay completely away from her.

He did not love her.

And he certainly wasn't going to wed with her.

And he wasn't going to dream about her ever again.

Five days later, Robin reined in his mount and stared at
the castle in the distance. He could have likely coerced
the captain into sailing farther north, which would have
saved him a grueling pair of days on horseback, but he
hadn't wanted to alert his family to his arrival. Better to
have it seem as if he had just come in from the lists. His
family would be about their various daily tasks and he
would walk in and feel as if he'd never left.

Except that five years had passed since he had last seen
his home. How much had it changed? How much had his
loved ones changed?

Nicholas cleared his throat. "Ready?"

"Aye."

"Mother likely won't be expecting us for at least another se'nnight."

Robin nodded, then looked at his brother. "She won't
recognize you. You've filled out a bit whilst we've been
away."

"So have you," Nicholas replied solemnly. "Save that empty space between your ears."

Nicholas was away before Robin could reconcile himself to the fact that he had reached out and grasped a fistful of air, not his brother's tunic. He spurred his mount into a gallop, trying to catch up to Nicholas.

By the time they reached the outer gate, Robin had forgotten why he had his brother's death on his mind. His heart lifted with every stride his horse took toward home. He had been away too long. Perhaps he would stay longer than a fortnight. After all, Artane would eventually be his. It might behoove him to remain a bit closer to home for awhile. He did have other fiefs in England to where he could escape if necessity warranted it. But to France? Not again quite so soon.

Perhaps it was a weakness, but he loved his home. Artane was a magical place and he greatly suspected it was his family that made it so.

He raced Nicholas up the long road from the outer gate, laughing at the direness and variety of curses he received from his father's men as they hastily moved out of his way. He slowed as he neared the inner walls and then walked his horse into the courtyard. Robin sat back and breathed deeply. Ah, to actually sleep a night in a bed that was his, eat at his father's table, relax in front of the hearth in the great hall without having to keep one eye over his shoulder.

Just as he was contemplating how best to enter the house and achieve the desired results, the front door opened and his father stepped out, rubbing his arms and stomping his feet to ward off the chill. Rhys blinked a time or two, then began to smile.

Robin dismounted and watched Nicholas walk by their sire with naught but a negligent wave. Rhys was just as busy paying him little heed. Perhaps to an outsider it would have seemed strange indeed, but he and Nicholas had decided upon the like long ago. Nicholas greeted their mother first and their father last; Robin the opposite. It had worked out so well after the first try they had kept to it. Robin walked up the steps and was immediately enveloped in a fierce hug. Robin gave his father a hearty kiss and slapped him on the back.

"Good to see you, Papa. What's for supper?"

Rhys scowled. "And to think I actually told your mother that I missed you . . ."

"Can we carry on this tender reunion inside? It's brutally cold out. I'd forgotten what a bloody frigid place England is."

"You swear too much," Rhys grumbled, pulling Robin inside. Once there, he hugged Robin again, until Robin thought his ribs just might pop. "Damn you, Robin," Rhys said hoarsely, "you didn't have to stay away so long."

"I had to," Robin said, feeling his eyes burn with an unwelcome kind of fire. "I had things to prove to myself. Things I couldn't prove here at home."

Rhys didn't answer, but Robin flinched at the affectionate slaps he received on his back. Rhys pulled away finally, blinking rapidly.

"Looks like you've grown a bit," he said.

"You saw me last year at court," Robin said dryly. "How much could I have grown since then?"

"Well," Rhys said, "it seems as if you have. Don't contradict me while I'm feeling so sentimental."

Robin straightened his cloak over his shoulders. "Care for a wrestle now so you can determine the true extent of the change, or shall we wait until I've had something to eat?"

Rhys took him by the back of the neck and shook him. "After supper. You'll enjoy your meal much more before your thrashing than after."

"No doubt," Robin said. He would indeed take his father on after supper and show him that five years of warring had turned his son into a man to be reckoned with.

The hall was deliciously warm compared to the air outside. Massive logs were burning in the hearth and various members of the family were gathered close, fussing over

Nicholas at the moment. Robin felt his palms begin to sweat and cursed himself. By the saints, he had no reason to be nervous.

But that didn't stop him from glancing about likely more than he should have. There were many souls coming and going in the great hall. There was surely no sense in not taking a look at them to see who they were. He looked back at the hall door, then turned and blinked in surprise. A young woman was rushing across the hall toward him. He thought she just might be his sister.

"Oof," he grunted as she launched herself at him.

"Oh, Robby!"

Robin gasped for air. "By the saints, Isabelle, you weigh more than my horse!"

Isabelle clung to him. "I've missed you so much, Robin. What'd you bring me from France?"

Robin let her slip down to the ground and looked at her in astonishment. When had his youngest sister grown up? She had been ten-and-one the year he left. He hardly recognized the slender girl who was certainly no longer a child. Had she been betrothed already?

"Presents, Robby," Isabelle reminded him.

What had he missed by not having watched her grow? The regret that washed over him, for he suspected this was not the first thing he had missed that he shouldn't have, was almost enough to make him weep. Then his sister began checking him over for baubles.

"Isabelle," he managed, "I watched Nick spend a fortune on presents for you and another fortune sending them home."

"A most generous brother," she said, industriously investigating the depths of his cloak.

"Why in the world would I have watched all that, then found myself fool enough to see more gold spent on you by me?"

She smiled up at him and the sweetness of her smile almost brought him to tears in truth. "You did bring me something," she said with a happy sigh.

"I brought you nothing, you greedy wretch," he said, giving her a fierce hug. He closed his eyes and prayed he wouldn't embarrass himself by an unmanly display of emotion.

"Robin . . ." she complained.

He lifted her face and kissed her quickly. "Did you miss me truly?"

"Aye."

"Come, you can do better than that."

She considered. "Desperately?"

"I may have brought you a trinket or two."

"Robin, I hardly slept a wink for missing you all this time. See the lines of worry on my face?" she said earnestly.

"Very well, I brought you several things, none of which you will see until I'm ready to show them to you." He was prepared to give her a further lecture on greed—for indeed he could see how else his guiding influence had been missed—but he saw another sight that deserved attention. "We'll discuss this further when I have time. Now I see that my favorite little slaves are waiting impatiently for their audience."

Isabelle moved just in time to avoid being trampled by Montgomery and John. The twins hugged Robin until he pretended to gasp for breath. Now these were children who had changed. They had to be at least ten-and-three by now. Robin remembered vividly holding both boys up over his head, one with each hand, countless times and their howls of laughter from the like. How he loved his youngest brothers. They were little imps, stirring up mischief even he had to admire. Now he wondered if he could possibly hoist them both any distance at all off the floor. Five years had done a goodly work upon them both.

"Move, little lads." The deep voice was accompanied by two arms that took the boys by the backs of their tunics and hoisted them away.

Well, apparently someone was still equal to that task. Robin felt his jaw slide down.

"Miles?" he asked.

"Who else?" Miles said setting the twins aside and making Robin a low bow. "At your service, spurs in hand."

Robin laughed. "Saints, but you've grown. I seem to remember picking *you* up when last we met."

"I doubt you would succeed now," Miles said, flexing an arm for Robin's benefit. "If you'd care to try?"

Robin caught sight of his mother. She was coming toward him purposefully, though he could already see the tears streaming down her face. "Later," he said, pushing his brother aside.

He reached her just as she had launched into a thorough scolding of him, and pulled her over to the hearth. No sense in not having the rest of him be warm while his ears were being blistered.

"I vow, Robin de Piaget," she said, frowning up at him with her fiercest frown, "that if another month had passed without some scratch on parchment from you, I would have finished your battles myself, then taken a switch to your backside for your lack of consideration!"

Robin pulled his mother into his arms and rested his chin on her head where she couldn't see his smile over her words. She continued enumerating in great detail the lengths she had planned to go to in instilling in him the smallest smidgen of manners, punctuating her reproof with various and sundry tugs on his hair. Robin closed his eyes and smiled at the novelty of using his mother as a resting place for his jaw. Though he'd outgrown her quickly, it never failed to surprise him that he was taller than she.

Then next he knew, she was sobbing. She shook with her weeping and Robin soon found that tears were coursing down his own cheeks. Perhaps it was unmanly to miss a mother so, but he didn't care. He loved her and damn anyone who wanted to mock him for it.

Gwen pulled back and began to check him over for

injuries. He laughed as he submitted to her poking and prodding.

"I am unscathed, Mama," he said with a gentle smile.

"You've grown so much," she said, with a frown. "Making it, of course, very difficult to take you to task. Mayhap I should seek out my blade when I've serious business with you."

"The saints preserve me," he said with a laugh. "I promise, my lady, that I will fetch you a stool, that you might scold me from a like height."

She shook her head with a sigh. "I vow I scarce recognize my sweet little lad whom I used to intimidate by looking down at him."

"Aye, I know," he said. "That lad went off to war to become a man."

"You were a man before you left, son."

Ah, how he wished he could agree with her! He sat her down in a chair, drawing up a stool and sitting before her. He gave her a brief recounting of his recent travels, leaving out the more unsavory parts, though he had the feeling she knew what he'd neglected to tell her. And while he talked, he kept one eye on the stairs leading up to the upper floors of the keep. There was no sense in not knowing just who was coming down to the great hall, was there?

His mother's questions distracted him for a time and when he looked again at the stairs, it was to see a young woman coming down them. He blinked a time or two, wondering if that were his sister or a ghost of his mother. He heard his mother laugh softly.

"Uncanny, isn't it?"

"Frightening is more the word I'd choose," Robin said, drawing his hand over his eyes. "She has certainly inherited your beauty, but 'tis a pity she hasn't inherited your sweetness."

Robin felt a sharp slap to the back of his head and scowled up at Nicholas who strode across the room and picked Amanda up to spin her around. Robin's frown deepened as Nicholas brought Amanda over to the fire. She was weeping. Well, let her weep. She had always loved Nicholas the best anyway and that was just as well, as Robin couldn't abide her sharp tongue or lack of manners.

"I see you haven't forgotten how to scowl," Amanda said, making him a deep, mocking curtsey.

"I'm not home ten heartbeats and already you're irritating me," Robin snapped. "Do you lie awake nights dreaming of how to torment me?"

"I wouldn't spare you the effort, Robin."

Nicholas laughed and pulled Amanda behind him as Robin rose with a growl. "Rob, you're pitifully easy sport. Don't let her rile you. She's already told me I'm hopelessly soft and need a few more hours in the lists each day. Now, give the lass a kiss of peace and let us have harmony for once between you two. Five years have passed and I would hope you would have matured. Come from your hiding place, Amanda, and don't plunge anything sharp into Robby's belly while he's trying to behave."

Robin gave Amanda a quick hug, fierce enough to silence her for a time, then kissed her briefly on both cheeks. "Now, begone wench, lest I remember the insults I must needs repay you for."

"Nick," Gwen said, reaching up to take his hand, "run fetch Anne from the chapel, would you? She's been out there for some time now. 'Tis far too cold for her."

"I'll go," Robin said, rising and pushing his brother aside before there could be any argument. "Nick would only fuss over her and that would irritate her."

"Don't you hurt her feelings," Amanda warned, poking him sharply in the arm on his way by. "You'll answer to me if you do."

Robin toyed with the idea of strangling his sister, then thought better of it. For one thing, his hands were so slippery with nervous sweat, they likely wouldn't have been able to get a good grip on her neck. Perhaps later, when he was calmer.

Though why he was so bloody nervous was something he couldn't answer. It wasn't as if he were seeking an audience with the queen. This was merely Anne of Fenwyck, the pale-haired girl who had grown to maturity in his home, who had been so painfully shy that he'd hardly noticed her.

He groaned as he slammed the hall door shut behind him.

When had he become such a liar?

He strode across the courtyard, pulling his cloak more closely around him. Bloody frigid country, this England of his. Why had he been fool enough to come back? He should have rather gone south to Spain. He had previously passed many months there quite happily. Indeed, he could have found himself spending his days lazing in bed with the countess who had once taken a fancy to him, strolling along the shore at night, enjoying the cool ocean breezes.

But those shores were a world away and it didn't serve him to think on them. He stepped up to the chapel, put his hand on the door and took a deep breath. Would she be pleased to see him? Or would she ignore him, brush past him, and leave him standing there like a fool?

Wondering about it was almost enough to make him wish he'd had a bit of a wash before he presented himself to her.

He opened the door before his thoughts turned him in any more circles. He slipped inside the dimly lit structure, then closed the door behind him silently. He'd forgotten what a small place this was, but perhaps 'twas large enough to serve his family's needs. Robin stood still until his eyes adjusted to the gloom. At least his years of moving quietly would serve him now. He would have a look at mistress Anne before she was even aware of him, and see if his memory had served him well or ill.

He found her immediately. One of his greatest strengths in battle was his sharp eyes, eyes that could distinguish the color of a man's eyes at fifty paces. And those eyes were currently riveted on the figure kneeling at one of the side altars, before St. Christopher, protector of those who went to war.

Robin didn't allow himself to ponder the significance of her choice.

He took a pair of steps forward, then stopped, finding himself rendered immobile. He held his breath, wondering if he were seeing a vision or if the sight of the beautiful woman in the deep green gown before him were real.

It could only be Anne. He would never mistake that cloak of pale golden hair for anyone else's. The candle-light flickered over it as it fell over her shoulders and down her back like a waterfall of spun gold. Her slender hands were clasped and resting on the altar before her. Her head was bowed, her lips moved soundlessly. Robin almost went down on his knees himself. Never in his life had he seen such a picture of tranquility, of goodness, of purity. Gone was the homely little girl with freckles, too-large eyes and ears that didn't seem to fit her face. In her place was a serene, lovely young woman.

He slowly walked to the front of the chapel and felt his way down onto a bench near her. He struggled to think of something clever to say—or at least something that wouldn't leave him sounding as witless as he felt.

By the saints, he'd never expected just the sight of her to leave him breathless.

He couldn't tear his gaze from her. Just looking at her seemed to ease his heart. For the first time in five years, he felt the tension ease out of him.

And it was because of the very woman he had promised himself he would avoid.

6

Anne felt a breeze blow over her hands as she knelt at St. Christopher's shrine, but she ignored it. For all she knew, 'twas her father come to fetch her and she wanted to put that moment off as long as possible. So she held her breath, kept her hands clasped before her, and waited for the inevitable, impatient clearing of a male throat.

The footsteps halted far from her, though, and she sighed in relief. Her fear of discovery was a foolish one anyway. Her sire never would have come to look for her here; it was her sanctuary alone. The other soul who had joined her was likely someone come to look for a little quiet as she had. With any luck, they wouldn't even mark her.

She bowed her head and continued with her prayer. It brought her peace, this ritual of hers. It was her daily trek to the saint's shrine to offer prayers at his feet, prayers that Robin would be kept safe, that he would return well and sound. She did not dare pray for the true desire of her heart. It was a miracle no saint could bring about, no matter his power.

Her leg trembled as she knelt on the hard wooden floor, but she didn't move. For all she knew, her sacrifice might mean the difference between Robin's life and his death. Though he would never know of it, and likely wouldn't care if he did, Anne made her offering willingly.

And when she was finished with Robin's needs, she spared a moment or two for her own.

Let me stay at Artane. Let me stay but another day or two.

She didn't dare pray for anything more. No saint could deter her father any longer than that.

She heard the footsteps begin again and come toward her, but she ignored them. It was likely Miles come to fetch her, or one of the twins. They could wait for another moment or two while she finished a few more supplications.

When she could truly bear the strain of kneeling no more, she crossed herself and opened her eyes. Getting to her feet would be difficult, but not impossible. Perhaps a bit of aid wasn't too much to ask for.

"Miles, if you please—" she began, turning her head to look at her visitor.

Only it wasn't Miles she saw.

It was Robin.

She couldn't have been more surprised if St. Christopher himself had been made flesh from her most fervent prayers. She gaped at the very man she had been praying for. It was impossible to look away. She could only hope she didn't look as foolish as she was certain she did. She made a small effort to close her mouth, but that was all she could manage.

By the saints, he was the last person she had expected to see that morn.

He sat on the long bench nearby, crushing her cloak beneath his heavy thigh. Anne took in the sight of him, marking the changes. His dark hair was long and unruly, falling over his forehead and into his eyes. His face was no longer the face of a boy, round with softness and charm. Five years had changed a young knight into a hardened warrior. His features were tanned, weathered, and very grim. His shoulders were broad, his empty hands wide and strong. His boots were caked with mud and his clothes were travel-stained.

She suspected she had never seen a more beautiful sight in her life.

She met his eyes but could read nothing in his gaze. He merely stared at her. She could readily imagine what he might be thinking, though, for she had been long in the chapel and the place was very cold. Her nose was likely red and her hands pale as death. It wasn't a sight guaranteed to bring a man to his knees pledging his body and soul.

Anne knew she had no choice but to rise. Perhaps in the effort, she might find some bit of wit remaining her. She turned away and put her hands on the shrine, praying she could manage to gain her feet. Robin was the last person she wanted to have see her weakness. She clenched her teeth together and tried to lever herself up using her good leg and her hands to push herself away from the altar. The action served her little but to force the blood of shame to her cheeks. If she wasn't careful, she would be sprawled at his feet.

This was not exactly how she had envisioned her next meeting with the young lord of Artane proceeding.

The altar was not the steadiest of crutches and her leg trembled so badly that Anne felt herself begin to waver dangerously. Instantly strong hands were at her waist, steadying her, lifting her.

Her mortification complete, Anne jerked away. The motion almost sent her stumbling in truth.

"By the saints," she gasped, "I don't need aid!"

Robin cleared his throat. "Well, I just—"

Anne straightened and looked at him with as much dignity as she could muster. It wasn't much, but her pride was all she had left at the moment.

"I was perfectly capable of rising on my own, thank you," she said as tartly as she could manage. This was

the very last thing she needed—to have Robin look at her
as if she were incapable of standing without aid.

Robin was beginning to scowl. It wasn't a good sign,
but Anne was too embarrassed to care.

"Fool that I am, I thought to ply a bit of chivalry on
you," he said gruffly.

"I already said I didn't need your help."

"I wasn't trying to help you," Robin returned shortly.
"I was trying to maul you. Does that improve your humor
any?"

Anne blinked furiously. She'd be damned before she'd
let his ill-concealed pity cause her more humiliation. She
pointed toward the door. "Your disrespect damns us both,
so begone."

"I'll leave when I bloody well please—"

"Now," she snapped. "For the last time, I don't need
your help, nor do I want it."

"I never suspected you did," he returned just as hotly.
He brushed past her and strode away with a curse that left
her ears burning. She waited until he was gone before she
picked up her cloak and pulled it around her, willing herself not to break down and weep. Her leg was throbbing
and her heart felt as if it had broken in uncountable pieces.

That was not how she had planned it, the reunion with
the man she loved. She was to have been elegant and
regal, bestowing her best smiles upon him as she sat
gracefully arranged in a comfortable chair. He would have
knelt at her feet, apologized profusely for having stayed
away so long, then showered her with praises about qual-
ities she hadn't even imagined she possessed.

Now, with but a few harsh words spoken, she had ruined everything. Perhaps it was just as well. If she
shunned Robin, he wouldn't have the chance to shun her.

She walked stiffly to the chapel door, trying to work
the cramp out of her leg. It was impossible. The chapel
had been colder than usual and she would pay the price
in agony for the rest of the day and far into the evening.

She stepped out into the frigid air and closed the door

behind her. She jumped when she saw Robin standing next to the door. He merely glared at her. She ignored him and started for the steps. Damn, who was the imbecile who had decided there should be all these steps up to the chapel door? Then she had at least eight wider ones to face before she would gain the great hall. She suppressed the urge to sit down and weep.

She saw Robin move toward her and quickly held up her hand.

"I do not need—"

"Stubborn baggage," he muttered under his breath as he put his cloak around her shoulders. "At least now you will not freeze as you take all afternoon to cross the court-yard."

Anne blinked back tears. "You needn't wait. I never asked you to."

He didn't reply, he merely descended the steps in time to her painful movements. Once she reached the ground, he stepped in front of her and took his sweet time ad-justing his cloak over her own. Anne might have thanked him for the chance to catch her breath had she not been so embarrassed. She pushed him away and started across the courtyard, her eyes fixed to the ground before her. A single false step and she would sprawl face-first in front of the only man whose opinion mattered to her.

She looked up to judge the distance and saw Nicholas come striding out of the great hall. He loped down the stairs with his easy gait. It was a lazy stroll that was so completely him that Anne felt herself begin to smile. How different Robin and Nicholas were. Robin was all fire and fury, roughness and strength; Nicholas was as serene and lethal as a finely polished steel blade.

And to be sure Nicholas possessed charm Robin never had, and likely never would. Even in his youth, Nicholas had been able to produce a look that had entranced every female from his mother down to the crustiest keeper of the larder. Anne had benefitted more than once from Nich-olas's ability to beg an apple or two and succeed. Robin could have begged for cloth to staunch a life-threatening wound and Cook would have just kicked him out of her way as if he'd been an unsavoury tablescrap. Robin did not possess Nicholas's pleasing ways.

"You fool," Nicholas exclaimed, casting a baleful glance his brother's way. "Can't you see she's in pain? Here, Anne, let me carry you back to the hall. You shouldn't be out in this chill."

"Leave her be," Robin growled. "She's not a cripple."

"She's a woman, dolt," Nicholas said, pushing Robin aside. "Women need to be cared for; something you never have learned." Nicholas put his hands on Anne's shoulders and smiled down at her. "By the saints, 'tis a pleasure to see you again. It makes me wonder what possessed me to go away when I could have remained at home and gaped at you."

Anne felt an unaccustomed blush apply itself liberally to her cheeks. It was a very unsettling feeling, one she didn't experience very often.

"Nicholas," she said at length, at a loss, "what a flatterer you've become on your travels."

"Flattery? Nay, 'tis but the truth." He lifted his hand and smoothed it over her hair. "Anne, you steal my breath."

And then Anne watched, open-mouthed, as Nicholas smiled at her again, a dazzling smile that fair knocked her to her knees. He put his hands on her shoulders, bent his head, and then, to her complete astonishment, he took a liberty she never would have anticipated.

He kissed her.

And then he kissed her again.

By the third time his lips had come down on hers so softly, she had almost regained her wits enough to breathe. She stood there in his embrace, feeling exceedingly foolish, and examined the feel of Nicholas's lips as they pressed against hers.

They were warm.

They were soft.

And then they were quite suddenly no longer there.

She opened her eyes in time to see Robin jerk Nicholas away and send him sprawling by means of a fist in the face. She stared at Nicholas as he rolled over and sat up, putting his finger to the corner of his mouth and looking at it as it came away bloody.

"Don't do that again," Robin growled.

Nicholas paused for a moment and then leaned back on his hands, slowly crossing his feet at the ankles. His lazy movements were geared, Anne knew, to irritate Robin as much as possible. Nicholas looked up at his brother tranquilly, a smile playing around the corners of his mouth. Anne had to admire his calm in the face of Robin's considerable wrath.

"Why not?" Nicholas asked. "Does it bother you?"

Anne wished she had something heavy and damaging on hand to throw at Rhys's second son.

Robin leaned down and jerked Nicholas up by the front of his tunic. "She's not yours to kiss, damn you. Now, keep away from her." He gave Nicholas a shove toward the hall. "I'll see her inside."

"She doesn't need to walk any more, Robin," Nicholas said, his gray eyes taking on the same glint Anne saw in Robin's.

"She doesn't want any help. She already told me so."

Nicholas snorted. "Knowing you, you didn't ask her the right way."

"She bloody didn't give me a chance to ask before she was telling me to go to hell!" Robin exclaimed.

Nicholas pushed Robin aside. Before Anne realized what he intended, he had scooped her up into his arms.

"She's had enough, Robin," Nicholas said firmly. "Go open the door."

"Damn you, Nick—"

"The door, Robin."

Anne watched Robin stomp up the steps, swearing furiously. He opened the door and left it open, disappearing inside the hall.

"Nicholas, I'm fine—"

"Be quiet," Nicholas said with a smile. "Anne, you didn't used to be this stubborn. Where in the world did you learn this unladylike trait?"

Anne smiled faintly. "From Amanda."

Nicholas laughed. "I don't doubt it for a moment. That girl is a terrible influence on you. I suppose it leaves me with no choice but to take on the task of rooting it from you."

She looked at his mouth as he carried her up the steps. He had kissed her. Why wasn't she trembling from head to toe? Nicholas was one of the most sought-after young knights in the realm. Not even Robin had so many women pursuing him, though that number interested her not at all. She should have been faint with joy that Nicholas had taken note of her. She looked at his face and studied the cut on his mouth.

"Does it hurt, Nicky?" she asked.

Nicholas winked at her as he shut the hall door with his foot. "Why? Thinking to ease my pain with another kiss?"

His head suddenly snapped back. Anne looked over his shoulder to see Robin with a fistful of his brother's hair.

"Put her down," he growled.

Nicholas jerked his head away. "You're sounding rather possessive, brother."

"Put her down."

"Once I'm by the fire, I will."

"Now, Nick."

Nicholas sighed and gently set Anne on her feet. Then he whirled and took Robin down to the floor. Anne didn't bother to watch them scuffle. If there was one thing in this world that could be counted on, it was that Robin and Nicholas would fight at least once a day. She had never seen two brothers closer, nor more ready to let fly a fist. Not even the youngest de Piaget brothers battled so often. She knew it wouldn't last long. An hour from now, Robin and Nicholas would be laughing together, as if nothing had happened.

She avoided the battle now being waged in the rushes and made her way across the floor. She smiled when young Montgomery bounded over and hugged her.

"Put your arm around me, Anne, and let's go over to the fire. How did you come by Robin's cloak? 'Tis powerfully dirty, don't you think? And it smells. I'll wager you can't wait to have it off you."

Anne leaned on Montgomery as he helped her across the floor, grateful for his aid. But she couldn't agree with him about Robin's cloak. It might have been dirty and it might have not smelled terribly fresh, but it was something he'd given her for her comfort.

The ring of swords startled her and she turned around to see what they augured. Robin and Nicholas were now taking blades to each other with great enthusiasm. Anne sincerely hoped Robin didn't cut his brother to ribbons.

"By the saints, take your quarrel outside, you fools!" Amanda shouted from where she sat near the hearth. "You're giving me pains in my head with your idiocy!"

Much cursing and many foul insults accompanied the pair out the hall door. Anne sat down before the fire, swathed in Robin's cloak, and wondered if she had the intellect equal to ferreting out the truth of what had just happened.

Nicholas had just kissed her.

Robin was furious over the fact.

And now they had departed outside to settle the matter with swords.

Anne put her face in her hands and started to laugh. It was the very last thing she would have anticipated for the middle of her day. She could hardly wait to see what the evening would bring.

It likely couldn't equal what she'd just experienced.

7

Robin sat back in his chair and fingered his goblet of wine. The family had sought refuge in the lord's solar, as was often their custom in the evenings. Robin was glad of it, for he was unsettled in his mind and he wanted none of the garrison knights watching to see what ailed him. At least he wouldn't have to confront Baldwin of Sedgwick. Rhys had sent Sedgwick off on an errand a few days earlier and he wasn't expected back for at least a se'nnight. Robin couldn't help but be relieved. Now, at least, the first meeting after so many years would come when he was prepared for it. He fully intended for it to end badly for his enemy.

Robin drank deeply and tried to let the wine soothe him. Tonight, unlike other nights, there was no minstrel to entertain them, nor any visiting noblemen to bring news from other corners of the isle. The entertaining of the family fell to Robin. He had begun the tale of his travels, but had found it difficult to keep to the thread of the story. His mood was fouled and he had finally bid Nicholas in curt tones to take over the exercise.

He knew the precise reason for his foulness. Damn Nicholas for being the first to steal a sweet kiss from

Anne's lips! Robin was passing certain she'd never been kissed before, if the look on her face had been any indication. Robin had been so stunned by his brother's boldness, he'd merely stood there and gaped. He couldn't tell if the kiss had pleased Anne or not.

It wasn't actually something he was interested in learning the truth of.

He stole a look at Anne and forced himself to breathe normally. Saints, she had changed! His first sight of her in the chapel had not shown him the extent of the transformation. When he had left five years earlier, Anne had been a plain, unlovely waif of ten-and-four. The Anne who sat across the circle from him was not the same girl.

Robin took a long draught of wine and then put the cup away. He leaned back in the shadows and let his eyes feast on the beauty before him. His father had always said one day Anne would blossom, but he had never believed it. Obviously his father had been right.

She sat in the chair next to Nicholas with her good leg tucked up under her. Robin could conjure up hundreds of memories of Anne in the same position, listening to the Fitzgerald brothers tell their gory tales of battle, minstrels singing praises to his mother's beauty, jongleurs performing their antics to amuse the family.

Gone was the homely little girl who had hugged her knee and watched the goings on with bright green eyes. In her place was a woman full grown. Her head was uncovered and the firelight flickered over her pale hair. One slender hand rested on her knee, her long fingers absently worrying the fold of her gown. Her left hand rested on the arm of the chair and Robin frowned. Her hand was too damn close to Nicholas's. His eyes flicked to his brother's and his scowl only earned him a grin in return before Nicholas continued on with his story.

Anne shifted in her chair and Robin's gaze was drawn to the way her long hair fell over her shoulder and down. With an effort he forced his eyes up past her flawless throat to her lips. They were slightly parted and he had the most overpowering desire to jerk her out of her chair and capture her lips with his own, just to see if they tasted as sweet as they looked.

She began to chew on her lip and the movement startled him into meeting her eyes. He stiffened as he realized he had been caught staring. She didn't smile, which made him think that perhaps she thought him as big a fool as he was. He rose abruptly, giving her the fiercest frown he was capable of. Damn her if she thought to laugh at him.

He bid his family a curt good-night and strode stiffly up the stairs. He walked all the way up to the battlements, feeling the need of a great amount of fresh air to clear his head. He never should have come home. If he'd just had the good sense to remain on the continent, he would have been perfectly content and happy. And now look. He was letting a slip of a girl ruin his night and make mincemeat of his heart.

As he leaned against the wall, the stiff wind blowing in from the sea cooled his passions. He shivered and then shook his head in disbelief. What was he doing? What did he care what Anne of Fenwyck thought? She could laugh at him all she liked. She was too prickly and disagreeable for his taste. And though she might have filled out a bit, she was still too frail. He liked a woman with a bit more to her, a woman who was lusty in bed and who made herself scarce out of it.

It was several minutes later that he finally made his way back down the stairs. What he needed was a good tumble. Perhaps he'd hie himself down to the kitchens, find himself the first attractive serving wench available and take her right there. Maybe he'd line up five or six of them and find relief from his torment. Relief from Anne.

But it wasn't to the kitchens that his feet led him so unerringly. He found himself in front of the chamber he shared with his brothers, and he relented with a sigh. So he was going to be as incapable of taking a woman tonight as he had been for months. It was hardly surprising.

He entered the chamber and lit a candle. He had a brief moment alone and there was little reason not to take advantage of it. He rummaged through his gear until he found what he was looking for. Taking his candle and his treasure, he retreated to the alcove and made himself comfortable on one of the stone benches there. He set the candle down, then took the box on his lap.

It contained his most precious possessions and there was not a time that he did not have it nearby. He opened it and examined what was contained therein.

There was the letter his mother had written him before he had been knighted, the crested ring his father had given him as he went off to war, and a gem which had been handed down from father to son for generations in the de Piaget family. Rhys had wanted Robin to bind the stone into a sword but Robin had never been able to bring himself to do it. He suspected there would come a time when he would wish to give the gem to his firstborn son. The thought of such a time gave him pause. A son. Now, that would be a thing to be proud of.

He fingered the four ribbons embroidered with his crest and then pushed them aside. They were dear to him, but not what he sought that night. From the depths of the box he pulled what he was looking for. He unwrapped the cloth surrounding it and held it up to the light.

The gold was so pale as to almost be white. It reminded him sharply of her hair. The paleness of the emerald did not do justice to her eyes, but it came damn close. He slid the ring onto the tip of his little finger and put his hand over his heart. Had Nicholas known of this foolishness, he would have laughed himself to death.

Then again, perhaps not. Nicholas was giddy enough to find the idea romantic. Robin was practical enough to find the idea idiotic. She would never wear his ring. She would laugh in his face.

Or perhaps she would accept him.

At the moment, he wasn't sure what would be worse.

Nay, the laughter would be worse. In his youth, he wouldn't have given that another thought. But that was before being laughed at became something he avoided at all costs. After the first time, he swore he would never be humiliated like that again. It was amazing how such a simple event in childhood could become such a heaviness in the heart of a man full grown.

Nay, she would have no chance to scorn him because he wouldn't come within twenty paces of her.

Besides, he had no tender feelings for her anyway. She was trouble embodied, trouble for his heart and trouble for his peace of mind. He had never loved her and he never would.

The door opened suddenly and Robin jerked in surprise. Damn, this was all he needed to make his evening of misery complete.

"Robin, are you in here?" Nicholas asked. "Mother feared you were unwell."

Robin shoved everything back in the wooden box and slammed the lid shut before Nicholas could see. He glared at his brother who stood near the doorway.

"There is nothing amiss with me," he said tightly. "I did but need a bit of peace from your witless babbling."

Nicholas bowed. "Of course, my lord. Now I can happily inform Mother that you are not ill, but merely mooning."

"I am not mooning!"

Nicholas only laughed as he turned and left the chamber. Robin would have followed his brother to beat him senseless, but he'd already taken his exercise of Nicholas that afternoon. That added to the weariness of traveling was likely enough for the day.

One thing was for certain, he wasn't about to expose his poor heart to the torments that might await it in his father's solar. He was momentarily tempted to see if any of his lads might be willing to visit the lists with him, then he discarded that idea as well. 'Twas late and what would serve him best was to be abed.

A pity he already could imagine his tossings and turnings and how those might lead to speculation by his brothers.

He leaned back against the wall and stared into the dimly lit chamber. He'd suspected coming home would be difficult. He'd never imagined what would await him here.

Though wasn't that why he'd had the ring made for her?

He closed his eyes and gritted his teeth. And he thought Nicholas was the one awash in romance!

Robin rose, put his treasure away, then put himself to bed. What he needed was a satisfying night's sleep and then a goodly bit of training on the morn. Perhaps he would inspect his father's garrison and see if he couldn't dispatch them all before noon. It was a worthy goal and one easily within his power to accomplish.

And it was something he could understand. This business of love and romance and a heart that pounded uncomfortably at the merest thought of a certain woman was not for him. If he were to find himself swooning, it would be because of a full day's labor in the hot sun, not because Anne had deigned to glance his way. Should his stomach be unsettled, better it be from a questionable bit of fowl than fear she would wed with someone else. And should he weep, better that it be tears of victory over a foe well vanquished. He had no intention of shedding any over a girl who had suffered one of the worst injuries he'd ever been privy to, yet pressed on with the courage any of his men would have been proud to call his own.

He snorted. Courage? Nay, 'twas stubbornness that drove her, and a perverse desire to see him miserable. Aye, that he was certain of.

How she managed to do the like with so little effort on her part was something of a mystery, but one he had no desire to investigate further.

Nay, the lists were the place for him and he would be there as soon as the sun cooperated in the morn and his father's men could be persuaded to indulge him. Far better to face things he could understand and best than to try to unravel the mysteries of womanhood.

Robin rolled over, pulled the blankets over his head and prepared to dream of war and bloodshed. It was much safer than the alternative.

8

Anne woke to find a very dim light trying to push its way through the bed curtains. Movement was beyond her at the moment so she simply snuggled deeper into the covers and put off the moment when she would have to leave the comforting warmth. There was no other sound in the chamber, so she assumed Amanda and Isabelle had already braved the chill to begin their days. For once, Anne didn't take issue with having been let sleep. Who knew how many more such mornings she might have to dawdle at her leisure? Soon enough she would rise and cloister herself in Gwen's solar with her ladies. There was sewing to be done, fine stitches for decoration to be wrought, and many other things with which to occupy her mind. At least she would have no trouble from her father that day and she had Rhys to thank for that.

Just the night before, when Geoffrey had arrived in Rhys's solar and begun speaking loudly of their impending return to Fenwyck, Rhys had begun tempting him with thoughts of a hunt. Miles amused himself by raising a kennel of hounds, and Anne knew their lure would be a powerful one for her father. Rhys had declared firmly that it would take at least a se'nnight to prepare and who knew how long to enjoy the outing. When she'd realized she had perhaps a fortnight's more grace, she had retired to her chamber and fair jumped for the joy of it. It wasn't as long as she would have liked, but perhaps Rhys could convince her sire of something else in time. This reprieve was enough.

But that didn't mean she was going to take unnecessary risks in encountering her father. Nay, 'twas best she seek something to eat, then retire to Gwen's solar. That might also spare her any unsavoury encounters with the other soul she fully intended to avoid—though she imagined he would be just as busy avoiding her.

She sighed, past fathoming why he did anything. One moment the night before he'd been looking at her as if she'd been a particularly appealing leg of mutton, then the next as if she'd been directly responsible for handfuls of dung set carefully inside his boots. What she had done to deserve either was anyone's guess. She'd simply been looking at him.

But simple things had long been beyond Robin's capabilities of enjoyment. Nay, all had become either life or death with him. He could never go to the lists for the sheer sport of it; with him it was either humiliate or perish in the attempt. Even chess was something he now turned into a full-scale battle. It hadn't always been so. They had played often during his illness and he had actually laughed the first time she had bested him. Gone was that mischievous boy who had spent so much time with her.

One day he had been laughing and the next cursing bitterly. She had never been quite clear on what had happened to change him so and he absolutely refused to talk about it. From that time on, he had shunned her. It had pained her greatly at the time. She liked to believe she had now moved past the hurt, but even thinking on it grieved her afresh. By the saints, what had happened to change him so?

He had not always been so troubled. She could remember much of the mischief he had combined when they had all been together while Artane was being finished. One night she had retired to the tent she had shared with Amanda to find a snake in her blankets—a dead one fortunately. She had retaliated by putting a dead rat under his pillow. It had taken her and Amanda all day to find one and then Amanda had been the one to kill it, as Anne had not had the courage. How Robin had howled when he had found it. The memory still made her smile.

But even with his boyish antics, he had possessed a sweetness she had come to treasure. He'd been just as likely to present her with a fistful of sweet-smelling flowers as he had some creature of dubious origins. She had adored him.

Then the fever had come. It had left half the village near Artane dead in its wake. Robin had been the only one of the family taken sick and for a time she had wondered if he would die too. He had been ten-and-four at the time and already very strong, else he might have lost his life. She had her own convalescence to endure, but she had spent as much time with him as allowed. They had played chess for hours when he felt strong enough. When he had become weary, she had read to him haltingly, and made up stories to amuse him.

It had taken him almost a year to regain his strength. And sometime during that year, he had changed. She had been up and hobbling about, amusing him as she could. Then one day her attempts to tend him had been harshly rejected. She would enter his room to entertain him only to find herself summarily ejected. Even if he spoke to her, he would not look at her, and his words were always clipped and curt.

He had thrown himself into his training. When others were inside the hall taking their ease, Robin had been out in the lists working. He became so ferocious in his sparring that the only ones who would tolerate his aggressiveness were his father and Nicholas, and Nicholas usually found himself vanquished in a matter of minutes.

Soon there had been no one to stand against him save Rhys. Robin had earned his spurs just before his nineteenth birthday and earned them he had. The lord he had gone to squire with was forever complaining to Rhys about how Robin ground his men to powder.

And then Robin had gone off to war. She had thought at the time that it was so that he might need not look at her anymore. Then she had come to suspect that it might have been to prove himself. There was no way of knowing, for 'twas a certainty he would not tell her of his own accord and she certainly wouldn't be asking him.

She sat up slowly, wincing at the protest her leg set up. There would be no vigils in the chapel today. Perhaps it was well that Robin was home. Her body needed a rest.

She rose stiffly and hobbled over to the window. She opened the shutters and leaned on the stone surrounding the opening. The sky was gray outside, which came as little surprise. Though she was passing fond of the rain, her father had done nothing but complain about the drizzle from the moment they had arrived. Anne breathed deeply, relishing both the smell of rainy sea air and no complaints to listen to. And with that lightness of heart and mind came feelings she couldn't deny.

Kind feelings.

Toward that very complicated soul she couldn't seem to put from her mind.

How could she harden her heart against that sweet dimple that appeared in his left cheek on those rare occasions when he grinned, or the wicked gleam in his eye when he was about some devilry? He was just as handsome as Rhys was, and that was something to marvel over for Robin's true sire was Alain of Ayre. Indeed, though Anne had never known Lord Ayre, she couldn't help but think that Robin looked a great deal like Rhys.

And she wondered just how such a thing could have come about.

Anne looked down from the rain-laden sky and turned

her attentions to the courtyard. Perhaps she would see aught there that would distract her from her contemplation of things she would never know. With any luck what she wouldn't see would be her sire waiting for her to rise so he could tell her that he'd changed his mind and they were returning to Fenwyck forthwith.

But it wasn't her sire who stared up at her.

It was Robin.

She was just as surprised by the sight of him as she had been in the chapel. She jumped away from the window and banged the shutters closed. It was well past time that she was up and doing. There wouldn't be anything left of breakfast if she didn't hurry downstairs.

She dressed quickly and ran a comb through her long hair. She contemplated donning a head covering, then discarded the idea. No one ever looked at her anyway. She would offend no soul she could think of. Perhaps she might break her fast then retreat to the sanctuary of Gwen's solar before her father managed to lay hands upon her person.

She soon found that the great hall, however, was not as empty as she had hoped it would be. One table was still set up near the hearth and men flanked it. Rhys sat at the head of the table with Nicholas to his left. Robin was just sitting down on his right. Members of Rhys's personal guard were there, as well as men Anne assumed belonged to Robin and Nicholas, for she recognized none of them. They looked to be deep in talk.

Then throaty laughter erupted and Anne doubted very much the talk was all that serious. At least her father was nowhere to be seen. But Anne wasn't about to invite herself to sit in council with the warriors before her. Yet before she could make her escape, Rhys had turned and beckoned to her. Though it was tempting to flee, she would have looked more foolish had she done that than if she continued on her course.

All the men at the table rose as she approached and she found herself for the second time in as many days blushing furiously. Nicholas gaped at her with his mouth open.

Anne looked at the other men and they stared at her in much the same manner.

Robin, however, seemed to be clenching his jaw.

She was unsurprised.

But the collective interest she was faced with caused her serious anxiety. And then a horrible thought occurred to her and she looked down hastily, fully expecting to see her clothes falling off in some embarrassing manner.

She frowned. She was laced in all the right places. She looked up again and was amazed to find that several of the men were giving her roguish grins. It flustered her so badly that she almost stumbled. Immediately one of the men jumped up and hastened to her side, offering her his arm.

"Sir Richard of Moncrief at your service," he said with a low bow.

She looked at him, knowing her mouth was hanging open most unattractively, but unable to help herself. Why was this fool being so polite? And why by the saints was he wearing that ridiculous smile? She knew very well who he was for he was one of Rhys's men. Why was he presenting himself to her as if she'd been a great lady?

"I need no aid," she managed, with as much dignity as she could muster.

"Then perhaps you would at least allow me to escort you to the table?"

A flurry of activity ensued as several men made a dash for one of the chairs put up next to the wall. The seat was brought and set down next to Rhys. Anne had the overwhelming urge to crawl into the rushes and disappear. She used every ounce of pride at her disposal to walk across the floor without displaying her limp overmuch, then sat as gracefully as she could.

And still she was the focus of attention.

"Anne," Nicholas said, reaching over his father and taking her hand, "you are a beauty. Don't you agree lads?"

A chorus of male voices assented with vigorous ayes. Anne pulled her hand away and looked at Rhys.

"My lord," she began and her voice cracked.

Rhys put his arm around her. "What is it, daughter?"

She leaned over toward him. "They're all staring at me," she whispered frantically.

"Ah, but the lads only find you lovely," Rhys whispered in return. "Perhaps 'tis that their manners need improving."

"I'll see to it," Robin growled from where he sat next to her.

"Ah, a bit of bloodshed," Nicholas said, rubbing his hands together enthusiastically. "How I love it when Robin pursues a righteous cause."

"Nay," Rhys said, thrusting out his hand and stopping what Anne was certain would have been Robin's leap over the table. "None of that, if you please. Anne, I would have a cup of wine if you felt so inclined."

Anne was grateful for the excuse to leave, and she recognized the request as such. "At once, my lord."

Half the table rose to their feet. There were equally as many offers to help with any such endeavor. Anne would have turned and fled if she'd been able.

"She can get the bloody wine herself," Robin snarled. "Sit down, the lot of you."

The men resumed their seats slowly, all save Nicholas.

"Nick, don't even think it."

Anne left before she had to watch Robin and Nicholas go at each other again. And she tried not to put more behind word or action than had been there to start. Perhaps Robin merely had a need to speak with the men and didn't want them going off on a foolish errand. Perhaps Nicholas only sought to annoy his brother and had found a way to do so completely.

Perhaps she would be better served by retreating to bed.

She shook her head and made her way to the kitchen. She procured a bottle of wine and a wooden plate piled high with sweetmeats, knowing Rhys's fondness for them. She returned to the hall, praying she would gain the table and then escape without anyone noticing her.

And then before she truly realized what was happening,

she felt her foot slip from beneath her. She tried desperately to keep bottle, plate and her person upright, but it was hopeless. The bottle slipped from her hands, plate and sweetmeats went flying and she closed her eyes, prepared to meet the rushes with an ungraceful thump.

But she never touched the ground.

She found herself cradled in strong arms and lifted up. She looked into Robin's face, which was only a hand's breadth from hers. She wanted to throw her arms around him, bury her face in his shoulder, and hide. Making a complete fool out of herself had not been in her plans that morning.

But instead, all she could do was stare into his gray eyes and hope he could see that she was grateful for the rescue.

He didn't move. Considering the fact that he could have dropped her where he stood, lack of movement was, to her mind, not an ill omen.

"Thank you," she managed.

That seemed to spark some sense of time and place in him. He set her on her feet with surprising gentleness, then stepped back. "The bottle can be replaced," he said gruffly, walking away.

Anne stood there in the middle of the great hall, shards of pottery, spilt wine and soggy sweetmeats at her feet and found she could do nothing else but stand and shake. She toyed with the idea of bursting into tears, but that wasn't very appealing. What she wished was that she had time to consider what had just happened.

Robin had rescued her. And to have done so, he had to have been watching her come across the hall. The bottle could be replaced? Did he mean, then, that she couldn't?

She shook her head, hoping that her foolish thoughts would spill from her ear and join the refuse on the floor.

Nicholas appeared before her, looking at her with concern. He was followed closely by several other of Rhys's personal guardsmen. One of the younger ones knelt before her.

"My lady, forgive me. I tossed one of the dogs a bone

at supper last night and saw him carry it over here. 'Tis my fault you slipped."

"I'll see him repaid," Nicholas said briskly, "if you like, Anne."

"Could we please return to the business of the day?" Robin exclaimed from his place at the table. "We've manly matters to discuss!"

Nicholas pursed his lips, dismissed the guardsman with a flick of his wrist, then smiled at Anne. "Manly matters be damned. What say you to a walk in the garden?"

" 'Tis chilly outside, Nicky," Anne said, wanting nothing more than to escape upstairs.

"I know."

She looked at him in surprise. "You know?"

"A perfect excuse to use all my efforts to keep you warm."

She laughed. She couldn't help herself. It was the most ridiculous thing she'd heard all morning. "Perhaps I would be better served to fetch a cloak."

"Now you insult my chivalry," Nicholas said, with a frown approaching one of Robin's milder ones. "My honor is besmirched and I demand satisfaction."

"Shall we do so with blades?" she asked, finding a smile came readily when induced by such charm. "Or should we settle for something less messy?"

"I'll think on it," he said. "Wait for me and I'll fetch my cloak for you."

Anne watched him make her a low bow, kiss her hand, then trot off to fetch something appropriate for her to wear. She snuck a glance at the table to find the men all dutifully discussing matters of war and training. Robin most pointedly gave her his back. But it was what she was accustomed to, so she didn't begrudge him the like.

Besides, Nicholas of Artane planned to take her for a walk in the garden. What need had she of anything more spectacular to pass the morn?

•   •   •

It was much later in the day that Anne found herself in her accustomed place in Gwen's solar. The fire was warm, the company fine, and Anne had something especially lovely under her needle. She set down her stitchery and let the pleasure of being home wash over her. She closed her eyes and imagined how it would be should such contentment be hers for the rest of her life.

It was with a start that she woke to find that conversation had waned and it was nigh onto time for supper. She sincerely hoped no one had noticed her napping, but no one seemed to be paying her any heed. Anne looked carefully about her at the women who were finished with their day's work.

Three of the women were wives of Rhys's personal guardsmen. Anne's stepmother never would have associated with women below her station and Anne had always admired Gwen's disregard of convention. The women were pleasant and witty and Anne enjoyed their company very much.

Amanda and Isabelle were there, of course, though Anne knew Amanda would have rather been out in the lists wreaking havoc with a bow or something equally as perilous—though Anne sometimes wondered if she shouldn't have learned a bit of that kind of thing herself. It would have served her well if she'd found herself attacked.

The remaining occupant of the chamber, save Gwen herself, was Edith of Sedgwick. Anne looked at her from under her eyelashes and wondered about her. She'd come to Artane when she'd been a girl of ten summers. Anne had been eight at the time, but she remembered vividly her first sight of the girl. She'd looked as if she'd been wearing the same clothes for years, for her skirts were well above her ankles and the cloth had been riddled with holes and rents. She'd smelled passing foul and her eyes had been full of a wild light.

Gwen and Rhys had taken her in, more because she was in need of aid than that she was Rhys's kin. Rhys's mother had been of Sedgwick and Rhys should have been lord of that keep, though Anne knew he had no desire for it. Rhys's cousin was lord there, at Rhys's behest, and Anne suspected that being Rhys's vassal didn't sit well with the man.

Baldwin was Lord Sedgwick's nephew and likely very much underfoot there, which was no doubt why he'd found himself packed off to Artane at the first possible moment. Rhys had taken the boy willingly enough, though only so he might always know what Baldwin was combining. Anne knew his reasoning well, though she couldn't say she'd been overfond of the logic. She had complained bitterly to Rhys about the torment through which Baldwin put not only her, but anyone weaker than he. Rhys had always remained firm. Baldwin would stay, but he would be watched closely. Apparently such scrutiny didn't bother Baldwin, for he had never seemed overly anxious to leave the comfort of Artane's supper tables.

Edith was much different from her brother, though, for she never complained and never wrought any mischief.

Anne looked at her dark head bent over her stitchery, then smiled faintly in acknowledgment when Edith lifted her head and caught her staring. The woman was fair enough, Anne thought, and passing pleasant when compared to her brother. Gwen was fond enough of her.

But Anne was, as she had been the first time she'd laid eyes on the girl, torn between compassion and fear, for despite her pretty manners, to Anne's mind the wildness had never quite faded from Edith's eyes.

"Ladies, let us be off," Gwen said, rising. "Anne, love, are you coming?"

"In a moment, Mother," Anne said, wanting nothing more than a moment or two of peace in which to think on events much more interesting than stitchery and women's gossip.

The women left and Anne remained in her chair, staring into the flames. It had been a most remarkable day. She was loth to let anything—supper, her father or other souls in the keep—disturb her contemplation of it.

Nicholas had entertained her the whole of the afternoon.

Robin had rescued her from a tumble on the floor.

There had to be a good reason for both, but she had no stomach for divining what it was. Likely Robin was feeling some sort of fraternal sentiment toward her and Nicholas saw an opportunity to irritate his brother by thwarting the same as often as possible. She could hardly credit Nicholas for true interest and it was even more foolish to think Robin might have any but the most indifferent of feelings toward her.

With a sigh, she threw her sewing into a basket at her feet and rose. It was dark and she was hungry. It was past time she descended to the warmth of the fire in the great hall.

She stepped out into the passageway. The torches were out again. It wasn't unusual, but it was unnerving. Anne peered into the dim passageway, but there was nothing to be seen. She turned and limped quickly to the stairwell, then started down the steps. She saw a glimmer of light around the corner and let out a sigh of relief.

And then she heard a faint sound.

It was the sound keys made when brushed together, or a chain of some sort.

Before she could truly be frightened by the realization that she'd heard a like sound before, she lost her footing and stumbled, her hands flying out to catch her balance. It was hopeless. Her weak leg gave out from underneath her and she tumbled down the remaining stairs, crying out as the edges of them slammed into her body. She rolled to a heap at the bottom and remained motionless, almost afraid to move.

"Anne!"

She heard Nicholas's shout and then the sound of his boots thumping down the passageway. Within moments he was kneeling next to her, gently running his hand over her arms and legs.

"Don't move," he commanded as she started to sit up.

"I'm fine," she insisted, pushing his hands away. It was only then that she noticed the pain in her wrist, pain that intensified as she moved it.

Nicholas took her wrist in his hand and gently ran his fingers over it. "It isn't broken," he said, frowning over it. "We'll bind it with stiff cloths and keep it immobile—"

"By the bloody saints, what is happening here?" Robin bellowed from down the passageway. Anne lay back with a groan. The last thing she needed was to have Robin see her in such an undignified sprawl. She made a halfhearted attempt to toss her skirts back down over her knees.

"Nick, you fool, move out of my way," Robin growled, shoving his brother aside. "Anne, what's befallen you? When will you learn to be more careful? These stairs are steep, much too steep for you to walk down them in the dark. Must I watch over your every move to see you do not kill yourself?"

Anne could have borne his tirade in silence, but his strong hands roaming over her limbs, checking gently for further injuries was something she could not bear.

And then she felt his hand on her ruined thigh. She shoved it away and sat up, backing away from him. "Don't," she gasped.

"Anne—"

She could hardly believe his actions. Had no one ever told him there were parts of a woman a man simply didn't touch?

"Leave me be," she managed. "I'm perfectly sound."

"I see," he said stiffly. "Nicholas can see to your injuries, but I cannot."

"He wasn't pawing my leg!" she exclaimed.

"Believe me," Robin snapped. "I meant nothing by it."

She expected nothing less, but his words hurt her just the same. "My only injury is to my wrist and I can bind that well enough myself," she said. "Favor some other wench with your impersonal touch."

Robin's eyes flashed in the torchlight. "There are many who long for it, I can assure you of that."

"Then find one and avail yourself of her," Anne said, turning her face away. "I can see to myself."

"Then see to yourself and trouble me no further with your accidents."

There was a grunt from Nicholas and Anne could only assume Robin had elbowed him out of his way. Robin's curses trailed behind him as he left, then finally died away. Anne lay in silence, grateful for the pain in her wrist that numbed the pain in her soul. Robin would never want her. Why had she ever allowed such a dream to have a place in her heart?

The most sensible thing to do would be to stay out of his way and pray he decided to return to the continent quickly. Perhaps once he was gone, she would rid herself once and for all of the foolish notions she had entertained. Even a simple man wouldn't have wanted a maimed wife. Robin wasn't a simple man, he was the future lord of Artane. He had little patience and even less heart. She would likely be better off with a man of her father's choosing. At least she would know she was wanted for her dowry.

The sound of cloth being torn distracted her and she looked up. Nicholas had stripped off his tunic and was currently tearing the latter into shreds. Anne averted her eyes from his bare chest. She continued to look away from him as he bound her wrist securely. Then he helped her to her feet.

"I'll have to feed you while you rest that wing for a bit," he said with a smile. "Will you oblige me? It has been many months since I last had the honor of serving a maid so very fetching and sweet."

She sighed. "Nicholas, stop, please."

Nicholas put his arm around her shoulders and led her down the final set of stairs to the great hall. He sat her down and smiled at her. "I'll run and clothe myself. Save my place. Or I'll be forced to kill anyone who's taken my seat," he said with a mock frown. "Father wouldn't approve of bloodshed at his dinner table."

Anne nodded absently, then frowned when Nicholas squatted down next to her chair.

"Do you feel unwell, Anne?"

She shook her head. "Nay. Why?"

"I just wondered if you'd felt dizzy and lost your balance. You did lose your balance, didn't you?"

She nodded, forcing a smile to her lips. "Of course, Nicholas. I'm just clumsy. I'll be more careful in the future."

He nodded and rose, seemingly content with her answer. Anne sighed in relief once he had gone. At least Nicholas wouldn't ask any more questions she'd have to answer with a lie.

Nay, she hadn't lost her balance.

She'd been pushed.

9

Edith stood in the alcove of the tower chamber and stared out the window. It soothed her to do the like. There was no sea near Sedgwick, and very little wind to take away the stenches of castle life. The sea here was so many things.

Savage.

Violent.

Beautiful.

It was the thing she loved best about Artane. It was also one of the reasons she never wanted to leave the place.

Not that she had any intention of ever leaving, of course.

The argument behind her increased enough in volume that she could no longer concentrate on her contemplation of the waves. The dispute had been going on for some time, far longer than Edith would have permitted. Perhaps 'twas that her brother and Maude were so ill-suited to a battle of words. 'Twas a certainty they were not equal to a battle of wits. Edith turned and listened to them scream at each other things that made little sense at all.

"Enough!" she said loudly.

Both Baldwin and Maude looked at her in surprise.

"The entire keep can no doubt hear you," Edith said in a quieter tone. "Perhaps you might consider that as you shout yourselves hoarse."

The other two settled for glares to express their displeasure. Edith looked at Maude first. The girl was wild-eyed and disheveled from her hasty flight up to the tower chamber. Baldwin looked just as disheveled, but that was from his recent return to the keep. Apparently his errands for Lord Rhys had been unsatisfying, for he had only been gone a pair of days. Edith suspected that her brother was relieved to be back. He was consumed by the thought of slaying Robin; any time away from the keep had no doubt been a burden.

"And *I* say," Baldwin said, "that you should leave her be. Don't give him a reason not to come to the lists."

"He doesn't love her!" Maude exclaimed.

"And he does you?" Baldwin said.

Unkind, Edith mused, but true. She watched Maude's temper flush across her face and knew that the time for silence was over.

"Leave Anne to us," Edith said, turning to her brother. "She won't be a distraction."

"See that she isn't," Baldwin said. "And keep *her*," he said gesturing with his head toward Maude, "far from me. I can't bear her screeching."

"And you'll be in the lists?" Edith asked. "Honing your skills?"

"Waiting for him to come timidly from the great hall to face me," Baldwin said, starting for the door. "I'll humiliate him immediately, of course."

"Better that than killing him too soon," Edith agreed.

Baldwin only grunted and left the chamber.

Once he was gone, Edith turned to Maude.

"Pushing her was foolish," she said bluntly.

Maude shrugged and pouted. "She was there. I was there. It seemed the best thing to do."

"You could have killed her."

"And if I had?" Maude challenged.

"You are better off not knowing what would have become of you had you done so," Edith said pleasantly. "Now, let us turn our minds to something of a happier nature. I think we should torment her, aye, but not kill her. Understood?"

Maude looked unconvinced. Edith sighed. One more chance would she give the girl before she took action against her. She could afford no more disobedience. Her plans were carefully laid and she would allow no deviations.

Edith handed Maude a leather envelope. "Put this in wine and see that she drinks it. But use it sparingly."

Maude blinked. "Poison?"

"Very deadly. Use it sparingly," she reminded her.

Maude looked happier than she had in days. She clutched her treasure and departed the chamber without another word.

Edith turned away and resumed her position at the window. The sea rolled in ceaselessly, patiently, with a roar that was ever just on the edge of what she could hear. She loved the sea. Odd how she'd never known of it until she'd come to Artane.

Aye, 'twas right that now she'd found it, she never be forced to leave it. This pleasure would be hers for the rest of her life.

That also was included in her carefully laid plans.

10

Robin strode purposefully from the great hall, his squire trotting along dutifully behind him. Robin's mail shirt likely should have hampered his striding, but he was accustomed to the weight. What he wasn't accustomed to, however, was the intense irritation and stung pride that threatened to sap all his powers of concentration.

He strode to the lists, needing distraction more than he'd ever needed it before in his life. Though, in truth, how he could be more distracted than he was at present, he surely didn't know. He couldn't remember the last time he'd slept well and his appetite was failing. If he hadn't known better, he would have thought himself suffering from some slow, lingering illness.

Unfortunately, he knew exactly whence his frustration sprang and he fully intended to seek refuge in the lists and drive all thoughts of her from his mind. He would not think about her, nor about the fact that she had shunned him for the past two days, preferring the company of his lackwit younger brother. Anne's preference in men was a sharp sting to his pride. Nicholas's visage was no more pleasing than his!

Nicholas's skill in healing was nothing to sing praises

over either. Robin would have sooner trusted his precious flesh to a scullery maid than to his bumbling younger brother. Nor was Nicholas's disposition that tolerable. Fluff and prettiness was all his brother possessed. If Anne found that more appealing than a real man, then she was welcome to her folly and he sincerely hoped she earned stomach pains as reward from the sweetness.

Robin stopped in the outer bailey and looked about him to see what sort of sport would appeal to him most at present. There was the quintain, as usual, as well as hand-to-hand combat. Robin wasn't overfond of the bow, so he found himself not at all tempted by that.

And then he spotted him. Baldwin of Sedgwick. His nemesis, the one man he hated with all his soul. So, the wretch had returned from whatever errand he'd been sent on. Robin had no doubt the lout had been lurking about in the countryside, robbing unwary travelers and stirring up like mischief wherever he could. But now he was home, and Robin was in the mood for sport. He smiled. The morn was shaping up nicely indeed.

In the past, he'd cursed his father for keeping Baldwin at Artane, but Rhys had insisted. His theory was that it was far easier to watch an enemy at close range than it was to let him go and wonder where he would strike next. Patrick of Sedgwick was actually Rhys's uncle, though no one at Artane would have any dealings with the whoreson. Rhys's mother had fled Sedgwick to escape harsh treatment and 'twas very late in life that Rhys had even discovered he was kin with them.

The hatred between Artane and Sedgwick ran deep and truly nowhere did it run deeper than in Robin. Robin had the nagging suspicion it might be his undoing some day, but for now he was young and strong and Baldwin was nowhere near his equal. It was past time to repay Baldwin for a few of his insults.

He strode over to the near end of the jousting field and took the reins of a horse away from a squire. He swung up into the saddle, snatched a shield out of the poor lad's hands and picked up a lance. Baldwin was at the opposite end of the field, leaning casually against the outer bailey wall. Robin stood up in the stirrups.

"Sedgwick!" he shouted. "Are you man enough to come against me, or will you remain clinging to the wall like a woman?"

Baldwin's response was immediate. Robin settled himself in the saddle and smiled grimly, already planning his strategy.

"Rob, your helmet!" Nicholas bellowed from near the wall.

Robin waved his brother's words away—foolishly no doubt, but he was past reason. Besides, Baldwin hadn't the spine to put a lance through his eye, not with so many witnesses about. Robin waited until Baldwin was prepared, then put his spurs to the warhorse's side. He guided the mount with naught but his knees as he positioned both the shield and his lance. He struck Baldwin full in the center of his chest, sending him toppling backwards. Robin wheeled his mount around and dropped to the ground. Aye, this was the sport he longed for. He waited impatiently until Baldwin had risen, then waited for Baldwin's attack.

"Whoreson," Baldwin spat, lashing out viciously.

"That is *my lord whoreson* to you, Sir Baldwin. Ever you forget your manners. Perhaps I should teach you a few this morning."

Baldwin's largest flaw, and a fatal one it was, was his temper. Robin had been too young to take advantage of it in his youth, but he had studied Baldwin long, marking all his weaknesses for future use. Now he was older and the future had come.

"I'll kill you this time," Baldwin snarled, his eyes blazing.

"Indeed," Robin drawled. "And find yourself dangling from the end of a rope come nightfall, I'd imagine. But I wouldn't worry over that possibility, Baldwin. My sisters could best you in a swordfight. I daresay I can manage the feat as well."

Robin heard Nicholas's hearty laughter from behind

him and knew that his brother and likely his father were looking on. Five years ago, having his father watch him would have unnerved him completely. Five years of warring had done much to work that unsurety out of him. He was confident in his skill and had no doubts that he could best anyone on the field. Except perhaps his sire. Even at two score and five, Rhys of Artane was still a master.

But Robin was his father's son and had learned well his craft. He continued to toy with Baldwin, pretending to fall back only to attack with parries that left Baldwin stumbling in surprise.

And when Baldwin let his guard slip, Robin shunned his sword, stepped in and caught the man under the chin with his fist. His foe slumped to the ground, senseless.

Robin felt wonderful. It was the first time in months he'd felt a genuine smile come to his face. He shoved his sword into the ground, cracked his knuckles with a happy snap and came close to beating on his chest in a most victorious fashion.

"A wrestle!" a young voice cried.

"Aye, a wrestle!"

Robin looked about to find his youngest brothers racing toward him. He smiled indulgently as he motioned for his squire to come relieve him of his mail shirt. Let the children come. It was the least he could do when he'd had such success already.

So he took them on, two on one, and allowed them to win. Of course, it was a lengthy battle. No sense in giving the lads less than a full sense of victory.

"We have you!" Montgomery cried, sitting on Robin's chest and waving his fist over his head triumphantly.

"And so easily done," John agreed with a war cry that set Robin's ears to ringing.

Robin only lay in the mud with them sitting upon him, and laughed at their boasts. His own pride had been mightily assuaged and he was ready to concede almost any other battle. Robin put his hands behind his head and sighed in contentment.

He suspected that life simply could not improve.

His brothers were eventually pulled off him and a hand extended. Robin allowed his father to pull him to his feet.

"Tolerable, for a whelp of your size," Rhys said gruffly.

Robin laughed and clapped his father on the shoulder. "Ah, such high praise, Papa. I think I might blush."

"Let us go sup, then perhaps you'll indulge me this afternoon. I've yet to find a lad to stand against me and I find my swordplay has suffered because of it." He grabbed Robin around the back of the neck and shook him. "I'm glad to have you home. Perhaps now I'll have some decent sport."

There was simply no compliment higher than that. Robin had to cough to cover his grin of pleasure. Nicholas groaned.

"Father, his arrogance is excessive as it is. I pray you, do not add to it more than necessary."

Rhys pursed his lips. "You both have more arrogance than is good for you, but I'll not complain. I will complain, however, about your short stays in the lists, Nick. I daresay you and I are the only sport for Robin, yet you will find yourself unable to stand against him if you do not train harder."

Nicholas waved a dismissive hand as he started back to the hall. "I've been tending Anne, Father. 'Tis a much more important task than tending Robin, believe me."

Robin stiffened and would have gone after his brother immediately had his father's heavy hand on his shoulder not kept him in place.

"He's baiting you, Rob," Rhys said quietly.

"I could not care less what he does with Anne," Robin said, trying mightily to sound more uninterested than he was. "Let him wed her if he wills it." He looked behind him for his squire. "See to my gear, Jason. I will be within."

"As you will, my lord."

Robin turned and walked with his sire across the lists. Rhys refrained from speech until they had reached the steps leading up to the great hall. Then he paused. Robin steeled himself. He knew something of great import was about to be distilled on his pitiful ears. His father was wearing that look. It wasn't often that he wore it, but Robin had learned to pay heed when he did. Robin could only hope it was something he could bear to hear.

"Anne is a very special woman, Robin," Rhys said slowly, "and she will require a sure hand and a loyal heart to win her trust."

Robin felt as if he should say something, but there was naught to say. His father had it aright. If Anne needed anything, 'twas a loyal heart.

"Nicholas coddles her overmuch and I daresay she doesn't care for it."

"I've told him that," Robin muttered.

"That isn't the way to win her," Rhys continued.

Robin waited, but apparently no more wisdom was forthcoming without some prompting on his part. Somehow, though, he wasn't sure he wanted to hear the remainder. He turned his face away and scowled as he looked out over the courtyard. It was filled with ghosts, shadows of him and Anne when they were growing to maturity, teasing and playing together. Robin could still remember how she had seemed to worship him and how it had empowered yet humbled him at the same time. Ah, the fervent vows he had made as a callow youth, vows to become a man she would be proud of, a man worthy of her goodness.

And then she had been trampled and he had been humiliated. She had withdrawn and he had let anger and bitterness fill his soul. Had he been a fool? Was it truly possible to undo the past and have her?

Robin took a deep breath and let it out carefully. He put his shoulders back. Best have the question over with and the answer received before he lost what courage he had remaining him.

"And how would a man win her?" he asked carefully.

Rhys clapped him on the shoulder. "Why would you care?"

Robin watched, open-mouthed, as his father entered the hall, leaving him standing outside on the step. He doubted he would have been more surprised if his father had clouted him on the nose.

But there was some truth in what Rhys had said. What did he care?

The problem was, he did.

The hall door opened and Robin fully expected his father to come back out and finish what he'd started. Unfortunately, the soul who stepped outside was none other than Geoffrey of Fenwyck. Robin tried a weak smile.

"My lord."

Geoffrey looked at him with intense dislike. "Oh. 'Tis you."

Robin made Geoffrey a bow. Surely a bow couldn't go wrong.

But when he straightened, it was to see Geoffrey give him a look he might have given a plump and steaming pile of dung he'd narrowly avoided plunging his foot into. Fenwyck then grunted and brushed past Robin without further comment.

Apparently the girl was not to be won through her sire.

Then Robin clapped his hand to his head, hard enough to make himself flinch, though likely not hard enough to rid himself of his unwise thoughts. He was beginning to wonder what would be worse for him—winning Anne or not. If this was the state he was to be left in by the deed, perhaps he was better off without her.

He entered the hall to find Nicholas and Anne sitting close to the fire. Nicholas was hovering over her as if she'd been a plate of sweets he intended to devour as quickly as possible whilst allowing no other a taste.

Robin was momentarily tempted to move his brother by force, but thought better of it. Then again, there was no sense in leaving Nicholas free to accustom himself to Anne's nearness.

"Nick, a word!" he called as neutrally as if he had nothing more important to discuss than what might stand to arrive upon the supper table within the hour.

"I'm busy," his brother returned, not looking away from Anne.

Robin decided then that perhaps familial murder wasn't such a poor idea. He gritted his teeth as he crossed the room, trying to keep his fingers loose and not clenched into a purposeful fist. He stopped directly beside his brother.

"Your horse, I believe, has thrown a shoe," Robin said. "You should see to it."

Nicholas only looked at him and raised an eyebrow. "I believe Father has a blacksmith for that kind of thing. Why don't you take the beast yourself? As you can see, I am much occupied at the moment."

"I believe this is something that requires your personal overseeing. You wouldn't want to have your horse lamed by your inattentions, would you?"

"I'm sure my horse will keep for a few more moments."

Robin looked at his brother and hoped the lad could see his own death in Robin's eyes. Nicholas merely smiled serenely. Robin knew his brother was enjoying himself immensely and that irritated him further.

"You should go," Robin growled. *"Now."*

"Can't," Nicholas said cheerfully. "Have things to do here."

Robin seethed silently. Well, short of taking the oaf by the ear and hauling him out of the hall bodily, there was nothing more he could do to distract Nicholas from his purpose.

And then Robin espied the empty stool next to Anne.

Robin planted himself upon it with all the alacrity of a pig leaping upon fresh slops. He looked at his brother archly, daring him to issue a challenge—any sort of challenge which would allow Robin the opportunity to justifiably beat him senseless.

"You've mud in your hair," Nicholas remarked. "And something else that smells rather foul. Perhaps you should go have a wash?"

Robin was halfway to his feet, his fists at the ready,

when the import of his brother's words struck him.

Did he smell foul?

Unchivalrous and unrefined as he might have been, even he knew that a man did not leave a favorable impression on a maid if he reeked of manure. Robin found himself crouched uncomfortably between standing and sitting and could do nothing but surreptitiously sniff, on the off chance that Nicholas had things aright.

He smelled dung, but that could have been on his boots. It was acceptable on one's boots, of that he was certain.

And then, just as he was trying to decide whether he should continue on to a stand or gracefully return to a sit, he felt the lightest of touches on his arm.

" 'Tis but a bit of mud, Nicky."

It was the voice of an angel and Robin felt the import of it wash over him like a soothing wave. He hardly dared look at her, lest he see laughter lurking in her eyes, but he found himself powerless to stop. Her face was turned away from him so he couldn't divine her expression, but her hand was still upon his arm. Before he could truly unravel the mystery of her touch and what it might mean, she had removed her hand and clasped them both in her lap again.

That was enough for him.

Robin sat.

And he glared up at his brother.

" 'Tis but a bit of mud, idiot," he said with a growl.

"It doesn't smell of mud," Nicholas said, sniffing enthusiastically. " 'Tis definitely dung. Anne, have a care lest the stench leave you faint."

Robin suddenly found himself staring into pale green eyes and he could do nothing but blink stupidly in return. Then she smiled a bit and the sight almost felled him where he sat.

"Montgomery and John boasted of their victory," she said. "It was kind of you to give it to them, even if it left you the one lolling in the dirt."

"Dung," Nicholas repeated. "Dung. Possibly something even more foul. Is that possible, do you think, Anne?

Something fouler than dung? Whatever it is, Robin seems to have rolled himself liberally in it."

Anne turned her head to look at a small commotion near the hall door. Robin looked at Nicholas and glared.

"Death," he mouthed.

Nicholas's returning look was full of meaning Robin couldn't mistake.

His brother intended to woo Anne. And he wanted Robin out of his way.

Before Robin could rise and throttle him, Nicholas had taken his leave of Anne and crossed the floor to greet Fenwyck as he entered the hall.

"Perfect," Robin muttered. He turned to Anne, intent on asking her if she cared to escape the hall before they had to watch what would surely be one of the more nauseating events in history—namely Nicholas flattering Anne's father—but Anne was already pushing herself to her feet.

"Best see to supper," she said.

And then she was gone.

Robin was tempted to offer her his aid, but that would have removed him from earshot of Nicholas and Geoffrey and he had no intentions of missing out on any of that conversation—should he be able to stomach it. There was no sense in not knowing exactly what his brother was about.

It would give him something to say when he eulogized the fool.

For there was not a means conceived in either Heaven or Hell by which Nicholas de Piaget would woo and win the lady Anne. Robin wondered why he had begun the morn with such confusion clouding his brain. Anne was his. She had always been his. And if Nicholas thought differently, it was past time Robin disabused him of that notion. Then he would turn his own thoughts to how Anne might be won.

Then he caught a whiff of himself. Perhaps Nicholas had it aright. Well, there was no sense in giving either Fenwyck or his daughter a reason to think poorly of him.

Robin left the hall at a run, planning on a quick wash, then a return for eavesdropping.

11

Anne stood near the hearth and watched several things that currently unfolded before her.

There were the preparations for supper, of course. That was nothing unusual. Anne had made a visit to the kitchen, assured herself that everything was proceeding as Gwen would want it, then returned and watched the hall be laid for supper. That was an appealing enough sight, for she was hungry, but it was not what held her attention.

Her father was currently holding court with Nicholas. Anne couldn't help but feel a bit grateful for that, for it saved her the bother of having to dodge her sire's meaningful glances. Indeed, since he'd begun to speak with Nicholas an hour ago, he seemed to have forgotten that he had meaningful glances to send her way.

And then Robin entered the hall. His hair was dripping wet, as was the majority of his tunic. Anne suspected that perhaps his brother's words had spurred him to action after all. She watched as he walked up to his brother and her father. Nicholas elbowed him aside and stood before him, apparently blocking Robin's access to her father. Robin merely made himself a place on Nicholas's other side.

Her father pushed him out of the circle that time.

Anne continued to watch their little dance with astonishment. By the saints, what were they about?

"It looks, sister, as if you might be here longer than you think," Amanda said.

Anne looked at her foster sister, who had suddenly appeared at her side. "What do you mean?"

"They're trying to woo your sire," Amanda said wisely. "I've seen it dozens of times. Doesn't look as if Robin's having much success."

"My father doesn't like him, I don't think."

Amanda snorted. "It pains me to tell you this, Anne, but I can understand completely. Robin's impossible. Intolerable. I can't imagine what you see in him."

The sigh escaped her before she could stop it. And once it was out, there was no sense in not following it up with the words.

"He's beautiful," she said.

Amanda grunted in a most unladylike manner. "I'll give you that, but his manners more than make up for that."

"He can be very sweet," Anne protested.

Amanda turned and looked at her with an open mouth. "Sweet?" she echoed.

"Occasionally," Anne clarified.

"I don't think your father agrees."

Anne looked at the dance in progress to find Nicholas and her sire making every effort to keep Robin outside their conversings.

"Mayhap Nicky offers for you," Amanda said quietly.

Anne shook her head. "He only does it because he thinks, for what reason I cannot fathom, that the doing of it will irritate Robin."

"Men," Amanda said grimly. "Why can they not confine their games to the battlefield?"

"The thrill of conquest," Anne said. "Why else?"

"Ugh," Amanda said. "Here they come. I will slap them both if I stay."

And Anne's last hope of a pleasant dinner walked

away. She looked to find both Robin and Nicholas coming her way, fierce frowns adorning both their faces.

Anne couldn't help but wonder why Nicholas of Artane seemed determined to fair stitch himself into her clothes. She couldn't believe he was interested in her. And she couldn't imagine that her father would give her to him. He was the second son and Fenwyck would never settle for that.

Besides, Nicholas would be fortunate indeed to last the evening, what with the glares Robin had been casting his way. Perhaps the battle would be conceded before it was fought. Not that it would have done him any good to fight it anyway. Robin had her heart in his keeping, whether he knew it or not, and whether he wanted it or not. She watched him walk toward her and wondered how it was she could watch him from a distance and understand him so well, yet when she drew to within ten paces of him, her logic fled. When he glared down at her with flashing eyes, her temper immediately rose to the surface and found voice. Or she retreated and wept. She'd done that often enough in the past. Her feigned cheerfulness served her only until she reached the safety of her chamber.

She jumped slightly as she realized Nicholas was standing in front of her, looking down at her with a smile.

"Green becomes you," he said, raising her hand to his lips. "But so do all the other colors you wear. Anne, you are nothing short of stunning."

"Nick, stop slobbering on her." Robin pushed his brother aside and took her hand. "Come and sit, Anne. I want to look at your wrist."

Anne pulled her hand away so sharply, she fell against Nicholas. She pushed away from him just as quickly.

"My wrist is fine. By the saints, stop hounding me. The both of you."

Nicholas pushed Robin out of the way and offered his arm. "Will my lady permit me to escort her to the table?"

"Nay, I will—"

Anne turned and walked away before she clacked their

heads together. Perhaps they were amused by their game, but she was beginning to find it intolerable.

She took her seat and immediately found herself flanked by the eldest Artane lads. Robin couldn't have pulled his chair any closer; neither could Nicholas. Anne surrendered for the evening since there was indeed little hope of escape, unless she hiked up her skirts and climbed over the table. She sat back and sincerely hoped Robin and his brother would not begin a war with her as the main battlefield.

A servant leaned over and poured wine into the large cup she shared with Nicholas. The girl's elbow caught Anne sharply on the shoulder and Anne turned and looked up at the girl with faint annoyance.

But her annoyance changed to surprise when she saw the glare the maid was giving her.

She blinked. By that time, the girl's expression had become one of a long-suffering sort of sullenness that Anne had become well acquainted with at her father's hall. It was an unusual thing to see here. At Artane the servants were treated well; Fenwyck could not boast the same fairness.

The girl pulled away and retreated behind the table. Anne turned back to her meal and shrugged off her bewilderment. She'd been imagining things. Perhaps the girl had thought Anne at fault for being in her way.

And then she heard a sound that set the hairs on the back of her neck to standing:

The unmistakable jangle of a bracelet.

Anne looked behind her in surprise, but the girl was gone. She looked around at the table and wondered if she nigh on to driving herself daft. Tankards were clanking as they were thrust together, spoons rattled, daggers clanked as they met with spoons. Then Anne looked down the table to see Isabelle holding her arm aloft. A bracelet gleamed in the firelight.

Anne blew out her breath in relief. Her relief was magnified by the fact that she hadn't been fool enough to tell anyone of her fears. The saints only knew what sort of rumors that would start—about her state of mind this time.

Nicholas tasted the wine, then turned the cup and held it for Anne. She looked down at the golden goblet, knowing that if she put her lips in the most convenient place, it would be the same place Nicholas's lips had been. It was a lover's custom. Anne lifted her eyes and looked into Nicholas's gentle expression.

"Drink, my love."

Anne began to do just that when her movement was stopped abruptly by a brawny arm in her way. Robin snatched the cup away and poured the contents into the pitcher a page standing behind him was carrying.

"Drink it all yourself, lad," Robin growled.

"Thank you, my lord!"

Anne opened her mouth to retort when she caught sight of his thunderous expression, which was directed over her head at his brother. She shut her mouth and leaned back against her chair.

"If you two are going to do battle," she said with a sigh, "please do it outside."

"Robin is a bit testy, love," Nicholas said cheerfully. "I don't think he's been sleeping well."

"She is not your *love*," Robin growled.

"Look, Anne, at the fine meats before us tonight," Nicholas said, closing his fingers gently over her wounded wrist. "What will you have? The fowl looks particularly fine this eve. Or perhaps the eel. Nay, I think we'll start with the boar. I can smell the fine sauce from here."

Anne watched as Nicholas's fingers were removed from her arm and Robin's placed there. He pulled her right arm gently toward him until she had no choice but to shift in her chair so she faced him.

"I'm trying to eat," she said pointedly. "And with your brother, if you don't mind."

"Nick can feed you whilst I look at this," Robin said gruffly. "I don't trust his methods of healing."

Anne forced herself not to tremble at his touch. Impersonal or not, it was gentle. She stared at his long, tanned fingers as they unwrapped the binding on her wrist, then she felt his calluses as he trailed his fingers gently over the bruised flesh. He lifted his head and looked at her.

"Does it pain you still?"

Anne had difficulty finding her wits to speak. It had been years since she had been this close to Robin. Or, more accurately, been this close to Robin and not been either shouting at him or giving him a false smile before she fled to weep in private over his harshness.

And he was no longer the hot-tempered lad of ten-and-nine. He was a man, not a boy, and being so close to him and having his hands on her skin made her want to bolt. Or faint. She couldn't decide which.

"Anne?"

She blinked. "It still hurts a bit when I move it."

"Has it occurred to you, then, to keep it still?"

She started to snap out a retort, then she caught sight of the faint twinkle in his eye. She blinked a time or two, certain her eyes were deceiving her. He couldn't be teasing her. Robin had forgotten how to jest years ago.

"I don't think the cloths are stiff enough," she managed.

"Then you should have let me tend it to start with," he said, sitting back and recapturing his brisk tone. "I'll have to splint it now. After supper. And I suppose I'll have to serve myself since you're unable to do it."

Anne pursed her lips. Apparently his lack of manners had robbed him of a supper companion, for he had no one with which to share his trencher.

Nicholas put his arm around Anne's shoulders. "Pay him no heed, Anne. He forgets he is now in a civilized hall, not out in his tent with his men. Here, I've chosen all the best pieces of meat for you. Shall I feed you, or can you manage?"

"By the saints, Nick, she isn't helpless. Stop hovering over her."

"I'll hover as much as I like, Rob. You aren't her lord and master. If she doesn't want me hovering, she can tell me so herself."

"She doesn't like to be fussed over, you fool."

Anne sat back and listened to them talk about her as if she weren't there. Robin was annoyed and Nicholas was fast becoming that way. She suppressed the urge to crawl under the table.

"And I say a woman needs to be fussed over. 'Tis nothing but the chivalrous thing to do."

"And I say you're treating her like a cripple. Her leg is weak, not useless, and her hands are perfectly capable of bringing food to her mouth. Don't pity her."

"I'm trying to woo her," Nicholas growled.

"She's *not* yours to woo," Robin returned, just as darkly.

"And just who are you to determine whom she belongs to?"

Robin rose so quickly, his chair almost toppled over. "Outside."

"Gladly."

Anne sighed as they both strode angrily across the rushes. It was another peaceful night in the de Piaget household.

But apparently they were fighting over her and that was something to be examined. Anne wondered if anyone would notice if she left the table to savor the miracle. She looked about her carefully.

Her father was deep in discussion with Gwen, which boded very well for her being allowed to escape the hall. The rest of the family and garrison were applying themselves industriously to their supper and the noise in the hall was formidable. Anne slipped out of her chair and made her way up the stairs. Perhaps a bit of fresh air would help her see more clearly.

Though she wasn't sure what it was she was supposed to see. Nicholas was flattering her, but it couldn't be more than that. Robin was doing the saints only knew what.

Perhaps he lusted after her wealth. Perhaps he was merely trying to thwart his brother.

Perhaps he had lost his mind somewhere in his travels over the past five years.

She clapped her hand to her head, and then turned her attentions to getting herself up to the battlements without getting killed. The memory of being pushed down the steps was almost enough to make her turn around and go back down to the light and comfort of the great hall.

But then she would have to face Artane's eldest lads when they returned from their brawl and she didn't think she was equal to that task. Besides, there were guards aplenty on the roof.

She would certainly be safer alone than finding herself squeezed between two Artane brothers who seemed bent on killing each other.

12

Robin whirled on his brother the moment they were outside, and slammed him back up against the hall door.

"Leave her be," Robin snarled. "She's not yours and she never will be."

"Let Fenwyck determine that," Nicholas said stubbornly.

"Damn you," Robin shouted, "she is *not* a mare at market! She is not available for you to look over and decide that a tryst with her would be amusing sport for the winter. She does not want a husband and even if she did want one, that man would not be you!"

Nicholas leaned back against the door and folded his arms over his chest. A lazy smile formed on his face.

"Is that so," Nicholas drawled.

Robin snagged his brother by the front of his tunic and dragged him down the stairs, feeling that the dirt would be more suited to beating Nicholas senseless than the top of the steps.

"She is not for sale," Robin growled, releasing Nicholas.

"Then you'd best pass those tidings to the garrison for I know of several who think she just might be."

"Who?" Robin demanded.

"Careful, brother," Nicholas said with a grin. "If I didn't know you so well, I would think you were jealous."

Robin grabbed Nicholas by the tunic and shook him. "Names!"

Nicholas only grinned again. "I wouldn't presume to sentence any lads to a thrashing from you, my lord. I suppose you'll have to discover their identities on your own."

"I know the identity of one man already," Robin said pointedly, "and that man would be wise to turn his attentions elsewhere."

"Why should I?" Nicholas asked pleasantly. "You've made no claim on her."

Robin had absolutely nothing to say to contradict that, so he contented himself with plowing a fist into his brother's belly and stomping back up the steps. Perhaps he would do well to keep a closer eye on mistress Anne, just to keep her safe. The first lad to look at her with lust in his eye would die a slow and painful death. It was a perfect reason not to let her out of his sight.

He strode back into the hall and immediately noted that Anne was not in her place. He fixed Amanda with a glare.

"Where is she?"

Amanda smiled serenely. "Gone."

"Where?"

"I daresay she thought to escape your foul temper by hiding on the battlements. She often goes there—"

Robin vaulted over the table and jogged to the stairs. He wanted to sprint there but didn't want anyone to think him anxious. By the saints, she could fall and kill herself and no one would be the wiser until they saw her body on the ground! What had possessed his father to allow her to wander up there without an escort?

He ran up the various flights of stairs to the battlements and burst through the door onto the walkway. He spotted her immediately and walked over to her without hesitation. He turned her away from the wall and began to pull her toward the door.

"What are you doing?" she gasped.

"Taking you downstairs."

"But—"

"Leading you along is the only thing which keeps me from wringing your neck here on the walkway, Anne. Do not argue with me."

She didn't. She wasn't exactly coming with him enthusiastically, but she wasn't fighting him either. Robin wasn't sure if he should be pleased or terrified by that.

He led her down to his mother's solar and shut the door behind them with his foot.

"Light a fire, won't you?" she asked quickly.

He looked at her, and felt himself grow weak under her gaze. By the saints, she had become a beauty. And it wasn't all just the fairness of her face. The quiet inner beauty she had always possessed had somehow found its way to the outside. It was no wonder half the garrison wanted to offer for her. The saints be praised that her father wouldn't give her to any less than a lord's heir. At least he had no reason to fear a mere knight stealing her away from under his nose.

"Robin?"

"The fire," he said, "aye, I remember. Do not start your harping on me already, mistress Anne."

She turned her face away. Robin led her to a chair near the hearth and cursed under his breath. He hadn't meant to hurt her feelings. In truth, he had no idea what he was about. He'd been fuming for a se'nnight that he couldn't seem to get Anne away from Nicholas, and now that he had her, he wanted to flee.

It was enough to make him want to throw up his hands and surrender.

He built up the fire, then sat back on his heels and looked at his lady. The moment he met her eyes, she averted her gaze. So she cared nothing for him. He couldn't blame her. He didn't care much for himself of late either.

He sat down and reached for a piece of kindling. She'd need a splint on her wrist. Nicholas knew better than to leave an injury such as that alone. Robin cursed under his breath as he worked. It should have been splinted and wrapped immediately. It would likely take her twice as long to recover from it now.

The rustle of fabric drew his attention and he looked up to see Anne rising.

"Where are you off to? Sit back down."

"I'm not going to stay any longer and listen to you curse me," she said stiffly.

"I was cursing Nicholas, not you. He should have splinted your wrist. Sit back down. I won't chase you the next time."

She hesitated, then she slowly sank back down to her chair.

And for some reason, that hurt him—likely because he knew he was hurting her. Didn't she know he would chase her as many times as she wanted? Didn't she have any idea that she was the reason he hadn't come home in five years? Didn't she have any idea that she was one of the reasons he trained until he dropped each day? He never, *ever* wanted to see her look at him and find him lacking.

Her insecurity broke his heart. Sweet, lovely Anne who should have had nothing but smiles filling her days, who deserved a gallant knight to court her, and a body that was perfect and didn't pain her.

Yet what did she have instead? A leg that was lame and a surly knight who couldn't string two words together to form a decent compliment.

Robin bent again to his whittling, not liking in the least the emotions that raged inside him. He could never give Anne what she needed, be what she deserved, and he was a fool to want to. He finished with the thin strips of wood and tucked his knife back into his belt. Then he looked around him for the cloth that had initially bound Anne's wrist.

She held it out and he took it. He laid the cloth on her lap and placed her wrist on it.

"Hold the splints, Anne girl, while I wrap it," he said, placing the wood where he wanted it.

"What did you call me?"

He looked up and met her pale eyes. "I don't remember," he lied. It had been a slip, an unwitting indication of his thoughts. He hadn't called her that since before his humiliation at Baldwin's hands. It had been his pet name for her, his alone. He'd broken Nicholas's nose the first time Nick had taken up calling her that. He resumed his work, feeling acutely uncomfortable. Gentleness was not in his nature. Soft words and silly endearments were not in his vocabulary. He was a warrior, not a woman, and he had no time for foolishness.

"I don't want you using this arm," he said as he tied the two ends of the cloth together. "No sewing, no cooking, no carrying. If I see you doing the like, you will regret it, and rest assured I will be watching you closely for the next se'nnight to see that you obey me."

"I am not one of your men, Robin."

He slipped his fingers under hers and rubbed his thumb over her knuckles. "I know that, Anne." He lifted her hand to his lips and kissed it roughly. He didn't dare meet her eyes.

And then he realized how foolish a thing it had been. He released her hand quickly and stood. " 'Tis time you were abed. Let me bank the fire and I'll see you downstairs. I don't want you tripping again." He carefully tended the fire, then brushed off his hands and turned to look at Anne. She hadn't moved. She was looking at her hand as if she'd never seen it before.

Robin wiped off his hands again and crossed the two steps that separated him from her. He held down his hand and called her name quietly. She looked up at him and her eyes were full of tears.

Robin suppressed the urge to run.

Anne put her hand into his and he gently pulled her to her feet.

"You're overly tired," he said gruffly. "Rest is what you need."

She nodded, but she didn't move. Robin hesitated, wondering what he dared do. What he wanted to do was pull her into his arms; what he dreaded was having her push away in disgust. Or would she laugh at him? That he couldn't have borne—

The door burst open and Nicholas stood there, disheveled. He met Robin's eyes.

"The page," he said, holding onto the doorframe for support. "The one you gave my wine to. That was Stephen of Hardwiche, wasn't it?"

"Aye. What has befallen the lad?"

Nicholas looked at him, his gray eyes wide with shock and horror.

"I think he's dead."

13

Edith walked sedately down the passageway, doing her damndest to appear calm. She nodded regally to whatever servant she passed and slipped by members of Artane's guard with as little notice as possible. She reached the base of the tower steps, took a deep breath and climbed them slowly. After she reached the landing, she took another deep, calming breath, opened the door and stepped inside the chamber. Once the door was closed behind her, she gathered all her reserves of control and asked the question she could not believe she was forced to utter.

"Dead?" she queried politely.

Maude was naught but a huddled mass against the wall, quivering and sniveling. Baldwin loomed over her with his fist raised. He turned to glare at Edith.

"Aye, dead," he snarled. "And this silly twit here was the one to do it."

And then he did something that forever damned him in Edith's eyes. He reached out and kicked Maude with all his strength.

It was one thing to kill a man. Even torturing a man was acceptable in several circumstances. Tormenting a woman could also be done, should the offense be grave enough. But beating a woman who was already cowering on the floor, who had no defenses, who was unable to fight back . . .

Edith knew that somehow she would have to reconcile that with what she was doing to Anne, but for now all she could see was herself in Maude's place, trying to avoid the battering fists and flailing feet of her own sire.

Then again, Baldwin was Sedgwick's get. What else could she expect?

"Cease," she said, striding across the chamber and pushing her brother away. She stood between him and Maude. "I'll see to her."

Baldwin drew his hand back, likely to slap her, but she stood her ground. She was certain he could see the hate in her eyes. When his own anger faltered and he lowered his hand, she knew she had won at least that battle.

"I should punish you as well for this," he growled.

"Do, and you'll regret it," she said calmly.

"You wouldn't dare."

"The only way to be sure would be to kill me now."

He looked to be contemplating it, then he cursed most foully and turned away. "That sport is too easy."

Of course. She pursed her lips at his contemptuous tone, but said nothing further. There was no point in trying to humiliate him. Robin had done that well enough that morn. She had watched them earlier and seen Artane dispatch him with barely an effort. Her brother's bluster was a great deal of wounded pride, surely, and perhaps encouraging him to assuage that pride would keep him out from underfoot until she could decide further how to proceed.

"Perhaps you'd find better sport in the lists," she suggested.

He glowered at her. " 'Twas a moment's misstep this morn," he said.

"Doubtless." She smiled at him sympathetically. "I suppose we all have them." Some fewer than others, but she didn't bother to point that out to him.

Baldwin pointed a shaking finger at Maude. "See to her. If you don't, I will, and rest assured, they won't find her to bury her."

Edith watched him leave the chamber and wondered if he actually had the spine for such a deed. He boasted of it often, but she'd never seen the fruits of his foul labors. She very much suspected that he didn't have the bollocks for the like. She wondered if he would even be capable of seeing through any of the tasks she intended to assign him.

Good assassins were always in such short supply.

Edith sighed and turned to kneel down next to Maude. She lifted the blubbering girl's face up and looked dispassionately at the swelling already apparent. There was one thing she could say for her brother: he knew how to use his fists to their best advantage.

"I told you but a little, Maude," Edith said quietly.

Maude only whimpered.

"The temptation was too strong, wasn't it?" Edith asked.

Maude nodded and sniveled.

Edith sighed. It looked as if Maude's usefulness had come to an end, at least for the immediate future.

"You'll rest now," Edith said. "No more schemes until you've rested. Indeed, I think it best that you do nothing more until I tell you otherwise. Understood?"

Maude nodded jerkily.

"I think beating a woman is despicable," Edith continued. "I would never do it."

"You w-wouldn't?" Maude asked.

Edith shook her head. "A clean death is much more dignified, don't you think? And in this intrigue we're engaged in, disobedience would merit the like."

Maude looked at her with wide eyes.

"You won't disobey again, will you, Maude?"

"Nay, Lady Edith," Maude whispered.

"Good," Edith said, smiling. "Stay here until you've recovered. If anyone asks you about your bruises, say you fell down the stairs. They won't ask any more."

"Aye, my lady."

"You'll do nothing until I tell you otherwise."

"Aye, my lady."

Edith nodded, rose and brushed off her hands. She left the tower chamber. Supper was over, the keep in an uproar and there would be no peace for her that night to sit and think on her plans. That likely wouldn't have served her anyway. Now it was best that she show herself to the family and express the appropriate horror and outrage. She could think on the morrow about how best to proceed.

Perhaps 'twas time she haunted the lists and watched Baldwin at his work. The saints only knew what kind of mischief she might find to stir up there. If nothing else, the fresh air might give her a new idea or two.

She shook her head as she descended to the great hall. Too much poison. By the saints, was she required to do all this herself?

14

Anne stood on the steps leading up to the great hall and watched the scene before her in the courtyard. There was the wagon, of course, bearing young Stephen of Hardwiche's body. The lady Gwennelyn was already mounted. Rhys's men were preparing to go, checking their gear and such.

Rhys stood apart with Robin, no doubt giving him last minute instructions. Anne watched Robin listen and marveled at his patience. He certainly hadn't shown any with her the night before. He'd been gruff in his mother's solar as he splinted her wrist and she very much suspected that he had been cursing her right along with his brother. Once Nicholas had arrived with the grim tidings, Robin had dragged her down the steps behind him, put her in a chair in the great hall, then ignored her for the rest of the evening.

Then again, he had kissed her hand.

In a rough, unpolished sort of way.

She looked down at that hand, then clasped it with the other and hid it back beneath her cloak. Her hands were white and they were shaking. She knew the reason why. It had come to her as she'd sat in the great hall the night before, looking at young Stephen's body laid out before the hearth. The solar door slamming she could have understood. Losing her footing on the stairs she also could have understood. She could have imagined being pushed.

But almost drinking wine that had killed a child?

That she could not ignore and the realization the night before had almost left her faint.

Someone was trying to kill her.

She'd sat in her chair the night before and trembled. She'd watched the goings on around her and shaken with the horror of it all. She'd said nothing of it to anyone. It had seemed almost too foolish a notion to give voice to. After all, who was to say the wine hadn't been meant for someone else?

Cook had found the lad slumped in a corner of the kitchen, an empty jug at his elbow. It could have been drunk by anyone, though Anne remembered vividly Robin's rudeness in snatching the cup from her and giving it to Stephen. Had he not done so, she would have found herself in that baggage wain, dead and not minding at all the journey back to Fenwyck.

It was enough to weaken her knees.

She found herself sitting on the steps before she knew she intended to do so. Then before she could understand how she had gotten there, she felt hands on her arms. She was shaken so forcefully, her teeth began to clack together.

"Are you unwell?" Robin demanded urgently.

"Stop shaking me," she said. Her head was starting to spin uncomfortably. "Robin, please stop."

He knelt down on the step beneath her and looked at her with clouded eyes. "Why did you sit?"

"My head pained me," she lied. There was no sense in telling him the truth. He likely wouldn't believe her anyway.

A long shape sat on the step next to her. Anne looked to her left to find Miles there. His customary grave look was even graver than usual. He put his arm around her, then looked at his brother.

"Rob, think you 'twas poison?"

"What else could it be?"

"Bad eel?"

Robin glared at his brother.

Miles shrugged apologetically.

"Well," Robin said, "I know of no malady but strong poison that could kill so quickly. It could be nothing else."

"But why?" Miles asked. "Who would want to kill a hapless child?"

"I don't know. And I don't envy Father the trip to Hardwiche."

"Stephen was the favored son," Anne whispered. "The youngest, but the most well beloved."

"At least your sire goes with him," Miles offered. "That may help. They are related, aren't they?"

"Aye," she said. "My stepsister's husband is Hardwiche's youngest brother."

"Well, then," Robin said with pursed lips, "perhaps your sire will be of some use after all."

Anne looked up to see her father standing behind Robin. He was less than gentle in pushing Robin aside.

"Anne, a word," he said curtly.

Robin regained his balance, stood, and offered Anne his hand. Between that and Miles's arm still around her shoulders, Anne found herself on her feet.

"Shall I stay?" Miles asked with a slight frown.

Anne watched her father push Robin and send him stumbling down the stairs. Miles was hauled away by his tunic and sent on his way with much the same results. Anne looked at her sire.

"That was unnecessary," she said simply.

"And that is the last I'll hear of that kind of disrespect from you," he said angrily. "I can see that being here breeds that in you and I'll not have it any longer. I'll return within the month. Be prepared to leave when I arrive."

There was nothing else she could do to delay her day of reckoning and she knew it well. She swallowed with difficulty. "As you will, Father."

"No more reprieves, Anne. Rhys fair talked himself into a faint trying to convince me I should leave you here until winter. I'll not do it, do you understand?"

"Aye, Father."

Geoffrey grunted, then turned and walked down the stairs. She caught a side view of the glare he gave Robin before he continued to his horse. Anne watched him mount and ride through the gates without a backward glance. Well, at least he was leaving, though she suspected it was under protest and with a great deal of reluctance. Her freedom would last another pair of fortnights. It was the best she could ask for.

The rest of the company followed suit, followed by the wagon bearing the boy's body. Anne didn't breathe easily until the gates were shut.

Once the dust had settled, Robin strode off to the lists, likely to reduce whatever lads he could find there to nothing. Miles made her a low bow, then disappeared after his brother, likely to clean up whatever bodies were sure to be littering the lists after Robin's work was finished.

Anne sat back down on the steps and watched until the courtyard was completely empty. She tortured herself with visions of her being the one to be leaving, riding down the way to the outer gates, looking back for a final sight of the home she loved so much. It was enough to bring tears to her eyes.

And it was such a ridiculous thing to do, she could hardly believe she was wallowing in her misery so fully— and so unnecessarily. There was no sense in ruining her last few days of freedom with grim thoughts about the future. The future would arrive in its own good time. The best thing she could do would be to enjoy what time remained her.

She stood, stretched and carefully made her way down the steps. One of the pleasures she enjoyed at Artane that she didn't at Fenwyck was the freedom to walk where she willed it. She hugged the walls of the lists as a general rule, for the distance was manageable and aid was ever near her should she need it.

She steadfastly refused to think about the fact that this morn she might also have the pleasure of watching Robin while she took her own exercise.

It took her longer than she would have liked to reach the lists, but even so she couldn't complain. The day was fine, the sun shining and her cloak protected her from the chill. It couldn't last, the weather and her freedom, so she savoured it fully while she could.

She walked along near the wall, trying to keep out of anyone's way. The lists were never empty, but since Robin and Nicholas's return, they were a busier place than usual. Apparently Robin had surrounded himself with men who were as driven as he—either that or his hand-picked guard feared he would truly do them in if they didn't train as hard as he did.

As usual, she set herself a goal, for there was no sense in not pushing herself while she could. She would make one circuit of the lists before she allowed herself to look for Robin. Her second trek could be made while stealing glances at him every few paces. The third time, should she have the means of managing it, she would look at him fully and not be shamed by it. If she managed to walk that much in one morn, she would deserve whatever pleasure she could take for herself.

She continued on her way slowly, forcing her leg to straighten with each step she took, to accept her weight, to work the muscles that would have rather remained idle. As the pains shot up through her leg into her hip, she cursed herself soundly for having been so inactive. Sitting and sewing peacefully came with a heavy price she had paid often enough in the past. She should have known better this time—

"Anne!"

A man's scream made her jerk her head up in surprise,

then she shrieked as she was knocked to the ground. Her breath had been completely driven from her. If that had been the worst of it, she would have been relieved. But having a mailed man sprawled atop her was fast crushing the life from her.

"Move," she mouthed, trying to suck in air.

A mail coif was shoved back from the wearer's head and Anne had a mouthful of dark hair as the man turned his head to look back over his shoulder.

"Robin," she gasped, "I cannot breathe." Unbidden tears of pain sprang to her eyes. He was pinning her leg under his thighs and she thought he just might break it soon. "Please!"

Robin heaved himself off her and rose, leaving her lying in the dirt. Anne tried to sit up, but found she couldn't. All she could do was stare up at the sky and wonder if by some miracle her form would ever again draw breath.

It returned slowly, but moving was still beyond her. She looked above her and saw that Robin was holding the head of a mace in his hand.

"Whose is this?" he bellowed.

A knight fell to his knees. "My lord, it was an accident!"

"You bloody whoreson, you almost killed her!" Robin thundered. He jerked the knight to his feet and shoved him. "Did your master never teach you to check your weapons? A bloody good thing you're my father's man, else I'd kill you where you stand!"

"I'd sooner kill myself than harm the lady Anne," the knight said fervently. "I vow it, my lord. I checked it before I wielded it."

"And I say you didn't," Robin snarled. "If the lady Anne's life is so precious to you, why is it she almost found herself without a head on her shoulders thanks to you?"

The knight looked as devastated as Anne felt. She knew him to be one of Rhys's guardsmen and a goodly warrior. She couldn't believe he would actually try to harm her.

Then again, she never would have believed anyone would try to poison her, either.

Robin looked about him, cursing loudly and fiercely. "Miles!" he shouted.

Anne realized that Miles was kneeling at her head only because he grasped her briefly by the shoulders before he stood and faced his brother.

"Aye?"

"Take this fool and put him in the dungeon."

The knight protested his innocence, but evidently Miles's reputation was not far behind Robin's, for all it took was a drawing of his blade to have the man falling suddenly silent. Anne couldn't twist her head to see what the outcome of that would be, but she assumed Miles had prodded the poor man toward the great hall.

"Sir Richard," Robin snapped, "see that all these weapons are checked again. By you personally."

"Aye, my lord."

"You will find yourself in the dungeon with Sir Edward if you fail me."

Anne lifted her eyebrow at that. Richard of Moncrief was Rhys's man and she was half surprised he took the insult from Robin. Then again, she'd never seen Robin quite so fierce before. She was almost flattered at his concern.

Then she found herself in his sights.

And she sincerely wished she were capable of getting up and hastening away.

He stomped over and glared down at her for a goodly moment before he took her by the arms and hauled her to her feet.

"And you!" he shouted. "What in hell's name were you thinking to come out here?"

Her breath had returned enough for some speech, though she suspected it wouldn't be enough to cool Robin's temper. "Well, I walk here often—"

"This is no place for a woman," Robin bellowed, "especially one who hasn't the sense to watch where she's going. I never want to see you out here again by yourself, is that clear?"

Had she actually had pleasant feelings toward this man? She was a fool.

"I'll go where I please—" she began haughtily.

"You'll be locked in your chamber if you don't obey me! Mindless wench, what were you thinking?" He shook her. "You could have been killed! Do your daydreaming somewhere besides the lists."

Anne had never been so embarrassed in her life. The garrison was standing not fifty paces away and she knew she couldn't have been fortunate enough not to have had them hear Robin's chastisement. She jerked herself away from Robin and turned to go back to the hall. She took only a pair of steps before her leg gave way and she fell to her hands and knees. Her mortification was complete.

Robin came to stand before her. "Pick yourself up and hie yourself back to the house," he growled. "You have no place here, Anne."

Anne watched his booted feet retreat and knew deep inside her that she had never hated Robin of Artane as much as she did in that moment.

Richard of Moncrief squatted down before her and held out his hands.

"Let me assist you, my lady," he said quietly.

"Get away from me, you baseborn wretch," she spat, her grief and shame crashing over her in a fierce wave. "I need no aid." She lifted her head and swept the rest of the men with a glare. "Begone! I'm no cripple, damn you all! Go!"

Anne knew she should rise, but she couldn't. All she could do was remain on her hands and knees and bow her head. At least that way she didn't have to look at the cluster of men that no doubt still watched her. Though they had retreated, she knew they were still there. And what a sight she must have made!

And it was a sight she would no longer provide for

them. She lifted her head long enough to look for something by which she could lever herself to her feet. There was a bench pushed up against the wall, but it was a goodly distance away. It would have to do, for she could see nothing else useful.

She began to crawl.

15

Robin put his hands against the bailey wall and leaned against it, trying to catch his breath and ease the pain in his chest. He closed his eyes and prayed he was imagining things. With the handful of days he'd just endured, perhaps 'twas understandable that his wits were not at their sharpest. There was much of coincidence in this life. Perhaps he had just experienced a greater share of it of late than a normal man might.

Then again another man might not have seen the woman he loved in a crumpled heap at the bottom of the stairs.

Another man might not have recently stopped that same woman from drinking wine that would have poisoned her to death.

Another man surely wouldn't have watched the heavy spiked ball of a mace go flying through the air toward that woman's head. That was the most unsettling of all. 'Twas naught but chance that had left him walking toward her. He'd scarce turned in time to save her.

He couldn't shake the feeling that this had gone far past happenstance.

He pushed back from the wall, dragged his hands

through his hair and blew out his breath. He would go
back to the hall and apologize to Anne. She would likely
think he had spoken to her harshly. If she knew he'd done
it out of fear and not malice, perhaps she would forgive
him.

He turned, but before he could begin to walk, he saw
a sight that was almost as terrible as the one he had almost
been privy to.

Anne on her hands and knees, crawling.

He looked at her in dismay. By the saints, he'd never
meant to reduce her to this!

She was making her way toward a bench. Just that effort looked to be costing her much. He spared the garrison
a brief glance and saw a variety of emotions on their
faces. Pity for the most part. Even Sedgwick's expression
was a serious one. That was just as well for him. Robin
would have likely killed him for anything else.

And then a handful of the men turned to look at him
and Robin was faintly surprised to see anger in their faces
and a goodly amount of accusation—as if he had been
the one to put Anne in that position!

But hard on the heels of that came the realization that
indeed he had. He could only speculate on the humiliation
she felt and that he could certainly take credit for. That
surely wasn't the worst. The saints only knew what kind
of damage he had done to her by crushing her as he had.

Well, better crushed than dead. He met those damning
looks with a glare of his own, then strode over and
stopped in front of Anne.

"Anne—"

"Move," she said in a raspy whisper.

Robin's mail voiced a loud protest as he bent, took her
by the arms and lifted her to her feet. She swayed drunk-
enly and he clasped her to him. His hoped his mail would
not pinch her—though he doubted it could be any more
painful than what he'd already done to her.

"Release me," she said, trying to push away.

That was the last thing he would do. He could not stomach the sight of her on her hands and knees again. He put one arm under her knees, one arm behind her back and swept her up.

"Put me down, you blighted bugger," she gasped.

Robin ignored her slander, knowing that he had been the one to teach her to curse in her youth.

He also ignored the flat of her hand across his face. He supposed he deserved it. He had humiliated her, but damnation, what did she expect? Was he to let her be killed without any effort made to stop it?

He continued to ignore her steady stream of curses as he carried her back to the hall. Had he ever thought of Anne as shy and retiring? Why, the woman could make a hardened warrior blush with her foulness.

"Anne, please," Robin said, exasperated. "I believe I've been left with little doubt about what you think of me."

Her curses gave way to tears. Robin felt his own eyes begin to sting. That he had been the one to wring such weeping from her was almost his undoing. He gritted his teeth and climbed the steps to the hall door. Damnation, what else was he to have done?

The great hall was empty save Amanda sitting by the fire. Robin paused, then scowled. His sister was staring off into nothingness as if she had naught but maidenly dreams as her most pressing occupation. He glared at her as he passed and was faintly gratified to find she had obviously felt the like, for she looked up in surprise.

"What happened?" she asked.

"I'll tell you later," Robin said shortly. "Fetch Nicholas to Father's bedchamber and don't eat or drink anything until we've had a chance to talk."

She blinked, then looked at Anne in his arms. "What is he babbling about, Anne?"

"By all the bloody saints, Amanda, will you for once just obey me?" he demanded. "Fetch Nick and do it now!"

His sister rose with a sigh he was certain she had intended should blow him over, but at least she was on her feet.

Robin paused, then another thought occurred to him. "After you've sent Nick, fetch Miles, the twins and Isabelle as well," he called after her. "Bring them upstairs."

Amanda waved him away and left the great hall. Robin continued on his way up the stairs and down the passageway to his parent's bedchamber. No sense in not appropriating the finest for his lady while he was lord of Artane. He kicked open the door and then set Anne down on her feet in the passageway.

"Stay here," he commanded, taking a torch off the wall. He drew his sword and entered the chamber, pushing the firelight into each corner and checking under the bed. By the saints, a body wasn't even safe in his own home anymore.

He returned to find Anne leaning heavily against the doorframe. He put his arm around her shoulders, led her into the chamber and placed her in a chair near the hearth. He built up the fire, taking more time than he needed to, but he knew he had things to say to his lady and he wasn't all that certain how to begin. It was time enough to gather at least a few of his thoughts. Once he was finished with his task, he remained on his knees and turned to look at her.

Her cheeks were smudged with dirt. Except, of course, for those trails of cleanliness her tears had left in their wake. Robin couldn't bear to see what might be revealed in her eyes, so he turned back to the fire. He took a deep breath for enough courage to put to her the questions he had to.

"You didn't fall down the stairs, did you?" he asked quietly.

She was silent for a moment or two. "Nay."

He dragged his hand through his hair and looked up at the ceiling as he let his breath out slowly. So it was as he feared. But who could possibly want to hurt her?

"Merciful saints above, Anne," he said with a sigh. "Who have you irritated lately besides me?"

He looked at her. She was looking at him, but her expression was not what he had expected. The hatred in her glance chilled him to the bone. He had been accustomed to looks of ill-disguised affection and undisguised annoyance, but hatred?

"Anne . . ." he began slowly.

She turned her face away and remained silent.

Robin would have cheerfully handed over all his teeth to have possessed a bit of Nicholas's glibness at that moment. The only looks of hatred he was accustomed to receiving were from those he prepared to put to the sword. He'd never had such a chilling glance from a woman.

Then again, he'd never left a woman trampled in the dirt before, either.

Perhaps Anne was angry with him over that. She had reason to be, he supposed. Perhaps she did but need a few moments to regain her composure and realize he hadn't done it out of malice. Perhaps if he turned her mind to other things, such as their current problem, she might forget that he had been the one to crush her. He cleared his throat purposefully.

"I could have believed you were clumsy enough to fall down the stairs," he began.

Anne didn't move.

Robin frowned at her lack of response, but continued on. "I also could have believed that Stephen had eaten something that made him feel poorly," he continued, "but Nick was up all night retching and mace heads do not simply fly off without some kind of aid. There is more to this than simple coincidence."

Still she made no move, gave no indication that she had heard him. Robin sighed heavily and rose.

"Very well," he said. "Perhaps rest is what you need. Let's have your boots off, then I'll carry you to bed. You'll be perfectly safe here for the present."

"Do not touch me."

Robin stopped before he did just that. " 'Tis nothing I wouldn't do for Amanda," he said stiffly, "though with likely less care than I'll use now."

"Go away, Robin."

Robin stared down at her, his anger warring with his concern. Her pale hair was coming loose from her braid and strands of it fell around her face. She breathed poorly, as if it pained her to do so. He paused. Had he broken anything, falling on her as he had? He reached out and touched her hair as gently as he could.

"Anne, do you have pain anywhere?"

She ignored him. He watched as she slowly and with a good deal of effort turned herself away from him.

Robin sighed and stepped back. Well, 'twas obvious he would have none of her thoughts at present. Perhaps later, when her temper had cooled.

He was momentarily tempted to ask Nicholas to pry the tale from her, then he thought better of it. The last thing he wanted was Nicholas and Anne alone in the same chamber together. Nicholas would be charming and gallant and say just the right things. Robin would return to find Anne having swooned directly into his brother's arms. Nay, far better that she be forced to talk to him.

He would, however, reserve the right to talk to his brother himself. Despite Nicholas's flaws, which were indeed many and mainly sprang from his great love of the fairer species, he had a head for strategy. Robin had benefitted more than once from discussing tactics with his brother.

"I'll return as soon as I may," Robin said.

Anne said nothing. Indeed, she made no move to even indicate that she had heard him.

Robin was unsurprised, and in spite of everything, that almost cheered him. He'd known she wouldn't speak to him. At least he was learning to predict her reactions.

He left the bedchamber and closed the door behind him. The passageway was well lit, but even so there were patches of gloom along the corridor. Robin peered into them, but saw nothing amiss. He decided then that a guard would have to be posted outside the door. More than one set, likely. Indeed, the best thing to do was likely to have someone inside with Anne to protect her.

He paused.

Who better than he to be that guard?

He turned the thought over in his head until he saw his brother coming down the passageway. It was a thought worth pursuing, but later, when he had determined just how dire circumstances were. Perhaps Nicholas would be more able than he to judge if events were accidental, or if Robin had discovered something more sinister.

For once, Robin hoped his imagination had overpowered his good sense.

Nicholas came down the passageway, then stopped across the passageway from Robin. Robin looked at his brother and was momentarily chilled by the thought of how close he had come to losing not only Anne, but Nicholas too. Irritating though he might have been, Nicholas was his brother, after all, and Robin loved him dearly. It had been a passing unpleasant night, what with Nicholas being violently ill for the whole of it. He didn't look much better now.

"What?" Nicholas rasped. He swayed, then leaned heavily against the wall. "I've no stomach for riddles today."

"A mace head flew off a weapon today," Robin said.

"And?"

"If I hadn't thrown Anne to the ground, it would have struck her in the face."

Nicholas's jaw slipped down. "Nay."

"Am I imagining things," Robin asked, "or does there seem to be a pattern here?"

"No one else nearby? No other possible targets?"

Robin shook his head. "I was walking toward her, but it wasn't aimed at me."

Nicholas looked even paler, if that was possible. "It would seem," he said weakly, "there is something foul afoot."

"I thought so as well."

"Could we sit to discuss it?" Nicholas asked. "I vow I'll fall to my knees if I must stand any longer."

Robin moved to aid his brother only to find Amanda already there. She moved silently enough, when she wasn't screeching her complaints at him. She put Nicholas's arm over her shoulders and helped him into the bedchamber. Robin waited for the rest of his siblings, who were coming down the passageway. And as he watched the souls he loved coming toward him, he realized that perhaps keeping them all protected was a more serious concern for him than he had realized before. Though these attacks seemed to be directed at Anne, who knew who the true target was?

Robin herded his family into the bedchamber, then shut the door and bolted it. He watched them take places near the fire. Nicholas sat near Anne, but even Robin had to concede that he looked too ill to take advantage of his position. Amanda first fussed over Anne, then drew up a stool at Nicholas's feet and sat. Montgomery and John sat on the floor flanking her. They leaned against her on either side and wrapped their arms about her as if she'd been a kind of bolster put there especially for their comfort. Isabelle and Miles fought over the remaining chair. Perhaps Miles's chivalry was in full bloom that day, for he conceded the battle quickly and sat at her feet.

"Rub my shoulders, will you, Iz?" he asked.

Robin watched the normal goings-on in his family and wished heartily that he could do naught but enjoy them. But he was responsible for his kin. Not only was he answerable for his own actions, and theirs as well, he was answerable for their safety. He was beginning to wonder if his sire had made a mistake in entrusting him with these souls.

He shook aside his thoughts. The responsibility was his and he would not shrink from it. He had no choice but to bring something very foul into their midst, so best be about it while he could. But once he found the culprit, this loss of their innocence was something else he would make the fiend pay for.

He took a deep breath. He could keep them alive and

unharmed. After all, warring was what he did best. Perhaps his sire hadn't chosen amiss. He stood behind Anne's chair and prepared to give them the tidings.

"Would someone care to enlighten us as to why we've been dragged here?" Amanda asked tartly.

Robin pursed his lips. Not even a chance to start before she was at him. Perhaps Amanda could be left to the wolves whilst he concentrated on the rest of his family. At least then he might have a bit of peace.

"We are here," he said briskly, "because there is something afoot in the keep and 'tis my task to see it discovered and rooted out."

"And you know this because..." Amanda asked slowly.

"Because Anne has almost lost her life three times in the past fortnight," Robin said. "I cannot credit it to coincidence."

"Perhaps the fiend was targeting you," Amanda said, "and missed."

Miles laughed, but quickly covered it up with a cough. "Sorry, Rob," he said. "I know this is no matter for jesting."

"Aye, how do you know 'twas for Anne?" John asked.

"Aye, maybe 'twas a garrison knight Rob wore down to his bones," Montgomery offered enthusiastically. " 'Tis a surety there would be several of those."

And then they were off, those souls Robin had just recently vowed to protect, apparently having no lack of names to suggest as to who might be such a likely lad. Robin listened to them list his victims and was torn between a bit of pride that the list was so long and annoyance that his siblings seemed not to realize their peril.

All except Nicholas who sat behind Amanda, sprawled wearily in his chair, drumming his fingers on the arm as if he hadn't a care in that empty head of his. But at least the dolt wasn't smiling. He was too sick for it and Robin couldn't help but find a bit of comfort in that.

And then there was Anne. Robin moved slightly so he

could see her face—then he wished he hadn't. He'd never seen her look more weary or grieved. And when he caught her gaze, she favored him with a look of such ill-disguised ill-will that he flinched. He opened his mouth to defend himself, but she looked away so purposefully that he shut his mouth with a snap. It would do him no good to plead his case now, not with all the rampant speculation that was going on about him.

Amanda rose suddenly and held down her hands for Anne. "Come, sister," she said ·quietly. "Let me put you to bed. You look as if you need rest."

Miles was instantly on his feet to aid them. Robin moved to help, but Anne pushed his hand away. His first instinct was to blister her with a caustic remark, then he bit his tongue. In truth, he couldn't blame her for her actions. She was likely afeared for her life, bruised mightily from his protection and angry that he hadn't helped her up in the first place. Perhaps sleep was what she needed to restore her to her good sense.

He watched Miles and Amanda care for her, and as he did so, his earlier thought came back to him.

He could sequester his siblings in the lads' bedchamber. Nicholas could keep watch over them. And when Nick had to be about some other business, Miles could take over the duty. The girls and the twins would be perfectly safe. Nicholas was infinitely capable of seeing to them. Miles was hard on his brother's heels when it came to swordplay and he was devious enough to anticipate any foul intent from a murderer.

But even Nicholas would have to admit that such an arrangement left mistress Anne to be watched over.

And who better to do that than him?

Alone. Where she could not escape him. And then perhaps for once in their sorry lives, they might have speech together that did not involve insults and shouting, and then Robin might discover the lay of her heart once and for all.

He was, after all, the best warrior in the keep. 'Twas

only fitting that he be the one to guard her. She was Fen-wyck's heir. She needed to be protected at all costs.

"Well," he announced, "that's enough discussion. I'll look into the matter. Until it's solved, everyone will hie themselves to the lad's chamber. Lads, leave only in pairs. Girls, don't go out without either Nick or Miles."

Nicholas frowned at him. "I think it best we remain all in the same chamber, brother. If we have a war within our own keep, far better that we remain in a single body."

As if Robin would allow his brother and Anne to be in a chamber together! Nicholas had already fair draped him-self over Anne for the past fortnight. Best get him as far away from her as possible. Robin turned to Amanda and gave her the sternest look he could muster.

"Take the little ones to my chamber."

Amanda pursed her lips, but nodded readily enough.

"But," Nicholas spluttered, "you can't mean—"

Robin turned to Miles.

"Nick and I have aught to discuss. 'Tis your task to protect the family until we've arranged our strategy."

Miles rose without comment or question. It was, though, a goodly while before he managed to get every-one out the door. Robin listened to his siblings suppose and surmise until he was near to screaming at them to get themselves gone. They had no useful suggestions and if he had to listen to the little lads discuss once again what kind of poison could be put in wine to kill so quickly, he would have silenced them himself.

But Miles was successful in the end and Robin couldn't help but feel faintly satisfied about it. At least there was someone in the keep who would obey him.

Once the door was closed, Robin looked over at the bed. There was no movement there. It was possible Anne was asleep, and Robin prayed the like was true. At least she wouldn't have to hear the argument that was to come. Nicholas was still lazing in his chair, but Robin knew that such a display of tranquillity couldn't last for long.

He put his shoulders back, took a deep breath and pre-

pared for battle. He would have loosened his sword in its
sheath, but that might have alerted his brother to what he
was about. Besides, a sword fight would awaken Anne
and that was something Robin wanted to avoid. His plan
would be put into action before she awoke and could add
her voice to Nicholas's.

And he hoped he wasn't about to make a colossal mistake.

16

"You're *what*?"

Anne winced at the force of that thunderous shout.

"Be silent, you fool! Say nothing else until I've made certain you haven't woken Anne."

Anne held her breath. It was very difficult to feign sleep with Robin coming over to stare at her and muttering under his breath loudly enough for the entire chamber to hear. One day she would have to tell him he did that when he thought too hard. She suspected he didn't know, and would likely have been highly irritated to learn of it. It gave away far too many of his secret thoughts.

Robin cursed as he stomped away.

"I've already decided this," he whispered sharply.

"Robin, you cannot be serious!"

Anne wished she had heard Robin's initial declaration, but damn him if he hadn't found it in him to whisper then. She had a feeling without hearing anything else that Nicholas had it aright. Whatever new strategy Robin had proposed could be nothing but madness.

She shifted on the bed and her body set up a clamor that fair left her gasping. And with that renewed wash of pain came back all the ill feelings she had acquired for the acting lord of Artane.

She despised him. She loathed him. She never wanted to feel his hands on her again. And she especially never wanted to be crushed beneath his heel again, as if she'd been a particularly noisesome species of insect he was bent on destroying.

" 'Tis the only way." Robin's deep voice was firm.

"Have you gone mad?" Nicholas continued, sounding as if he fully believed that his brother had accomplished the like. "Her father will slay you if he learns. Not to mention what ours will do!"

"By St. George's throat, Nick, I'm not about to bed her," Robin retorted.

"I should hope not. She's a virgin, for pity's sake—"

"She's the same as a sister to me—"

"Merde," Nicholas snapped. "She is not your sister and keeping her prisoner in this chamber is equal to fornication, you fool! Do you for one moment believe anyone will think her virtue unmarred once they discover she's spent the night in your bed?"

"Saints, Nick, it isn't as if I'll be joining her," Robin growled. "I'll sleep here before the fire. Her precious virtue will remain unsullied by my filthy hands."

"Let her sleep with us—"

"Nay! She'll stay with me. I'm the only one here who can protect her."

"Ha," Nicholas said scornfully. "I'm perfectly capable of doing it. Indeed, I think I might be a better choice."

"When I'm dead," Robin snarled. "And not a moment before. Your task is to see that Amanda and Isabelle are kept safe. Give the girls the bed. The lads can sleep on the floor."

"I still say we should all remain together!"

"And I say we shouldn't!"

There was silence for a goodly amount of time and Anne began to wonder if Nicholas and Robin were looking at each other, trying to decide where to cut first. And then Nicholas spoke.

"I see," he said quietly.

"You see nothing."

"You'll not see this end as you wish it, Robin."

"Won't I?"

"You will not. I fully intend to woo her."

"And as I continue to tell you, Nick, she isn't yours to woo."

"Why not? Think you she's yours?"

When the sun falls from the sky and turns us all to ashes, Anne thought sourly. Robin of Artane was the very last person she intended to be wooed by—as if he would make the effort to do the like!

"Post a guard outside where you sleep," Robin said. "Should anyone attempt an attack, they'll find themselves facing a sword, not a sleeping idiot. You can manage that, can't you?"

"Your confidence in my skill is nothing short of staggering, my lord."

"Saints, Nick, someone tried to kill Anne not once but thrice! This is not a matter for jest."

Nicholas grunted. "I was not making it such. And as far as this other business is concerned, I like it not at all."

Anne didn't either, but saying as much would tell the men that she'd heard everything they'd said and she had no intentions of that.

"It matters not to me what you like."

"I have not given up my fight," Nicholas said. "Her father certainly prefers me to you."

"He doesn't know you very well," Robin snapped.

"I'll make it a point to see that he does—"

"Oh, by the saints, will you cease!" Robin exclaimed. "Go do something useful, such as finding us a meal. I daresay Anne will be hungry when she wakes and doubtless too weary to move. Feed a taste of everything to the dogs first. Who knows who this cur will choose as his next victim."

Nicholas sighed deeply. "Aye, you have that aright."

"And help me off with this mail before you go."

"Ah, demoted to his little lordship's squire. Rob, how I do love being your brother."

Anne heard Nicholas lose his breath with a *whoosh* and prayed he wouldn't retaliate. Truly, pretending she was sleeping through a brawl would have been more than she could have managed.

There was a muffled thump and a sigh. "Better."

"Must I help you with your boots also? And need I mention that strutting about Father's bedchamber naked would be something I would certainly have to take a blade to you for?"

"I'll endeavor not to offend Anne with my sorry form. I would appreciate something to eat. Now."

"I'll return with a meal and stay to see if it agrees with Anne."

"You'll deliver it, then go. I do not need your aid in seeing her fed."

There was a goodly bit of silence after that and Anne wondered if they were trying to glare each other into submission. Well, at least there was no ringing of blades as of yet.

And then Nicholas sighed heavily. "I think you're making a mistake."

"I've no doubt you do."

"You'll not have her, Robin."

Robin only grunted. Anne listened to them both cross to the door, then heard the footsteps pause.

"And be forewarned," Nicholas said. "You'll repay me for my serving you thusly. Fetching meals," he grumbled. "Acting the squire. Saints, I'm past all that!"

The door opened, then closed softly. Anne remained motionless, listening to Robin rustle about the chamber. There was the sound of steel against wood as she assumed he had laid his mail shirt over a chair perhaps, or a trunk. Then she heard two distinct thumps—his boots coming off perhaps. Muted footsteps crossed the room, then she heard the rustling and popping of a fire being brought back to life. The scrape of a stool across the floor sounded overloud to her ears and she took advantage of the following sigh to roll over so she faced the fire. She waited until silence had descended again before she opened one eye a slit and looked to see what Robin was about.

He sat facing the fire, with his back to her. His head hung down, leaving only the thick hair flowing over his neck exposed to her view. His broad, bare shoulders were hunched, his long, muscled back bowed. He looked enormously weary. And, for a small moment, she had the urge to go to him, to put her hands on his shoulders and work the stiffness out of them, to drag her fingers through his hair and soothe him.

But nay, Robin wouldn't care for that. Even in his youth, he'd never cared for it. Nicholas, on the other hand, had dropped everything at even a hint that she or Amanda might be willing to scratch any part of his person. Robin had shunned anything like such petting, calling it a most unmanly pursuit. Nicholas had always called him a fool for missing out on such lazy delights. Anne had wondered if Robin secretly longed for such affection, but he had never relented.

And he wouldn't relent tonight. He would likely shrug off her hands and bark some unfeeling curse at her. And it would wound her, as it always did.

Or as it would have in the past, she corrected herself. Now, it wouldn't bother her. Since she had protected herself with this newfound dislike for the young lord of Artane, his derision and shunning of her wouldn't hurt her in the slightest. Indeed, it would only confirm the opinion she should have had of him from the first. He was an unfeeling worm of a man with no heart and no chivalry. A gallant knight did not crush his lady in the dirt, then leave her there to pick herself up. Nay, she would have no part of a man who possessed such poor manners.

Then why did the fact that he had saved her life, albeit roughly, make her want to weep?

Another knock sounded on the door and Anne immediately closed her eyes. She remained perfectly still as Robin answered the door.

"Guards?" Robin asked.

"Your own men," Nicholas said quietly. "At this door, and the lads' chamber down the passageway. Jason will come here as well."

"What of Sir Edward?"

"Weeping in the dungeon," Nicholas said, with disgust. "A pitiful excuse for a knight if ever I saw one."

"Leave him there," Robin said curtly. "Perhaps it will loosen his tongue."

"He swears he had nothing to do with this."

"Do you believe him?" Robin asked.

"He's one of Father's men. I can't imagine this kind of disloyalty."

"Well," Robin said with a heavy sigh, "leave him there for a day or two and let us see if aught else happens. Now, if you don't mind, I've a lady to protect and I don't need your aid."

"Robin, I still don't know about this—"

"I know what I'm doing. Your task is to see to the rest of the ruse. And have a care with Amanda. Wouldn't want the wench to die before I have a few more goes at her backside."

Nicholas snorted. "I'll be sure and give her your best, brother."

"You fed some of this meal to the dogs?"

"Aye, and all are still breathing."

"Good enough."

Anne heard the door close, then watched him walk over to the hearth and set down a basket full of food she could smell from where she was. It had been hours since she had last eaten and her belly protested the delay rather loudly.

"Anne?"

She realized he was looking at her and she knew feigning sleep was foolish. "Aye?"

"Come eat," he said, turning his back on her and sitting on the floor.

Ah, such a paragon of chivalry. She sat up, wincing at the way her body protested such a simple act. She felt as if she'd been beaten. Or flattened by a very heavy, mailed knight. Perhaps being struck by the mace would have been less agony than this. She pushed herself up from the mattress, swayed, then regained her balance with a quick step forward, one that rattled her teeth. She shuffled across the floor carefully, too angry at Robin's rudeness to be embarrassed by her ungainly walk. The least he could have done was rise off his slothful backside and offer her his arm!

He didn't even look up as she stood next to him, trying to decide the best way to reach the floor short of falling. Robin made a sound of impatience.

"Sit down, Anne."

She gritted her teeth. "I'm trying."

"You're dawdling."

"Damn you, Robin, you could help me!"

He looked up at her and his eyes were dark, so dark she couldn't tell their color. "You don't like to be coddled, so I'm not coddling you. Sit down and eat, Anne, while there's aught to spare."

She wanted to strike him. Aye, she didn't want to be coddled, but she wouldn't have scorned a gallantly offered hand now and then. She blinked back tears of frustration and looked for something with which to lower herself. If she bent her leg without something to hold onto, it would have collapsed under her. Her body was sore enough without any new bruises. She took hold of the heavy stone of the hearth and used it as a crutch, holding herself up with it while she knelt on her good leg, her lame leg stretched out in front of her. She scraped her hands on the stone, but at least she made it to the floor without mishap.

Other than losing her pride on the way down.

She scooted back to where Robin was sitting and glared at him. He averted his face hastily.

So she sickened him. At the moment, she couldn't have cared less. She hated him. She repeated that over and over in her head as she helped herself to roast fowl and bread, washing it down with wine contained in a bottle she took right out of Robin's hands. And when she was finished, she moved to her right a bit, so she could face her captor.

"I don't want to stay here with you."

He looked into the flames. "You needn't fear for your virtue."

Anne laughed bitterly. "Ah, as if that mattered. You know as well as I that my virtue or lack thereof will never come to light. No man would have me anyway."

"Daft wench," Robin muttered.

"Men do not purchase lame wives for themselves."

"Silence," he said sharply, fixing his gaze to hers. "You speak foolishness."

Anne lifted her chin. "The truth is, I do not wish to stay here, because I can't stomach being in the same chamber with you."

"Your alternative is likely death. I daresay you can endure me if the other is your choice."

"I would prefer death," she said haughtily.

He dashed the contents of his cup into the flames, setting up a sharp hiss. "Somehow, that doesn't surprise me," he said. He jumped to his feet, jerked on his boots and snagged a tunic from off the back of a chair.

The door banged shut behind him.

Anne turned back and looked into the fire dispassionately, pointedly ignoring the sting behind her eyes. Robin's every movement, his every breath spoke of his distaste, his revulsion for her. And why not? Why would he ever feel anything else where she was concerned? Though he certainly had frightened off the more timid heiresses in England, the bold ones hadn't been fearful.

Tales of his mischief had reached her ears, tales from court, tales from the continent. Rhys had been furious over the bastards Robin had sired, though he was certain the number had been exaggerated. What did it matter if it had? She had seen some of the women who had bragged of having Robin in their beds. Beautiful, elegant women who were perfectly formed, perfectly coiffed, perfectly mannered. And not a one of them had walked with a limp. Why would he ever have looked at her, when those were the choices offered him?

Besides, Nicholas wanted her. Hadn't he said as much? Hadn't he courted her father with more enthusiasm than Robin had likely ever used for anything but a pitched battle?

It made it all the more unfortunate that Nicholas was not the brother she loved.

She closed her eyes, ignoring the tears that crept from beneath her eyelids.

17

Robin leaned back against the door and let his breath out slowly. Then he realized there were guards leaning against the opposite wall. Perfect. That was all he needed to add to his irritation—tidings of his bewildered state being bandied about the garrison hall. He straightened and gave them his most lordly look.

"No one enters," he commanded.

"My lord?" Jason asked from where he appeared at Robin's side.

"Stay here," Robin said. "Watch over the lady Anne."

Jason nodded with wide eyes. Robin turned to his guard, received more nods, then turned off down the passageway before he did anything else foolish. At least the guards were his own men so they could be intimidated if necessary. And they were men he trusted. Anne would be safe enough by herself. Indeed, now that he'd had more chance to think about it, he suspected that she might be safer without him. The only thing he knew with certainty was that he would be rotting in Hell before Nicholas was alone with Anne in that chamber.

Robin stomped down the steps, wishing he could unclench his jaw but knowing it was useless to try. His anger was too near the surface for that. By all the bloody saints, what was Nicholas about? He didn't love Anne, of that Robin was sure. But Nicholas wasn't cruel, so Robin also had to concede that his brother wouldn't be toying with her for his own sport. And he wouldn't use Anne to torment Robin.

It was a damned perplexing snarl.

Well, at least there were a few things Robin could understand. One was that his sire would be away for at least a month and that meant Geoffrey of Fenwyck would be gone for at least that long as well. Perhaps in that time he could invent a strategy to improve his standing with Anne's sire.

The other problem was who to watch over Anne while Robin saw to the business of the keep. His earlier vows aside, he knew it would be impossible for him to remain with her every moment of each day. Someone would have to be recruited to take on the duty whilst Robin was about his affairs.

But 'twas for damned sure it wouldn't be Nicholas. Robin suspected Miles might be equal to the task, so that was something to think on. Miles would likely find Anne more amenable to his company anyway.

And that reminded him of Anne's last words and he found himself scowling. So she couldn't bear his company. She might change her mind when she came face-to-face with a sword. Indeed, she might discover that she needed him after all. But for himself, what he needed was a goodly amount of ale. Perhaps that would drown out her slanders.

He found his brother sitting alone in front of the hearth, a cup in his own hands. Robin sat down across from him and reached for the jug. He assumed by the way his brother continued to breathe that the brew was safe enough.

Only once he had a cup of ale in his hands, he found that his taste for it had disappeared. He stared into the fire and didn't fight the realizations that seemed determined to catch up with him.

Someone was trying to kill Anne.

Anne would have rather died than stay in the same chamber with him.

And Nicholas was likely in higher favor with Anne's sire than he was.

It had been, Robin decided grimly, a decidedly unpleasant day.

"I would suggest you go to bed," Nicholas said, "but I know where that would lead you and I vow that won't happen."

Robin looked at his brother and couldn't even muster up enough irritation to thrash him as he might have another time.

"You needn't fear for her," Robin said wearily. "She cares nothing for me."

"Oh?" Nicholas said, his ears perking up. "Think you?"

"Aye, I know it. She cannot abide my presence."

"How perfectly lovely," his brother said, sounding as if nothing could have pleased him more.

It was that tone that woke Robin from his stupor. He eyed his sibling with disfavor.

"I daresay she wouldn't have the stomach for you either, if you'd been the one to bury her in the dirt this afternoon. At least I saved her precious skin. What have you done for her of late, save leaving a goodly amount of slobber on her hands?"

"I would make a fine husband for her."

Robin didn't even bother to reach for his sword. He shook his head slowly and prayed he wasn't making a mistake by speaking with seriousness to Nicholas.

"You might," he agreed, "but you do not love her truly. Do you?"

Nicholas, for a blessed moment Robin wished had gone on for the rest of eternity, was silent. Then he sighed. "I could learn easily enough."

"She's mine, Nick," Robin said, plunging ahead before

he lost his courage. "And she has been from the moment I clapped eyes on her."

"You put a worm down the front of her gown, Rob. I doubt she remembers that with fondness."

"What was I to do?" Robin asked crossly. "Go down on bended knee and profess my love? I was but a lad! Lads do things that only lads would do."

Nicholas stared at him for several moments in silence, then turned and looked into the fire for a like amount of time. Robin suspected he was trying to decide if the fight were truly worth it. Robin hoped he chose well. He would have hated to have run his brother through, but Anne's hand was at stake here.

Assuming she would have him.

But he would stand a far better chance if he didn't have Nicholas underfoot. Besides, he had spoken the truth. Nicholas might have loved her, but it was a brotherly affection. Robin could not possibly imagine the two together. Nicholas would pamper her overmuch, she would grow restive under his care and they would be unhappy within months.

But that was beside the point. She was *his*, not his brother's. She had always been his.

Assuming, of course, that he could convince her of that.

Nicholas sat back suddenly and sighed. He raised his cup. "Very well, I concede the battle."

"Wisely done," Robin said, feeling a rather unhealthy sense of relief.

"I still say I would have made a fine husband for her."

Robin suppressed a shudder at the thought of Anne's sweetness coupled with his brother's. Too much for one family, to his manner of thinking.

"Find your heart's desire elsewhere," Robin said. "Far away from Anne, if you please."

"I could have loved her. I do love her."

"As a sister," Robin said, hoping the glint he knew to be in his eye left a deep impression upon his brother.

"Your feelings for her are of a fraternal nature, nothing more."

"Her sire prefers me," Nicholas said, a small smile beginning to play around his mouth.

"He'll accustom himself to me in time. And if not to me, then to my inheritance."

"You have that aright, at least. I can see the advantages of being the firstborn."

And for once, Robin could too. He put his shoulders back. "See to the keep, will you? I go to keep watch over Anne."

"Watch your back."

"I fear no one," Robin said confidently.

"Anne might stick you while you sleep."

Robin grunted as he rose. There was truth in that. Perhaps he would do well to redon his mail before he took his rest. "Come to me first thing on the morrow," he said. "We'll plan how best to see the day's tasks accomplished between the two of us."

Nicholas nodded. "As you will. Oh, and Rob?"

Robin stopped. "Aye?"

"Sleep on the floor," Nicholas suggested.

As if he dared sleep on the bed! Anne would do him in for a certainty then. Robin gave his brother a flick on the ear for the sheer sport of it, then retreated up to his sire's chamber.

And as he walked down the passageway, he felt a shiver go down his spine. One day he would walk the same passageway, only he would be Lord of Artane.

Assuming Anne didn't slay him before he could outlive his father.

He shook aside his thoughts and approached the door. After confirming with his men that no murderers had entered and no stubborn wenches had escaped, he entered and bolted the door behind him.

He saw Anne immediately, lying before the fire in her cloak. He scowled. Didn't she know she would catch her death from a chill? He crossed the room quietly and squatted down next to her, grateful for the time to gaze at her in peace.

It was a miracle she hadn't been betrothed already. Indeed, she should have been. He remembered very well the year she had turned ten-and-five and her sire had arrived with what he deemed to be a suitable mate: a lad of a score and five. Robin had been beside himself with jealousy but completely unwilling to show it. Fortunately his father had had more sense than Anne's and talked Fenwick out of the plan.

After her accident, there had been no more offers of marriage. Robin couldn't have been happier about it. Men could not see her for her leg and he was perfectly content to let them be blind.

Aye, she was a beautiful creature. Vexing, but beautiful. How could any man look down at those angelic features and not be moved to lyricism? Unless he was Robin of Artane and found himself tongue-tied in her presence. Robin smiled grimly to himself. Perhaps it was his thoughts running amok in his brain that confused his tongue so. He'd done his damndest never to think of her while he was away.

But since his return to Artane, he'd thought of nothing else. Especially whilst he'd watched his lackwit brother try to woo her. Saints, but he wanted to strangle Nick for the deed! In the past few days, he'd been reduced to staring at her from the shadows in the evening, watching the way the firelight played over her hair and fair skin, the way her hands tortured her gown or smoothed it down, depending on her mood. And he'd wanted to sweep her up in his arms and stalk off with her, never to release her again. But he hadn't. Anne didn't like stalking and she didn't care for him either. She wanted a chivalrous, gallant knight with fine court manners and pleasing ways.

Which was precisely what he wasn't. A man had no use for fine manners and minstrelsy when he was tromping across blood-soaked ground and trying to keep his head on his shoulders. You bloody well didn't ask permission before you cleaved a man's skull in twain!

He sincerely doubted he could remember how to play the fine lord and didn't know if he cared to stir himself to try. After all, he had acquired a reputation for ruthlessness. It would be a pity to lose it simply because his men saw him trailing after Anne like a moonstruck calf. Nay, it was best he remain hard and cold. It would save his good standing with the men, and it would also save his pride, as he had no doubts Anne would spurn him at every turn.

He frowned down at his charge, noting the dark shadows under her eyes and the creases that didn't leave her brow, even in sleep. Sleeping on the floor had been foolish. Her muscles would stiffen up and leave her in pain the next day. What the girl needed was a few lessons in how to care for herself.

Robin paused. That wasn't such a poor idea after all. He'd known a man who had had his leg crushed, in much the same way as Anne's. And now the man was fit and hale, claiming that hot baths and the rubbing of his muscles with oil were what had cured him of his stiffness. And he had forced himself to strengthen the muscles each day. That was surely what Anne needed to do. Taking her for walks outside would give him relief from being prisoner inside his own chamber and it would aid her as well. And though he was certain she wouldn't allow him to touch her leg, he could show her what she needed to do.

And it would give him one more reason to be near her. Even gruff, surly knights longed for the company of their ladies.

He put his hand on her arm. "Anne, wake up. You cannot sleep here before the fire."

"Go away," she muttered, pulling her arm away.

Robin paused and reconsidered. Perhaps this would be more difficult than he thought. Fortunately he was a man of action, so he heeded her words not at all. He lifted her up into his arms.

"You're hurting me!"

"I'm hardly touching you," he retorted. "I'm just carrying you to bed. You needn't sound as if I'm beating you."

She bit her lip and said no more. Robin gently deposited her on the bed and pulled a blanket over her.

"Will you be warm enough?"

She nodded, not meeting his eyes. Well, the girl was half asleep. He couldn't blame her for not showing him any gratitude.

He pulled his cloak off the back of a chair and sat down before the fire. After putting more wood on the blaze, he rolled up in his cloak and tried to make himself comfortable on the hard wood. It was no easy task, and he was certain that come morning he would regret his actions. But it was a small bit of chivalry and perhaps in time Anne would come to appreciate it.

Robin tossed and turned on the floor for a goodly while before he gave up and sought the comfort of a chair. He sat with his chin resting on his steepled fingers and gave thought to the mystery with which he'd been presented.

It was a surety that Stephen of Hardwiche had not been the killer's true target. The accident that morn in the lists had left him with no doubts about that. But why would anyone want to hurt Anne? And who in the keep could possibly have anything to gain by it?

Robin's first suspect was Baldwin, of course, but even that made no sense. Baldwin's quarrel was with Robin, not Anne. And Baldwin couldn't possibly know of Robin's feelings for the girl. Why would he hurt Anne, if Robin were the one he hated? Besides, Robin couldn't credit Baldwin with the imagination to think up such a scheme. Nay, it had to be someone else and for a reason none of them had seen yet.

Robin sighed and pushed away those thoughts. He would begin his training before sunrise and hopefully something would occur to him then. Perhaps Amanda and

Isabelle could be deposited inside the chamber; they would be company enough for Anne. Miles could be left with them. Nicholas was no longer a problem, which left Robin free to think on other things.

And first among those was helping Anne recover from the crushing he'd subjected her to. Perhaps that would induce her to think more kindly of him, though he suspected that she would have less than genial feelings toward him after what he planned to do to her leg.

He rested his head back against the chair and closed his eyes. On the morrow. He would see to it all on the morrow.

18

Maude of Canfield stood at the end of the passageway with folded linens clutched in her arms. She had just watched Robin go into the lord's chamber. She shook. Indeed, she trembled so badly, she had to clutch the cloth to her to keep from dropping it. But it wasn't from fear.

It was from anger.

She could scarce believe her eyes. He had gone inside that chamber to be with *her*! It was all she could do not to run screaming down the hall and pound on the wood to bid them cease.

But she couldn't do that. There were guards aplenty in the passageway, guards likely put there to protect *her*. And Maude had seen the dogs downstairs, tasting all that came from the kitchen.

She would have to find another way. And soon. Before anything happened between them. She had to stop Robin before he made a terrible mistake. And *she* would pay dearly for the pain she had already caused Maude.

Maude leaned back against the passageway wall and indulged in her memories. She'd had Robin to herself for almost a fortnight. Of course, she'd only had him in her bed one night, and that after a solid fortnight spent work-

ing to get him there. And once she'd had him, who had
come between them?

She had.

Maude pushed away from the wall, turned and retreated
back down the passageway. She would have to wait, but
she wouldn't wait long. Edith might have had a plan, but
it required too much waiting. To be sure, Maude wanted
to avoid Baldwin's fists again, but perhaps he could be
dodged as well. Besides she didn't trust either of them.
She'd been promised that she would have Robin and she
had yet to be allowed to speak to him. Not only that, her
most glorious beauty had been shorn straight from her
head, leaving her with ragged locks that would attract no
simple man, much less Artane's heir.

Nay, she would wait no longer. *She* would have to
leave the chamber eventually. And when she did, Maude
would be waiting.

A pity, though, that she didn't have Edith's skill with
weapons. Maude had watched her on the journey to Artane. She'd dispatched a ruffian or two with blades she
seemed to produce from some hidden place on her person.
She'd killed without noise, or apparent pleasure.

It had been frightening to watch.

Maude put her shoulders back before she entered the
kitchens. Never mind that she didn't have such skill herself. Edith might have been handy with a blade, but
Maude was handy with her wits. And she had far more
than she'd ever been given credit for. She would just have
to use them. Because once *she* was dispatched, then Robin
would be free.

And then Maude would have what she'd been promised.

19

Anne woke to an empty bed. It took her a moment or two of panic to realize that she wasn't in her lone bed at Fenwyck; she was at Artane. But she wasn't in her usual chamber. She was in Rhys and Gwen's bedchamber.

With Robin.

There was a hearty bit of snoring going on so she could only assume that he still resided within the walls. She had vague memories of him carrying her to the bed and laying her down. She quickly determined that she was still wearing all her clothing, save her shoes, and she couldn't decide if she should be disappointed by that or not. Had she been naked, at least she could have taken a blade to him in good conscience.

A pressing need presented itself almost immediately and she groaned as she struggled to sit up. How was she to take care of such a thing with Robin loitering about? Perhaps she could leave and seek out a garderobe before he was alerted to her plan. She bit her lip as she swung her legs to the floor. By the saints, she felt as if every bit of flesh she possessed had been bruised. At least now, though, her wrist was the least of her pain. She was heartily tempted to crawl back beneath the blankets until she felt better.

"Anne?"

Damn, but the wretch had finely tuned ears.

"Go back to sleep," she said firmly, hoping he would recognize the tone and obey without question. She waited until she thought Robin might have fallen back asleep before she shifted her weight and put her feet on the floor.

The bedcurtains were jerked back to reveal Robin standing there rubbing his face sleepily.

"What in heaven's name are you doing?" he rumbled. "Escaping?"

"I've needs to attend to."

He yawned widely, then pointed to a corner. "There's the chamber pot. Make use of it."

"Robin!"

He blinked. "What? What have I done now?"

"I will not do this with you here!"

"Anne, we're going to be together in this chamber for several days. You may as well accustom yourself to it now."

"I will not," she said. "You'll have to leave."

"I brought in a privy screen yestereve. Surely that's sufficient to protect your modesty."

She gritted her teeth. It wasn't just her modesty she was worried about, but she was hardly going to admit that she doubted her legs would hold her up long enough for her to finish the deed.

"It isn't that," she muttered.

"Ah," he said, wisely. "Foolish of me not to think on that. You'll require aid."

Anne glared at him. "If you think for one moment that I'll ever allow you close enough to me to aid me in this, then you're a bigger fool than I thought. Get out of my way. I'll use the garderobe."

He began to frown. "You'll not leave this chamber."

"I am not your prisoner." She forced herself to her feet.

"Aye, you are. Until this mystery is solved, you'll go where I tell you and stay when I command it."

"What difference does it make to you?" she asked hotly. "Whether I live or die?"

"It doesn't matter to me," he said, through gritted teeth. "That's why I almost took a spiked ball in my head yesterday and that's also why I didn't get a wink of sleep last night from sleeping in that bloody chair!" His voice had risen with every word until it had become a shout. "I'm a lackwitted fool and you're a shrew! Now, use the bloody pot and get you back in bed."

She was momentarily tempted to burst into tears, but she would be damned before she gave him that satisfaction. So she folded her arms over her chest and gave him what she hoped was a formidable glare.

"Get out," she said through clenched teeth.

"Nay."

Almost before the thought had taken shape in her head, she watched her hand reach out and snatch the dagger from his belt. She watched with faint admiration as that same brave hand pointed the little blade at Robin's chest.

"Move," she said.

Robin looked down at the knife, then snorted. "You wouldn't use that on me."

"The temptation is almost overwhelming," she said.

Damn the man if he didn't stand there without making a hint of a move to protect himself. Anne wished she had the spine to stick him firmly between the ribs, hopefully in a place that would pain him greatly. Perhaps it would be a slow, agonizing death. Nothing would have pleased her more than to sit at his bedside and watch him linger on for several weeks before expiring in a great, painful rush.

"You, my lady," he said, continuing to stand there as if he hadn't anything more pressing to do than argue with her, "will use the pot."

"Robin, you great oaf," she said in exasperation, "I am *not* one of your men to be ordered about!"

"Would that you were! 'Twould make this all much simpler!"

She poked at him with the dagger. "Move and do it now. I've no more time nor breath to waste on you. Even you should be able to recognize the difference between your father's bedchamber and your tent on a battlefield."

"Aye," he returned in irritation, "my father's chamber has a pot! Were you in my army, you'd be standing behind a tree!"

Robin of Artane was gruff, irritating, hopelessly rude. And he was lacking in the most basic principles of chivalry. Anne decided that it was futile to waste any more breath on him. She tossed his dagger at him point first and pushed past him while he was trying to fend it off. She crossed the chamber as quickly as her battered form would allow only to find Robin blocking the door before her. She glared at him.

"Robin—"

He looked at her, then slowly held up his hand in surrender. "I have no liking for this—"

"I care nothing for what you do or do not like."

"But if you are determined—"

"Very."

He sighed. "You are the most stubborn woman I have ever had the misfortune of—"

She pushed him aside before he could finish. He pushed readily enough, which made her realize that it had no doubt been something he'd allowed. Had he planned to thwart her, he would have been as immovable as stone.

He caught the door with his hand and stopped her before she could open it fully.

"At least let me come with you and keep watch," he said quietly. "Then should someone attack, you will be safe."

She looked up at him.

And then she wished she hadn't.

His expression was grave, but it wasn't the gravity a man wore like a shield when he faced a distasteful business or considered an unpleasant turn of events. His concern was plain to the eye—even her eye. His gray eyes seemed almost black in the torchlight and his weariness was easily seen. It would have been easy enough for him to send her on her way and abscond with her place on the bed.

Yet there he stood, ready to guard her on her journey to the garderobe.

"Robin, it isn't as if we're walking into a pitched battle," she said, beginning to feel slightly ridiculous.

"And if we are, Lady Anne, 'tis my privilege to protect you."

And with that, he took her hand and pulled her out the door behind him.

Anne followed him, trying to dredge up the loathing she'd felt for him the night before. She dug deep for any shred of anger or irritation she'd felt over the past fortnight. Fortunately, as her body protested each and every movement she made, she had no trouble rediscovering any of those feelings.

But struggling mightily to fight its way through the press of hurt and anger was a tiny feeling of something very quiet and very precious.

It was his privilege to protect her.

The words softened her heart and his actions warmed her soul.

It was rather unsettling, on the whole.

And then there was the feeling of his hand holding hers so securely behind his back. Mayhap he wanted no one to see what he did. 'Twas also likely that perhaps he feared being seen doing the like with her would shame him. But he didn't release her until he had seen her safely inside her destination. And he took hold of her hand again the moment she had come back out into the passageway.

"My lord Robin!"

Anne found herself crushed between the passageway wall and Robin's substantial self so quickly, she lost her breath. She heard Robin's sword come from its sheath with a purposeful hiss. Then she felt him relax.

"Jason, by the saints," Robin snapped, "do not steal up thusly!"

"Forgive me, my lord, but the lady Amanda sends word that she is weary of her confinement."

Robin sighed deeply, then resheathed his sword. He turned and looked at Anne.

"Still breathing?" he asked.

"Barely," she wheezed.

He sighed, and put his arm around her. "Jason, fetch Amanda and Isabelle to my father's chamber. Have Miles come too."

Anne found herself escorted carefully back to Artane's bedchamber where she was made comfortable in a chair while Robin saw to the fire. He said nothing, and he apologized not at all for squeezing her yet again between himself and an unyielding surface. Perhaps he was becoming too accustomed to doing the like. Anne watched him as he worked, his strong hands steady and sure as they tended the fire. Whatever else his flaws, she couldn't deny that he was infinitely capable of protecting her.

He finished with his task, brushed his hands off and sat back on his heels. He looked at her.

"I need to train," he said, "and I have the business of the keep to see to."

"I know."

He frowned. "I hadn't planned to leave you at all, but I can see now that isn't possible."

"Of course."

"I will return, Anne."

She found that she could do nothing but nod. She knew she should have been telling him to keep himself gone as long as possible, that she had no desire to see him again, nor did she need his protection.

But that little feeling of softness toward him was beginning to work a foul work upon her common sense. She was almost swayed enough by it to thank him for his efforts.

"I'll see food sent," he continued. "Need you something to occupy your hands?"

"I suppose so," she said. "Since you won't be here to throttle."

But she found that she couldn't even manage any venom to deliver with that last sting. Robin looked unimpressed and rose with a half-hearted snort.

"I'll find you your sewing," he said. "And if that doesn't distract you, you'll have my sister to listen to for the morn. By the saints, you can hear her complaining already!"

There was truth in that. Anne had no trouble hearing nor understanding Amanda, likely because Robin figured so prominently in her slander and those were words Anne had used more than once herself.

The door burst open and Amanda swept inside. "I will not be kept prisoner in my own house!" she exclaimed. She stomped over to Robin and poked him in the chest. "And you'll not keep Anne here either, you fool! Have you no thought for the gossip you've caused already?"

Anne watched Robin grit his teeth. She looked down. His hands were clenched as well—never a good sign.

"My duty is to protect her," he said tightly. "And if that means keeping her prisoner in my chamber, then that is what I shall do."

"I could likely protect her with more skill than you—"

"Amanda," Anne interrupted with a gasp.

"Well," Amanda said, with an amazing amount of bluster, considering whom she had just insulted. "I could."

Anne looked at Robin, wondering if he would take a blade to his sister and prove her wrong. There was one thing a body didn't do and live to tell of it and that was insult Robin of Artane's skill with a blade. Rumors of his bastards might have reached her ears with questionable accuracy. Tales of his defending his abused honor rang true with every word.

But Robin was either weary from his night in the chair, or he was trying to impress them all with his calm. He merely unclenched his hands, wriggled his jaw a time or two as if he sought to relieve a cramp there, then took a deep breath.

"Sister," he said with admirable restraint, "I have sworn to keep Anne safe. I will not have her blood on my hands when there is aught I can do to save her life. And if that means keeping her in my chamber from matins to lauds and every hour of prayer in between, then that is what I will do!"

"Ha," Amanda said, with a scowl. "But my blood you would likely wash off those hands readily enough."

"Would I?"

"Aye, you likely would!"

Anne watched the exchange with fascination. Robin and Amanda had ever been at each other with words and pokes of stiff fingers, and she had oft wondered if it might come to bloodshed some day. But somehow this time the game had turned entirely more serious and she couldn't help but wonder about the outcome.

"Then, sister, you know me not at all," Robin said quietly, "for I would not have your blood on my hands either if there were aught I could do to protect you."

And with that, he grasped Amanda by the shoulders, pulled her close and kissed her gently on the forehead.

And then he strode from the chamber.

Anne looked at Amanda. Her foster sister's jaw fair rested upon her chest. Anne couldn't help the laugh that seemed to come from a very tender portion of her heart. By the saints, Robin could be sweet when he willed it. And to leave Amanda speechless? Now, *that* was a feat worthy of a minstrel's best efforts.

"The oaf," Amanda managed finally. She looked at Anne. "Did you see what he did?"

Anne smiled. "I did."

Amanda scowled. "Bloody wretch. He's a fool if he thinks that will keep me in this chamber for the whole of the day."

But Anne noted that Amanda sat without further comment and she didn't complain about her confinement. And when Miles arrived with food and stitchery, Amanda accepted the both with no disparaging remarks about her eldest sibling.

Anne took up her stitchery but her heart wasn't in it. She finally put it in her lap and stared blindly into the chamber, reliving the morning's events and wondering mightily over them.

It had been, she decided finally, a most exceptional morn.

She could scarce wait to see what the evening might bring.

It was very late in the day when Robin returned and shooed his siblings out of the chamber. Anne rose with difficulty only to find herself almost plowed over by men bringing in a large wooden tub. Water followed and she was treated to several looks of frank speculation that she had trouble ignoring. She could feel her face flaming and she lifted her chin in answer to their challenge. She had done nothing amiss. Besides, 'twas no affair of anyone's what she did or where she slept. As if Artane's servants would actually believe she had shared Robin's bed!

She was, however, very relieved when the men were gone and Robin had bolted the door behind him. She shook her head regretfully at the sorry state of her life. She was locked inside a chamber with one of the realm's fiercest warriors, a tub of bathing water sat not five paces from her, yet she was relieved to be free of potential rescuers?

By the saints, she was losing her mind.

"Make haste while the water is hot," Robin said, startling her.

"I beg your pardon?"

"Get in," Robin said, gesturing toward the tub.

She could only gape at him, speechless.

Robin rolled his eyes. "I want you to bathe, Anne. You're stiff and sore; your muscles will benefit from it."

Anne had taken her share of baths, under protest of course until she had seen the benefit of it for her leg, but bathe in front of Robin of Artane?

Not even should the Fires of Hell themselves be warming the water from beneath the tub and several demons be prodding her toward the bath with their forked tails.

Anne looked for a place of refuge. Well, the bed had served her well enough the night before. She set her sights on that haven and made her way toward it. She soon found, however, that Robin had somehow gotten in her way. She moved ungracefully to one side only to find him again before her. He reached for her and she slapped his hands away.

"What do you?" she demanded.

"I am endeavoring to aid you. Can you lift your arms? Nay? Bend over, then, and I'll pull your dress off you as gently as I can."

Anne could hardly believe what she was hearing. "I am *not* bathing in front of you, you imbecile!"

"I can tell you are stiff, Anne. 'Tis nothing I wouldn't do for one of my men."

"I am not one of your men!" She had the overwhelming urge to clout him on the head and bring sense back to him. "You are not removing my clothes," she spluttered. "Especially in front of yourself!"

He sighed and dragged his hand through his hair. "I'll turn my back and you can do it."

"I don't trust you!"

He flinched, as surely as if she'd slapped him. Anne felt a sudden surge of regret, but that left quickly enough at his next words.

"Why would I stir myself to gape at you, Anne?" he said angrily. "You said yourself that no man would want you."

Tears sprang to her eyes at the words that felt more like

a blow. But before she could decide if she should walk or run from the chamber, she found herself with Robin's hands on her shoulders.

"Anne," he said, "by the saints . . ."

Anne held herself stiffly away from him. Mayhap 'twas better that there be no mystery regarding his feelings for her. If he truly found her so revolting—

But if that were the case, then why was he trying to pull her into his arms?

She watched as he took her hands from off his chest, opened her arms and stepped closer to her. He gently released her hands, then with a tenderness she could hardly credit him with, put his arms around her and drew her close. Anne was so surprised by it all, she couldn't find her wits to move.

And then she felt his hand skim hesitantly over her hair.

It was her undoing.

She knew she should have still been angry with him. She knew she had just cause to keep the fires of her hurt burning long into the rest of her life.

But she also couldn't deny that she had likely hurt him just as intensely.

She wondered if there would ever be a time in their lives when they might have speech together without some kind of altercation marring it. And hard on the heels of that thought came the one that troubled her most: was there even a point in worrying about that? For all she knew, she would be packed off to some uncaring lord and never see Robin again.

The feeling of Robin's hand on her hair slowly and surely caught her attention through her miserable thoughts. She sighed lightly. There was no use in fretting over her future. Perhaps she would be far better served to think on her present. Besides, how often did she find herself in Robin of Artane's arms, with both of them silent?

And then there was the hesitancy of his touch.

As if he truly sought to be gentle with her.

She very slowly, and very carefully, turned her head and laid her ear against his chest. Robin gathered her more securely to him and she felt him sigh. His cheek came to rest on top of her head. He made no move, said no word. He simply stroked her hair and held her close. Anne closed her eyes against the sting there. Even so, she couldn't stop a tear or two from leaking out.

And then a feeling washed over her so strongly that she could scarce stand through it once she realized what it was.

She had come home.

She stood for several minutes with him exactly thusly, until she knew that the feeling of being in Robin's arms was forever burned into her soul.

And then she felt him stir and knew the moment was gone. But that mattered not; she could recall it now at any time.

She pulled back and looked up at him. For the first time in years, gone was the roughness in his expression, gone was the mask he wore, the one he likely believed protected his heart. She looked at a man who returned her look with an expression that though it might not have been considered gentle by some, was gentle enough for her.

"I didn't mean . . ." he began, then he shut his mouth and tightened his lips, as if he had already said more than he intended.

"Nor did I," she said quietly.

He pursed his lips, but a hint of a smile escaped just the same. "Perhaps you shouldn't trust me, Anne. Many a beautiful woman has been ravished in her bath."

"But I'm not—"

A large hand was suddenly over her mouth.

"Enough," he said simply. "Go soak before the water cools so much that it no longer serves you."

She escaped his hand. "And you'll be outside, I take it?"

"You may need my help—"

"Robin!"

"Anne, I give you my most solemn word of honor that I will not look at you whilst you bathe."

She scowled at him.

He sighed. "I'll hide within the bedcurtains. Will that soothe your maidenly reserve?"

She folded her arms over her chest.

"Bloody hell, I'll tie a cloth over my eyes!"

"Well," she said slowly, "that might suffice me."

"I've given you my word," he reminded her.

And Robin was as good as his word. That much she could never doubt of him.

Besides, hadn't she said she trusted him? She had to have meant it or she wouldn't have said it. Or so she told herself as she watched Robin cloister himself inside the bed hangings. She watched the bed for several minutes, just to assure herself that he wouldn't pop out to see how she fared. Once she was convinced he would remain where he was supposed to, she turned and limped over to the tub. He was right about the benefits of a good soak. With any luck at all, she might have a bit of time to contemplate what had just transpired between them.

It felt like a bit of a truce.

She stripped off her clothes, biting her lip to keep from groaning as she did so. She sighed as she saw the bruises covering her body. It was a wonder Robin hadn't broken half her bones with the way he had thrown himself atop her. She couldn't deny, though, that he surely hadn't meant to hurt her, nor could she deny that he certainly had saved her life. That was worth, perhaps, a bit of forgiveness. She eased herself down into the tub and a groan escaped her before she could stop it.

"Anne, are you hurt?"

"Nay," she said quickly. "I am well."

Robin's gasp was harsh in the stillness of the chamber. "Merciful saints above, what have you done to yourself?"

"Robin, nay!" she exclaimed, frantically trying to cover herself with her arms as she heard the bed curtains snap back and his feet hit the floor. "You vowed you would not look—"

"That was until I saw this!" he exclaimed, his footsteps approaching rapidly. "Lean up, Anne."

"Oh, Robin, please," she begged. "Please leave me in peace."

He was silent for some time and she might have thought him returned to his place if it hadn't been for the little mutters he was making under his breath. And then he cleared his throat.

"Anne, you're bruised terribly."

She felt his fingers trail over her upper back, then his hand stopped.

"I did this yesterday, didn't I?"

"Of course you did!"

"The rest of you is likely just as bruised, isn't it?"

"If I say aye, will you go?"

He was silent for so long, she almost turned to look at him to see what he was thinking. She could hear him shift hesitantly.

"Should I, um, wash your hair?" he asked gruffly. "As my penance?"

"Nay. I'll manage."

"I wouldn't hurt you."

"I know," she said, wishing mightily that he would choose a more opportune time to beg her pardon. "Now, will you please go? Make your penance later."

"I fear I was too frightened yesterday for gentleness."

Anne gritted her teeth. By the saints, she was naked in her bath and he was continuing to carry on as if they'd been strolling in the garden!

"Anne, did I break anything, do you think? Do your ribs pain you? By the saints, your leg!" He reached around and put his hand on her bare knee. " 'Tis no wonder you're stiff—"

"Robin!" she shrieked. "Get away from me!"

"Anne, I was just trying to help—"

"I'm naked, you fool!"

He jerked his hand back instantly. "Of course."

"Go back to bed," she commanded.

He immediately padded back over to the bed.

"Close the bed curtains," she commanded.

He got back onto the bed and jerked the curtains closed.

"Don't open them."

His sigh likely came close to blowing the curtains from their moorings.

"Promise?" she prompted.

"Aye!"

Well, at least he was shouting at her again instead of trying to tend her. Anne waited until Robin had stopped shifting on the bed, then quickly washed her hair and bathed.

And then she merely sat in the water and let it ease the stiffness from her. She hadn't been at all sure of the practice before her wounding, but Gwen had put her into so many tubs of hot water over the months following that she'd acquired a taste for it.

It was agony to lift the buckets of rinse water, but she wasn't about to ask Robin for help. It was bad enough that he had seen what she hadn't been able to cover with her hair and arms. Not only had Robin seen, he'd touched!

She wondered if such a thing might count as a loss of virtue.

She dressed quickly, then sat down in front of the fire on a stool to comb out her hair. She heard Robin rustle about the chamber, but she didn't look at him. She didn't dare. By the saints, he'd seen parts of her that no one had in years!

Before long, she felt his hand on her back.

"The men come to take out the tub. Nick is bringing us something to eat."

Anne nodded and didn't look at the lads who came to take away the remains of her bath. She could only speculate about what their glances would say now. Best not to know.

"Surviving the lion's den?"

Anne looked up at the sound of Nicholas's voice. He stood next to her, looking much improved from the day before.

"We haven't killed each other yet," she said with a smile.

"Anne," Nicholas began, "you needn't stay here if you don't wish it—"

"She stays and you go," Robin growled, taking hold of Nicholas by the back of his tunic. "See that the garrisons are put to bed."

"And just what is it you plan to do this eve?" Nicholas asked.

"Don't worry," he said as he propelled Nicholas toward the door. "We'll find some way to amuse ourselves."

"Keep your hands off her."

"Leaving me free to put them on you repeatedly if you don't cease with your babbling. Go protect the babes."

Anne listened to the door shut and then looked up at Robin as he came back to the fire. "You needn't stay—"

"If you wish me to go, I will," he said briskly.

But he wasn't moving.

And neither was she.

She could easily remember the feeling of his arms around her and the tenderness with which he had touched her hair. She took a deep breath. No sense in not keeping her part of the truce.

"Stay," she said, "if you like. I won't argue with you."

"For once," he grumbled. He picked her up, stool and all, and moved her closer to the fire. "You'll chill."

Well, perhaps it wasn't as gallantly spoken as Nicholas might have done it. Anne couldn't deny that it was chivalry all the same.

Robin's interpretation of it, of course.

And as she watched him mutter under his breath as he laid their supper out, she couldn't help a small smile.

Mayhap he grumbled about her, but then again, perhaps not. All she knew was that they were little grumbles she was growing accustomed to and had begun to look on with a small bit of fondness.

Perhaps there was hope for them after all.

20

It was well into the next morning that Robin found himself lingering at the lord's table in the great hall. He stared blindly into the distance. Another day gone by and he was no closer to solving his mystery. He had looked over the lads carefully in the lists that morning, searching for the slightest hesitation when meeting his eyes, or the slightest shifting uncomfortably when he spoke to them.

There had been nothing.

Not even Baldwin had flinched when Robin had glared at him. He'd received his customary sneer in return, but no offer to cross blades. Robin had watched Sedgwick train and suspected that the fury behind it had to do with a desire to redeem himself from his previous humiliation at Robin's hands. Robin couldn't have been happier about it.

How lovely it was to be the victor for a change in that fight.

But no one else had looked at him askance. His own men, he trusted. Nicholas's lads, which were only a handful anyway, were equally as known to Robin, and there was surely no murderer amongst them.

That left only his father's men as possibilities, and

Robin had methodically dispatched them that morn in hand-to-hand combat and found not a one of them either lacking in skill or moving about in a suspicious manner. Sir Edward had been interrogated and released from the dungeon when Robin had determined his innocence. It had left the knight free, but Robin without a culprit.

He was beginning to wonder if he might not be unequal to the task of unraveling the tangle.

Of course some of that trouble he could certainly lay at Anne's feet. Who could have possibly foreseen that holding her in his arms could have worked such a foul work upon his good sense? He could remember with perfect clarity the very moment she had ceased to fight him and had come willingly into his poor embrace. He'd felt a peace descend upon him softly and surely until it reached into his heart and stilled all but his gentlest feelings.

Had he not liked it so much, it likely would have frightened him witless.

But what *had* frightened him had been the sight of her bruises. He had hurt her badly; he could only hope she knew how deeply he regretted having had to do the like. He was only grateful he'd seen the mishap coming. And that led him back to wondering just what foul fiend had Anne in his sights. Or was it Anne? Surely an assassin couldn't have been so inept to have been targeting him, yet managing to find Anne each time.

He rubbed his eyes suddenly with the heels of his hands and rose. He would accomplish nothing by just sitting and stewing. 'Twas a sure sign of his muddled state that he'd even been caught doing the like. But perhaps he could be forgiven it, given the day he'd had.

Of course, it might have begun more pleasantly if he hadn't been suffering from another miserable night's half-sleep in the chair. He'd retreated to the lists at dawn only to find them a mud pit that even a sow wouldn't find to her liking. If the lists had been unpleasant, his return to the keep had been even more so. He'd been assaulted by his father's steward immediately upon his return to the hall, even before he could snatch a morning meal. That had taken far longer than he'd wished, but he'd had no choice but to make decisions about foodstuffs and the like. And if that hadn't been trouble enough, he'd heard himself agreeing to take on his father's court of justice tasks.

Though now that he'd had a chance to sit and think for a bit, he could see that overseeing such a thing might prove to be very interesting. Perhaps there was some soul aggrieved enough to think to punish them all by hurting Anne. Aye, that would be worth a day's time.

But now all he wanted to do was seek a bit of peace and quiet. His siblings were above and likely needing a report from him, but after he had finished with them, he would see if Anne wasn't amenable to spending the rest of the afternoon in his sire's solar. She was likely growing weary of the bedchamber.

He made his way upstairs and walked quietly down the passageway. The guards were at their posts, though they looked less than happy to see him. A sense of foreboding immediately assailed him.

"What?" he demanded as he neared them. "Is my family within?"

"Aye," one of the guards said hesitantly. "Most of them."

Robin threw open the door before the man could say more. After all, it was their responsibility to keep murderers from entering. He hadn't instructed them to forbid anyone from leaving.

It took him but a moment to ascertain that everyone was within—except Nicholas and Anne.

"I'll kill him," Robin growled. He looked at Miles. "You couldn't stop him?"

"Anne wanted to go," Miles said.

Amanda rose, gathered up a handful of cloth and shoved it at Robin. "Take this to her."

Robin yelped as he grabbed hold of a fistful of needle. "Saints, wench, what are you trying to slay me with?"

"Believe me, brother, if I were trying to slay you, I wouldn't limit myself to a paltry needle."

Robin started to glare at her, then he caught the look on her face. Her heart wasn't in her slander and Robin felt an unaccustomed sense of fondness for his sister. He frowned anyway, though, so she wouldn't see it. There was no telling what she might do with the knowledge of such a weakness.

"She wanted to go?" he asked.

Amanda shrugged with a sigh. "She was restless and Nicky offered to take her to Father's solar. He thought it was safe enough."

Miles came to stand next to Amanda. He put his arm around her and smiled faintly at Robin. "If you want my opinion, I think she wanted to look for you."

"Though why she'd want that is a mystery to all rational souls," Amanda added.

Robin scowled. Well, at least Amanda hadn't completely lost herself amongst those foreign feelings of kindness she'd been having toward him. That was somewhat reassuring.

"Oh, Amanda," Miles said, giving her a slight shake, "you are a cruel wench."

"And you're a mindless twit," Amanda said, turning a frown on her younger brother. "What know you of what Anne wants?"

"I have eyes," Miles said placidly. "A woman does not spend a goodly part of her time watching the door if she isn't waiting for a man to come through it."

"She could have been waiting for a meal," Amanda said tartly.

"You have not a shred of romance in your soul," Miles returned with a bit of a laugh.

"No time for it," Amanda said. She looked at Robin. "Well? What are you standing there gaping at? Off with you and seek out your lady before Nicholas escapes with her."

"Right," Robin growled, then turned and left the chamber. He looked at his guards. "No one enters or leaves without my permission. Use your blades if necessary, especially on my sister Amanda."

He received four fervent nods, though he could tell that at least one man was having second thoughts about the last. Even Robin would concede that his sister was beautiful. Perhaps they could prod her where it wouldn't mar her face.

He made his way quickly down to his father's solar, then burst inside. That the door wasn't bolted only increased his ire.

But just as a torrent of words were about to gush from his mouth, the scene before him and the possible significance of it reached his poor, overworked mind.

Nicholas was sitting in one of their father's chairs, reading some manuscript or another. Robin couldn't have cared less which one it was, or even that his brother was doing something so useful with his time. What struck him immediately was that Anne was not sitting in his brother's lap. Nor was she sitting in the chair next to him. Robin's relief was followed immediately by concern that she wasn't where she should have been.

And then he spotted her in the alcove, sitting on one of the benches there and looking out the window. He would have chastised her for sitting in such a perilous place, but even he had to admit that since the solar was on the second floor, it was unlikely that she would be harmed with anything put through the window. And she looked so contemplative that he couldn't begrudge her her post.

But he could begrudge Nicholas the company. He caught his brother's eye and motioned to the door.

"I'm comfortable here," Nicholas said.

"You'll be less so very shortly if you don't go," Robin informed him. "Get out."

Nicholas sighed, returned the manuscript to its trunk and left, without further comment or protest.

That seen to, Robin bolted the door and then turned to Anne. She hadn't turned to look at him and that made him nervous. He cursed under his breath as he threw her sewing into a chair, snatched up a blanket and crossed over to her. Apparently she hadn't the good sense to keep warm, else she would have been sitting next to the fire. 'Twas a wonder she had survived as long as she had without him looking after her.

He wrapped the blanket around her shoulders, sat down next to her, then hesitated. Casting caution and his pride to the wind, he gently slid his fingers under her hair and pulled it free of the blanket.

"Why are you sitting here in the chill?" he asked, his voice rough despite his efforts to gentle it.

"I love the rain," she said, still not looking at him. "It softens things so, don't you think?"

He snorted. "Try sleeping out in it for weeks at a time and see how you feel about it."

She looked at him over her shoulder and smiled faintly. "Always the sensible one."

"Always the dreamer," he returned.

She shrugged, turning back to her contemplation of the garden below her. "Life is easier thusly."

He sucked on his teeth, wondering what to say now. The first foray into conversation hadn't gone exactly as he would have liked. There was certainly no warm welcome for him in her words. Had he imagined the cessation of war between them the night before?

And why had Miles thought she had gone seeking him? She had likely been hiding from him. Well, best to know now, before he was disappointed later.

"I left you in the bedchamber," he began.

"I was restless."

"And your life meant so little to you that you couldn't endure a bit of that in exchange for safety?"

"I took Nicky with me."

"And how was he to save you? Talk your assailant to death?"

She did turn then and to his surprise, Robin found her smiling at him. "He can wield a sword, Robin. Surely not as well as you can, but he isn't past all hope."

Robin grunted. "Then you haven't been watching him in the lists of late, if that is what you believe."

"Oh, Robin," she said with a shake of her head.

Robin rubbed his arms. "Could we seek out the fire, at least? 'Tis bloody cold here."

She shook her head. "Let me look out a bit longer, if you please."

He sighed. "As you will." But he rose and fetched her another blanket. No sense in not saving her from herself. He returned and laid it over her legs.

"Thank you," she said.

"It was nothing I wouldn't do—"

"—for your mount, I know," she finished.

"What a stubborn baggage you are, and I was going to say 'twas nothing I wouldn't do for my sister." *Or for you*, he added silently.

"She would no doubt appreciate it, as do I. Here, come take your mind off the matter. See you the mist yonder?" she asked, pointing over the castle walls.

"Aye."

"Don't you find it beautiful?" she asked. " 'Tis full of all manner of ghostly shapes, don't you think?"

Robin knew she had turned her head to look at him, but he couldn't pull his eyes away from the scene before him. By the saints, he wished he could see nothing but promise in that drizzle. Unfortunately, the sight struck him so strongly with a memory, he couldn't pull himself away from it.

"Will you know what I see?" he asked slowly, not intending it as a question. "I see Coyners in France in October, two years past. I see bloody ground before me and the mist obscuring the fallen men around me. I hear the screams of my fellows and of the enemy, screams of the horses, battle cries echoing in the air." He took a deep breath and let it out slowly, finding himself hesitating to say more.

And then he felt a hand come to rest atop his. He took a deep breath and continued on.

"I taste fear in my mouth, I smell blood and death about me, I hear the whistles of arrows and blades. The rain soaks me to the skin, chills me, makes the ground beneath me slippery and treacherous." He smiled bitterly. "I killed a score of men that day, in the rain, and watched the drizzle wash away their blood from my sword and my clothes."

"Oh, Robin, I'm so sorry."

He shook his head. But as he looked in her eyes, he prayed he would see something there that would ease the heaviness in his heart. He wanted her to know what he'd seen and how desperately he'd wished in his innermost heart that she would want him home, that she would want him next to her, that she would be proud of what he had become.

Tears spilled over onto her cheeks. Robin shook his head.

"I didn't say that to grieve you."

"You fool," she said with a groan. "I know that."

He looked down at his interlaced fingers and saw that his knuckles were white. Anne's slender fingers were resting atop them.

"I'm sorry, Robin."

"There's nothing to be sorry about," he said with a sigh. "War is war. There is no glorifying it. 'Tis a bloody business."

"Are you returning soon?"

Now, if that wasn't a question to be answered carefully he didn't know what would be. He didn't dare look at her. Did she want him to go back to France, or did she want him to stay? He could scarce bear the thought of knowing.

But a coward he wasn't, so he took his courage in hand

and looked her full in the face. "I'm not sure."

"Your father needs you here, Robin."

Ah, of course. His father would need him. He sighed. There was no mention of how she needed him, but he knew he couldn't have expected the like.

"He's been terribly lonely without you."

Robin pursed his lips. "He has plenty of other sons."

She didn't reply.

Robin couldn't move; he could scarce believe what he'd just said. It was out, his worst demon. He looked away, unable to meet her gaze. So his sire had been the baron of Ayre, a powerful man in his day. Robin would have torn the blood out of his own veins if it would have meant Rhys de Piaget's blood flowed through them. It was possibly the one thing he wanted the most, and the one thing he knew he could never have.

Save Anne, that was.

"You are his firstborn, Robin," Anne said gently. "He loves you very much."

"He may tolerate me," Robin said stiffly, "but you know as well as I that I am not his firstborn. Miles has that honor. My sire was a miserable whoreson." He slanted a look her way, wondering if she would agree with him or not.

She merely smiled gently. "Was he? Perhaps when you're a better frame of mind, I'll give you my thoughts on it."

"There is no thinking to do on it, Anne. You cannot change the facts."

Her smiled turned amused. "You are an impossible lad, aren't you, Robin? I don't think I've ever met a more stubborn soul."

"I am not a lad. I'm a man full grown. Your disrespect is, at the very least, highly insulting."

She leaned back against the stone wall, but she didn't take her hand away from his. Robin didn't dare move, for fear he would frighten her away. She stared out over the courtyard again.

"Don't you remember how we loved the rain when we were small?"

He forced the tension out of himself. Aye, he remembered well. Rainy days had been his favorite, the only time he had had full days of leisure. He had passed them with Anne as a rule, finding that her sweetness was much preferable to Nicholas's teasing or the other lads' sharp, judging eyes. They had spent hours in this very spot, playing chess or simply talking softly as Rhys carried on with the business of the keep. Robin had boasted of the fine warrior he would become and she had remained silent, listening to him raptly. She had been such a shy, dreamy child and he had been her protector, her champion. He'd taught her to play chess on the same bench they now occupied, allowing her to win time and time again, merely to hear her laugh at him.

Aye, he had loved her dearly.

He had never allowed her back after his humiliation. She'd tried to come, knocking on his door softly, begging him to let her in. In time, the knocking had ceased and he had been alone to squelch his tears with harsh young pride.

"Do you remember how you used to lie using my legs as your pillow and pay me to sing to you?"

He blinked away his hard memories and looked at her. "What?"

"Don't you remember?"

"I remember no such thing. I never had time for such foolishness. And even if I'd had the time, I certainly wouldn't have been forced to pay you."

She smiled sadly. "Your memory is short, my lord." She rose and limped slowly over to the fire. Robin watched her take up her sewing trinkets and sit down on a chair near the hearth. She bent over her work; all Robin could see was the glint of firelight on her pale hair.

He leaned his head against the wall. Pay her?

Ah, of course. Now that he thought on it, he remembered very well. He'd never considered her request for his

aid a payment at all. She'd begged him to take her to
Mass each morn, as she couldn't bear the teasing of the
pages. Morning after morning he had escorted her there,
keeping his arm around her to shield her from prying eyes
and taunts. He'd never understood why the pages teased
her so. Perhaps she hadn't possessed Amanda's striking
beauty, but she'd been a comely child. Shy but comely.
Children were cruel and Anne had suffered because of it.

Well, Mass was over for the day, but perhaps he could
serve her in other ways. He'd meant to see her work her
leg anyway. Perhaps taking her on a stroll through the
passageways would be exercise enough. He could keep
her safe. The walk would do her good and it would certain
keep him from babbling anything else foolish for an hour
or so. Aye, this was something he could do for her and
succeed.

He rose and walked across the chamber purposefully.
He stopped before her and held out his hand. "Let us
walk."

She paused in her work and looked up at him. "I beg
your pardon?"

He took her sewing and put it aside, then held out his
hand again. "Come walk, my lady."

"Freedom?" she asked, looking as if he'd promised her
something far more desirable than a bit of painful exercise.

"Aye," he said, pulling her to her feet. Then he thought
better of his haste and looked about him for what he
would need. He strode over to a trunk and opened it.

"What seek you now?" Anne asked.

"This," he said, pulling out a cloak his mother had worn
several years past. He drew the cloak around her shoulders, pulling the hood up over her head and covering her
glorious hair. He looked down and was surprised to see
her face fall.

"What is it?" he asked.

"Nothing," she said quietly.

He was tempted to give her reaction more thought, then

thought better of it. He would get her out the door whilst she was still amenable to the idea. He led her to the door, opened it, then looked out to see that the passageway was empty. He turned and looked at Anne. She seemed to have lost much of her enthusiasm for the prospect, but perhaps she had begun to realize that it wouldn't be all pleasure. He took her hand and pulled her out of the solar behind him.

"We'll go slowly at first. I don't know why you've let yourself favor that leg, Anne, but you shouldn't. The less you use it, the more it will pain you."

She jerked her hand away. "If my limp distresses you so, begone then."

He looked at her in surprise. "You need to work your leg, Anne. I'm here to see you do it properly."

"Very well, then," she said flatly. "Do what you will. It matters not to me."

Women. Would he ever understand them? Perhaps it was only Anne who baffled him. The women at court he could understand. They wanted him, ready, in their beds. They couldn't have cared less about his chivalry or lack thereof. He pleasured them well and they were left with a tale to tell their solar companions the next day.

But Anne was different. Robin couldn't understand her and he suspected he never would. He likely never had. From the looks of things, she couldn't bear his touch. And his generous offer to help her regain her strength had obviously displeased her.

He was tempted to sit down until his poor head stopped aching.

Saints, he'd never felt so unsure of himself. At least with women at court he knew how to comport himself. A single lifting of one eyebrow was all it usually took to have his bed warmed. He lifted his eyebrow seldom indeed, though.

He didn't want to speculate on why.

He walked the corridor with Anne and cursed under his breath. Damnation, he wasn't adept at gentle wooing. Demanding, aye; taking, surely; but wooing? Nay. He'd never had to.

She stumbled and he instantly caught her around the waist. Once she was steady, he tucked her hand under his arm. She jerked it free so hard, she almost went sprawling. Robin turned to her and put his hands on her shoulders to keep her upright. Before he could speak, she'd yanked her hood back.

"Begone from my sight, you heartless swine," she spat.

Robin felt his jaw slide down. "By the saints, Anne, what in the bloody hell have I done to you *now*?"

"You hypocrite. You cover my face so no one will see me, yet you hold on to me as if we were lovers. Find some wench more foolish than I to ply your unsavory trade upon."

She turned on her heel and limped away. Robin stood, rooted to the spot. Hypocrite? *Hypocrite?* Damn her, the only reason he had kept her covered was to keep her safe! As for walking as lovers would, the woman had no idea what that meant. Perhaps he would do well to show her, that she never mistook a gallant touch for anything else again.

A shaft of pale light fell over her as she passed by a stairwell.

And he could have sworn there was a faint jingling sound in the distance.

"Anne!" he gasped, leaping forward.

She was so startled, she tripped and went down. A crossbow clattered down the stairs and came to rest at her feet. Robin skidded to a halt next to her. He gaped down at the weapon, still cocked, then looked up the stairwell.

"Guards!" he thundered suddenly. He looked down at Anne, torn. He could either go up the stairs himself after the murderer and leave Anne alone, or he could take her to his sire's chamber and lock her in, and never let her out again.

He looked at Anne and found that she wasn't moving. He cursed, waving a fond farewell to any hope of seeing who had attempted to harm her. He knelt next to her and gently drew her up.

"Open your eyes," he commanded. "Anne, look at me!"

She threw her arms around him and clung to him. Robin was too unsettled to be surprised. He looked up as several of his guardsmen thumped down the steps and came to a teetering halt before him.

"Did you see anyone?" Robin asked.

"Nay, my lord," his captain said. "Just the normal servants and guardsmen."

Robin took Anne in his arms and rose to his feet. "Anyone you would remember?"

He watched them think, then frowned at four shaking heads. Well, he supposed he couldn't fault them overmuch. There were servants and men-at-arms aplenty in the keep, and the passageways were certainly not off-limits to them. Robin sighed, bid his men follow him as he carried Anne up the steps and down to his sire's chamber.

His siblings rose almost as one as he entered. He ignored them and sought the fire, sinking down into a chair with Anne still in his arms.

"Anne, you're safe," he said quietly. "I'll not leave you again, I swear it." He wasn't sure how he would manage that, or if it would even be safe to keep her at his side. But for now, it was the best he could say to her.

"W-who is d-doing this?" she said, her teeth chattering.

"I don't know, but I'll find out."

"What happened?" Miles demanded from Robin's side.

"Aye," Nicholas said, coming to stand before him, "what mischief has been wrought? And why weren't you more careful?"

Robin explained and answered and thought he might go mad if his siblings didn't give him peace. And just as he thought he might have satisfied their poking and prodding, Anne tried to push out of his arms.

"I can't sit with you like this," she said, trying to escape.

"You've been sitting with me like this for a goodly

while already; you'll survive a bit longer. Besides, I'm powerfully rattled. You'll need to hold on to me, very tightly, lest I break down and sob."

"Don't mock me!"

"Aye, don't mock her," Amanda added, cuffing Robin smartly on the ear.

Robin threw his sister a glare before he turned back to his lady. "I'm not mocking you. Can't you feel how I tremble?"

He wasn't about to tell her that fear was only part of the reason he trembled. By the saints, when was the last time he'd held her in his arms? When he'd been ten-and-four? At nine, Anne had hardly been the woman of his dreams.

"Robin, why does someone want me dead?"

"I don't know." By the saints, he wished he did.

She nodded, then sucked in her breath as she tried to stretch. Robin realized that he had her leg pinned against him, paining her. He sighed and rose with her in his arms. He carried her to the bed and laid her down. He covered her with a blanket, then turned back to his family, prepared to clear them from the chamber.

They didn't want to go, he could see that, but he couldn't stomach any more of their questions. He also thought he might get Anne back in his arms if they were alone and that wasn't something to be taken lightly. Besides, Nick and the twins could head up a search of the keep while Miles kept the girls safe. He himself had enough to do with his father's court to hold on the morrow. What else could he possibly find more important to do with his time that day than woo?

Then something else occurred to him. He looked at Anne. "I covered you up to keep you safe, not because I was ashamed of you."

"Robin—"

"Understood?"

She sighed. "Aye."

He knew she didn't believe him, but damn it, he didn't

care. She would believe him if it were the very last thing she ever did. He'd see to it personally. He hadn't earned the reputation for being ruthless for naught.

He straightened and threw his siblings out. Nicholas, however, seemed loth to leave. Robin considered. He needed to plan a strategy, but he found that somehow it was the last thing he had the stomach for.

Just how was it a battle-roughened knight with flawed manners went about wooing a delicate lady? Nicholas would surely know. Nicholas could charm an abbess out of her clothes.

Robin hesitated at the doorway and frowned. He'd be damned if he'd ask his *younger* brother for advice. Nicholas would likely offer it to him with a straight face, then go off and howl over it until he was ill. Robin didn't need his suggestions anyway. Hell, it wasn't as if he didn't know Anne already. They'd been raised together. She liked . . . well, she liked . . . He sighed. He had no idea what she liked.

He straightened. It would just take him a bit to remember it. After all, he hadn't had much to do with her for the past ten years. A girl's tastes changed. But he'd go to hell before he'd admit his ignorance to Nicholas. The last thing he needed was to be faced with that irritating smirk at every turn.

His brother stood and approached him. Without thinking, Robin threw a fist into his brother's belly. Nicholas doubled over with a cough.

"What'd I do?" he gasped, straightening.

"Stop your smirking, you arrogant whoreson," Robin growled, hauling him outside into the passageway. He glared at his guardsmen for good measure, then pushed his brother in the direction of the steps. "You know exactly what you've done."

"You're daft! What do I have to smirk over?"

Robin gave him another shove. "I can woo her without your suggestions, fool."

"Woo her?" Nicholas spun around to look at him. "Woo her?"

There was the smirk. Robin was easily as irritated by it as he knew he would be.

"If it were me . . ." Nicholas began.

"It isn't, so shut up."

"I would prepare a bit of fine verse about her beauty," Nicholas continued, backing up as he spoke. "But perhaps rhyming isn't one of your skills."

Robin clenched his fists and wondered if clouting his brother strongly on the head might rid the dolt—and the rest of England, poor isle—of his own skills in the like.

"A ballad, then," Nicholas said. "Can you play the lute?"

Robin gritted his teeth. His brother knew he had no skill with minstrelsy, nor much else that didn't involve a blade and an opponent in which to stick it.

"Dancing?" Nicholas asked doubtfully.

How he continued to think so deeply and continue walking, Robin surely didn't know. It had to have come from all that time spent capering about great halls to music. A damned unmanly pursuit, to his mind.

Nicholas sighed heavily. "I don't know how you'll manage it, Rob—"

"Go!" Robin bellowed.

Nicholas winked, turned and loped down the stairs. But Robin knew he couldn't be so fortunate as to escape one final barb.

"Brush her hair," came the faint suggestion. "Even you could manage that."

Robin blew out his breath, rolled his eyes heavenward and turned back toward his bedchamber.

21

Maude pressed herself against the door of the garderobe and tried to catch her breath. The smell didn't help her in that effort, but she wasn't used to much finer, given the state of her sire's hall, so she made do. And as she took very deep breaths to calm her racing heart, she decided something.

Weapons of war were not her forte.

It had been a good hour since her failed attempt on Fenwyck's get, an hour in which she had wondered if now her own life might be the forfeit. Lady Edith's words had rung in her head with such force, she thought she might faint from the fear they inspired.

A clean death is much more dignified, don't you think? And in this intrigue we're engaged in, disobedience would merit the like.

You won't disobey again, will you, Maude?

Maude put her hand over her racing heart and closed her eyes. She would die if Edith discovered what she'd done, she was certain of that. There was no mercy in that woman's soul, despite her pretty tones.

But damn her, what did she expect? For Maude to stand

there, doing nothing, watching Robin fall under that blond witch's spell?

If only she hadn't dropped the bloody bow before she'd managed to get it around the corner.

Well, at least the guards hadn't marked her. She was both flattered that she was able to escape notice so neatly and insulted that she was able to escape notice so neatly. Many a man had thought her memorable.

Many.

She took one final, cleansing breath and opened the door. The passageway was refreshingly cool and pleasant and she felt quite calm as she made her way along it.

To the kitchens, of course. There was no sense in lingering about in a place where there were no witnesses to any mayhem that might be combined against her.

Especially by Edith of Sedgwick.

Maude shuddered and quickened her pace.

22

Anne shifted in her chair, then forced herself to turn her attentions back to her stitching. She had much to be grateful for, she knew, not the least of which was the fact that she was in Gwen's solar and not her bedchamber. Things indeed could have been much worse. She looked up and smiled at the sight of her companions. Miles was sitting next to her, reading. The twins were playing chess in the corner. Amanda was laying out for them all an enormous list of Robin's flaws and Isabelle was chiding her for the like.

It was, on the whole, a most typical morning.

Or it would have been, had she not feared for her life every step she took outside the lord's bedchamber.

She wondered if Robin felt the like when he went into battle. It was odd to think that someone else moved and breathed with the thought of another soul's death consuming them. Nay, battle was not for her. She very much suspected she wouldn't have the stamina for it.

A movement startled her and she looked to her left. The only other occupant of the chamber was Edith of Sedgwick. Anne had been faintly surprised at Robin's having allowed Edith to join them in the solar, but no doubt he had his reasons. She suspected that Robin felt sorry for the girl. After all, she'd had to endure Sedgwick for several years. That and the fact that she hadn't been able to escape her brother's foul presence even at Artane was likely enough reason to pity her.

Anne watched her and wondered about her. They were of an age, and Anne wondered why it was Edith had never found herself a husband—or, more to the point, why Edith's sire had never found a husband for her. She wasn't uncomely and she wasn't unpleasant to have speech with. Though Anne had to admit that there was something in Edith's eyes that she couldn't dismiss.

A coldness.

Edith caught her staring and Anne looked away quickly. She took up her stitchery again and made an effort to look busy. She could only be grateful that it was almost sunset and time to cease working. She'd passed far too much of the day in speculation and that was never good for a body. What she needed to do was force Robin to sit and have speech with her. He'd passed the evening with her the night before, but there had been little in the way of conversation. He had brought the steward up and they had talked far into the evening about matters that would arise today in Artane's court. Anne had listened and remembered, that she might tell Rhys that Robin had done well—at least as far as her opinion went. His questions had been piercing and unrelenting. Anne had suspected the steward had been very much relieved when he'd been allowed to go.

The sudden jingle of a bracelet almost wrenched a scream from her.

"By the saints," she gasped. "What was that?"

Isabelle held up her arm. "Robby gave it to me." She looked at Anne, a puzzled expression on her face. "Haven't you seen it?"

Anne forced herself to take slow, even breaths. As she looked at Isabelle's wrist, an unruly, impossible thought assailed her.

Could Isabelle be behind this?

She shook her head sharply to clear it. Never had a more absurd notion come into her mind. There was nothing but deep affection between her and Artane's youngest daughter. Not only that, it was impossible to believe Isabelle capable of such malice. Nay, 'twas foolishness.

"It's beautiful," Anne managed.

" 'Tis the second one he bought me," Isabelle said, twisting her wrist this way and that and watching the bracelet. "He said the first one was uglier though, and perhaps 'twas a good thing he lost it."

Amanda snorted. "He can hardly hold a thought. It shouldn't surprise you that he couldn't manage to keep hold of your bracelet."

"How kind of him to find you another," Edith said, smiling. "He is a good brother."

"Aye," Isabelle said, giving Amanda a pointed look. "He is at that."

"You must wonder, however," Edith said, "where it was that he lost it."

Isabelle shrugged. "It matters not to me."

"I think," Edith said slowly, "that I've seen one like it."

"Have you?" Isabelle asked.

"The location escapes me," Edith said with a frown. She looked up and smiled brightly. "It doesn't matter, I suppose. 'Tis enough that Robin found you another."

"Aye," Isabelle agreed. "And I'm happy someone else besides me thinks so. Anne does, of course, but Amanda is truly impossible when it comes to Robin."

Anne watched Isabelle and Edith carry on an animated discussion of Robin's good points. Amanda snorted and muttered her way through the same list, leaving Miles chuckling now and again. But no one else in the chamber seemed to find anything unsettling about the girl. Anne shook her head. Perhaps she was the one who was going daft. Edith had likely had a miserable childhood. Perhaps 'twas only that which Anne saw lingering in her eyes.

The door opened suddenly and the lord in question himself stood there. Anne looked up at him and couldn't squelch a small tingle of pleasure at the sight. She resolutely pushed away any thoughts of how long she might enjoy such pleasure. For the moment she was home and Robin seemed determined to keep her well within his reach. She could hardly ask for more.

Edith stood suddenly, her sewing dropping to the floor. Anne watched as Robin retrieved it for her, then handed it to her. As Edith passed him out the door, she favored him with the same smile she gave to everyone. Anne couldn't help but think that it was tinged with something.

Triumph?

Anne clapped her hand to her forehead. By the saints, she was losing her wits. It had to be too much confinement. Perhaps Robin had learned something that day that might purchase her a bit of freedom.

"Miles, take the children back to our chamber," Robin said shortly.

"Children?" Amanda echoed. "Just who do you think—"

Anne found herself relieved of her sewing and drawn to her feet before she knew what Robin intended. He put his arm around her and led her to the door.

"Nick will be up later to see how you fare," Robin threw over his shoulder.

He paused, looked up and down the passageway, then pulled Anne out with him. She found herself tucked securely at his side as he made his way to the stairwell. She was surprised to watch him draw a dagger before he preceded her down.

"This is madness," she whispered.

His only reply was a grunt.

Once they had reached the lower floor, Robin again drew her close and walked with her down the passageway. His guards were outside the bedchamber door.

"Anything?" Robin demanded.

"Nay, my lord," said one. "Nothing."

Robin sheathed his dagger, then led Anne inside the chamber. He led her to a chair, but Anne shook her head.

"I'll pace for a bit," she said. "I've been idle too long this day."

"Would that we could both take a turn about the lists," he said grimly. "I too have suffered too much confinement this day."

"Did you learn aught?" she asked, coming to stand next to him.

He knelt before the hearth and brought the embers back to life. "Aye, more than I ever wanted to know about the pettiness of mankind."

She smiled at his disgruntled tone. "You've sat with your sire often enough on these things, haven't you? It should have come as no surprise."

He scowled at her. "Aye, but it was never my own sorry self trying to mete out justice. By the saints, Anne, why can these souls not treat each other kindly?"

"Why indeed," she mused.

He opened his mouth to speak, then shut it and pursed his lips. "Is that a barb especially for me, Lady Anne?"

She shook her head with a smile. "For us both, my lord."

"After today," he said, "I vow I would be happy never to bicker again."

"Even with me?" she asked.

He paused. "Aye," he said. "Especially with you."

Damn him, would he never cease to take her off guard? She cleared her throat, desperate to redirect his attention. The very intensity in his eyes made her nervous.

"Could you say the like about Amanda?" she asked, grasping for something to distract him.

He looked up at her with a glint in his eye. "She is my sister. You, however, are not."

Before she could recapture the breath she'd lost hearing *that*, Robin had risen, dusted off his hands, then made himself comfortable in a chair. He looked up at her.

"Come here." He patted his knees.

"I beg your pardon?"

"Come sit here. Now."

"Absolutely not!"

He hooked a stool with his foot and dragged it in front of him. "Here then. I want you over here."

She lifted her eyebrows as far as they would go. It would have been more effective if she could lift only one as Robin and Nicholas could. She hoped her look was haughty enough as it was.

"Now why would I want to come over there when you haven't the manners to ask me politely?"

He leaned forward. "Because you don't want a chivalrous knight. I'm sure of it. Now, come you here while my humor is still sweet."

"Why?"

"Your place is to obey me, not question me. Did my mother teach you nothing?"

"She taught me to think for myself!"

"More's the pity."

She looked at him narrowly. "What are you going to do? Throttle me?"

"As I said before, you are not my sister. You're safe from that fate."

Anne considered, but before she could make up her mind just what he was about, he had risen, led her over to the stool and very gently sat her upon it.

"My concession to chivalry tonight," he grumbled as he sat down behind her. "Are you close enough to the fire? Too close?"

"Fine, but what—"

He put his hand on top of her head to keep her from turning around. "I've never met a woman who could talk as much as you do. Your silence would please me greatly."

She opened her mouth to let fly a retort, then she felt his hands trying to remove her wimple and veil. She didn't wear them much, as a rule, but Robin had insisted that morning that she might have her hair covered and thereby retain some anonymity.

"Vexing contraptions," he grumbled.

"Robin," she said, swallowing hard, "what do you?"

He sighed so hard, he blew her veil over her face. "I plan to brush your hair," he said in annoyance. "If you could just let me be about my work!" He gave a hearty tug, and her headwear came off in his hand.

She felt his hand slide gently down her hair, his touch belying the gruffness of his tone. And speech deserted her. She heard Robin's chair scrape against the floor as he moved closer to her. She knew he was closer because his knees were touching the back of her arms.

She closed her eyes and swallowed convulsively the moment she felt the brush touch her scalp. By the saints, she could scarce believe she wasn't dreaming. Nay, that was his hand wielding the brush so hesitantly, as if he feared to hurt her. And he thought himself ruthless. It was perhaps well none of his men could see him at present or they would have had a different tale to tell.

She trembled as he pulled the hair gently back from her face.

"Hurt?"

"Nay," she whispered.

Once he was certain no tangles remained, he began to drag the brush through her hair with long, chill-inducing strokes.

She shivered.

His hand stopped. "Should I cease?"

"Aye, if you don't value your skin."

He snorted out a laugh. She looked over her shoulder at him, surprised. It had been years since she'd heard Robin do anything akin to it. But he only put his hand atop her head and turned it around again.

She closed her eyes and simply enjoyed. She waited for Robin to grow bored and stop, but he seemed perfectly content to do nothing but continue with his work. He brushed her hair, then he began to trail his fingers through it. Finally he merely skimmed over it with the flat of his hand.

"I can see why you cover your hair," he said quietly.

"Can you?" she asked. "It compares poorly with Amanda's and Isabelle's. Theirs is so rich and dark."

"And here I was thinking yours was like pale, spun gold," he said, sounding amused. "I thought you covered it not to shame them."

She couldn't stop herself from turning around to look at him in surprise. "You didn't."

He smiled and the sight of it was so beautiful, she could scarce look at him. "Anne," he said, with a slow shake of his head, "you do yourself too little credit."

"I have eyes that work perfectly well," she said tartly.

He took her hands in his. "As do I, and I know what I see. You've no reason for shame in their company, for you are indeed their equal."

She felt her jaw slide down, but could find nothing to say to that. Surely, he didn't think her beautiful.

"Well," he said, frowning a bit, "perhaps not Amanda's equal."

She shut her mouth with a snap. There, now he began to sound more rational.

"Her tongue sours some of her beauty, I think, whilst yours does not."

She watched as he brought her hands to his mouth and kissed them. A shiver that started in her poor, captive fingers worked its way down her arms and up to her head. She was certain her hair was beginning to stand on end. His smile faltered and he looked at her with a seriousness she had rarely seen him wear.

"Anne . . ."

Anne watched in astonishment as he leaned toward her. By the look on his face, she very much suspected that he intended to kiss her.

And *that* was enough to fair send her falling off her stool in surprise.

She watched one of his hands reach toward her and

slide under her hair to touch the back of her neck. Robin bent his head, his eyes never leaving her face. She didn't dare breathe, didn't dare blink, didn't dare even think too hard lest she break the spell.

He was going to kiss her.

The moment she had waited for the whole of her life was about to commence.

"Anne," he whispered, his lips a hand's breadth from hers.

And then a fierce banging on the door almost sent him tumbling into her lap.

Anne caught him before he pitched fully into her arms. He straightened and blinked, as if he'd just been struck strongly on the head.

"Robby," a voice called, accompanied by more banging. "I've brought supper. Open up."

Robin blinked at Anne. He looked as dazed as she felt.

"I'm going to kill him," he managed. "I vow I'll do it this time."

The banging on the door continued. "Hurry. The trencher is heavy!"

Anne watched Robin heave himself to his feet. He stomped across the chamber and threw open the door.

Nicholas barged in, elbowing Robin in the belly to gain passage. Anne watched him shove supper into Robin's hands, then cross the chamber to her. She couldn't even smile. All she could do was look at him, mute.

"What have you done to the girl?" Nicholas exclaimed. "She looks positively bewildered."

"He brushed my hair," Anne whispered.

Nicholas sat down in Robin's chair and made himself comfortable. "I'm ready for a demonstration, then. Robby, come show me how 'tis done."

Nicholas was summarily hauled to his feet by his hair.

"State your business, then go," Robin growled, shoving his brother before he set supper down on the floor.

"And leave you alone with her? Never."

"Have you any tidings for me?" Robin barked.

"Nay."

"Then begone. We've no need of you."

"I disagree—"

Anne watched Robin propel Nicholas into the hall with all the efficiency of a shepherd's hound. The door was slammed shut and bolted. Robin turned slowly and looked at her. Anne could do nothing but stare back at him. She watched him take a deep breath, then put his shoulders back.

She had the feeling he would not be thwarted in his plans this time.

And that was enough to weaken her knees so greatly she wasn't sure she could stand.

He marched purposefully across the chamber toward her. He stopped before her, took her by the arms and pulled her to her feet. Anne swayed, then put her hands on his chest to steady herself.

Robin wrapped one arm around her waist, then slid his hand under her head again to cup the back of her head.

"Oh," she said involuntarily. By the saints, she had never expected to have these kinds of tingles overcome her at the mere thought of kissing Robin of Artane.

She had certainly never felt the like when Nicholas had kissed her.

And then she had no more time for thinking. Robin bent his head, gathered her more closely to him, and captured her mouth with his. There was no other way to view it.

It was no polite kiss.

She shivered.

So did he.

She found herself slipping her arms up around his neck. It seemed the thing to do, because she was sure that way she would have a better chance of using him to keep from falling to her knees. She closed her eyes and gave herself up to the devastating sensations that rocked her to her very core. He kissed her again and again until she wondered if she would ever again take a normal breath.

And then, if that hadn't been overwhelming enough by itself, he kissed her deeply.

She lost all rational thought. All she could feel was Robin's hand in her hair, his mouth on hers—

She sincerely hoped his eyes were closed so he couldn't see her blush. Her mouth had never been investigated by anyone besides the barber surgeon when once she'd had a sore tooth and he'd been peering inside, not using his—

Robin kissed her mouth closed with a brief, hard kiss, then stepped back a pace. His chest was heaving. He looked flushed, which eased her mind greatly for she suspected that she looked the same.

He said nothing. He merely held her by the arms and stared at her with an intensity that fair burned her to cinders where she stood.

Then he blinked and cleared his throat.

"Dinner," he rasped.

"Aye," she managed.

" 'Twill grow cold, else."

"Likely," she agreed.

But she ached like she had never ached before with the desire to go back into his arms and never leave them. By the saints, having a taste of what it could be like to be encircled in his embrace was overwhelming.

Never mind how it felt to be kissed by him.

She suspected that she would never be the same.

23

Robin waited impatiently for his squire to see to his mail. He shrugged his shoulders and rolled his neck, trying to work the kinks out of it. Too many more nights spent either in the chair or on the floor would be his undoing. It was one thing to know that naught but the ground was available; 'twas a far different thing to be sleeping ten paces from a bed, and a comfortable one at that, and knowing that all that kept him from it was good manners.

And it surely wasn't as if he possessed those in abundance.

Though after kissing Anne the night before, he was almost certain that lying abed with her would be a very bad idea indeed.

"Be quick, Jason," he whispered.

Anne slept still and Robin wished for her to remain that way until he could make his escape. He wasn't sure how she would view the events of the previous evening once she'd had a chance to digest them in her sleep.

He knew how he felt, though. And not only had he stolen that first mind-numbing kiss, he'd bested her twice in chess, which had led to many other simple tastes of her sweet lips. He hadn't dared kiss her again as he had at first. He was still reeling from it. And that was one of the reasons he had slept on the floor and not in her bed.

He held up his arms while Jason helped him into his surcoat, then belted his sword about his waist. He felt his heart begin to soften toward his squire, who was always so diligent about caring for his gear. He supposed perhaps it was a menial task for the future baron of Ayre, but the saints only knew he'd done his share of menial tasks as a squire.

Robin clapped Jason on the shoulder. "I'm in the mood for sport this morn, lad. Perhaps you'll care to provide me with it."

"Me?" Jason said, his surprise poorly hidden.

"Aye, you," Robin said with a half smile. "You're a fine enough swordsman. I should know, as I'm the one who has trained you."

"Of course, my lord."

Robin paused. It was on the tip of his tongue to tell Jason he was sorry for the terrible places he'd dragged him, all the battles, the endless sieges, the dangerous courts. It was a wonder Jason could still smile.

"Have you had such a poor life, Jason?"

Jason looked at him as if he'd never seen him before. "My lord, are you unwell?"

Well, perhaps that was answer enough. Robin turned Jason toward the door and gave him a gentle push. "Fetch Miles and return. He'll be capable of protecting Anne for a bit."

Jason trotted off dutifully. Robin sighed as he adjusted his sword at his side. Jason would leave soon enough to make his own way and Robin would be sorry for it. He was a good lad, likely all the better for not having grown to manhood at Ayre.

Not that it was such a foul place. After all, Ayre was his, because of his sire. Robin had never had any desire to live there, or to be its lord in truth. Jason's father, John, had been Alain of Ayre's youngest brother and had willingly taken on the task of seeing to Ayre.

John was a fine lord and Robin had never had any complaints about his care of the soil. Jason would likely make just as fine a lord when the time came. Robin smiled to himself. At least he knew if Jason displeased him, he could yet thrash the lad in the lists. It wasn't such a poor way to settle a dispute.

Robin looked at the bed. Anne slept still, surely. He hesitated, then moved to take hold of the bed curtains. Just a small peek to assure himself that she slept well. He couldn't be faulted for that, could he? He pulled the curtain back and looked down at her, her face scarce revealed by the dim light in the chamber.

She opened her eyes and he jumped in spite of himself.

"I thought you slept still," he managed.

She shook her head.

Robin forced himself not to shift uncomfortably. He'd kissed the woman before him senseless the night before and now he felt as callow as a young squire. Did she regret it? In how many ways had she found him lacking?

"I need to train this morn, to clear my head." *To give you time to decide if you want me or not*, he added silently.

She nodded.

"Miles will arrive presently."

"Thank you."

He nodded, then made his way out of the chamber before he did anything else foolish. He waited until his brother arrived, instructed him to stay out in the passageway until Anne had risen, then pushed Jason in front of him down to the great hall. Robin stopped for a cup of ale, grateful to be doing something besides sitting and stewing.

"My lord?"

Robin frowned at him, hoping to dissuade him from speaking.

"My lord," Jason said again, shifting uncomfortably, "ah, the lady Anne . . ."

"What about her?" Robin demanded.

Jason clasped his hands behind his back. "Ah," he began, looking completely miserable, "about her virtue, my lord. I hesitate to speak of this . . ."

Five years ago, Robin could have lifted Jason off the ground with one hand and held him suspended there while he shouted at him. Jason was now ten-and-six, and much heavier. And much braver, Robin thought grudgingly.

"She's a maid still," Robin grumbled.

"But, my lord, I know it has been many months since you have taken a woman—"

"Enough," Robin interrupted sharply. "It isn't my habit to despoil virtuous maidens, and you know it well."

Jason nodded, miserably. "But, my lord, when Fenwyck learns . . ."

"I'll see to him when the time comes, if that time comes. What you don't seem to understand, little lad, is that there is no safer place for her than my chamber with my sword before her. Unless you think you are more capable than I of protecting her?"

"Of course not, my lord. You are a master."

Robin grunted and set his cup down. "We'll go to the lists and I'll prove it to you again."

Jason trailed behind him obediently. Robin rolled his eyes at the number of times Jason cleared his throat as they walked out through the inner bailey and out the gate to the lists. Finally, he could stand it no longer. He whirled around.

"What?" he demanded.

Jason bumped into him, then jumped back and made a small bow. "Nothing, my lord."

"Stop quivering. I've yet to lay a hand on you, you pampered puss." It was true. He might have hardened his heart against others in his life, but he'd always harbored a soft spot for the young lad with bright blue eyes who had looked at him as if he could do no wrong. "Speak your mind freely, Jason. As I have the feeling you'll do anyway," he muttered.

Jason wiped his hands on his thighs. "My lord, I know

you and the lady Anne haven't been close in years past—"

Robin grunted.

"But, well, have a care with her, won't you?" Jason asked, looking up at Robin earnestly.

"I gave you my word she would remain a maid."

"I speak of her heart, my lord," Jason said quietly.

Robin looked at his squire, seeing him in a different light. The lad was no longer a child, but a lad on the verge of manhood. Robin folded his arms over his chest and looked Jason over carefully.

"What would you know of her heart? Or any woman's heart, for that matter?"

Jason reddened. "I am not ignorant of the ways of men and women, my lord."

"Of course you aren't."

"I speak of matters of the heart, my lord, not of bedding." He paused and took a deep breath. "She loves you, my lord."

Robin pursed his lips. "Of course she doesn't. She wants a chivalrous lout with a sweet tongue and gentle manners."

Jason shook his head. "I must disagree. She may say that is what she wants, but her eyes tell a different story. She is quite easy to read if you look closely enough."

"And just what would you know of reading a woman, boy?"

"I know how Isabelle looks at me," Jason insisted. "And I know how I feel about her. 'Tis all in the eyes, my lord—"

"Isabelle!" Robin gasped, finding his tongue. "My sister Isabelle?"

Jason blushed to the roots of his hair. "A slip of the tongue, my lord."

Robin lunged and took Jason down to the dirt. "Isabelle," he repeated, incredulous. "Jason, she's a *child!*"

"Old enough to be betrothed," Jason insisted.

Robin couldn't decide if he were more shocked about Jason telling him that Anne loved him, or knowing the identity of the woman who held Jason's heart. How had this come about? They hadn't been home a month!

"But you hardly know her!"

"Ofttimes, it doesn't take long," Jason managed.

"Does my father know?"

"Saints, nay," Jason said quickly, shaking his head. "He'd likely have me strung up if he did."

"Have you touched her?" Robin demanded.

"I wouldn't dare!"

Robin grunted. "See that you don't, or you'll answer to me." He rolled off his squire and heaved himself to his feet. "Daft, Jason. That's what you are. She'll give you gray hairs before you earn your spurs." He hauled Jason to his feet.

"Will Lord Rhys give her to me, think you?"

"Why you'd want her is a mystery to me."

"She's beautiful. And kind. And I want to be braver and more gallant when I'm with her. Isn't that reason enough?"

Robin shook his head. "I suppose so, lad."

Jason walked next to him with his head bowed. "Would you speak kindly of me to him if he asked you of me?"

Robin took Jason by the back of the neck and shook him. "I'll see how you show this morn, Jason, before I decide what I'll tell your lady's father about you."

Robin was surprised he hadn't known about it sooner. Was he truly so unobservant, or was Jason better at hiding his feelings than Robin had given him credit for?

Robin watched Jason critically in the lists. The lad had become a fine warrior in the past ten years. Robin even felt himself begin to smile as he marked Jason using some of Robin's own techniques against him. Perhaps Isabelle could do worse than this lad.

It was a goodly while later that Robin finally called peace and put his hand on Jason's shoulder.

"Well done, Ayre. Your father will be most pleased with you."

"And yours?" Jason smiled. "Will he be pleased also?"

Robin frowned. "Little lad, you should rather be more concerned that I am pleased with you. My father is not your master, I am."

"My lord, I know you are pleased with me. And you do not hold my love's fate in your hands. I daresay you likely feel the same about my lord Fenwyck."

"Be silent," Robin hissed. "Think you I wish for everyone to hear your witless words? Moon all you like over my sister, but do not expect me to join you."

"Of course, my lord," Jason said quickly. "I meant it only in jest."

"And Fenwyck's opinion matters not to me," Robin added with a growl. "I could best him on any field."

"Aye, you could."

Robin looked up as Nicholas approached, grinning lazily like the idiot he was. Robin scowled at his brother.

"What do you want, dolt?"

Nicholas put one hand on Jason's shoulder and the other on Robin's. "You two are as chatty as two ladies-in-waiting. Discussing your ladyloves?"

Robin knocked his hand away. "We were discussing the best way to disembowel a grinning fool. Jason, perhaps you should test my theory on this fool here."

Nicholas only laughed and slung his arm around Jason's shoulder. "It sounds as if he has a fine case of it, doesn't it Jason?"

"I couldn't say, my lord," Jason answered, yawning. "My lord Robin thinks a dagger vertically down the belly is most effective. What say you?"

Nicholas grinned and winked at Robin. "You know, I think he kissed her last eve. I couldn't tell if she was pleased by his attentions or so ill she was dazed. Perhaps you'll come with me tonight and you can decide—"

Robin sheathed his sword and shoved his brother. "She was not displeased!"

Nicholas threw back his head and laughed heartily. "St. Michael's bones, Rob, you are a besotted pup."

Robin drew his sword with a curse. Nicholas grabbed

Jason by the shoulders and put him between them. "Now, now, brother. You wouldn't want to disembowel your squire. Jason, what has put him in such a terrible temper? Could it be love?"

"This isn't amusing anymore," Robin snarled. "Release the boy and face me like a man, if you're capable of it. Or have too many evenings spent honing your skill with the lute left you unable to put your fingers to the hilt of your blade?"

Nicholas had shoved Jason aside and drawn his own sword before Robin could blink. Robin countered his brother's parries with thrusts of his own, ones that should have silenced Nicholas permanently, or at least warned him he was close to being so silenced. Nicholas wasn't paying Robin's warnings any heed, if his attack were any indication. In the back of his mind, Robin was vaguely impressed with his brother's detachment and precision. But he didn't spare it much thought. His mind was on fire and he went with the heat, not caring if he cut his sibling to ribbons before he came to himself.

It wasn't how he usually fought. He knew he had a warriorly reputation for recklessness, just as Nicholas did for being cold and methodical. But even in the heat of battle, while the blood was thundering in his ears and his fury was all-consuming, Robin never released that small part of his mind that was perfectly calm, perfectly rational, perfectly sane. It was the logic that controlled his strategy.

He couldn't find that calmness at present. He was embarrassed. He'd known Nicholas would make sport of him, but to keep harping, to speak loudly enough that others could hear—that he hadn't expected even from his hopelessly romantic sibling. Damn him, he should have had more respect! Whatever intimacies Robin shared with Anne were not fodder for conversation in the lists.

Not that he'd share them again. Bloody hell, if this was what kissing her earned him, he'd never come within two feet of her again!

"Robin!"

He heard Nicholas's warning shout and jerked back the moment before Nicholas's blade would have gone through his arm. As it was, there was a fine rent in his tunic sleeve.

"By the saints, Rob, what were you thinking about?" Nicholas exclaimed, dropping his sword and coming toward him. "I almost cut your head off."

Robin had no good answer for that. "Jason, come with me," he said, shrugging off Nicholas's hand. "Nick, see that the men attend to their work. This is not a day of leisure."

"And you will be?" Nicholas asked.

"Making certain that all is well inside," Robin said. He strode through the lists, wanting nothing more than to escape notice until he could regain his composure.

"Artane, a moment!"

Robin saw Baldwin coming toward him with a purposeful glint in his eye. He cursed and waved the man away. He had no time for him this day.

"Stop," Baldwin exclaimed. "Stand and face me!"

Robin paused and glared at him. "For what purpose? To best you again? Was last time not sufficient?"

Baldwin drew his sword with a flourish and a curse. Robin muttered under his breath and drew his own blade. Perfect. Could his day deteriorate any more than this?

He set his squire out of harm's way and drew his own blade the moment before Baldwin's reached him. He might have been distracted with Nicholas, but he suffered no such affliction now. Baldwin was furious and Robin supposed he couldn't blame the man. After all, he had humiliated his cousin badly on their first and only encounter. Perhaps Baldwin had listened to the recent laughter of Robin's family over and over again in his head until his temper was past being controlled. Robin smiled pleasantly as he easily deflected Baldwin's paltry attack. Perhaps all those years spent warring had been a benefit after all. He'd faced much worse than this and lived.

"I'll kill you," Baldwin snarled.

"You continue to say as much," Robin answered, "yet I live still. How is this possible?"

"I haven't," Baldwin said, grunting with exertion, "begun my labors in truth."

"Haven't you?" Robin asked. "Please alert me when that day comes. I'll want to be ready."

Baldwin only snarled a curse in answer. Robin watched him as they fought and a thought occurred to him. Was it possible Baldwin was behind the attacks on Anne? No sense in not finding out.

"Are you coward enough to attack a woman?" Robin asked suddenly.

Baldwin sneered. "I wouldn't spare one the effort. Why, when I've your death to think on?"

"Why indeed," Robin muttered. He found, suddenly, that he tired of this confrontation. Though he could surely understand his father's desire to keep Sedgwick in his sights, he wondered if that necessity hadn't passed. Should he remain at Artane, he would suggest to his sire that life would be more pleasant without Baldwin's smirk to endure each day. And 'twas a certainty Baldwin was no sterling swordsman.

Robin went on the attack and took as little time as possible to dispatch his foe. Baldwin's sword went flying, and he came at Robin with his fists. Robin sighed, tossed his blade at Jason, and showed Baldwin as quickly as possible that he knew how to use his hands as well as his weapons. When Baldwin tripped and went down heavily onto the field, Robin walked away without another word. He had had enough. Perhaps he would find another tunic and see how Anne fared.

It was his duty after all.

And he wasn't one to shirk duty.

It would also give him ample time to see if she looked on him with disgust. He could have sworn he'd felt her shiver the night before, but that could have been with revulsion.

By the saints, he didn't even trust his own instincts anymore.

"Jason."

"Aye, my lord," Jason said, handing Robin his blade.

"Help me off with this mail upstairs, then use the rest of the afternoon for your pleasure. You might train a bit more."

"Aye, I could."

"Or you could deliver a message to my sister Isabelle for me."

"If you required it of me, I daresay I could force myself to."

Robin smiled before he could stop himself. "Ah, Jason, I have ruined you for polite company."

Jason shook his head. "You have taught me much, my lord. I could not have asked for a finer master. And I would gladly accept any advice you could give me in the matter of wooing this headstrong wench of mine."

Robin had a hard time hiding his surprise. "Me? Rather you should ask my womanly brother."

"Nay, I would rather hear your words. Any man could win a woman with flattery. Isabelle is apparently unmoved by it. What else would you suggest?"

Robin gave it a good deal of thought until they made their way to Artane's bedchamber. Robin paused before the door. "Brush her hair for her," he said. "For the life of me I don't know why, but they all seem to like it."

"And kissing?"

"If you kiss my sister before she wears your ring, I'll disembowel you. Lengthwise across your belly. We decided that was a much more painful and prolonged death, didn't we?"

Jason gulped. Robin opened the door. "Come inside, Jason, and help me. Then you are free for the day."

Anne gasped the moment he entered. She rose and started toward him. "What happened to you?"

"Nothing," he said shortly.

"Nothing?" she echoed. "Your clothes are fair to falling off you and this is nothing?"

Robin ignored Anne as Jason pulled off his mail shirt. He pulled off his tunic as well. Then he looked at her.

And all his irritation over Nicholas's teasing vanished. Being the object of Nicholas's jests wasn't that painful. He could always thrash his younger brother if need be. And, besides, did any of that matter when he held Anne in his arms, felt her trembling mouth beneath his, touched her smooth skin and silky hair? Nicholas could laugh as long and as loudly as he liked. He had no woman of his own.

Robin caught Anne's empty hand and brought it to his lips. "I am well."

"You're unbloodied," she corrected. "Well is still undecided." She looked at Jason. "Who did this?"

Jason laid Robin's mail shirt over a trunk. "Nicholas, my lady."

"Is his skill so poor that he tripped and fell on you with his blade bared? Or was he mooning over some wench? Aye, I can see that readily enough."

Robin snorted. "As can I. Jason, I want a meal. See to it before you seek out my sister, would you?"

By the swiftness of his leave-taking, Robin suspected his squire had a mind to woo himself. Poor wretch.

Robin made himself comfortable in a chair before the fire and passed a goodly hour watching Anne surreptitiously as she sewed. There came a point, though, when he couldn't bear just the watching anymore. He leaned over and before he could give it more thought, kissed her softly.

She looked at him in surprise.

"What?" he asked. "Must I best you at chess before I kiss you?"

She looked at him in silence for so long, he began to grow uncomfortable.

"Anne, what is it?"

She shook her head. "I vow I do not know you."

"Don't you?"

"Why are you doing this to me?"

"Why not?" he said, tossing the words off casually. Saints, what was he supposed to say? *I'm wracking my poor head for ways to please you?*

"You bastard," she said through gritted teeth. She rose ungracefully to her feet and glared at him. "I'll not be sport for you."

Sport? He felt his temper rise swiftly, but before he could give vent to it, Anne had limped over to the alcove.

And then he could have sworn he heard a sniffle.

Ah, by the saints. He rolled his eyes as he heaved himself to his feet. He stepped up behind her and put his arms around her waist, dropping his chin to her shoulder.

"Anne, you aren't sport for me."

"Of course not," she said curtly. "Why would you even take sport of a cripple, much less anything else?"

"Cease with that talk," he exclaimed. "You know it angers me when you speak of yourself that way."

"How would I know?" she demanded. "You've hardly spoken to me since it happened, except to curse me."

"That isn't true."

"Aye, it is."

He stood there and considered her words. Was it true? Not at first. At first, they had recovered together. Ah, but then he'd tried to defend her honor and Baldwin had humiliated him. Had he spoken to her since? Unlikely. He put his hands on her shoulders and turned her around to face him.

"Anne . . ."

"Please don't hurt me," she wept. "I couldn't bear it, Robin. I vow I couldn't."

"Anne, why would I hurt you?"

"You hurt me just by being here," she said. She pulled away from him and turned toward the window. "I beg you to go. Please."

Robin felt his heart still within him. "You want me to leave?"

"Aye," she said. "I want you to go."

Robin didn't want to, but he couldn't see what else to do. Anne wasn't turning to face him. So he turned and walked soundlessly from the chamber. He hardly noticed that he wasn't wearing his boots. He nodded to his men, then continued on down the passageway. At least Anne would be safe with his guards at her door.

Her weeping haunted him all the way down to the great hall.

The next day Robin still sat in a chair before the fire in the great hall and stared into the flames before him. He hadn't moved since the afternoon before and already it was afternoon again. Anne's words rang over and over in his head. She didn't want him. He'd come home for naught. She found him lacking. Hadn't she said as much? What else could she have meant by telling him if he stayed he would only hurt her?

Booted feet stopped next to him and a long frame settled into the chair facing him.

"Rob, what is it?"

Robin spared his brother a weary look before he turned back to the fire. "I regret there is no longer anything for you to laugh about," he said heavily. "Forgive me for not providing you with more sport."

"Now, Rob, how often do you provide me with something to tease you about? And I'm sorry about almost cutting you. You know I didn't do it purposely."

"I know." Robin sighed. "It was my fault. I was preoccupied."

"Speaking of your preoccupation, why aren't you with her?"

Robin met Nicholas's gray eyes. "She bid me leave her," he said flatly.

"Perhaps she needed a moment of privacy."

"She bid me go away, Nick. For longer than merely a moment of privacy. She said I hurt her merely by being near her. You tell me what that means if not that she cannot bear the sight of me."

Nicholas looked into the fire. Robin watched his brother's expression sober and his heart sank even further. So it was obvious to Nick too. Robin groaned inwardly. How could he have ever imagined that she would come to care for him? It was obvious that someone like Nicholas was what she wanted, a man with polish, a man who wouldn't hurt her with his rough edges.

Nicholas leaned forward with his forearms on his knees.

"If I told you something honestly, from my heart, would you hear me?"

How much worse could he hurt than he hurt at present? Robin nodded slowly.

"And you won't immediately discount my words as the ramblings of your younger, empty-headed sibling?"

"Difficult, but I'll try."

Nicholas didn't smile. "Robin, I've jested with you in the past about things, about women and your poor tastes, but you know I only did it because I love you so well. And I think you take yourself far too seriously." He smiled briefly. " 'Tis a younger brother's duty to torment his elder sibling and, since you never let me forget that you are the saints only know how much my senior, I have ever repaid you by teasing you. But I'm in earnest now."

Robin didn't move. "Go on."

"I'm certain you would see this as well, were you able to step back a few paces and look at what has happened between you and Anne over the years. She loves you. She's loved you for as long as I can remember. And after our little morning at Baldwin's mercy, she loved you still. But what you don't know is that she never saw what happened—"

"And she'll never know of it," Robin growled. "If you say one word to her about it, I'll kill you."

Nicholas shrugged off the threat. "That isn't the point. What you don't understand is that she has no idea why one day you were welcoming her into your sickroom and the next you were casting her from it. She thinks it is something she did."

"Of course she doesn't. She's done nothing to me. Short of making me daft each chance she had."

"You're not listening to me, Robin. Anne doesn't trust you."

"But I'm not planning to hurt her. Can't she see that?"

"Based on what? How you've never wavered in your devotion before?"

"I never did," Robin snarled. "My feelings for her never changed."

Nicholas looked at him so long in silence, Robin felt like squirming. Then he realized what he had said and how far he'd laid open his heart to his brother.

"She irritates me as much as she did when she was eight," he said quickly, hoping he'd put enough gruffness in his voice.

Nicholas smiled gravely. "Did you just hear yourself?"

Robin scowled at him in silence.

"Rob, you just admitted to loving her, then you denied it. Is it any wonder Anne's frightened witless of letting you close to her? How would you feel if she told you she loved you, then immediately made light of it?" He put his hand on Robin's shoulder and shook him gently. "Don't be a fool, Robin. You love her and she loves you. Somewhere, deep in that hidden heart of yours is a place she needs to see. I don't expect any of the rest of us will ever see it, but Anne deserves to. Be as gruff as you like with her in public, but don't do it in private." He rose and looked down at Robin. "She's far less likely to hurt you than you are to hurt her. I'd certainly trust her with my heart."

Robin watched him walk away. He fought with himself until Nicholas reached the hall door.

"Don't you dare," Robin called after him.

Nicholas smiled and made him a small bow before he left the hall. Robin turned back to his contemplation of

the fire and his brother's words. He had no trouble seeing
the truth of the matter. How could Anne possibly have
known why he pushed her away? For all she knew, he
could have shunned her because of her limp.

He felt the room begin to spin. Had she actually thought
such a thing? Pieces began to fall furiously into place.
She thought no man would want her because she was
crippled. And why shouldn't she think that? He had
shunned her after her accident. It would have been easy
enough to assume that was the reason why. She hadn't
seen his humiliation at Baldwin's hands; he'd threatened
anyone who ever spoke about it so severely that it had
likely become past history in everyone's mind but his.
Robin put his head in his hands and groaned. It was his
fault. His stupid, foolish pride had hurt the very last person he had wanted to.

He rose, needing to pace. Was it too late? Nay, it
couldn't be. He wouldn't allow it. It would likely take
time, but perhaps he could win her trust again. He could
never offer her flowery words and prettily sung ballads.
Perhaps she would take him as he was, flawed and rough.
Perhaps she could gentle him. If anyone could, it would
be Anne.

But first a bath and a change of clothes. He'd borrow
something of Nicholas's, then present himself at his
chamber and hope that Anne would unlock the door.

24

Anne sat in the alcove with her knees drawn up and hugged to her chest. It was a painful way to sit, but she didn't care. The pain in her thigh numbed the pain in her heart. She'd hardly moved from the spot since Robin had left her there. His sire's bedchamber was the very last place she wanted to be, but she remembered vividly the sound of a crossbow clattering at her feet. If nothing else, she was safe where she was.

But once the culprit was discovered, she would be out of the lord's chamber immediately, never to return.

She was past weeping. She hadn't wept the night before, which had almost surprised her. Either she was too tired for the like, or she had expected Robin's words. Or perhaps it was that Robin truly did not love her and thus her tears need not be spent over him. She could hardly believe he had kissed her as he had. Perhaps boredom had driven him to it, or that he wasn't free to bed several of Rhys's serving wenches in rapid succession. Well, he was welcome to them. She wanted no part of him.

She was also a very great liar.

She sighed and leaned her head back against the wall. More was the pity that she loved him. And despite his words, she couldn't help but believe he harbored some affection for her.

Unless he could truly kiss her as he had without his heart taking part in it.

Was that possible?

A soft knock sounded on the door, interrupting her thoughts. She groaned as she unfolded herself from the seat and made her way haltingly across the floor. The knocking continued until she gained the door and pulled back the bolt. She opened the door and flinched once she saw Robin standing there.

He looked as if he hadn't slept since he'd left the night before. Likely because he'd been ravishing as many of his father's serving wenches as possible. She pursed her lips and turned back toward the alcove, leaving the door open. He could come or go as he pleased. She didn't care.

She was very surprised, when she sat down, to find Robin hovering in front of her. He covered her with a blanket, then stood there with his hands clasped behind his back.

"Are you comfortable?"

She didn't look up.

"I'll build you a fire."

He walked away, not waiting for an answer. Anne looked out the window. She heard Robin tending the fire, then heard his sound of dismay when he saw the untouched food. She closed her eyes and listened to the sound of wine being poured into a cup and that cup being set on the stone of the hearth. Wine would have been good. It might have soothed the chill in her heart.

She heard Robin's firm footfall as he walked to her. He shuttered the windows.

"I've made you a place by the fire."

"I'm not interested in it."

Anne didn't protest when he picked her up in his arms. Why bother? He wouldn't listen to her anyway. Had he been capable of listening, he wouldn't have come back.

She saw the nest of furs and pillows and then found

herself set atop it. A heavy chair had been set there to support her back.

"I'm not a cripple," she said stiffly as Robin arranged a pillow behind her back. "I need none of this."

"Anne, this has nothing to do with your leg. I would certainly be more comfortable sitting this way."

"You seem to have no trouble sleeping on the uncomfortable floor."

"I'm accustomed to sleeping on the ground. I even slept in a tree once. The floor seems as commodious as a stack of goose-feather mattresses. Well, perhaps not a stack. Saints, woman, must you be so contrary?"

She looked at him, ready to give as good as she got, only to find him looking at her kindly. It was enough to irritate her into silence. She turned her head and tried to ignore him.

It didn't last. He nagged her until she ate. And after she could barely breathe, which satisfied him, he put a cup of warm wine in her hands.

She drank it, merely to have him cease troubling her, then she rose and walked to the alcove. Her leg was slowly beginning to pain her less. Perhaps she could credit Robin and his endless walking her about the chamber for that.

"I would like to do something to please you," he said quietly.

It was difficult to hide her surprise. By the saints, life with this man would be more complicated than she could stomach. Perhaps she would truly be better off without him.

"As a penance," he added.

"For what?"

"For speaking foolishness last night."

She waited, but apparently that was the only detail she would have from him. He looked very unwilling to say any more and that left her to speculate on just what he'd said the night before that he found foolish. There was ample material there, so she took his words and put them aside for future contemplation. What she did understand, however, was that she might very well have him at her mercy.

"Take me outside," she said, without hesitation.

He scowled. "Nay."

"To the chapel then."

"And if I say you nay, the fate of my soul hangs in the balance."

She waited, listened to his sighs, but remained unmoved by them. Finally he grumbled and rose. "Very well."

She felt a surge of victory. "I'll fetch my cloak."

"You will not kneel at St. Christopher's shrine today."

Perhaps she had no more need of prayers, now that Robin was returned safely. And she suspected her supplications hadn't gone beyond the chapel ceiling anyway, for 'twas a certainty that her pleas for him to love only her had gone unanswered. She had no idea what jest her saint sought to work upon her, but she would have no more of it.

No more of Robin's kisses, either.

She made that decision as Robin put her cloak around her shoulders. Aye, she would have no more of that and if he offered, she would refuse. Perhaps she would extend the courtesy to Nicholas again, should he be so inclined.

Though she had to admit, and it galled her to do so, that Nicholas could not compare to Robin in that kissing business.

Damn Robin anyway.

She walked toward the door. Robin caught her by the arm before she managed it, and looked down at her gravely.

"Forgive me," he said.

"For what this time, Robin?"

He looked about him helplessly, as if he sought an answer lurking in the bed curtains, or perhaps lost behind a tapestry. That Robin of Artane was actually apologizing, albeit for nothing in particular, was something of great note. She began to wonder if that was what he had been thinking on the whole of the night. Perhaps she would do well to suggest he spend another night determining just what it was he'd done that merited such groveling.

A contrite and supplicating Robin was an interesting thing to see indeed.

"For many things," he said, at length.

"When you can tell me what it is I should forgive you for, then I'll think about it. Until then, walk me to the chapel."

He began to mutter under his breath, and she suspected his mutterings included several uncomplimentary things about her. She supposed, however, that if he couldn't come up with anything decent to apologize for, he wouldn't be equal to the task of spilling the contents of his heart.

One thing was certain, he wasn't concentrating on her. Anne watched him as he swept the great hall with his gaze as they entered it. The trip to the chapel was made with even more care. Whatever else his faults might have been, at least he was capable of keeping her safe. She was grateful for it.

He led her into the chapel and sat down with her near the altar. Anne bowed her head and said her prayers.

When she was finished, she looked next to her. Robin sat with his hands folded in his lap and his eyes closed. His long, dark lashes fanned over his cheeks, reminding her of how long she'd always thought his eyelashes to be in his youth. He had been such a beautiful boy. And he had become a beautiful man. He had every bit of Rhys's handsomeness, along with a bit of ruggedness that was his alone.

And she felt her traitorous heart begin to soften yet again. She could hardly believe he had been sitting so quietly for so long. In his youth, Robin had always given the impression of being headed in a dozen different directions at once, even while standing still. Nicholas could be lazy. Robin had never known how. Anne frowned. He drove himself too hard trying to ever prove himself worthy. Of what, she didn't know. Had he no idea how very much Rhys loved him? Or Gwen? Anne could bring up hundreds of memories of Rhys bragging about his heir and what a fine man he had become. Robin likely wouldn't have believed the words if he'd heard them. As far as he was concerned, he was still proving himself. In truth, all he was doing was exhausting himself. He'd proved himself years ago.

Anne reached up and before she thought better of it, tucked a lock of hair behind his ear. Robin opened his eyes and slid a look her way.

"Did you think me napping?"

She couldn't help but smile. "I confess I did."

Robin reached for her hand and held it between both his own. "Nay, Anne. I've much to be grateful for. I was giving thanks and had only reached the middle of my list. I believe I stopped just after being grateful for Anne of Fenwyck's beautiful green eyes and before her fiery spirit. Perhaps I will save the rest of your virtues for another time."

"Nay, finish. It won't take long."

" 'Tis fortunate for you that I know you are not in earnest. The saints only know how I might have to repay you for that slight to my lady."

His lady? She looked down at her hand between his work-roughened hands and shook her head. Ah, that she could actually believe his words. It would have been a sweet thing indeed.

He squeezed her hand. "Let us go back. All this piousness has left me with a powerful hunger."

Anne let him pull her to her feet and followed him from the chapel. He kept his arm around her as they left the building and started across the courtyard. Anne tried to ignore the stares they received. Perhaps it wasn't seemly . . .

"Are you so ashamed of me then?"

She looked up at him. "Of course not."

"Then why do you pull away?"

"What will they think?"

"They will realize I'm keeping you warm. And if they're very quick, they'll realize I'm being noble and chivalrous."

"Indeed."

He pursed his lips. "I am making an effort, Anne. Credit me with that."

"Is it so difficult, then?" she asked.

"What? To walk with you so politely when the barbarian in me thinks it would be more to my taste to haul you into my arms and stalk off with you? Aye, 'tis very difficult."

"Kind of you, then, to make the effort."

He snorted as he drew her closer and led her up the stairs. Anne couldn't stop a sigh of relief when the hall door was shut behind her. She hadn't felt unsafe outside with Robin there beside her, but she couldn't deny that knowing she was behind heavy doors was a reassuring feeling.

Then she caught sight of Amanda standing before the hearth, tapping her foot purposefully, and wondered if she might not have been safer outside.

Amanda pulled Anne away the moment they reached the fire.

"Amanda," Robin rumbled dangerously.

"Go find my foster sister some wine," Amanda threw at him. "She's chilled."

Anne soon found herself sitting before a roaring fire and squirming under Amanda's sharp glance.

"Has he touched you?"

"Amanda!"

"Has he?" Amanda demanded. "By the saints, I'll take my blade to him if he has."

"Amanda, he's been perfectly—"

"—chivalrous? I don't believe that for a moment, sister. Robin isn't capable of it. Now, you leave him to me. I'll tell him just what will happen if he doesn't comport himself properly."

"Amanda, I'm certain—"

"Aye, I am too. I've lost count of the number of his bastards—"

Anne gasped as Amanda was hauled up to her feet. All she saw then was Robin's back as he dragged his sister away. Anne watched as Robin backed her up against the back wall of the hall. The sound of him slapping his palms against the stone echoed in the chamber. But she heard nothing after that. And when Robin and Amanda came back over to the fire, Amanda was wearing the expression she usually wore after Rhys had chastened her for something. Robin sat down in the chair opposite Anne and glared up at his sister.

"You may pour us wine."

"I'm not pouring you anything, you arrogant cur—"

Amanda shrieked as Robin jerked her over his knees. He held her there with two heavy forearms over her shoulders and lower back.

"I fear I didn't hear you," he said pleasantly. "What was that?"

"Miserable whoreson!"

Anne jumped as Robin gave his sister a healthy whack across her backside.

"You were saying?" he said.

"Damn you, Robin, let me up!"

"That is *my lord Artane* to you, you disobedient shrew. Now, will you comport yourself as a lady, or do I beat decorum into you?"

"You, my lord Artane, are a mannerless pig!"

Anne hastily covered her mouth with her hand to hide her smile.

"Robin, release her!" Nicholas vaulted over the table and stood over his brother, bristling with anger.

"I'm teaching her how to behave herself. Sit you down, lest you force me to teach you as well."

"You might try," Nicholas scoffed.

"Nicky," Anne said warningly, catching a full view of

the dangerous glitter in Robin's eyes. "I daresay now is not the time to push him."

Nicholas leaned over the back of Anne's chair. "Haven't you kissed him today, Anne? Surely that would sweeten his mood."

"Cease," Anne said, feeling herself beginning to blush uncomfortably. Never mind that she fully intended never to kiss Robin again. She had very vivid memories of past experiences with the like. "My lord Artane does not wish to be teased today."

"Then let us certainly honor his wishes," Nicholas said, inclining his head. "Go ahead and beat the wench, Rob."

"Nicholas!" Amanda wailed. "Robin, release me."

"If you can behave, aye, I might."

"I won't say another bloody word about your scores of bastards. Now, let me up!"

Nicholas reached over and pulled Amanda away. "Saints, Amanda, use your wits! Does it not occur to you that Anne might not want to hear about that?"

Anne waved away his words. "Nay, 'tis nothing." By the saints, this was the last thing she wanted to discuss! A quick look at Robin's face told her that he likely felt the same way.

"It would certainly mean something to me," Nicholas said. "Amanda, exert yourself to be less thoughtless in the future."

"If you two are finished babbling," Robin growled, "you may go. And, Amanda, remember the feel of my hand on your backside. It will be there as often as is needed to teach you the manners Father never did."

"Ha," Amanda said scornfully, but she kept herself well out of Robin's reach. "Take me back upstairs, Nicholas. I fear what I might do if left here to retaliate."

Anne looked into the fire until she and Robin were alone. She couldn't look at him.

"Anne?"

She continued to look at the flames. "Aye?"

"I have something to apologize for."

"What?"

He sighed. "My lack of discretion in the past."

"It matters not."

"I would hope it would. It would certainly matter to me. If you had taken a lover, don't you think I would hunt him down and geld him?"

She looked at him reluctantly and decided that, given the look in his eye, he might have. She pursed her lips. "And what am I to do with all your past lovers, my lord? Take blades to them?"

"There are far fewer than I'm credited with and 'tis best if you forget them. I certainly have."

"Ah, but have they forgotten you?"

He winced. "You say the damndest things, Anne."

She only looked at him.

"All right, damn you," he snapped. "I'm quite certain that whatever sorry nights I spent in anyone's bed has completely escaped the poor wench's memory. You've no need to fear anyone coming to regale you with tales of my prowess. Satisfied?"

"And why would that bother me anyway?" she asked politely.

His mouth worked silently for the space of several breaths, during which time Anne began to wonder if she had misjudged him. He was seemingly concerned that she not be assaulted by any of his former lovers, concerned that she believe their number to be fewer than he was credited with, and now he could not muster up a decent answer as to why it should trouble her.

And, most notably, he had apologized. More than once.

He spluttered a moment or two more, then cursed as he stood abruptly. "We shouldn't be here. It isn't safe. Come with me upstairs to Father's solar. We'll have supper."

Anne soon found her hand in his. More was the pity that she was starting to become accustomed to the like. She sighed and followed Robin up the stairs and down the passageway to Rhys's solar.

Supper arrived soon enough and with it Robin's siblings. Anne sat silently during the meal, bemused by Robin's apologies. She found herself watching him with new eyes. His grumbles, she noted, were directed at those who had somehow either touched his heart or awakened his ire. He was, to be sure, gruff and impossible, but she suspected that beneath those growls lay a great deal of love for his family.

It was a highly enlightening meal.

It was also a very typical one, except that Robin threw a bite of everything he planned to eat to the dogs first. Anne wasn't allowed to eat until he'd tried it then on himself. Other than that, supper was a normal affair. Amanda and Robin bickered. Nicholas tried to keep the peace and finished off supper by challenging Robin to a wrestle. And for once in his life, Robin refused. Anne had never seen him do the like and she wondered what it could possibly mean.

Robin excused them and led her to his sire's bedchamber. He sat her in a chair and took the stool before her.

"Comfortable?"

When the alternative was the bed, aye, she was comfortable enough. And then the thought of the bed brought the thought of bedding to mind and Anne began to blush.

"I never should have said aught about any of it," he said, "but it was something to apologize for."

"So it was," she agreed.

He looked at her in silence for a moment, then rose and held out his hands. "Let me plait your hair for you, then I'll put you to bed. Too much apologizing is exhausting. You'll no doubt need your rest to listen for another round of it on the morrow."

"More apologies?" she asked with a smile. "How delightful."

He scowled at her as he lowered her to the stool. He sat behind her and began to brush her hair. Anne closed her eyes and savored it. He would have made a fine maid.

He plaited her hair deftly, then sat back. Anne stood and turned to look down at him.

"Thank you," she said.

He nodded solemnly. "Off to bed with you, then. And don't fret over me. I'll be perfectly fine here in the chair or on the floor."

She pursed her lips. "You said you had no trouble sleeping on the floor."

"That was before I exerted myself brushing your hair."

"Then don't sleep on the floor," she said, then she bit her tongue. She should have been glad of his discomfort, but somehow she found she couldn't be.

He looked at her in surprise. "Truly?"

"Well, you could sleep in your clothes," she said pointedly.

"Couldn't," he said, shaking his head. "Too uncomfortable."

"Robin—"

"The bed is large and I give you my word of honor you will remain untouched." He cleared his throat. "You needn't strip, if you'd rather not."

Anne could hardly believe he wasn't putting up a larger fight about sleeping next to her, but perhaps he was weary of the floor. She frowned at him.

"Douse the candle and close your eyes. Far away from me, if you please."

He did so and Anne took off her gown while she had the chance. She crawled into bed in just her shift and prayed it was enough to protect her modesty.

Anne listened as Robin's clothes fell to the floor with soft thumps and she prayed he had clung to some sense of decorum and left something on. The bed creaked as he slid in from the opposite side. She took a deep breath.

"Robin?"

"Aye."

"Are you wearing anything?"

"Naught but my sweet smile."

"Robin . . ."

"Your virtue is safe. I vow it."

"Oh, Robin—"

"Hush, Anne. Go to sleep."

Well, she'd made the offer after all, and 'twas likely too late to toss him from her bed. She closed her eyes and prayed she hadn't made a very large mistake.

One thing was certain, she would not sleep at all.

25

A brisk knocking on the door roused Anne from a deep slumber. She pulled the bed curtain aside, but the chamber was still dark. It had to be surely the middle of the night. Why would someone be knocking in the middle of the night? Had war come to Artane?

"By the saints," she said, starting to get up. Then she realized several things almost at once.

She was abed with Robin.

She had apparently fallen asleep in spite of her fears she never would.

And someone was at the door who would, unless she did something very quickly, enter and discover that she was abed with Robin and had fallen asleep where likely no maid with any virtue would have dared.

She clutched the blanket to her chin. "Robin," she whispered frantically. "Someone knocks!"

"Tell 'em to go away," he mumbled, burying his head under a pillow.

She jerked the blanket off him. "Go answer it, you fool!"

He groaned and rolled from the bed. Anne heard the hiss of a candle being lit, then saw much more of Robin than she'd ever intended. Robin padded to the door, rubbing one eye sleepily with his hand. It was then that Anne realized she had never seen a naked man before. Boys, aye, but a man?

Never.

Especially one in that condition.

She could only assume he was, well, not at rest as it were. But perhaps the condition came naturally to him, for he made no mention of it. Indeed, he seemed not to notice it.

He grumbled as he pulled back the bolt and jerked open the door.

"What?" he demanded.

There were so many gasps, Anne hardly knew where to start in identifying them.

First there was hers, when she watched Robin's sire push his way inside the bedchamber, torch in hand.

Then there was Robin's, when he realized his father had come home, and at least a fortnight early at that.

Then there was Rhys's when he caught sight of not only his son in his naked glory, but Anne peeking from within the bed curtains.

And if Rhys's gasp had been loud, Geoffrey of Fenwyck's was deafening. He strode into the chamber, ripped open the bed curtains the rest of the way and glared at her. Anne clutched the blankets to her throat. She half wondered if her father would take a mind to beat her.

But apparently he had other prey in mind.

"You whoreson!" he bellowed, turning and launching himself at Robin.

Anne fell out of bed, then struggled to her feet, pulling the blanket out and wrapping it around her.

"Father!" she shouted, praying her father wouldn't throttle Robin. He had his hands around Robin's throat and had slammed him back up against the wall. "Cease! He's done nothing—"

"Nothing?" her sire bellowed. *"Nothing?"* He released

Robin and whirled on Rhys. "Artane, I vow I'll kill him if it's the last thing I do!"

Rhys said nothing. He didn't have to say anything. He looked first at her and she saw him absolve her of any part in the current situation. Then his steely gray eyes slid to his son. Anne had to admire Robin's calm in the face of what would surely be a wrath he had never seen from his father before. Rhys's eyes missed no detail. Robin stood panting against the wall with his hands by his side, not attempting to shield his nakedness. Anne watched his father look down. Robin flushed and rubbed his throat.

"Think you I would be in this condition had I just bedded her?" he asked defensively.

"Think you it makes one wit of difference if she is a virgin or not?" Fenwyck bellowed. "You fool, what possessed you to do this thing!"

"I had a very good reason—"

Anne's father roared. Anne clapped her hands over her ears, praying her sire wouldn't do anything she would regret, such as kill Robin.

"My lord," Robin began.

"Silence!" Geoffrey drew his sword, but Rhys put his hand out.

"My friend, kill him and you kill your daughter's husband."

"Husband!" Geoffrey gasped. "How can you possibly entertain the notion that I would give my child to this bold, honorless whoreson!"

"Because he could very well be the father of your grandchild," Rhys said calmly.

Anne stole a look at Robin, then wished she hadn't. His expression was grimmer, if possible, than his father's. She didn't want to speculate on his thoughts.

"Geoffrey, come with me to my solar," Rhys said. "We'll reason together there."

"I'll go nowhere—"

"My solar," Rhys bellowed suddenly. "It serves us nothing to stand here arguing."

Anne found herself in her father's sights once more before he cursed his way from the chamber and slammed the door behind him. She hoisted the blanket up a bit higher and turned her sights to Robin's sire.

And then she wished she hadn't.

She had never seen him look so grim before. If it had been possible, she would have given anything to have disappeared before him rather than see the censure in his eyes.

"I would suggest you two retreat to separate chambers to dress," he said evenly, "but I can see 'tis too late for that. Robin, I will expect you in my solar immediately. Do not keep me waiting. Unreasonable delays will not soothe my temper and I assure you, you do not wish to increase my ire this night." He turned, then paused. He looked back over his shoulder at Robin. "I expected more from you than this."

With that, Rhys left the chamber, closing the door softly behind him. Anne looked at Robin, but he wouldn't meet her eyes.

"Robin," she began.

He shook his head, once, then walked over to his trunk. He pulled on his clothes silently. Anne limped over to the fire, heavily favoring her right leg, and pulled her dress over her head. By the saints, this was a disaster.

"Robin . . ."

He didn't look at her, or acknowledge that he'd heard her. He simply pulled on his boots, belted his tunic and left.

Anne stood in the middle of the chamber and wrapped her arms around herself. She had done nothing wrong. There was no reason for the shame that coursed through her. Robin had just been protecting her, though she had to admit that sleeping in the same bed with him had been very ill-advised. Her generosity had certainly been unwise, though she had hardly expected her sire and his to return home and assume they'd lain together.

Though what else were they to think?

Anne sighed and considered her next action. She could

remain where she was and wait for her fate to come to her, or she could go to meet it. She hadn't been invited to Rhys's solar, but there was no reason she couldn't eavesdrop and find out what was going to happen.

And possibly keep her father from killing the man she loved.

She opened the chamber door and saw Robin's guards still there. They looked at her with expressionless faces and she could only speculate on what they were thinking. She lifted her chin and pushed her way past them. They fell into step behind her and she stopped and looked at them.

"I'm out for an intrigue," she said, "and do not need a cluster of knights clomping along behind me."

One of the men made her a low, creaking bow. "My lady, we are bid guard you by my lord. We cannot fail him."

"And my sire is liable to kill him unless I make exceeding great and silent haste," she returned.

They did look at each other then, and a pair of them shifted uncomfortably.

"One man," she said, looking at their apparent leader. "You. But come silently."

It was only after she was creeping along the passageway that she realized how bold she had been in ordering Robin's men about. She shook her head. A pity she had found her tongue when it likely wouldn't serve her.

She paused before Rhys's solar door and motioned Robin's man behind her. The door was shut, but that was remedied easily enough. The growling going on inside would likely cover whatever sound she might make disturbing the sanctuary. She pushed the door open only far enough to hear what was being said.

"I overlooked your indiscretions in the past," Rhys was saying, in a voice so cold that it sent chills down Anne's spine, "but this is no common slut you've bedded."

"I didn't bed her!"

"You've kept her a virtual prisoner in your chamber for how long? A fortnight—"

"I had to!" Robin exclaimed. "She's fair lost her life

four times. Did you not see my guard outside? Did you not think to wonder why they were there?"

"Likely to protect you from prying eyes!" Fenwyck bellowed. "Enough of this, Rhys. I'll have him in the lists!"

Robin's snort almost made Anne smile, if she could have managed it given the circumstances. At least Robin had no lack of respect for his own skill, and her father's lack of it in his eyes.

"Would you have done aught differently?" Robin demanded. "Would you not have done whatever you could to keep her safe?"

"My actions are not under discussion; yours are."

"I had no choice!"

"You were naked in her bed!" Rhys thundered. "A fortnight in my chamber, Robin. Think you any sane man would believe you haven't touched her?"

"Believe what you will," Robin snapped. "I'm no liar."

"And I say you're a bloody wretch who deserves to be hanged!" Fenwyck bellowed. "Rhys, I demand retribution!"

"You'll have it," Rhys replied, in that same, cold voice he'd used at first. "The wedding will take place immediately."

"You cannot force me to wed," Robin growled.

"I can and I will."

"I will make the choice myself!"

There was silence and Anne felt coldness steal over her heart.

Apparently that choice would not be her.

"To say I am disappointed in you, Robin," Rhys said quietly, "does not come close to describing the feelings that plague me at the moment. You will wed with the woman I choose for you and you will do it when I say you will. Or you will forfeit your inheritance."

Anne clapped her hand over her mouth to stifle her gasp. Surely Rhys could not be in earnest. What would Robin do without land?

And then Robin laughed. It was the most humorless laugh she had ever heard.

"That would please you well enough, wouldn't it?" he said, laughing again. "Give it all to Miles, Father. Give him the title, your lands, your gold. Give it to your son of the flesh. Give him Anne while you're at it, for I bloody well won't be told what to do by you or by anyone else!"

"Aye," Rhys said hotly, "you will. You will wed Anne as soon as the priest can be roused."

"I will wed when and where I choose," Robin snarled. "If you would but listen—"

"To what?" Rhys demanded. "What pitiful excuse can you make for your actions? By the bloody saints, Robin, she was in your bed! Hell, it wasn't your bed, it was *my* bed. I should beat you for that alone!"

"There was nowhere else!" Robin shouted.

"Enough," Rhys said curtly. "You'll wed within the hour. Go to the chapel and give yourself over to prayer—"

"You take your pious demands and go to hell!" Booted feet crossed the chamber with heavy stomps.

"Robin—"

"And why are you home so early?" Robin demanded, apparently stopping just short of the doorway.

"We met Hardwiche on the road," Rhys said shortly.

"And how did you know Anne was in my chamber?"

"A servant told us as we came into the hall," Rhys said impatiently. "Now, as for you—"

Anne pulled back into the shadows of an alcove a heartbeat before Robin jerked the door open, then slammed it shut behind him. She was too stunned by the events of the middle of the night to do aught but watch as Rhys left the solar hard on Robin's heels, or her own sire who followed right behind.

She was still as stone, wondering if she would ever again breathe a normal breath.

So, Robin didn't love her. What else was she to divine from his words? If he'd wanted her, he would have taken her no matter the means.

And then she gasped as her father suddenly reappeared
before her. She had never seen him angrier. It took every
ounce of courage she had to face him and not cower, but
she did it.

"Did he force you?" Fenwyck demanded.

What would it serve her to explain anything to him? In
his present mood, he likely wouldn't believe her anyway.

"Nay," she said simply.

He clapped his hand to his head. "Then you went to
his bed willingly? You foolish girl, what were you thinking?" He grasped her by the arm and jerked her down the
passageway.

"My lord!" Robin's guardsman said in alarm.

Geoffrey snarled a curse at him and continued to pull
Anne along. "I suppose the only thing good to come of
this is you will be wed after all. To Artane's get, since
he's ruined you for anyone else." He grunted in disgust.
"I suppose I can trust him with my lands, though I daresay
I shouldn't. I couldn't trust him with my daughter. Perhaps he has more sense with soil than he does with
women."

Anne listened to her father cite a listing of both Robin's
flaws and good points, but she couldn't agree with any of
them. She knew one thing and one thing alone:

Robin of Artane did not wish to wed her.

But she suspected he would have to.

Her sire opened the door to Rhys's chamber and pushed
her inside. "Stay here," he grumbled. "I don't like this,
but obviously 'tis the only thing to be done. Do whatever
it is you have to to make yourself presentable. And do it
quickly. I don't want the bastard changing his mind before
we get to the chapel."

And with that, he shut the door, leaving Anne to her
thoughts.

And they were not pleasant ones. She had wanted to
stay at Artane. She had prayed she would stay at Artane.
She had hardly dared hope that she might remain there as
Robin's bride.

She had never envisioned having all of it come about because of a sword in Robin's back.

The humiliation of it was almost more than she could bear. Anne found herself envisioning the day that would stretch before her and she almost sat down on the floor and wept. If Robin appeared at the altar, he would do so by means of his father's guard forcing him there. How would Rhys wring any acceptance of the marriage from his son without bloodshed? Even if they could get him to the chapel, Robin would likely cut down half his sire's garrison to be free of the place.

Free of her.

Had he felt any affection for her over the past fortnight, had there been anything tender growing in his breast, it was gone now. By the saints, the thought of him repudiating her at the altar was almost more than she could take.

But that was hardly her fault.

Anne felt her chin lift the slightest bit. No one had asked her opinion on the matter. Never mind that inquiring about such a thing never would have crossed her father's thoughts even had he been drowning in his cups. No one had asked if she wanted to wed Robin, if she had any affection for him, if she thought she could stomach the rest of her life spent in his company.

If she was going to wed anyone, she would at least wed someone who wanted her—for her dowry if nothing else.

She turned and headed toward the bedchamber door. She wasn't powerless to decide her fate. She would leave the keep, hopefully unnoticed in the confusion. Perhaps there was a place for her at court until her sire's temper cooled. Then she would have another look at his choices for her mate and she would wed one of them based on his lust for her lands. Lust was lust, perhaps, where a husband was concerned. She threw open the door, fully prepared to escape.

And she came face-to-face with her sire leaning against the far wall with his arms folded over his chest. Robin's guards were conspicuously absent.

There would be no escape.

But before she could say anything, the lady Gwennelyn came down the passageway and swept her back inside the bedchamber. The next thing Anne knew, she was ensconced in her foster mother's tender embrace.

"Sweet Anne," Gwen said, pulling back and smiling ruefully, "what folly has Robin pulled you into?"

"What folly?" Anne asked, feeling suddenly very near to tears. "This farce of a marriage?"

Gwen shook her head with a gentle smile. "Love, 'tis no farce. Things will settle themselves in time, I daresay."

"He is unhappy—"

"As are you, I imagine," Gwen said. "I doubt this is how you would have wished your wedding day to go."

"It wasn't as it seemed," Anne said.

"Aye, I know," Gwen said. "Nicholas gave me the entire tale and I don't fault either you or Robin for your actions. Indeed, he could have done nothing else with his most precious of treasures."

"His horse was safely in the stables at all times," Anne said grimly.

Gwen laughed softly. "Ah, my Anne, you know I speak of you. Robin has his father's stubbornness and 'twill likely take him a goodly amount of time to come to his senses. If you're patient, you'll no doubt be rewarded."

Anne didn't want to tell Gwen that she had lost all her wits when it came to Gwen's firstborn son, so she remained silent. And she said nothing when Gwen combed out her hair and found a simple circlet to place over a sheer veil. She supposed she looked bridal. She knew herself that she was certainly virginal.

But she suspected no one else would believe it.

She couldn't find anything to say as Gwen walked with her to the chapel a goodly while later. She wasn't looking forward to seeing Robin, for she could only imagine what had transpired in his sorry life over the past pair of hours.

She hoped it hadn't included bloodshed.

Of any but his, of course.

26

Edith woke to the sound of screeching. Actually, she'd been awake for longer than she would have liked, as there had seemingly been a great deal of shouting. She had been almost certain she had dreamed the like.

"Oof," she said, as she felt something collapse onto her sleeping pallet. She sat up and pushed the offender off.

"Oh, Lady Edith," Maude gasped. "You must awake!"

"I already am," Edith said curtly, not daring to hope that the other two women in the chamber hadn't been awakened too. It could have been worse. The entire community of Gwen's castle ladies could have been sleeping in their accustomed chamber. The ones who had been left behind were either too deaf to hear Maude's squeals, or too stupid to understand what they meant. She looked at the girl in the faint light of dawn and was unsurprised to see a look of complete panic.

She sighed. "What is it now, Maude?"

"Lord Rhys has returned!"

"How lovely, but you needn't alert the entire keep to the fact."

"He's found them in his bed together!"

Edith paused. Now, that was a tidbit she couldn't have

hoped for. "How interesting. How did he happen upon that?"

"I told him, but that isn't the worst of it!"

Edith could scarce wait to hear more. She yawned. "Go on, Maude. And hurry so I can return to my slumber."

"They're set to wed!"

Edith smothered her yawn abruptly. "Robin and Anne? How do you know?"

"I heard it myself!" Maude wailed. "I'll never have him now."

"Well, men take lovers—"

"I'll not be his mistress!"

Edith refrained from pointing out to the twit that his mistress was what she had already been, though perhaps that was giving a single night of lust too lofty a title.

"I fear, little one," Edith said sympathetically, "that there is nothing you can do."

"I'll the wedding!"

"How?"

"I'll the priest!"

Edith sighed.

"Kill *her* then."

Edith felt a tingle of alarm go through her. Not yet. That wasn't her plan. Torment Anne, aye. Make her life a misery and thereby torment Robin, aye. But kill her?

That would come last.

Once all the rest had been seen to.

Edith put a restraining hand on Maude's arm, and held her trembling limb still. "You've naught to fear," she said soothingly. "I daresay Robin will not allow this to happen." *And if he does, all the better for my plan. To lose a love would be painful. To lose a wife, perhaps a wife with child?*

It was almost enough to send shivers down *her* spine.

"Think you?" Maude asked, lifting up her tearstained face. "Think you truly?"

"I'm certain of it. Now, off with you and make no mischief. I will see to it all."

Maude nodded, less happily than Edith would have liked, but at least she was seemingly in agreement. Edith laid back once Maude had left the chamber and gave herself over to contemplation of this new turn of events. Perhaps Maude's attention could be turned to the other children.

A handful of dead lads and lasses.

She smiled. What a lovely wedding gift that would be.

She rose to dress. If she wanted to be at the wedding, she would have to make haste.

27

Robin continued to walk blindly down the passageway, ignoring his father's continuing commands that he stop. Well, at least he couldn't hear Fenwyck behind him bellowing out any more threats of death and dismemberment by means of a very blunt sword and other painful implements. Had he been in different straits, he might have found Anne's sire to be quite imaginative.

But he wasn't in different straits.

So he continued to walk, lest he be completely unmanned by breaking down and sobbing. By the saints, all that he had struggled for the whole of his sorry life had been ruined.

His father found him lacking.

There were simply no words to describe how badly that hurt, how deep the agony went. Robin couldn't breathe. He could only walk and hope that when he stopped, the pain would stop. He had no idea where he was going. All he wanted to do was escape from his father's condemning glance.

An eternity later, he found himself in the chapel. It wasn't where he wanted to go, but it was where his feet seemed bent on taking him. He strode to the front and sat on a bench near St. Christopher's shrine. He stared at the likeness grimly, wondering why Anne had bothered with all her prayers there, kneeling on that cold floor. What had they served her? To acquire a husband whose fondest desire was to run from the scorn in his father's eyes?

And from that sprang his second greatest hurt: the scorn he would no doubt see in Anne's eyes.

Should he ever have the courage to look in them again, that was.

She'd seen him in his fully-flawed glory that morn. She'd watched him be reduced to a lad of seven or eight summers by the censure in his father's voice, watched him do nothing but stand there and whimper at his father's chastisement. If he'd been a man, he would have hauled Anne into his arms, told his father to go to hell and arranged for the wedding himself.

Instead, he'd let himself be ordered about like a whipped whore's bastard and trudged off to his father's solar to receive his due. By the bloody saints, he was a man full grown! He hardly had need to listen to his father's lectures. He'd known immediately that marriage was the only course of action. In truth, he'd known that before he joined Anne in her bed. He was beginning to wonder if he'd known it before he'd locked her in his father's bedchamber with him alone as company.

He dropped his face into his hands and groaned. This was not how he would have had it. He should have courted her. He should have swallowed his pride and asked Nicholas for ways to woo her. He should have humbled himself and gone to her sire to ask for her hand. Perhaps he himself wasn't much to rejoice over, but his inheritance was vast and his skill with the sword unmatched. He suspected that he might even manage to keep her lands producing as they should if given the time to prove himself on that sort of battlefield.

And if nothing else, he should have gone down on his knees before Fenwyck and assured the man that Anne was loved and would be treasured above all else.

Not that Fenwyck would believe him now.

Nor, he suspected, would Anne.

He shook his head in disbelief. It was barely dawn yet his entire life had been changed already. Anne's too. It wasn't how she deserved to be wed—with swords at their backs.

Her ring.

Robin jumped to his feet. That at least he could provide her. And perhaps that small token might salvage at least some portion of the morn for her. She might not believe that he loved her, but surely the ring would say something, wouldn't it?

He started toward the back of the sanctuary, then froze. His father stood leaning against the door, his face fixed in an uncompromising frown.

Well, damn him, it wasn't as if Robin planned to escape. He started toward the door and almost immediately found himself facing a drawn blade.

"Oh, by all the bloody saints," Robin said in disgust.

But his sire didn't move. His adopted sire, Robin corrected himself. The man whose approval meant everything to him didn't move. The condemnation Robin saw in Rhys's eyes was almost enough to break his heart.

Had he had a heart to be broken, that is. Robin turned and resumed his seat on the bench. And as he did so, he felt his heart chill and harden. Perhaps this was for the best. Perhaps wanting to please his sire had been a foolish dream. Indeed, he suspected it was. He was likely well rid of it.

In fact, perhaps he was well rid of his desire to please Anne as well. Aye, he thought as he sat on the bloody uncomfortable bench at the front of the chapel just a handful of paces from where she had knelt the saints only knew how many times praying for him, perhaps all the events of the morn had come about for a reason. What had possessed him to believe that giving his heart to anyone would serve him?

Nay, 'twas best that he keep it protected. He would do as his father willed and wed with Anne.

And then he would be off once again to do his manly labors.

In France, perhaps.

After all, a man was expected to do his duty, no matter where that duty took him. Aye, he would travel as far away as he could and put all his energies into warfare where they were best suited. It couldn't be construed as fleeing from his troubles. No one would suspect why he'd left. Anne would be free of her father's desires to see her wed. She would remain at Artane and she would be happy. Robin suspected that was what she wanted the most anyway. And if that were the case, her ring would be better off left in the bottom of his box.

It had been a foolish idea anyway.

He heard the door open behind him, heard voices and footsteps but made no effort to identify them. He looked up as the priest moved to stand behind the altar. He frowned. Surely the betrothal would take place inside the great hall, not the chapel. 'Twas the custom, was it not?

And then his father's scribe was ushered up to stand next to the priest. Robin smiled without humor. Well, it looked as if the betrothal agreement would be signed here before Mass. Perhaps his sire feared he would escape should he have had a bit of open ground between the hall and the chapel.

And then a heavy hand came to rest on his shoulder. Robin didn't look up, for he knew to whom the hand belonged.

" 'Tis time," Rhys said.

Robin didn't look at his sire. He merely rose and took his place before the altar, standing stiffly. He could have sworn he felt Anne's presence before he heard her uneven steps coming down the aisle behind him. She came to a stop beside him. He hardly dared look at her and when he did, he wished he hadn't.

She was so pale, she looked as if she might faint. Robin

wanted with all his heart to reach out to her—his earlier resolutions aside—but he didn't dare. If she pulled away or flinched at his touch, he wasn't sure how he would bear it.

So he kept his face resolutely forward and hardened his heart.

It was the only way to protect it.

And then he felt control of his own life slip through his fingers. The betrothal agreement was laid before him. He knew that 'twould be his father's right to list his holdings. He wouldn't have been surprised in the slightest if Rhys had retained all that Robin would have eventually inherited had things been different.

He lifted his chin. Rhys's lands didn't matter. He had his own lands, lands that he had inherited from Ayre. Those would have been more than sufficient to appease Anne's sire.

Then again those and the choicest of Rhys's own lands would likely have had the lout falling on the floor in a fit of rapture.

To his surprise, though, Rhys did not deny Robin anything that was due him. And when he heard no thump behind him, he assumed Fenwyck had known all along what Robin would bring to the union.

His true surprise, however, came from Fenwyck's recitation. He would have assumed that many of Geoffrey's holdings would have gone to his stepdaughter and her husband. Apparently Fenwyck either distrusted the lad entirely, or he thought Robin capable of managing his fiefs.

Either that or Robin was considered the lesser of two unpalatable alternatives.

Not that Robin cared about Fenwyck's lands. What Geoffrey didn't realize was that, despite his rich soil, the true prize was the woman who stood next to him, the woman who was starting to sway a bit.

Robin almost reached out and put his arm around her.

But that would have meant he loved her and that wasn't something he was going to admit to. Not now. Not when he planned to leave as quickly after the ceremony as possible—

"Robin, *turn!*"

The shout had him spinning almost before his brother's words registered in his poor abused head. He and Nick had protected each other for years with that simple command. It had been instinctive to obey.

And then he felt everything slow as if the pace of the world had ground to a halt. He found himself with his dagger in his hand. He watched in amazement as a body came flying down the aisle toward them with arm upraised.

And then he thought he heard the jingle of a bracelet.

Robin took a step forward, his rage and frustration overcoming him. He had looked for this soul for days, cursed his own inability to flush him out. Now that he had him in his sights, he would accept no defeat. He thrust upward with all the anger that lay simmering beneath his hurt.

The hooded figure cried out, gurgled out a curse then fell toward Robin. Robin shoved the body away and watched him collapse to the floor, a wickedly long dagger still clutched in his hand. A bracelet encircled the assassin's wrist. Robin stared down at the figure, then looked at Anne.

There was a slash down the back of her skirt and blood splattered everywhere.

And then just as suddenly as events had slowed, they quickened until Robin could scarce keep up with what he needed to do. He took a step backward, grasped for Anne and hauled her close. "Are you hurt?" he demanded frantically. "Did he cut you?"

She only shook her head and clung to him.

Robin wrapped his arms around her and held her head against his chest with her face turned away so she might not see. Nicholas knelt next to the body. He gingerly turned him over. Robin couldn't stop a gasp at the sight.

It wasn't a man.

It was a woman.

And one not unfamiliar to him.

The young woman looked up at Robin. "Failed to stop it," she managed, then gurgled her last breath.

There was absolute silence in the chapel. Robin looked about him and noted the expressions on the faces there. Shock for the most part. Even Fenwyck looked to be taken aback.

"A servant, Artane?" he managed.

"Aye," Rhys answered slowly. "But recently recommended and retained, though."

Robin wondered if now would be a good time to mention that Maude was a lord's daughter. Or that Robin had a very personal, intimate acquaintance with her.

Not that it was something he remembered with fondness. Looking back on it now, he wondered how he had ever found himself in her bed. She was greedy, grasping and tenacious.

Or had been, rather.

Aye, even with shorn hair, she was unmistakable. Robin watched Nicholas close Maude's eyes, then look up at him. Robin knew his brother knew. Though he likely could have counted on Nicholas's silence, there was little point in it. The tale would come out eventually. He might have been a coward that morn, but he would be such no longer. 'Twas a man's right and privilege to be truthful, no matter the cost.

He could only hope the cost wouldn't come too dear this time.

"She's no servant," Robin said heavily.

All eyes turned to him and Robin wished heartily that he could sink into the floor. Even Anne pulled back to look at him. Robin looked away from the crowd, avoided Anne's eyes and settled on staring over the altar only to meet the condemning gaze of the priest.

Bloody hell.

"One of your lovers, perhaps?" Geoffrey said, his voice laced with scorn.

Damn the man. "Aye," Robin said shortly.

"Maude of Canfield," Nicholas supplied. "It would seem, Rob, that she wasn't overfond of the thought of your nuptials."

"Well," Rhys said grimly, "at least we have our assailant."

I'm thrilled, Robin thought sourly. What impeccable timing.

"And she's blond," Geoffrey added, no less scornfully. "We know where your tastes run—"

"Enough," Robin said, glaring at his future father-in-law. "My past is my own and no affair of yours. You insult your daughter and I'll have no more of it."

"I intended to insult you," Geoffrey said curtly.

"Then do so in the lists. I've no stomach for a fight with words." Robin turned to the priest. "Wed us. Now."

"But," the priest said, gesturing to the cooling corpse behind Robin.

"Now," Robin growled. "We'll forgo Mass today."

"Perhaps that's wise," the priest agreed. "Especially in light of . . . well . . ."

"Oh, by the saints, cease with your babbling!" Fenwyck bellowed. "Get on with the bloody ceremony!"

Robin gritted his teeth and wondered if clouting his lady wife's father in the nose could possibly worsen the events of the day. There he stood with blood on his hands and clothes with a dead lover at his heels.

And then he heard someone begin to be violently ill.

He turned to see Isabelle being heartily sick. Miles was trying to help, but turning very green very quickly. The twins had clapped hands over their mouths and Amanda's eyes were beginning to roll upward in her head. Robin watched as Nicholas caught her before she slumped to the ground.

And Anne began to weep.

At least they wouldn't have to stand there and listen to any more recitations of holdings. Robin signed the contract with a curse, then shoved the quill into Anne's shaking hands. He doubted anyone would recognize her name as her own, nor would they believe it hadn't been signed under duress. Nevertheless, the contract was made before witnesses and 'twas legitimate. Never mind that several of the witnesses were too far gone in various states of incapacitation to be useful.

"The blessing," the priest began.

"I doubt it will help," Robin said grimly. He put his hands on Anne's shoulders, ignoring the blood that covered him, and kissed her very briefly. He pulled back, fully prepared to bolt and make for France.

Then he noticed his bride.

She was looking at him.

He couldn't tell if her expression revealed abject horror or complete misery.

Or was that wry amusement?

The sight of her stunned him so, 'twas as if he'd never before seen her. And as he looked at her, and realized that she was indeed his, he began to question the idea of France.

It was, after all, a very nasty place to be in winter.

He considered. He could remain at Artane. The lists were fine. He could ensconce himself there for great stretches of time. At least that way he could look on Anne from afar now and again.

The lists. Aye, that was the place for him. Soon, before he began to entertain any other foolish thoughts.

Such as being Anne's husband in truth.

He reached out and swept her up into his arms before anyone, mainly Anne, could protest. Without comment, he turned and stepped over Maude's body and approached his mother.

"See to Anne, will you?" he asked.

"And where do you think you're going?" Fenwyck demanded.

"To the lists."

"Go if you like," Rhys said, "but your mother won't be here to tend Anne."

Robin blinked. "She won't?"

"I won't?" Gwen echoed.

"You won't," Rhys said shortly. "We're leaving."

"But we just returned home," Gwen protested.

"Fenwyck has invited us for a lengthy stay," Rhys said.

"I have?" Geoffrey said, looking less than delighted about the prospect. "I don't remember that."

"Children," Rhys said, "collect your things. We'll leave within the hour."

Robin let Anne slip down to the ground and she took a step away from him with more enthusiasm than he would have liked.

"You're leaving?" she asked Gwen, sounding quite horrified by the prospect. "Now?"

"Not a bad idea," Geoffrey said, coming to stand behind his daughter. "No use in staying for the bedding anyway, especially given that she isn't a virg—"

Robin let his fist fly. He watched himself plow that fist into his father-in-law's face and wondered absently at the wisdom of it. Fenwyck lay sprawled on the floor, apparently too stunned by the blow to move. Robin smiled in grim satisfaction.

"Speak disparagingly of my wife again," he said, wishing Fenwyck would heave himself to his feet so he could brawl with him truly and repay the lout for several annoying things said to Anne, "and you'll not find me so lenient."

Fenwyck groaned, but did not move.

Robin sighed regretfully, then took Anne's hand. "Come, Anne. Let us leave the rabble to their plans."

He didn't wait for her to agree or disagree, he merely pulled her behind him out the chapel.

"Cheeky bastard!" came the sudden bellow from behind them. "I'll kill him yet myself!"

Robin grunted. "At least he isn't permanently damaged."

Anne choked, a soft sound that made Robin wonder if

she were laughing. He looked down at her, but she had bowed her head and he could not see.

He slowed his pace to match Anne's once they were down the steps and a goodly distance from the chapel. He released her hand, then stole a look at her to see how she would react.

She merely clasped her hands in front of her and continued to stare at the ground.

Ah, so perhaps she truly could not bear him. Robin frowned to cover his consternation. He shouldn't have been surprised. Perhaps the best thing he could do was keep his distance from her. He would resurrect his plan to return to France—

Which he now couldn't do, given that his sire was leaving again.

He cursed his father under his breath. Had the man anticipated Robin's thoughts and thwarted them before Robin could act? Damn him.

Robin waited as Anne mounted the steps to the great hall, then he opened the door for her and crossed with her to the hearth.

"I will don my mail and train," he said.

She only nodded. She didn't meet his gaze.

"What chamber will you have?"

She did look up at him then. "What?"

"Well, I didn't suppose you would want to continue in my sire's. 'Tis the finest, of course, but after this morning . . ."

"But I thought," she began, then bit her lip and fell silent.

Robin wasn't sure how to react to that. Did she expect to share a chamber with him? He took a deep breath.

"Mine is comfortable, but I daresay Amanda's is cleaner. You can have whichever you choose."

"Of course," she said quietly.

Robin scowled. Damn her anyway, what did she want him to say? *Come share my bed?* She was his wife, after all, though he hardly dared claim his rights.

"Father's then," he said in exasperation. "You can decide later on a more permanent solution."

He looked down at her. There was blood spattered on her hands. Her gown sported an enormous rent in the back and he had likely been the one to muss her hair clutching her to him as he had.

Before he could think better of it, he reached out and put his fingers under her chin. He lifted her face and looked at her. She was pale and teary-eyed and lovely. It was all he could do not to drop to his knees and apologize right there for having ruined her wedding day.

But for all he knew, she was ready to weep because she found herself his wife.

So, he slowly dropped his hand and took a step backward, never taking his eyes from her. And when he could bear it no more, he turned and walked away. He heard his squire trailing dutifully along behind him and prayed Jason would keep himself silent. He also hoped for men in the lists, for he was in sore need of something to take his mind off the sorry state of affairs in his life.

The only good thing had been that at least now they knew who had been trying to hurt Anne. Robin shook his head as he made ready to wage mock war. Maude of Canfield. Who would have thought a simple dalliance would lead to such trouble?

But Fenwyck had been right. Maude was blond. There was a reason for that and Robin hoped Anne wouldn't think overlong on what that reason might be. It would likely horrify her more than the day of her nuptials had.

28

Anne stood near the fire in Rhys and Gwen's chamber and watched the flames twist and dance. It was mesmerizing and she wondered how long she had been standing there, unseeing. She finally pulled herself away and sat. She wasn't sure she could face thinking on the events of the day, but she knew she had little choice. It was necessary to resolve a handful of things in her mind and putting that off wouldn't serve her.

She leaned her head back against the chair and sighed. One good thing to come of the day was that her assailant was dispatched. Anne looked down at her hands. Washing them had made them clean again, but she suspected it would take her longer than that to rid the memory of blood on them from her mind. Or the horror of knowing how close she had come to having Maude of Canfield's dagger in her back. Bless Robin for his quickness.

Yet at the same time, she couldn't help but pity the girl. How miserable she must have been to have found herself driven to such lengths. Anne wondered if she had loved Robin so deeply, or merely been furious that he had left her in his wake, as it were. Perhaps a little of both. All Anne knew was that at least now she might walk freely about the keep without having to look over her shoulder. Maude had perhaps earned her reward for her actions, and there was surely nothing Anne could do about it but to put it behind her and look forward.

It was in the looking forward, though, that she found her most vexing concern. Perhaps it did her no good to think on it, but she couldn't help but wonder if Robin would ever make her his wife in truth. He certainly hadn't sounded as if that were in his plans.

She smiled to herself. How greedy she had become. A month ago, it would have sufficed her merely to remain at Artane by whatever means available. Now that she was wed, she found she wanted more than just a place to lay her head. And it was Robin's fault. Had he never kissed her, never held her in his arms, never even for a brief moment become her safe haven, she never would have wanted more.

But she did.

She closed her eyes with a sigh. Perhaps there would come a time when he would be so starved for company that he would seek her out. Rhys, Gwen, their youngest children and her sire were already departed, so he would not have them to converse with. She suspected, though, that Robin was very thankful her sire had gone, even though he had departed complaining loudly about the condition of his nose. Anne couldn't help a small smile over that. She couldn't deny that he had deserved it. And she couldn't help but have warm feelings toward Robin for having done the deed.

If that wasn't defending her abused honor, she didn't know what was.

But that was something she would think on later.

Amanda, Nicholas and Miles had not gone with their parents. They were instead making for one of Nicholas's holdings nearby. The three of them got on perfectly and Anne almost envied them their companionship. They would likely enjoy themselves immensely.

She wondered if she would enjoy the next few days.

Not to mention the rest of her life.

The door opened behind her and Anne leaped up out of habit.

"Only me," Nicholas said with a smile. "You can be at ease now, remember?"

"It has been a less than leisurely day, my lord."

He shook his head. "Leave it to Robin to do things any way but the most simple. At least you can cease worrying about your safety. That should bring you some comfort. Well, as comfortable as you can be given that you're now Robin's wife."

"Nicky, I cannot jest about that," Anne said. "Truly, I cannot."

Nicholas dropped onto a trunk a pile of things contained in a sack. "Rob's gear," he said, then crossed the chamber to take Anne's hands. "Give him time. He's a bit thickheaded."

"I daresay time is what I have the most of," she said with a sigh.

Nicholas kissed her very chastely on the forehead. "Don't leave him out in the lists all day. It's raining and he'll mold. Either that or he'll rust and think on the complaining you'll need endure."

"I'm sure he'll come in eventually."

"And I'm just as certain he won't. The lad is possessed."

"By something foul, to be sure," Amanda said, coming into the chamber.

"Perhaps he'll find sense," Miles said, trailing her, "now that he's wed his ladylove."

Anne snorted. "I doubt I'm that."

Miles only nodded knowingly. "That and more, I daresay." He slung his arm around Amanda. "Think on us while you're residing here in comfort."

Anne looked at Nicholas. "You're for Wyckham?"

"Aye," Nicholas said. "I've a few repairs to make—"

"It has no roof," Amanda put in, wrinkling her nose. "Nor a decent garderobe, I'll wager."

Nicholas only smiled pleasantly. "Sunshine and a goodly amount of exercise taken while trudging to the forest to see to your unmentionable needs, sister. What more could you ask for?"

"A goose feather mattress and a decent meal or two."

"Which we will not have if Amanda's at the fire," Miles said affectionately. "The cooking will obviously fall to me."

"The saints preserve us," Amanda said, looking green again.

"I'll cook," Nicholas said with a sigh. "I'll put on the roof. I'll build you a cesspit to be the envy of all in the north, Amanda. Will that suit you?"

"I'll see your work, then judge."

Anne laughed in spite of herself. "And here I was envying you your little holiday together. Off with you, and pray send me word now and then that all three still breathe."

Nicholas made her a bow, then pulled his brother away. "Come with me, Miles, and let us see to our lady's baggage. I vow she intends to reside in comfort judging by the weight of it."

"I will not live in a tent," Amanda called after them. Then she turned to Anne and hugged her tightly. "I'm so sorry, Anne."

Anne shook her head. "Nay, all is well."

Amanda pulled back and raised her eyebrow. "You were wed with my father's sword bared, Robin's dead lover cooling at your feet, and Isabelle heaving her porridge into St. Gertrude's shrine. I imagine you could have wished for a better start to this than that."

" 'Tisn't the start that matters so much," Anne said, praying that was true. " 'Tis the finish that's important."

Amanda looked unconvinced. "Well, you have him, whether you will it or no. I wish you good luck of him. If he mistreats you, send word and I'll come thrash him for it."

"He won't."

"He's a clod, Anne. I know you love him, but I vow I can't understand why."

"Are you trying to help?" Anne asked in exasperation.

"Well, aye—"

"You aren't. Go. Enjoy your sunshine and bitter air. I'll pray it doesn't rain overmuch. Did you bring a cloak?"

"Nicky brought me one home from France. It will serve me well enough."

"Then off with you."

Amanda hugged her tightly, then ran from the chamber in a flurry of skirts. Anne followed her, closed the door and started to bolt it. Then she realized there was no need. But to think how close she had come to death. If Robin hadn't turned so quickly. If he hadn't saved her life . . .

She turned away from that thought and from what she'd seen that morn. Robin had wed her and given her the gift of Artane to enjoy for the rest of her life. Perhaps that would be enough.

She turned, leaned back against the door, and surveyed her domain. Gwen had bid her make free use of the chamber and vowed they would be gone for at least half a year. Anne suspected it wouldn't be that long, but still there was no sense in not making the chamber hers for the time she would have it. Once the unremarkable task of unpacking had been accomplished, she could turn her mind to other things.

Namely, how she would survive a life with Robin of Artane if he intended to spend all his time in the lists.

And then she would worry about why he apparently preferred the sport of his fellows to her company and what that boded for her marriage to him.

She pushed away from the door and turned her mind to her task. Her clothes had been brought for her and laid upon the bed. It took her little time to put them away, for she had left much behind at Fenwyck. Not as much as her sire would have liked at the time, but enough that she had precious little here to call her own.

Robin's gear was not much more. Anne opened his

sack and put his clothes into his father's trunk. He had no trinkets as such and she came close to folding up the rough linen bag when she realized there was something else inside it. She reached down and pulled out a battered wooden box.

And she wondered just what it might contain.

Her conscience warred with her curiosity. She shouldn't look. These were Robin's private things, things he likely wouldn't want anyone perusing.

But then again, they might give her some insight, some hint into the contents of his heart. Wasn't that reason enough to paw through them like a thief?

She got to her feet, quickly bolted the door, then retreated to the alcove. There was precious little light from the gray sky outside, so she fetched a candle. She set it a goodly ways away from the box, lest she set the contents on fire, took a deep breath and opened the lid.

Laying on top of everything else were four things she recognized immediately. Ribbons she herself had fashioned for Robin at various times in his life. The sight shocked her so, she could barely lift them out.

She looked at the first, a wide ribbon she had embroidered for Robin during his illness. She remembered vividly sitting by his side and listening to him tease her about her clumsy attempts. But it had been gentle teasing and he had accepted her finished gift with a grave smile and a hug that had almost broken her ribs. He had vowed he would never be without it. Later she had been certain he had been lying. Now, she knew he had been telling the truth.

The next three had been fashioned by more skillful hands. She had given them to him at his knighting, at his first tournament, when he had gone off on the crusade. To her knowledge, Robin had never worn any of them. But the ribbons before her told her a different tale.

She could hardly believe he had kept them.

She took the favor she had given him at his knighting and trailed her finger over his crest, over the black lion rampant with the aqua eyes. There were no scars on that one, though she could see even now where the knot had been tied to hold it around his arm.

The next ribbon was the one she had given him at the first tourney he'd attended after his knighting. She looked at one end of the ribbon. Those were not her stitches mending the thing and she could only surmise that Robin had done the honors himself. And that could only mean that somehow it had been cut from him. Perhaps he had it after all.

She took the last ribbon in her hands. There was hardly anything left of it. She remembered well how she had snuck into his chamber and left it for him on his pillow on the night before he'd left for the crusade. It looked as if he'd worn it continuously—or so she told herself. His clumsy stitches were all over it. The crest was unraveling and the ribbon was in shreds. But it was clean, as if it had been cared for tenderly.

Anne set the ribbons carefully aside, still so stunned by the finding of them in Robin's box that she could scarce see for the tears that threatened to spill down her cheeks.

She brushed them aside, though, for she had more to look at and little time in which to do it.

There was a letter there and she opened it without hesitation. And she found herself weeping in earnest at the words Gwen had written there, words of encouragement, words of love. It was no wonder Robin had kept it close.

She put it aside and pulled out a heavy silver ring, stamped with his crest. She remembered when Rhys had given it to him, though to her knowledge, Robin had never worn it.

She paused. Why was that?

She supposed that perhaps he might not wear it because it certainly couldn't be comfortable to wield a sword with a ring on his hand.

Or did it go deeper than that?

She held the ring up to the candlelight and looked at it thoughtfully. Did Robin not wear it because he didn't feel he had earned the right? His words in Rhys's solar came back to her. *Give it all to Miles, Father. Give him the title, your lands, your gold. Give it to your son of the flesh. Give him Anne while you're at it.*

Was that truly what he thought? She shook her head, marveling at his stupidity. Rhys could not possibly love a son more than he loved Robin. Nor could a son possibly look any more like his sire than Robin did Rhys. She wasn't sure how such a thing might have come about, but there was little doubt in her mind over it.

She shook her head and put aside the ring. Perhaps one day she would have the answer to that mystery, as would Robin, and he would be at peace.

Nestled in the bottom of the box was a heavy gem and Anne recognized it at once. Rhys had given it to Robin, desiring him to bind it into a sword. No doubt that gift resided herein for the same reason the ring did. She could almost hear Robin saying it.

This should go to a son of his flesh.

Anne stared out the window. Could Robin be Rhys's in truth? That would mean that Gwen and Rhys had lain together while Gwen was married to Alain of Ayre. How would Robin react if he were to learn he was actually Rhys's bastard son? By the saints, she didn't want to see the shouting match that would ensue from that. Nay, perhaps 'twas best she keep her suspicions to herself. Perhaps Rhys himself didn't know. Though how he could doubt it, she couldn't imagine. But souls were ofttimes blind— Rhys and Robin being perfect examples of the same.

She put aside the stone, read another pair of letters from Robin's parents, then paused. The last thing remaining was something wrapped in a bit of cloth. Slowly, she unwrapped the cloth and caught her breath.

It was a ring. Anne held it up to the light. It was the most beautiful green stone she had ever seen. The gold was so fair, it looked to be silver.

It was sized to fit a woman's hand.

Anne was so tempted to try it all that the impulse fair felled her on the spot.

But what if she tried it on and it didn't fit?

Or worse, it did?

She curled her fingers around it, brought it to her chest and closed her eyes. By the saints, this had been a poor idea. What had she been thinking to grope through his things? She deserved this. Nothing good ever came of eavesdropping and she could now add to that rummaging through one's husband's private things. She was a fool and she deserved the pain she'd just brought upon herself.

All the same, now she had come this far, there was no sense in not finishing the deed. She took the ring and slid it onto her finger, the finger that should have worn a betrothal ring.

It was too big.

But not by much. Better too big than too small, she conceded. Should such a thing have been for her, could it have been easier to have it made smaller or larger?

A pity she knew nothing of goldsmithing.

Before she could wallow any longer in her foolishness, she rewrapped the ring and placed everything back in the box as it had been—or as closely as she could remember. Perhaps if Robin thought she had been meddling, then he would shout at her and she could question him.

She placed the ribbons back carefully on the top and took small comfort in that. He had saved what she had given him. That was enough for her at present.

He had also wed her and saved her life, and the latter more than once. There were many reasons to have kind feelings for him. She put his box in his trunk, shut the lid and sat down upon it to give the morning's events further consideration.

Robin had surely been wounded by his father's doubt of him. Now that she looked back on what he'd said, he hadn't disparaged her. She suspected he'd felt a goodly amount of shame at his father's rebuke, especially given the fact that Robin hadn't been allowed to explain himself.

He would have taken that as a personal affront and she could only imagine how that would have angered him.

Or hurt him.

She turned that thought over in her mind for a goodly while. Aye, perhaps that was it. Perhaps he felt he'd been embarrassed in front of her and that distressed him. The thought of Robin of Artane being embarrassed on her account was so ridiculous she felt her cheeks begin to burn. She could hardly believe she was actually considering such a thing. By the saints, she was a simpleton. Her opinion could not possibly matter to him. His sire's, aye, but not hers.

She looked back over the events of the past fortnight, though, and she had to concede that he might have some affection for her. She suspected that if he'd been toying with her, he would have bedded her, not simply asked for a virginal kiss or two.

And there was her wedding to consider. Anne sighed deeply. It certainly wasn't how she had envisioned it, though now she wondered how she could have imagined anything else. Robin had defended her, wed her and clouted her father in the nose all within moments of each other.

Only Robin could have done the like.

And there was the look he'd given her once he'd deposited her inside the hall. She'd known he expected an answer of some sort regarding where she would sleep, but for the life of her she'd had none to give. She had assumed she would sleep with him, though she'd certainly avoided thinking on consummating their marriage.

She frowned. Was it that he had no intention of doing the like?

She sighed and shook her head. There was nothing to be done but see to dinner, drag Robin in from the lists and hope that things sorted themselves out in time. With everyone gone, they would have no one to distract them. It might happen that they would be so desperate for conversation that they might speak to each other and then who knew what might happen?

Anne rose and left the bedchamber. She saw to supper, blessing Gwen for having taught her so well that the servants honored her requests without question. At least in this aspect of being Robin's wife she would succeed.

She put her cloak on and made her way out to the lists. It was dark and a substantial rain was falling. Anne walked carefully over the slippery ground, holding her skirts up well out of the mud. She'd changed her gown for something less blood-spattered and it was almost all she had to wear unless she filched something of Gwen's.

And then without warning, she ran bodily into someone.

She jerked back with a cry only to find herself facing Edith of Sedgwick. Anne looked at her in surprise.

"Edith?" she asked. "Are you unwell?"

Edith only stared at her in such an unsettling manner that Anne almost turned and ran. The woman was dripping wet, as if she'd been standing out in the rain for the whole of the afternoon. Her face was haggard, her eyes empty and her cloak askew on her shoulders. Indeed, she looked as if she'd suffered a great tragedy of some kind.

"Edith," Anne repeated. "Are you unwell?"

Edith shivered once, violently, then blinked and looked at Anne.

Or looked through her, rather.

Without another word, Edith stepped around her and started back toward the great hall. Anne didn't wait to watch and assure herself the other woman had reached her goal. She hiked up her skirts and hastened to the lists as quickly as she could. Would that Rhys and Gwen had taken Edith along with them.

She saw the light of a torch in the distance and felt relief flood her at the sight. It took her little time to join Jason under a wooden shelter that rested against the outside of the inner bailey wall. He was shivering and the torchlight flickered as a result. He made her a low bow.

"My lady," he said, straightening and frowning at her. "What do you outside in this weather?"

She shook off the unease that Edith had inspired in her. "What do you think I'm doing?" she asked dryly. "Someone has to fetch him in for supper." She looked out into the gloom. "Where is he?"

It looked as if all the men had gone in, for there was no one there. And then she caught sight of a figure running in the distance, keeping close to the wall. She'd seen Robin running about in such a fashion more than once, but usually only after he'd finished off his own men and there was no sport left for him. But that had generally been in dry weather. She could hardly believe he was doing such a thing when the chances of him landing facedown in the mud were very good indeed.

"He won't come in," Jason said, sounding as if he very much wished Robin would.

Anne glanced at Jason to find he looked miserably uncomfortable, and it looked as if his discomfort didn't come completely from the rain. "What ails you, Jason?" she asked.

"I'm sorry," he said hesitantly. "I know it isn't my place to apologize for my master, but he should be inside with you. I tried to speak to him about it, but he flicked my ear most vigorously and bid me be silent."

Anne looked at Jason for a moment, then turned to watch Robin thoughtfully. A day ago she might have been terribly hurt to think he would rather be in the lists than at her side. She likely would have either cursed him and hardened her heart, or she would have retreated to her chamber and wept.

But now things were different. She'd had a peek into his heart. She suspected that Robin was doing his damndest to outrun his demons.

Well, he could run until he dropped, but it wouldn't change a thing for him. Perhaps in time he would come to realize that. But it was his realization to make. All she could do until then was try to keep him fed so he would have the strength to keep running.

She watched him continue to make his way around the lists toward her and Jason. He came to a halt before her, then leaned over with his hands on his thighs and sucked in great gulps of air.

"What . . . do you . . . here?" he wheezed. "You'll catch . . . your death."

Anne pursed her lips, unimpressed. "Come inside and eat."

He straightened. "I'm not . . . finished."

"You are for the moment. You are welcome to return after I've seen you fed."

He looked at her, his eyes inscrutable in the torchlight. His hair was dripping into his eyes and his surcoat clung to his chain mail. Anne wondered if Nicholas had it aright and Robin would actually rust. What she did know, however, was that Robin looked a bit like a drowned rodent of some sort and he was the one who would catch his death if he didn't come inside and warm up.

The other thing she noticed was that he wasn't arguing with her. He was merely watching her as if he couldn't understand why she was there. Was he so surprised, then, that she would come to fetch him? That made her pause. Perhaps she would be unwise to act on her newfound knowledge of him. Would she be better served to be aloof?

She shook her head, wondering if perhaps standing outside was beginning to turn her common sense to mush. She would not resort to foolish games. She would treat Robin with respect and courtesy. If he at some point decided to unveil his heart to her, she would accept it gracefully.

And if he never did the like, she would accept that as well—though perhaps not as gracefully.

It was enough to know he had kept her ribbons. He had cared for her gently over the past fortnight. He had wed her that morn. She suspected that not even his father could have forced him had Robin been truly determined not to.

But she wouldn't make the first move. That was for Robin to do.

He pushed his hair back from his face and frowned. "A small meal. Then I'll return."

And then, miracle of miracles, he offered her his arm. Anne accepted, ignoring the water that began to pool in her sleeve and the way her slippers squished in the mud. She had won a victory and she had nothing to complain about.

"A meal." Jason sighed happily from behind them.

Anne smothered her smile and walked on.

29

Edith of Sedgwick stood in the tower chamber, perfectly still despite her garments, which were soaked through to her skin. She would not shiver. It was a weakness and she would tolerate no weakness, neither in herself nor others.

Perhaps 'twas a good thing Maude was dead.

She had watched Lord Rhys carry the body off with him on his journeys. She imagined that Canfield wouldn't care much about his daughter's death. She'd been a plague to him for quite some time. And no one would blame Robin. It had been a matter of defense.

Which led her thoughts in a new direction.

Having a legitimate reason for murder was never a poor thing.

The door opened and slammed shut behind her, sending her candle flame flickering wildly.

"Can you believe it?" a voice exclaimed.

Edith closed her eyes and reached down deep inside herself for patience. It was all she could do not to turn on her brother. Was he such a fool he couldn't see how Maude's death had fouled her plans?

"He took all his bloody children with him!" Baldwin exclaimed.

Edith had cursed over that bit of misfortune as well. First Maude running amok and now Artane having taken Edith's other potential victims with him.

It had not been a productive day.

"And why did he leave the eldest three behind?" Baldwin demanded. "How does that serve me?"

"They didn't stay," Edith said. "Off to Wyckham, I believe."

"How am I to wed with Amanda, now that Robin has wed with Anne?" Baldwin spoke as if he hadn't heard her, which, knowing him, he likely hadn't.

Edith pursed her lips. "Mayhap you can—"

"My prey," Baldwin interrupted, looking as baffled as if a fox had suddenly slipped from under his nose. "They're gone!"

"Surely you can track them."

He blinked, then began to pace—never a good sign. Edith sighed and waited for him to spew some other bit of rot.

"I'll track them," he announced suddenly.

"You'll need help," Edith suggested.

"Ah," he said, nodding, "of course. That can be hired." He resumed his pacing. "I'll see to Rhys and the brood he has with him, then turn my sights to Wyckham."

Edith sincerely doubted he would find Rhys and his brood unattended enough for slaying. They would likely ensconce themselves in Fenwyck for a goodly time. And Rhys was no fool. He'd been a mercenary himself in his day, and his family was full of spies for the French king. If anyone could escape Baldwin's clumsy attempts at murder, it would be Rhys. Likely half-asleep and well into his cups even.

But seeking lads to aid him would keep Baldwin occupied and that was not something to be dismissed lightly. Edith listened to him plot and scheme, encouraged him when needed, then watched him leave all in a bluster.

And then she turned her attentions back to her own dilemma.

Her own plans were ruined.

Ruined.

Someone would have to pay for that.

She suspected she would have little trouble deciding upon whom.

30

Joanna of Segrave swept into Artane's great hall at sunrise, happy to be off her horse and more than happy to be at her journey's end. She pointed her cook toward the kitchen entrance and sent him off with instructions to make the best of things. Though Gwen and Rhys set a fine enough table, Joanna was not prepared to settle for anything marginal at supper. She had work to do and no time to worry about trivialities such as the condition of her daughter's larder.

The hall was oddly quiet and it puzzled her until she made her way to the lord's table. One weary soul slept with his face mashed against the wood. His squire kept him company, his own head lolling back against his chair, his mouth wide open to accommodate his snores.

Joanna lifted the first's head by his hair and was greeted by the sight of bleary gray eyes.

"Are you drunk?" she asked bluntly.

"Grandmère," the man said with a sweet smile. "How lovely . . ."

Joanna let his head resume its resting place with a none-too-gentle thump. "Robin, where is your bride?"

"Hmmm," Robin said, smacking his lips a time or two and then drifting back off to slumber.

Joanna slapped the table with both hands hard enough to make Robin's squire choke on his snorts and throw himself suddenly to his feet. Robin only continued to sleep on blissfully. Joanna fixed Jason with a steely glance.

"Have you answers for this, lad?"

"He trained until but a few hours ago, my lady," Jason said, snapping to attention.

"And his bride?"

"She allowed it."

Apparently there was more to the tale than she could divine at first glance. Joanna looked at Robin's squire, then at Robin, then she considered.

Once she had heard Robin had returned to Artane, she had immediately decided to take up her journey north. 'Twas far past time the boy was wed and she had been determined to see it happen. Though she had never taken part in such matchmaking in the past, she had decided perhaps it was a new vocation to pursue. She had been blessed with a love match in her youth and had mourned her late husband for years. She had watched her daughter have her own long years of difficulty while waiting for her marriage to Rhys de Piaget to come about. Joanna had waited for Robin to come to his senses for too long.

She had encountered her daughter the evening before on the road to Fenwyck and a hasty retelling of the past fortnight's events had left Joanna no less determined to see Robin happily settled. Anne deserved to be properly wooed and it was a certainty that Robin didn't have the skill to do it on his own. It was a grandmère's duty to see to that education, especially when that grandmère was so immeasurably suited to the task.

It was for that reason that she had brought a score of souls possessing various talents related to the art of life at court. If Robin couldn't learn to behave with those bodies as his instructors, then the boy was truly hopeless and

Joanna would have no choice but to leave him to his own devices.

And pity Anne for it.

And if she waited much longer to begin her labors, she would have no great-grandchildren to fuss over before she found herself in her own grave. The time for action had come.

"A bucket of water, young Ayre," Joanna commanded.

Jason's eyes widened quite dramatically. "But, my lady—"

"You're a quick lad to see my purpose," Joanna said. "Be even quicker about fetching me what I need."

Jason gulped and nodded, though it was done none-too-enthusiastically. Joanna watched him fight his way through the gaggle of souls who currently sought to gain entrance into the hall at the same time. She looked over her little flock and was pleased with what she saw. These were various and sundry souls who had wound up at her keep for equally various and sundry reasons, not the least of which was her fondness of all things refined. That and, she supposed, the quality of the meals her kitchen had consistently produced since shortly after she had become mistress of Segrave. Whatever the true reason, she had amassed a following of impressive proportions and each man a master at his craft.

And now young Robin was about to have their expertise distilled upon his poor, unchivalrous self.

Whether he willed it or no.

The noise in the hall had become almost impossible to speak and be heard over. No matter. She had no intention of shouting to wake her grandson. She waited patiently until Jason returned with his heavy bucket of water. Then she gestured pointedly at Robin.

"Douse him," she commanded.

Jason looked as miserable as if she'd commanded him to plunge a blade through Robin's heart. "But, Lady Joanna . . ."

"I'll tell him 'twas my idea."

"Forgive me, my lady, but that won't matter."

Joanna searched her wits for something that would mo-
tivate the lad, short of having her guards poke him with
their swords. She'd known countless men over the years
who had been swayed by their bellies, but she suspected
Robin inspired a loyalty in Jason that not even a decent
meal could influence.

That, she decided, was a point in Robin's favor.

She tried another course. "Jason, the sooner he wakes,
the sooner he can be taught the ways to win over his
lady."

"My lady?"

"Chivalry training, Jason. I've brought his teachers with
me."

Jason looked over his shoulder and his eyes widened.
"Them?" he squeaked.

"And none other," she said. "Now, wake him please,
and let's get on with this."

Jason shook his head, took a deep breath and pulled
back the bucket. "He won't like it, my lady."

"They never do, my lad."

Jason closed his eyes, blurted out a heartfelt prayer,
then he took a deep breath and let fly the water. Robin
leaped to his feet with a howl. Joanna found the bucket
thrust into her hands and Jason under the table before she
could protest. Robin had his sword drawn and looked as
if he planned to kill the first person he clapped eyes on.
But since that person was her, she merely smiled pleasantly at him.

"A good morrow to you, grandson," she said, setting
the bucket down on the table.

He stood there and spluttered for several moments, then
realization apparently began to dawn. She watched his
fury battle with his respect for her. It was very engaging
and she did her best not to laugh at him. Finally, he swallowed his ire and made her a low bow.

"Grandmère," he said. "Forgive me for not being at my
best this morn to greet you."

She waved away his words. " 'Tis nothing, Robin, my love."

"How lovely of you to visit," he continued.

"I'm not here to loiter without a purpose," she said. "I've come to work."

"Work?" he echoed in horror. "You?"

"Aye," she said calmly. "I've a task to see accomplished."

"And that would be?"

She waved expansively to her little flock behind her. "Why, your civilizing, of course."

He was speechless. Joanna smiled in satisfaction.

Perhaps this wouldn't be as difficult as she feared.

31

Robin stood behind his father's table and stared in horror at the souls that now filled his father's hall. Minstrels and various other artistic sorts, the lot of them. If Robin hadn't been so weary, he would have fled to his father's solar and bolted himself inside for the duration. Not even a man of the staunchest courage could face that rabble and not feel a bit anxious.

"Ah," his grandmother said in satisfaction, "there is your lady. Anne, my dear, how fare you?"

Robin looked to his left to see Anne coming down the last pair of steps into the great hall. He wondered absently how much of the proceeding madness she had been privy to. And he realized in an instant just how laughable he appeared, standing there drenched and gaping.

"Lady Joanna," Anne said, coming around the table and taking his grandmother's hands. "How lovely to see you. I see you brought your courtiers."

Joanna laughed. "You flatter an old woman, love. I'm hardly holding court, but you know I can't bear to be away from my little pleasures for long."

"I'm sure we'll enjoy them as well," Anne said.

No doubt, Robin thought sourly. Anne wasn't the one

Joanna intended to torment with the louts. He could well imagine what his grandmother had in mind for him, for he had spent a goodly amount of time at her hall and seen the goings on there. But he'd be damned if she would turn him into one of the perfumed peacocks strutting before him now.

Though he had the feeling, judging by the look in his grandmother's eye, that that was precisely what she had in mind.

He suspected that he had just lost control of his own fate.

"You'll need chambers," Anne said. "You are welcome to take Lord Rhys's finest, of course—"

"She is not," Robin said, turning to look at Anne in astonishment. He turned to look at his grandmother. "The girls' chamber is in fine shape."

Joanna only waved a hand negligently. "As you will, Robin. We can see ourselves settled. Perhaps you have things to see to?"

Robin felt her pointed gaze sweep him from head to toe. He scowled at her. By the saints, he wasn't the one who had put himself in this drenched state!

"I need to train," Robin said.

"Didn't you just finish training?" Joanna asked.

Robin frowned. She would have him cornered if he weren't careful. "A man cannot train too much," he said firmly. She could hardly argue with that.

"Surely," his grandmother said just as firmly, "there are many things you must see to *inside* the hall. Though you would no doubt know much more about the manly workings of a keep than I."

Robin snorted before he could help himself. His grandmother had managed Segrave alone for well over a score of years—and managed to keep herself free of the various suitors who considered her a fine widowly prize. Hell, she could likely run the entire realm without perspiring. At over three score years, she was a formidable woman with an iron will.

But Robin was, after all, her grandson and a goodly amount of that wily blood flowed through his veins as well. He leaned on the table and gave her his most disarming smile. He didn't use it much, but he knew it was effective.

"I should at least see to my men," he said. "I won't neglect you, Grandmère."

"It isn't me I'm concerned with," she said, leaning on her side of the table and putting her still very beautiful visage close to his. She lowered her voice to a whisper. "You are freshly wed, my boy, are you not?"

He scowled at her. " 'Tis a marriage fraught with complications, my lady."

"Then you'd best be at the unraveling of them straightway, don't you think?"

"When I think, Grandmère, I always find myself in trouble."

His grandmother laughed, put her arm around his neck and kissed him on the cheek. "Ah, Robin, my love, I have missed you. Go be about your play, then come indulge me in a bit of conversation. I can see we've much to discuss."

And he could see by the purposeful glint in her eye— her sweet words aside—that his reprieve would be short-lived at best. So he grunted at her, fixed his squire with a pointed look, then started around the end of the table.

Only to come face-to-face with his bride.

It wasn't that he had forgotten she was there. It was, well, it was that he had forgotten that she was his. Yet as he stood there like a half-wit and gaped at her, he wondered how he could have lost sight of such a thing.

She looked disgustingly well-rested. Serene even. She certainly didn't look like a maid who had spent her wedding night alone, sobbing into her pillow because of it.

"You slept well?" he asked, because he could think of nothing else to say.

"Well enough," she replied, looking up at him solemnly. "You, my lord, have table marks still in your cheek."

He scrambled for an explanation. "I didn't want to wake you," he said, feeling very quick on his feet considering the amount of sleep he'd had.

Anne only smiled a small, gentle smile in return. "I'll have a meal ready for you after you've finished in the lists, if you like."

Robin frowned at her. Was she seeking to feed him to death? He wondered, absently, why she wasn't shouting at him for having left her alone. Unless, of course, she was relieved about that. Though she didn't look all that relieved. She looked, well, serene.

It was enough to set his teeth on edge.

A meal from his lady, then tortures from his grandmother to endure. It wasn't much of a day to look forward to. Mayhap he would be better off to hide in bed.

But nay, Anne would fetch him. For all he knew, his grandmother's minstrels would come fetch him and he wasn't sure he could bear the humiliation of that.

The lists. He clung to that thought with his last shreds of dignity. He grunted at his lady as he set her aside and walked away. He heard Jason fall into step behind him. Joanna's gaggle of artists scattered before him like frail leaves blown by a fierce wind.

"Ah, Anne my love, how good it is to see you," came floating along behind him and Robin suppressed a shudder. The saints only knew what havoc his grandmother would combine upon his wife.

He paused at the door, wondering if he should perhaps separate the two for the morn. He looked over his shoulder and cursed. Too late. His grandmother had already swept his wife up and was propelling her toward the stairs. He had no doubts they would barricade themselves in one of the solars for the saints only knew what kind of conversation. He stroked his chin thoughtfully. With any luck at all, it might be conversation that included him. Favorably.

Then again, it might not.

He might have had Anne's hand, true, but he wasn't certain he had her heart.

Was it too late to win that?

He looked about him at the supposed masters of various arts and found himself scowling in spite of himself. He was to find himself aided by these? Peacocks, the lot of them.

He left the hall before he did them any damage. After all, they might have a suggestion or two he could use. It was possible.

But he doubted it was very likely.

With one thing and another, it was late in the afternoon before he managed to get himself inside the hall again. Preparations were just being made for supper and Robin looked forward to a hearty meal. Things certainly smelled good. Perhaps one of his grandmother's lads had been hard at work. Robin followed his nose, which led him in a straight path back to the kitchen, only to find his way blocked by a stout figure of a man holding a cooking implement of some kind as if he intended to do damage with it. Robin stopped and folded his arms across his chest in his most intimidating pose.

"Move," he said without preamble.

The cook bristled. "The lady Joanna commands that you attend her in the lord's solar."

Robin pursed his lips, but decided that it was passing unfair to cut down a man who thought so highly of a wooden spoon, and likely wielded it with the same enthusiasm. Who knew what he would find at his place if he offended the man? He'd heard of souls receiving very unpalatable servings at his grandmother's table for naught but a look askance. Who knew what sorts of nasty tidbits bloodshed might bring him?

So Robin, who never backed away from a fight or found himself intimidated by another soul, stepped back and conceded the battle. He could do nothing less for the sake of his poor belly.

He made his way to his father's solar, sighing heavily with every few paces. He paused before the door, took a deep breath and prayed he could control his temper. He suspected that even though he had forborne slaying his grandmother's cook, he might not have that counted in his favor if he decimated the rest of her entourage.

He opened the door and peeked inside.

It was worse than he had feared.

His sire would have come undone had he been privy to this sight. Every available surface was covered with either cloth, baubles or his grandmother's *artistes*. And, worse yet, all eyes were turned his way.

Robin toyed with the idea of escape, but he suspected that the delicate souls before him were no doubt very fleet of foot. The humiliation of being chased down by his grandmother's minstrels and such was just more than Robin could contemplate. So he took another deep breath, let it out slowly, then entered the chamber.

The door was shut behind him and bolted. Immediately.

"Ah, Robin," his grandmother said, smiling what he could only assume she believed to be a disarming smile at him. "We have been anxiously awaiting your arrival."

"No doubt," Robin said as sternly as possible. Best to begin as he intended to finish—with some shred of dignity remaining him.

"Our first task," she continued just as pleasantly, "is to see you properly groomed and dressed." She gestured expansively to a tub set before the hearth. "In there, if you please."

Robin grumbled but didn't argue. There was little harm to be found in a bath now and then, despite what some thought about the perils of soaking in water. And Robin had to admit that there was something almost comforting about having his grandmother wash his hair for him— something he was certain she hadn't done in years.

But once his head was free of the soap and he had

shaken the water out of his ears, he noticed the murmuring going on directly behind him.

"I say we cut it."

"Nay," another said thoughtfully, " 'tis goodly hair."

"Unfashionably long, though."

"Perhaps it could be trimmed here and there," offered another.

"Nay, cut away a goodly amount," insisted the first. "Don't you agree, my lady?"

"I defer to your expertise, Reynaud," Joanna said blithely. "Lads, be prepared to hold him down if he fights."

Robin struggled to turn around and fix his would-be-assaulters with a glare. "I don't want my hair cut."

The three looked at him as if he were a new breed of vermin they must needs eradicate or face a lifetime of misery otherwise.

"Cut it," Joanna commanded.

"I like it long!" Robin exclaimed.

One of the three came at him with a knife and Robin looked about him frantically for a weapon. He caught sight of his gear—safely tucked behind his grandmother's slender form. And then he found himself ringed by a collection of men whom he likely could have dispatched with his bare hands alone.

Then again, maybe not. He looked at them and found in the group a lad or two with a glint in his eye that spoke of ample time spent in places much less civilized than Segrave's great hall. Robin sank back into the tub in a wary crouch.

"Very well, then," he said. "But I'll not have my head bared as these fools in court do." He clutched the sides of the tub. "Not too short," he repeated.

The knife began its foul work and Robin closed his eyes. There was no sense in watching his poor hair falling about him in ignominious heaps.

After that torture was over, he was instructed to rise. He didn't dare touch his head for fear of what he wouldn't find there any longer. So he dried himself off, then allowed himself to be dressed. The clothing was fine—even he had to admit that, though he did it in the sternest manner possible. There was no sense in allowing his grandmother to think she could do with him as she liked.

But then some lout or other approached him with footwear. Robin gaped at the toes of the dainty shoes.

"What is that foul protrusion?" he demanded, pointing a shaking finger at the same.

"The latest fashion from Paris," the shoe bearer said, fondling the toe with a rapturous sigh. "Lovely, isn't it?"

It was without a doubt the silliest thing Robin had ever seen and he could hardly believe these dolts intended that he should wear the like on his feet. His were manly feet that demanded boots that could withstand mud and dung and all manner of manly elements. He sincerely doubted that he could cross the rushes in these without falling straightway upon his arse. And, given his luck of late, he would likely impale his eye upon the toe of his shoe in the process!

"Absolutely not," Robin said, folding his arms.

Several daggers appeared out of voluminous sleeves and his grandmother cleared her throat meaningfully.

"Damnation," Robin snarled as he surrendered his feet to a humiliation they had never before had to endure. It did not bode well for the rest of the evening.

But when two seamstresses materialized from the crowd and came at him with baubles, needles and thread, Robin knew action had to be taken.

"You will not," he said to the two women, giving them his most formidable glare, "attach those to my clothes. Absolutely not. Never. I refuse and resist."

"Tie him down," his grandmother said with a sigh.

"What?" Robin screeched. He listened to himself and could hardly believe the sound was coming from him. He never screeched. He bellowed. He snarled. He commanded legions with a mere shout alone. Yet look what pointy-toed shoes and shorn hair had reduced him to.

And then before he could reconcile himself to the fact that his grandmother had indeed been in earnest, he found himself overpowered, overwhelmed and overcome. The wave of mankind receded and Robin found himself in a chair. Tied to it, actually, and completely unable to move. He glared at his grandmother.

"If you think—"

"I think you wish to win your lady," his grandmother said shortly, "and we are here to help you do it. The sooner your lessons are done, the sooner she will be yours. Is that not what you want?"

Robin scowled, but said nothing. He gave his grandmother a short nod and closed his eyes as he felt his clothing being attacked. Perhaps she had it aright and what he needed to win Anne was a little civilizing. Perhaps she would see him dressed as a fine lord and take a liking to him.

Assuming she didn't laugh herself into a faint first.

"Feathers now," Joanna instructed. "And don't be shy, mistresses. He has many appearances of less-than-lordly stature to make up for."

Robin snarled out a curse, but that was the best he could do.

The saints only knew what Anne would think when she saw him.

32

Anne sat at a table in the healer's house and contemplated two things. One was that she actually had the freedom to sit in peace without wondering when a stray knife might find itself between her ribs. The other was the sight of the herbs lying in bunches before her. She recognized most of them, but that wasn't because she'd studied them diligently. She'd had them used on her so often during her convalescence that she could recognize most by smell alone.

That was not necessarily a pleasant skill to have.

"Rose," Master Erneis said, gesturing with a slender finger.

"Aye," Anne said absently. "I know."

"Good for several things, though I daresay the lady Gwennelyn has them for beauty alone. These come from well-established plants."

"They were laid along with the stone for the keep," Anne said.

"Long before my time," he offered. "I daresay Mistress Berengaria saw them planted though."

Anne smiled at his tone of reverence. She couldn't help but agree with him. Berengaria had been Artane's first healer, and the one who had seen Anne through her troubles. There had been a great many times when Anne had wondered if Berengaria had been adding something extra to her brews, though Anne couldn't have said what. Her hands had been steady, her knowledge of herblore ample and her gentleness a soothing balm. Anne had grieved mightily when Berengaria had found Erneis and brought him to Artane to train him in her skills so she might make her way in the world, but it hadn't been for Anne to say who should go or stay.

Master Erneis, however, seemed even now to labor under the woman's shadow. Anne couldn't fault his knowledge, though, or his skill. But he was, after all, just a man. Anne wondered mightily if Berengaria might have possessed a few skills that no simple healer should have.

"My lady?"

Anne blinked, then shook her head. "Forgive me. My mind wanders." She turned her attentions fully back to the table. Now that she was the lady of Artane, if only for a little while, it would behoove her to know more about the healing arts. That was why she had ignored her discomfort over the idea, forced herself to cross that courtyard with its smooth stone, and presented herself at the healer's house for a lesson.

Even though the smell was less than pleasant.

The door opened behind her and Anne couldn't help but feel a bit of relief over a possible reprieve. She looked behind her only to find Edith standing there. And in spite of herself, she shivered.

"Cold, my lady?" Erneis asked.

Anne shook her head. "Hungry perhaps. I should likely see to dinner inside. Thank you for your aid—"

She would have said more, but she caught a flash of silver and turned just in time to see Edith producing a blade from somewhere on her person. Anne shrieked, then watched the blade as it flew.

It pinned a rat to the floor.

Edith look at her with puzzlement. "My lady?"

"Nothing," Anne rasped. "I'm overwrought."

"I'll walk back with you—"

Anne held up her hand. "Nay, Edith, but I thank you most kindly for the offer. I wouldn't want to interrupt your business here."

And with that, she moved as quickly as possible to the door and out into the fresh air. Once there, she lifted her face and looked into the late afternoon sky.

By the saints, she didn't trust that woman.

"Lady Anne?"

Anne blinked, then saw Jason standing before her. She smiled in relief. Now that Jason was there, all would be well. Anne took his arm.

"The saints be praised," she said with feeling as they walked slowly. "Would that you had come hours ago while I was captive in the solar."

"Captive, my lady?"

"Joanna bade me stay until she had finished her work with your master. I vow if I'd had to put another stitch in a tunic, I would have gone mad. 'Tis only recently that I've escaped her."

Jason cleared his throat, a bit uncomfortably to her ears. "I daresay, my lady, that my lord has the same feeling."

Anne looked at him and smiled. "A difficult afternoon for him?"

"If he appears for supper, 'twill be nothing short of a miracle," Jason predicted.

"What could the lady Joanna possibly have done to him?" Anne asked in surprise.

"I couldn't begin to describe it," Jason said. "I'll leave it to you to see the results."

Anne kept her curiosity under control and ascended the steps carefully to the great hall. She watched her feet as she crossed to the hearth, lest she trip and take Jason down with her. He stopped and she stopped with him. She raised her head.

It was all she could do not to gasp.

Well, it was certainly Robin, but it was a Robin she had never seen before. She now understood what Jason had meant by stitches in tunics.

Never in her life had she seen a shirt so adorned with buttons, ribbons and—this she could hardly believe—feathers. Anne looked down and marveled at the pointed toes of his shoes. She could scarce believe Joanna had convinced him to put them on. She worked her way up past the hose, back up past the bedecked tunic and up to meet Robin's scowl. She couldn't tell if he was resigned or furious. She suspected it might be a bit of both.

Then there was his hair. It was substantially shorter, and Robin continually pulled on it, as if by doing so he could restore some of its length. One thing it did was reveal his ears, which she was certain she had never seen.

They were, she had to admit on closer inspection, perhaps ears that were better left under hair. They resembled his mother's a great deal and such substantial protrusions were her bane.

And then a most startling realization struck her.

He was wooing her.

His grandmother had laid out in great detail her plans to civilize Robin, once she had poked and prodded enough to learn that Anne wasn't praying for an annulment. Anne had listened politely, certain Robin would never, *ever* allow himself to be dressed up like a pampered lord at court.

Yet apparently he had.

For her.

Had she ever had any desire to laugh, it disappeared at the dangerous glint in his eye. She suspected that if she even came close to any expression of mirth, she would never be forgiven for it. So she put on the most serious look she could muster and moved to stand near him.

And then she sneezed.

Robin's look of irritation had turned to faint alarm. She watched him sniff about his person anxiously. He wrinkled his nose at what he found, but shrugged it off. He turned to her and made her a low bow, sending another waft of perfume her way.

She sneezed thrice in rapid, uncomfortable succession.

"Something in the hearth," she said quickly, waving her hand in front of her face. "Bad wood."

Robin's look of dismay didn't diminish much, but at least he wasn't making any more sniffing forays in his immediate vicinity.

And then the hall began to fill with garrison knights and the like, come to partake of their evening meal. Anne watched them catch sight of Robin and prayed—for their sakes—that they did not giggle.

Robin's men, who either had been trained very well or were so battle-hardened that they were no longer surprised by anything, marched in and took their places happily at one of the lower tables. Rhys's men, ones who were either less well-trained in keeping their thoughts to themselves or had just rotated in for their yearly service, stopped so suddenly in the middle of the hall that they formed a knot of men who were suddenly staggering about, trying to keep their feet.

Robin's expression darkened considerably.

The gaping turned to grinning on some faces and Anne had the feeling those men would pay dearly for their sport at Robin's expense. Robin gave her a curt nod before he strode across the rushes and stopped but a hand's breadth before the foremost man.

"Something amuses you?" Robin demanded.

"Nay, my lord," the man said, but he was unsuccessful in wiping the smile completely from his face.

Robin looked at the rest of the men gathered there. "Anyone else unable to repress their chuckles? Ah, I see a few lads here who find something to tickle them."

"The feathers on your tunic, my lord," one of the men said with a guffaw.

Robin found that man, put his arm around his shoulders and led him to the other lower table. He beckoned to the other men and bade them sit as well.

Anne suppressed a shudder.

"Enjoy your meal," Robin said, patting the shoulder of the first man he'd seated. "Then meet me in the lists."

There was a small chorus of ready ayes. Robin walked back to the hearth a satisfied smile on his face. He made Anne a low bow.

"My lady?"

She could hardly contain her surprise. "You aren't going to kill them?"

Robin shot his grandmother a quick look and Anne turned in time to see her sharp shake of the head. He sighed.

"Apparently not. But fortunately my sire has a fine healer. I imagine he'll be busy with much stitching tonight."

"Robin," Lady Joanna warned.

"Maiming, Grandmère," Robin growled. "I promised no death, did I not? But that doesn't mean they can't be taught a lesson in respect."

Clearly someone had informed the most outspoken of the lads of Robin's reputation because there was a groan and thump as one man fell backward off the bench and cracked his head soundly against the floor under the rushes. Robin merely raised his eyebrow and offered Anne his arm.

She took it, wondering absently just how Robin intended to teach anyone any lessons in the lists while wearing those shoes. He barely made it to the table without pitching forward half a dozen times.

She soon found herself on his right while his grandmother sat on his left. As she smothered a sneeze and began fanning away as surreptitiously as possible Robin's perfume, she suspected that this might be one of the longest meals of both their lives.

"Ah, food," he said as the dishes appeared before him. He placed his trencher directly before him and began piling a goodly amount of food atop it.

"Robin," his grandmother whispered fiercely, "what do you?"

Robin's sigh fair blew over his wine goblet. "I'm eating. I'm allowed to do that, am I not?"

He pulled off a huge piece of the trencher as well, and managed to get it most of the way to his mouth before aged, bony fingers came to rest on his arm. *Rest* was, perhaps, not the word for it. Anne watched in fascination as Joanna slapped her fingers on Robin's arm and jerked it down.

Anne watched Robin turn to look at his grandmother. Joanna was making motions that he should replace the bread. Robin shook his head forcefully enough to send several feathers on his shirt flapping. His grandmother whispered something to him in urgent undertones. Robin cursed, then put the bread back on the table and made an attempt to rejoin it with the mangled trencher.

His grandmother began to sigh.

"What have I done now?" Robin demanded.

"Share your trencher with Anne, Robin," Joanna exclaimed. "By the saints, boy, where have you been dining the past few years? At a trough?"

Robin grunted, but said nothing.

Anne soon found the trencher closer to her than it had been, but not by much. Robin almost managed to eat something, but he was again thwarted.

"The best pieces go to her."

"Grandmère, I am fair starved to faintness!" Robin exclaimed.

"That doesn't matter."

"It matters to me!"

"What should matter to you, grandson, are your manners!"

Robin growled, then snatched a goblet and drank before he could be stopped.

"Wipe off where you've sipped, then offer it to your lady."

Robin took the cloth that covered the table, wiped the

rim of the cup, then began to wipe the rest.

"Best remove all my traces," he grumbled. He then offered it to Anne with a scowl. "It would seem, my lady, that 'tis only *now* the cup is fit to drink from."

Anne raised the cup to her lips, then couldn't control the hearty sneeze she left lingering in said cup. Robin pursed his lips at her, then looked at his grandmother.

"What now, O Wisest of Advisors?"

A sharp slap to the back of his head left him hunching down over his half of the trencher. Anne couldn't blame him. Between the perfume that emanated from his person and the feather that seemed to be protruding from his shoulder and lingering beneath her nose, it was all she could do to down anything at all for her sneezes. She had to admit it was with a sense of relief that the end of the meal came. Robin seemed to be just as relieved. He shoved his chair back from the table without hesitation the very moment he was allowed to.

"Jason!" he bellowed. "My boots!"

He stood, ripped off the tunic he wore, scattering feathers, buttons and assorted other baubles across the table and floor. Several of Joanna's following gasped in horror and leaped up to rescue their work. Robin sat down, jerked off his shoes and flung them across the great hall as well. Anne could have sworn one of Joanna's lads began to weep.

Robin stood up with a purposeful clearing of his throat. Mail was brought and donned. He turned and Anne found her hand grasped in his. He leaned over, then was stopped by his grandmother's hand on his shoulder.

"You don't kiss," she said.

Robin turned and gaped at her. "What?"

"Isn't that so, Stephen?" she asked one of her lads.

"Aye, my lady," Stephen said, bounding over enthusiastically. " 'Tis a new thing at court, but very well thought of, to my mind. The gentleman bends over the lady's hand and feigns as if he kisses it. It leaves less spittle on her fingers, which might give her a distaste of him before he can pursue his suit with her."

Robin's jaw had gone slack. "What's the point then?"

" 'Tis all in the art, my lord. The art of wooing."

Robin looked at him, then looked at Anne. She had never seen a more perplexed look on a body's face. "He's daft," he said, then released Anne's hand and backed away. He looked at Stephen. "I'm for the lists where when a man comes at you with a blade, he means it! By the saints, I do not understand this wooing business!"

And with that, he vaulted over the table and strode across the great hall.

"Out," he said to his previously selected evening's entertainment. "I've business with you all outside. In the lists," he threw over his shoulder at his grandmother pointedly. "Where men are men and do manly things!"

The door banged shut behind him to be opened rather less enthusiastically by the men who followed him out. Anne watched them, then looked at Stephen and Joanna who were shaking their heads.

"I can wield a sword," Stephen protested. "And very well, if I might say so."

"Of course you can," Joanna said. "You've merely chosen to spend your energies of late in studying the finer points of courtly manners. There is no shame in that."

"Look at what he did to that tunic!" one of Joanna's seamstresses said, holding out the offended garment.

"And the shoes!" the apparent keeper of the footwear said with a great deal of distress. "He caught me between the eyes with one of these!"

"He's a barbarian," another man said with a shudder.

"Aye," Anne said happily.

"This will never do," Joanna said with disapproval. "We'll have to work on him again tomorrow, my friends. A good night's rest and up early before he escapes off to the saints only know where."

"He'll never submit again," a man said, a man who was sporting a very swollen and abused eye.

Anne could only assume he had tried to subdue Robin the first time.

"He will," Joanna said, looking at Anne. "If he wants the prize, he will."

Anne shook her head as she excused herself and made her way upstairs to Rhys and Gwen's bedchamber. Her bedchamber, she supposed, though it was certainly not meant to be hers alone. Robin had likely had enough civilizing for his lifetime and she would only be surprised if she ever saw him anywhere else besides the lists.

But as she made ready for bed, she couldn't stop either a final sneeze or a smile over his efforts that day.

Feathers and buttons indeed.

33

Robin awoke in his father's solar, but couldn't force himself to open his eyes yet. He remained rolled in a blanket on the floor and gave serious consideration as to whether or not all these machinations were worth it. Surely most men did not go through such tortures to woo their brides.

Nay, he thought with a snort, most men wed with women they scarce knew, much less loved, and the question of wooing did not enter into things. His was a different tale entirely.

He didn't begrudge Anne her due. After all, she'd had to endure his poor manners for years. And he'd ruined her wedding day with the unfortunate incident in the chapel, though he wasn't going to take responsibility for Isabelle losing her breakfast so abruptly.

In truth, though, he could scarce believe the events that had transpired on Artane's holiest ground. He should have been more vigilant. He should have taken more time to investigate, though in fairness to himself, he had looked the servants over carefully several times. He had never seen Maude, of that he was certain.

Or had he, and just not realized who she was?

He had to concede that perhaps that was possible. He

flexed his hands. Killing a woman—now that was something he had never had included in his lengthy list of
deeds before. He sighed heavily. It wasn't something he
would have done, or could have done, had he known who
it was who threw herself at Anne. How could he? No
woman had ever felt even a blow from him, or the flat of
his hand. Well, save Amanda, and he had only taken his
brotherly due of a friendly swipe or two at her backside.

Nay, women were God's most precious gift to man. He
believed it fully. He had never betrayed that belief.

He sincerely hoped Anne would understand. It was not
how he would have had her day proceed. He would do
much to make it up to her.

But even with all that on his conscience and a fairly
strong desire to redeem himself before his lady, he wasn't
sure he could bear another day of civilizing. Thrashing
the lads in the lists the evening before had been satisfying
enough, but he hadn't been at his best and he blamed his
grandmother for it. The anxiety he'd felt whilst trying not
to trip in those damned shoes before supper had drained
his strength. He would surely not be wearing anything else
so foolish on his feet.

He opened his eyes, then yelped in surprise. His grandmother sat in a chair next to him. Indeed, she was fair
sitting upon him and he could scarce believe he hadn't
heard her come in.

"You," he said, sitting up and willing his heart to stop
pounding, "are a wily old woman."

She only smiled, a feral smile that set the hairs on his
arms to standing. The saints only knew what she had in
store for him today.

"Am I?" she asked pleasantly.

"Aye, you are, but you can cease with your plans for
the day. I've business to attend to."

"Your business is taken care of," she said smoothly.

"What?" he exclaimed. "How could you possibly—"

"Know how to run a keep?" she finished. "I can do
many things, whelp, not the least of which is keeping your

father's lovely hall from falling into ruin for the whole of a single day."

Robin pursed his lips. "I have things only I can see to."

"I think not. I've put one of my lads in charge of your business. Things will proceed perfectly well without you attending to them for one day. Besides, you have other things to concentrate on today."

Robin wondered if it would be a mark against him to lock his grandmother in one of the guardtower upper chambers, far away from the keep proper, of course, where he could not hear her foul cursing of him. He could leave her there only so long as necessary—say until she tired of her current schemes and vowed to return home quietly.

"Dancing," Joanna stated firmly.

Robin shook his head. "I will not—"

"Aye, you will."

"Grandmère, I've business to attend to that cannot be entrusted to one of your frilly fools!"

She looked at him. Robin could see her thoughts whirling in her head and it gave him a bit of an unsettled stomach.

By the saints, she was a dangerous woman.

She nodded briefly. "Very well, then. Finish it by matins."

"Impossible. This afternoon, at the earliest."

"Noon, and not a moment longer, lest I be forced to drag you in by your ear."

Robin had several very vivid memories of his elegant grandmother doing just that in his youth, so he rubbed his ear protectively and glared at her. "I cannot possibly—"

"Learn to dance? Of course you can. Even your grandsire, God rest his soul and his cloddish feet, could sketch out a few steps after some instruction."

Robin paused. "How much instruction?"

His grandmother ignored the question and that convinced him that he was facing another day of complete misery.

"Noon," she said, rising. "Do not be late."

Robin watched her leave the chamber and as he looked at the door, another thought occurred to him.

He was almost certain he'd bolted it behind him the night before.

He scowled. Either he had slept like the dead because he'd been overwhelmed by his own perfumed stench, or his grandmother knew things she shouldn't and possessed skills no woman of her age should.

He didn't want to speculate on which it was, for either alternative was unpalatable.

He rose. Best use his time wisely whilst he had command of his fate.

He finished training at noon. He'd toyed with the idea of remaining out in the lists for yet awhile, just to see if his grandmother would actually make good on her threats. The other reason he'd been tempted was that Baldwin of Sedgwick had not deigned to grace them with his presence that morn and such had pleased Robin enormously. He had learned from one of his father's men that Baldwin had departed for points unknown the night before, which likely should have given him pause. But Baldwin was like unto cesspit odor, ever present and only disappearing long enough to catch a body unawares when it returned in its full glory. Robin suspected his cousin would blow back into the keep soon enough. For now, Robin was merely enjoying the respite.

Unfortunately his respite from his grandmother's torture was now over. There was no point in avoiding what she wanted him to do. He trudged back to the keep grimly, wondering just how well he would fare with her lessons in dancing. He'd danced a time or two over the course of his score-and-four years, but it had never been a pleasant event—either for him or the ladies so cursed to have him partner them.

Perhaps he had inherited his grandfather's cloddish feet.

Joanna was standing at the top of the steps leading up to the great hall, tapping her foot impatiently.

"I am not late," Robin growled at her.

She bestowed a smile upon him. "Indeed you are not. I was just preparing my feet for a vigorous lesson today."

"My feet would be much happier to find themselves propped up on a table where they could enjoy the music without having to participate."

Joanna took his arm and drew him into the hall. "Never fear, grandson. They'll find this much to their liking. First, though, we must put them in something more suited to dancing. Booted feet never a happy maid made."

He scowled at her. Had she invented that fiendish statement on her own, or was it something handed down from generation to generation of women bent on torturing their men with such frivolous behaviors? Even he, though, could see the logic of it. Better to step on Anne's feet in something besides his boots.

Robin found himself led over to the hearth where he was pushed into a chair, his boots removed and flimsy slippers placed up on his feet.

"Dancing slippers," one of his grandmother's peacocks sighed rapturously.

"Perfect," Robin muttered under his breath. Indeed, he muttered several things as his grandmother's little group of minstrels tuned their instruments and did whatever minstrels did to prepare themselves for a hearty round of torture. Robin had no musical gifts, nor much of an ear for it, so it all sounded like screeching to him.

He looked about the great hall and was somewhat relieved to find it empty. Well, save his grandmother's entourage. But there were no servants, no men-at-arms to see his humiliation. He lifted an eyebrow. Perhaps he had given his grandmother too little credit. She might have been bent on humiliating him privately, but at least she had made some little effort to save his pride publicly.

And then his grandmother cleared her throat.

The musicians ceased and all eyes turned to her. Robin looked at her as well. He knew she would likely pull his ear if he didn't.

She gestured expansively toward a cluster of souls near the middle of the floor in the great hall.

"Behold your dancing master," she said. "Wulfgar."

The gaggle parted. Robin felt his jaw go slack. He could scarce believe what he was seeing.

The man standing there cracking his knuckles enthusiastically was taller than Robin by no doubt half a head, and perhaps even broader through the chest and arms. He looked more suited to lifting mailed knights over his head and heaving them great distances than he did capering about to music.

"He will, of course, expect your full cooperation," Joanna said happily.

Robin rose with a sigh. He could take the man, of course, for he had no doubts of his own skill. But it would be a messy business and there would be a great deal to clean up off the hall floor afterwards. Besides, if a lout this size could learn to dance, perhaps Robin would find himself not unable as well.

He found himself relieved of his weapons suddenly and he submitted. Then he crossed the great hall, folded his arms across his chest and gave his dancing master his most formidable glare.

"Get on with it," he commanded.

The man made him a bow. "As you will, my lord. And as you can see, if I am able to move about so gracefully, so should you be likewise able."

"My thoughts exactly."

"Think of it as a battle, my lord," Wulfgar continued in a gravelly voice that sounded more accustomed to bellowing orders than gently instructing prancing steps, "and think of your body as your troops."

Robin stroked his chin. War? Aye, this was something he could understand.

"Your goal, my lord, is to negotiate the battlefield as

delicately as possible, guard your lady as you go, and reach your goal."

"Which would be the finish of the song?" Robin asked darkly.

Wulfgar laughed, a hearty laugh that made Robin think of tankards of ale shared in wayside inns after a successful siege. He felt immediately warm and comfortable and even managed a smile.

"Aye, my lord," Wulfgar said. "There is that as well. Now, let us begin."

Well, at least he wasn't required to clasp hands with the man as if they'd been lovers. Wulfgar maintained a perfect warriorly distance as he showed Robin what he needed to do.

Even so, Robin suspected it would be a very long afternoon.

But he was no coward. And if Wulfgar the Large could do the like, so could he.

Though he had to admit, once a small rest was called for, that this dancing business was much more difficult to do correctly than he had dared believe before. He stood there, panting, his head spinning with dancing strategies, patterns and tactics.

By the saints, 'twas enough to give a man pains in his head.

Not to mention his feet.

Robin walked gingerly to the high table only to see a sight that simultaneously brought a flush to his face and a chill to his veins.

Anne was sitting on the bottom step, her elbows on her knees, her chin on her fists, watching him.

Robin came to a dead halt. How bloody long had she been observing him? He wasn't sure if he should shout at her or ask her if she thought him skilled. He shut his mouth with a snap and scowled.

And then another thought occurred to him. Would Anne be able to do any of these steps with her leg? He'd learned many intricate caperings that morning. Would she be equal to them?

But before he could decide anything, he caught sight of his grandmother hastening to Anne's side.

"He learned well, didn't he?" she asked.

Anne smiled. "Aye, Lady Joanna. He's very skilled."

Robin paused and considered. Kind words from his lady. There was something in that.

"Come, my dear," Joanna said, raising Anne to her feet. "Come try a turn or two with him."

Robin wanted to bid his grandmother be silent, but perhaps she knew better than he what Anne could do where this dancing was concerned.

He found himself suddenly with his lady's hand in his and his mind completely free of all the things he'd recently learned.

Damnation.

When it was clear to everyone including Anne that he was hopelessly lost, Joanna bid the screechers of song and pluckers of lute strings cease. Wulfgar was summoned again to the center of the hall. Robin took Anne's right side and Wulfgar took her left and Robin watched his dancing master as they rehearsed their steps again. And as they did, Robin realized how ingenious his grandmother had been in her choice of things for him to learn. He did a great deal of foolish prancing about, but Anne was required to do little but walk a bit and look lovely. The dancing steps she took were graceful and she seemed to enjoy them, but he suspected they wouldn't tax her overmuch.

And when he was finally released from his tortures and allowed to take his place at high table, he escorted his lady there and sat with a happy sigh. He was vastly relieved to be off his feet.

Until, that was, his grandmother approached purposefully.

"We'll dance again tonight," she announced. "That Robin might trot out his hard-won skills."

Robin scowled, but realized he had no recourse. Besides, a sliding glance Anne's way revealed that she didn't look opposed to the idea.

Dancing.

He only hoped it was the last of the tortures his grandmother had in mind for him.

34

Anne sat in the alcove of Gwen's solar and enjoyed a bit of peace and quiet. She'd pulled the curtain across to give herself privacy, something she rarely did lest she offend everyone else in the chamber. But Artane's ladies had been dispatched to various locations unknown, Joanna was off marshalling her last reserves of patience by indulging in a nap, and the saints only knew where Robin was. She'd seen Jason earlier and he told her, as he headed toward the kitchens where any sensible boy of ten-and-six went when given leave, that he was enjoying a day of liberty and had no idea where his master was.

Anne could only hope Robin wasn't in the village, bedding as many willing wenches as possible.

Now, with her precious privacy, she could give herself over freely to the contemplation of her situation. She stared out the window and smiled to herself. Who would have thought that Robin of Artane, of all people, would have put himself through such travails just to please her? Her father would certainly have been surprised by it, Amanda appalled and Nicholas—well, Nicholas would have laughed himself to death, and that would have sparked several battles between the two so perhaps 'twas best Robin had made his forays into fine-lorddom by himself.

The curtain moved suddenly as if set to flapping by a stiff breeze. Anne jumped in spite of herself. Then she heard the voices in the chamber and relaxed. Her attacker was dead and her husband was on the other side of the cloth. She was safe.

"Very well," Robin said heavily. "Let us have this over with."

"My lord," said a voice whose beauty just in speaking made Anne catch her breath, "skill with the lute cannot be acquired if 'having it over with' is all you are willing to dedicate to its mastery."

"And how could skill with the lute possibly serve me?" Robin demanded. "It certainly won't save my neck—or my lady's if that romantic notion suits you better, ah, you, um, Master Lutenist."

"Geoffrey, my lord."

"Ah," Robin groaned, "not another one."

Anne smiled. There was no mystery regarding Robin's feelings for her sire. She settled back to listen, wondering greatly how it would all play out. She sincerely hoped Robin wouldn't decapitate the minstrel. He had a beautiful voice and for that alone he should be forgiven his part in Lady Joanna's scheme.

"Two lutes?" Robin complained. "By the saints, man, have you no mercy? There'll be no rest for me at all if you've two of those bloody things."

"One for me," Geoffrey said smoothly, "and one for you, my lord. Now, if you'll be so kind as to take the instrument. Hold it thusly, there you have it. Well done, my lord!"

"Leave off, will you?" Robin said crossly. "Even I can manage to hold it. 'Tis the playing of it that I'll never manage."

"If you can wield a sword, you can play the lute," Geoffrey promised.

"Hrmph," Robin grunted. "Is that what you say to all

the half-wits who find themselves in your vile clutches?"

Geoffrey laughed and it sounded more like a waterfall than a man's voice. Anne was half tempted to peek around the curtain and make certain her husband wasn't about to be enspelled by a faery or sprite from the woods. Surely no mortal man possessed such a beautiful voice. Joanna had very fine taste indeed.

"We will learn a ballad first, my lord," Geoffrey said. "But two chords and easy ones at that. Here, watch you my fingers and place yours precisely so on your strings."

Anne heard one strum of the lute and assumed, perhaps a little unkindly, that it hadn't been Robin to produce that sound. His next words confirmed it.

"Bloody hell, man, how do you expect me to fit my lumps of fingers on these spiderwebs!"

"Perseverance and patience, my lord. Perseverance and patience."

Neither of which, Anne learned as the morning wore on, Robin possessed in much of an abundance. Robin's cursing drowned out any hope of hearing anything else Geoffrey might have had to say.

"Take a deep breath, my lord," Geoffrey said, loudly enough to be heard over Robin's slander.

Robin, blessedly, was silent.

"One more time," Geoffrey cajoled. "For your lady, my lord."

Robin heaved a huge sigh of what sounded like immense frustration, then produced what might have been construed as a chord. There was an accompanying twang of a string struck improperly and, of course, the ever-present curse to follow, but at least it was an improvement.

"Well done, my lord!" Geoffrey exclaimed.

Robin was silent. Then he strummed again. It was quite a bit better that time; Anne wished desperately she could have seen his face.

"That wasn't completely hopeless, was it?" Robin asked, with something akin to surprise in his voice.

"You've made great strides, my lord. You will make a fine lutenist if you've the mind to try."

Robin snorted. "Nay, my brother plays much better than I ever could. There is no point."

"Ah, but who would your lady prefer to hear? Your brother, my lord, or you?"

There was a goodly bit of silence. Then Robin spoke.

"Another chord or two, if you please, Geoffrey. I'm certain a handful of minutes at this each day could only improve my swordplay."

"No doubt, my lord."

Anne leaned back against the wall and listened raptly to Robin's efforts to master something that was completely beyond his normal experience. She was almost sorry when Geoffrey told him he thought that perhaps they should cease with their lute lessons, lest Robin learn too much in the first day and overwhelm his lady with his skill.

"Then I'll be off," Robin said, sounding rather relieved.

"Ah, but what of verse?" Geoffrey said quickly. "Surely you don't want to neglect that."

"Don't I?"

"You don't, my lord."

There was a very heavy sigh and a thump, as if Robin had resumed his seat with extreme reluctance. "Very well. May as well plunge the dagger into the hilt while you've already begun your work."

"Well done, my lord," Geoffrey said. "I daresay you'll find this quite easy as well."

"If you say so," Robin said doubtfully. "What first?"

"First you decide upon a subject for your verse. I daresay you would likely have the most to say about your lady, aye?"

"Aye," Robin said.

And Anne could have sworn she heard a bit of wistfulness in that aye. Then again she could have been imagining it. With Robin, one just never knew. It could have been indigestion from all that dancing after last night's supper. She hadn't seen him about that morn. Either he had found the guard tower to be a fine place to hide, or his feet were still smarting from all their hard work learning the task his dancing master had set before him and he'd been abed recovering. Anne had to smile over that. Poor Robin. He couldn't help but be relieved when his grandmother turned her attentions to some other of Rhys and Gwen's offspring.

"Now, if you were to say something about your lady, what would it be?"

"She is the most profoundly stubborn woman I've ever met."

Geoffrey's little gasp of astonishment only told Anne that he hadn't spent all that much time with Robin yet. She pursed her lips. She could scarce bear the waiting until Robin truly found his tongue where she was concerned.

"But, my lord," Geoffrey said, sounding rather aghast, "you must say something complimentary about her."

"That was a compliment. Tenacity is a fine quality."

There was a bit of silence. Then Geoffrey apparently gathered the shreds of his innocence about him enough to recover his powers of speech.

"Try something else, my lord."

"Well," Robin said slowly, "she has more courage than any bruised and bloodied lout I've ever fought with. She's braved her own demons and come away the victor, time and time again. Aye," he said, sounding more enthusiastic, "the courage of half a score of the most sliced, bludgeoned and maimed men I've had the pleasure of hoisting a sword with—"

"My lord, you cannot sing of bloody battles and your lady in the same breath."

"Why not?" Robin demanded. "Bravery's nothing to scorn, man. I daresay you could think of worse souls to guard your back than my Anne."

My Anne.

Anne blinked back tears. It was the most unpolished

verse she'd ever listened to and she'd even heard a lay or two composed about her own poor self. But it was without doubt the most moving.

"Her eyes, my lord," Geoffrey pleaded. "Say something about her eyes."

"Well, she has two—"

"The color!" Geoffrey exclaimed. "Praise the color! Compare it to beryls, seacoasts, rare and exquisite jewels. Use your imagination!"

There was silence for a goodly amount of time—time during which Anne wondered if Robin was reaching for his blade. Then he cleared his throat.

"Her eyes . . ." he began slowly, "well, the color of her eyes is akin to . . . hmmm . . ." He trailed off and there was a bit more silence, then a foot stomped in triumph. "Akin to sage, aye, *sage* after it's sat in the sun too long."

There was a slap and Anne could only assume it was Geoffrey clapping his hand to his own forehead. Aye, that was definitely a groan and it was not coming from her husband.

"I told you," Robin said defensively, "that I've no head for poetry."

"The lute," Geoffrey said weakly. "We'll pursue the lute. You can sing other men's songs."

"Are we finished now?" Robin asked hopefully.

"Aye," Geoffrey said. "I doubt either of us can face any more today."

Anne heard the door open, followed by Robin's curse.

"Grandmère, no more today," he said firmly.

"You've lessons in bowing, grandson. Come with me."

"Nay," Robin said tightly, "I will not. Bowing will not win my lady."

"And mucking about in your boots will?" Joanna asked tartly.

"Perhaps not, but being the best damn bloody swordsman in England just might!" Robin returned hotly. "So I go, my lady, to continue to seek after that goal in the lists! With your permission?"

The door slammed shut and Anne could only assume that Robin hadn't waited for his grandmother to say him aye. She rose, groaned as she did so, and swayed. She caught herself with her hand on the opposite wall. Within a heartbeat, the curtain had been pulled back and Joanna stood there, a worried frown on her face.

"Are you unwell—"

The door burst open and Anne saw nothing but a blur as the curtain was jerked closed.

"Aye?" Joanna said.

"I've come to a decision," Robin announced. "You and my lady will present yourselves in the lists posthaste. I will woo her *my* way, Grandmère, and that will begin by demonstrating my prowess on the field. Fetch Anne, if you please, and come immediately where you may watch and admire."

Joanna was silent for a moment or two, then she cleared her throat. "As you will, grandson. I'll find your lady and bring her."

The door slammed shut and the curtain began to open. Before Anne could say anything, Joanna had spun around as the door was flung open yet again.

"See that she dresses warmly. And have one of your frilly lads make himself useful by bringing her a blanket or two."

The door slammed shut again and Anne sighed in relief. Joanna pulled back the curtain. She shook her head at Anne.

"Impossible lad."

"Of course," Anne said with a smile. "But I'm fond of him that way."

"Of course you are, my dear." Joanna took her hands and smiled. "Can you bear the chill outside, Anne? I daresay heads will roll if we neglect his commands."

Anne nodded to Geoffrey as she crossed the chamber. He, though, only stared at her in surprise. Anne was momentarily tempted to check her clothes and hair, then forced herself to assume the best, not the worst.

"Aye?" she said.

"You are his lady wife?" Geoffrey asked incredulously.

"Aye," Anne said.

"And he could find nothing to say but that your eyes were the color of sage?"

"What?" Joanna exclaimed.

"Apparently so," Anne said cheerfully.

Geoffrey shook his head. "*I* will compose his verses for him, for I have a great deal to say about your loveliness, my lady. Your lord has little imagination."

"Minstrelsy is not where his gifts lie," Anne conceded. "But he does the best he can."

Joanna snorted. "You're a besotted goose, Anne, and I pray Robin is someday grateful for it. Now, come and let us have this over with. I don't fancy an afternoon sitting in the mud, but there you have it. What we won't do to humor a man."

Anne walked with Robin's grandmother down to the great hall, then stopped her before the door.

"Are you disappointed?" she asked.

"Disappointed?" Joanna asked. "In Robin? Nay, he's cooperated much longer than I thought he would. He must love you greatly to have endured such tortures."

Anne smiled faintly. "He has submitted very well, for whatever reason. The one thing I'm sorry for, though, is the clothing. It was passing fine and he was handsome in it."

Joanna snorted. "It grieves me as well, but what use does he have for fine clothes when he ruins them in the rain anyway? I vow, Anne, you'll never be free of the mud and such he'll bring in on his boots."

"I think his manners may have improved," Anne offered.

"My dear," Joanna said, putting her arm around Anne and giving her a squeeze, "this was merely to bring him to his senses, for I was certain he would never arrive there on his own. You deserved to be wooed. It is Robin's right and his duty to woo you, and all the better if he does it as it pleases him. If I have in some small, insignificant way pushed him to do it sooner than his stubbornness might have allowed otherwise, then I am content."

Anne couldn't help a small laugh. "You are devious, my lady."

"From whom do you think Robin inherited that trait, if not me?" Joanna asked, with one eyebrow raised. "Now, come my girl, and let us be away before he comes to fetch us. Whatever other flaws he might have, he is at the very least a powerfully fine swordsman. I wouldn't want to force him to prove it by prodding us where he wants us."

Anne nodded and went to fetch her cloak. She made her way as quickly as possible down to the hall. Joanna was waiting for her at the door to the great hall, swathed in furs and followed by several lads carrying fine chairs, blankets and foodstuffs. Anne was only surprised not to see someone else toting supplies to build a pavilion.

"If we must be there," Joanna said crisply as Anne approached, "we may as well be comfortable."

Anne had no intentions of arguing. She walked with Robin's grandmother out to the lists, doing her best to keep her skirts well out of the mud. Hopefully her father would have some sense and send her the rest of her clothing. It wasn't all that much, but she possessed another gown or two and that might come in handy if she were required to present herself at the lists for any more admiring.

After all, Robin was wooing her *his* way.

And if that wasn't enough to bring a smile to her face, she didn't know what was.

Robin was tromping about, looking irritated until he saw them arrive. Anne watched him gape at the trappings that accompanied them, then shrug his shoulders. Anne soon found herself seated in a comfortable chair, her feet propped up on a padded stool, her person covered in blankets and furs and her elbow near a small table covered with foodstuffs and a cup of warm wine.

And she began to wonder if inviting Joanna north more often might be a very good idea.

"Primitive," Joanna said with a shake of her head, "but I daresay we'll survive it for a bit. Comfortable, my dear?"

Anne nodded happily, remembering all the hours she had spent watching Robin in the lists while trying to be inconspicuous. That had generally entailed crouching against the wall or making use of some uncomfortable bench or other. She suspected that with this kind of luxury surrounding her, she could watch Robin all day.

Which was, she suspected, his intention.

She looked at the field and blinked at what she saw. There was Robin on her left, standing by himself, cracking his knuckles and flexing his arms over his head. Facing him was the rest of Artane's garrison, made up of his own men and his father's. She frowned. Did he intend to fight them in a bunch?

She realized, an hour later, that he had planned to dispatch them one by one. She also realized, that same hour later, that such a thing was not beyond his reach.

Swords went flying. Men cried peace. Lads who were freshly knighted were humbled with quick strokes. Men who wore their years of experience solidly on their shoulders were eventually forced to concede victory.

And through it all, Anne could scarce take her eyes off her husband. Her wine went undrunk, delicacies went unnibbled and substantial meals were brushed aside in annoyance.

By the saints, he was beautiful.

She could only shake her head in amazement that such a man was hers, even in name only. Perhaps had she known the true extent of Robin's prowess, she might have been less free with her tongue at his expense. His strength was unflagging. He fought man after man without so much as a pause. His wits were unmatched, for she watched him never be drawn into any devious scheme to rid him of his blade. And his skill was unequaled, for no man bested him in that very long afternoon.

And when the line of challengers was no more, she

watched him throw his sword up into the air and laugh for the sheer sport of it.

She suspected that she might never recover from the sight of *that*.

He caught his sword, turned and strode over to them purposefully. He shoved his blade into the mud at his grandmother's feet and looked at her, his chest heaving.

"*That*, Grandmère," he said haughtily, "is what I do best. Can you find fault with it?"

"Of course not, Robin, my love," his grandmother said, looking at him serenely. "I never could."

Robin scowled, then turned his attentions to Anne.

"And you, lady? What think you?"

Anne swallowed with difficulty. "I think you, my lord, are . . ."

"Well?" he demanded.

"Magnificent," she finished, wondering if she looked as lustful as she felt. By the saints, 'twas all she could do not to leap to her feet, throw her arms around his sweaty self and bid him take her right there.

Robin blinked in surprise, but recovered quickly enough.

"A word I might have chosen myself," he said. "Now, come, my ladies and let us sup. You'll need your strength for the morrow."

"We will?" Joanna asked hesitantly.

"I've plans for you after my business is finished in the morn."

"Plans?" Anne asked.

"I will see you both in my father's solar at noon. Do not be late."

"Will you entertain us with the lute?" Joanna sounded rather hopeful.

"Ha," Robin said scornfully. "Tales of battle, Grandmère! Bloodshed! Victories!"

Joanna frowned.

"It will be very exciting," Robin promised.

Anne couldn't imagine anything more exciting than what she'd just witnessed, but she could be patient and see.

With Robin, one just never knew.

35

Edith stood just inside the outer gates and watched the little party begin to make its way back up to the keep. She could scarce believe the luxury in which Joanna of Segrave wallowed. By the saints, even a visit to the lists necessitated trappings Edith had never enjoyed during the whole of her life.

Perhaps striking at the old woman first would gain Robin's attention.

Edith wiped her hands on her hose, then looked down and cursed softly. The blood was too stale for wiping; 'twould take a proper washing to remove it and she would have to find water outside. She could not retrieve her clothes from their hiding place in the stable and enter the hall with bloodied hands.

She'd been out hunting.

It honed her considerable skills.

But rabbits were poor sport and not wily enough to truly give her pleasure. Nay, for that, she needed a creature with greater wits. And greater wits meant the use of more of her own for the chase. Not that the chase need be hurried, though. She had no need of haste. She was, after all, a very patient woman.

There would be time enough for all her plans. Maude's death had been a surprise, but perhaps 'twas nothing the wench hadn't deserved. Edith had told her to stay far away from the wedding, though she'd suspected Maude would have found it too powerful a lure to resist. She'd disobeyed.

Death had been what she deserved.

But that was behind Edith. Now, her own plans deserved her full attention. Hunting that day had given her new ideas to consider. For was it not all the game of stalking the quarry, flushing it out, then killing swiftly and without hesitation?

She very much suspected it was.

But first, clean hands.

It would throw her prey off the scent.

36

Robin leaped up the steps, then strode down the passageway to his father's solar. He'd had a fine day so far, what with great success in the lists, nothing broken, stolen or in an uproar in the keep, and now an afternoon of freedom in which to tell his favorite stories. Life improved with each day that passed.

Anne smiled at him a great deal these days.

Robin suspected it boded well for their marriage.

He burst into his father's solar and was highly pleased to see both his lady and his errant grandmother sitting before him, apparently prepared and waiting for him to astonish them with tales of his prowess in battle. Robin rubbed his hands together with great energy.

"Where shall we begin?" he asked, slamming the door shut behind him with his foot.

"With a large cup of something strong," his grandmother answered without hesitation. She blinked at him innocently. "To soothe our delicate constitutions, of course."

Robin snorted. He'd seen his grandmother flay more than one hapless suitor alive with naught but her sharp tongue. *Delicate* was not one of the words he would have chosen for her.

But he was in a fine mood, Anne looked happy to see him and he did have the whole of the afternoon and evening to trot out his favorite battle tales for their inspection and admiration. Filling his grandmother's goblet now and again was small payment for such pleasure.

So he filled, saw to the fire and moved a chair or two aside so as to have the most possible room for pacing, for he knew the sheer exhilaration of relating such breathtaking tales would drive him to movement. He looked to make certain his ladies were attending him, then rolled his shoulders, shook out his hands and stomped his feet a time or two.

"Let's begin in Spain, shall we?" he asked.

His grandmother sighed.

Anne smiled, though, so Robin took that as encouragement enough. And as he stole another look at her, he remembered telling her what a bloody business it was, and that almost gave him pause. For there was a very dark side to it, and dreams of it troubled his sleep quite often. There was a part of him that would have been glad never to engage in it again.

But there was also the glory and the toil and the satisfaction of an enemy routed, a victory won, a wrong righted. He put his shoulders back. 'Twas of that he would speak, for there were those tales aplenty.

"Now," he said, "I will tell you of a skirmish Nick and I had in a little town just outside Madrid. We likely shouldn't even have been there, but the weather was fine, the wine excellent and we heard there was a bit of gold in the deed for us as well."

It was also where Robin had found the stone for Anne's ring, but that he would tell her later, when he'd found the proper time to give it to her.

"Did you really need the gold?" Anne asked.

Robin blinked. "Well, aye. Always."

She looked at him in confusion. "But Robin, you have lands aplenty."

"Aye, but this was gold I'd *earned*. By my own sweat."

"And you don't protecting your holdings?"

It was going to be a very long afternoon if this was the kind of response he was going to get. He frowned at her.

" 'Tis a different matter entirely. I was just another hired sword, not Artane's son."

She looked at him for a moment in silence, then she smiled a bit. "I see."

And as he watched his grandmother take a hearty draught of her wine, he suspected she did as well.

"Damned foolish, if you ask me," she said tartly, "but men will be men. Be about your work, grandson. These old ears of mine can only stand so much talk of battle in one day."

Yet they could stand hours on end of string plucking and screeching, Robin thought with a grumble. He scowled at his grandmother for good measure, then took up his tale again.

"We were in Spain," he continued.

And once he was finished with that small skirmish, he moved to larger battles. He told his tales with complete accuracy, for there was no need to embellish or augment his part in them. His deeds spoke for themselves and he related them with as much humility as he could manage.

Then he told of humorous things, of arrogant knights shamed, foolish lords humbled and crafty innkeepers outsmarted.

And when he'd finished that, he turned to the most glorious of battles and the most daring of escapades.

The afternoon passed into evening.

Robin paused in his pacing to gauge the effect his most exciting tale yet had upon the women. He looked at his grandmother to find that her head was resting against the back of the chair and she was sound asleep. Every now and again a delicate snort would come from her lips.

His lady wife was not asleep—not yet. He watched her

smother an impressive yawn, then watched as she realized she was being observed.

"Interesting," she said, nodding. "Breathtaking. Truly." She smiled encouragingly.

Robin pursed his lips, hoping that she could see that he didn't much believe her enthusiasm.

On the other hand, he had to concede that she was smiling at him and listening with a pleasant, if sleepy, expression on her face. He couldn't complain about that.

He sighed and pulled up a stool in front of her. Perhaps he'd regaled the pair with enough tales of bloodshed and the like. He had a moment of peace with his lady; he might be wise to use it. His grandmother was snoring peacefully, albeit daintily, so their self-appointed chaperon wouldn't be looking at him pointedly if he made some unacceptable social blunder. He looked at his lady and was faintly surprised at the ease he felt in her company. Surely she had seen him at his worst—bedecked with feathers and all manner of baubles—yet she hadn't laughed at him. He'd stepped on her toes enough for a score of dancers, yet still she seemed to endure his presence well enough.

Yet now that he had her, he hardly knew what to do with her. More stories of battle seemed a bit inappropriate, even for him. He racked his pitiful brain, praying for some small bit of inspiration. He watched Anne shift in the chair and suddenly it occurred to him how he could amuse her. Or at least show her that he had thought of her over the years. After all, wasn't the avenging of your lady's honor a noble thing? Perhaps it was time she knew it.

"Anne," he said.

"Aye?"

"Do you remember Peter of Canfield?"

She paused, then a look of perfect stillness descended upon her face. "Aye," she answered carefully.

And remember him she should. Never mind that he was Maude's brother and Maude was someone he would rather avoid talking about. Peter had once trapped Anne in a stable and taunted her until she was hysterical. Robin hadn't been privy to it, though he'd heard tell of it through one of the little twins who had witnessed the event. Robin had thrashed Peter several times in the lists afterwards, but it had never seemed quite enough. Fortunately, another opportunity had presented itself.

"I saw him," he began, "in a tourney three years ago in France."

She didn't reply.

"It might interest you to know that I bested him in the joust and held him for ransom. I took, of course, all his gold, his horse and his mail."

"Of course."

"But I left him his tent."

She smiled faintly. "Good of you."

"Aye, it was. And whilst he slept in that tent in the midst of the lists, for he could find no one to help him move it, as his squire and sundries were too thrashed by my lads to aid him, I crept in and took what clothes I had left him."

"You didn't."

"I did," Robin said pleasantly. "Not a stitch remained him."

She waited expectantly.

"Now, the stands the next day were quite crowded with a great number of France's finest nobles. I, being the diligent soul I am, had noised about that there would be a great bit of entertainment that morn and 'twould serve all in the area to arrive early to see it."

She laughed. "Oh, Robin."

He couldn't help a smile himself. "As you might imagine, the lists were full when Peter came stumbling from his tent, naked. He was laughed off the field and out of France. He hasn't dared show himself at another gathering since."

Anne shook her head. "You are incorrigible."

"Well," he said mildly, "I do what I can for the cause of truth and right. Now, perhaps it would amuse you to hear the fate of Rolond of Berkhamshire. I remember him being such a fine, upstanding young lad in his youth."

Actually Rolond had been one of the worst. Robin could still remember hearing him call Anne ugly time and time again. Well, at least she was still smiling now. She hadn't been then.

"My memory fails me on his character," Anne said, "but I'll accept your word for it. What havoc did you wreak upon his hapless soul?"

"I was at court briefly a year or so ago," Robin began, "flattering and courting the king as was expected, when I happened to learn that Rolond and his substantial wife, Alice, were there. And let us not forget his mistress, Martha, who was placed in a nearby chamber."

She caught her breath. "You didn't."

Robin smiled modestly. "It was purely by chance that I saw Rolond go into his mistress's chamber. Fearing for his eternal soul, I hurriedly sought out a servant to inform his wife of the deep sin into which her husband was about to fall face-first."

Anne was watching him with a smile. "How thoughtful of you."

"Aye," he said, "it was. Now, as it happened, the servant wasted little time in passing on the tidings. It seemed just a moment that I spent hiding in an alcove—just to see that no stone was left unturned, of course—before Lady Berkhamshire came thundering down the hall with the fury of an avenging angel. She didn't bother to knock; she merely burst into the chamber. She rescued her mate from the clutches of that fallen woman, dragging him out with his hose down around his knees and his hands continuing to clutch what had surely been his mistress's ample bosom only moments before."

"You *didn't!*"

He smiled. "I can only take credit for being a spy and a teller of tales. Lady Berkhamshire provided the amusing sport. And the last I heard, dear Lord Berkhamshire hasn't

seen the outside of his walls since. It would seem his wife
rules with an iron hand."

Anne leaned her head back against the chair and smiled
at him. "You are a terrible troublemaker, Lord Artane."

"I have several more stories that I think you would find
just as amusing, should you wish for me to trot them out
for your inspection."

"My lord, you are so gallant."

He felt his smile falter. "It won't last."

"I wouldn't want it to."

He sighed. "I'm not fond of playing the gushing lord
at court, Anne. As you should have noticed by now."

"Robin, what makes you think that is what I want? I
never could stomach a man with affected manners and no
substance underneath them. I can't imagine why they're
so popular."

He tried not to show his surprise. "But surely you want
a chivalrous knight. Every woman wants a chivalrous
knight."

"Chivalry hasn't served me before, except from one lad
in my youth. I haven't had much use for it since." She
met his gaze unflinchingly. "There is more to love than
chivalry, Robin."

He could hardly believe she'd said the like, but there
was no hint of jest in her face. And what was this business
of a chivalrous lad in her youth? She couldn't be possibly
talking about him. Could she?

Robin looked down at her hands folded in her lap.
Then, before he could think better of it, he reached for
one and held it between his own. It wasn't as if he hadn't
held her hand before. But he'd never held her hand knowing that she was his, that it was his privilege to enjoy such
simple joys of marriage. He took a deep breath.

"Anne, I've much to beg pardon for."

"Again?" she asked in surprise.

Robin scowled. He wasn't all that encouraged by that,
but then again, he had many regrets so perhaps he de-

served to writhe in penitent agony for a bit. He stole a look at his grandmother to make certain she slept on, then looked back at his lady.

"I have," he said, mustering up all his reserves of courage, "treated you badly."

"Have you?" she asked. "When?"

She tried to raise one eyebrow, but both went up. He watched her prop one up with her finger and he almost managed a smile.

"You mock me," he said reproachfully.

"You're groveling. 'Tis most unsettling."

"Anne, I'm in earnest. I was a dolt in my youth and a fool in my manhood."

She cocked her head to one side and smiled faintly. "Perhaps I do want to hear this. Go on, if you please."

She was not giving him or his confession the consideration it warranted. He glared at her and wondered if an apology counted if given whilst the giver was powerfully tempted to throttle the receiver.

"I can stop," he growled.

She shook her head, still smiling just the smallest bit. "Nay, Robin, I daresay I will be glad of it when you've finished. But you aren't the only one at fault."

He grunted. "You can take your turn after I've had done. I'd best babble whilst I can stomach it."

"Then by all means, proceed, my lord."

He scowled at her again, just out of habit, then plunged ahead before his pride managed to close his mouth.

"I turned away from you in our youth—"

"Why did you, Robin?"

Damn her, he was never going to finish this if she didn't stop interrupting him. "It isn't important—"

"I think it's very important," she said. She looked at him expectantly. "Why did you?"

He was up on his feet pacing before he knew what his body intended. He realized just as suddenly that it would be uncomfortable for Anne to chase him and wring the truth from him, so he returned to stand before her. He looked at his grandmother.

Still sleeping.

He looked about him, hoping to find some corner that might be more private for the blurting out of his darkest secret.

There was nowhere else save the alcove; it had no light but perhaps that was just as well. Robin pulled Anne to her feet, waited until he sensed she had put weight on her leg and found it to be sturdy beneath her, then he led her over and sat with her on one of the benches. There in the shadows, he took her hand and held it tightly between his own. She said nothing, but he felt her clasp his hand. Robin took a deep breath, then felt his heart begin to pound and his limbs begin to tingle. By the saints, he never felt the like even before the worst of battles! He could scarce believe that relating such a simple, foolish event could cause him this kind of distress.

And then he felt Anne lean her head on his shoulder.

"Robin, perhaps 'tis too close still," she whispered. "If it grieves you this much, I'll not demand the tale."

He shook his head. "Nay," he began, and his voice cracked. He cleared his throat. "Nay," he said again, "you deserve to know. I was a fool then and I'll not repeat the mistake now." He blew out his breath. " 'Twas one morning near the healer's house. You had walked across the courtyard to the hall. I should have accompanied you. I don't know now why I didn't."

"You'd been abed with the fever, Robin. 'Twas a wonder you hadn't died."

Her hand fluttered between his briefly, then was still.

"Aye, well, whatever the reason," he continued, "I watched you and saw the . . . um . . . the—"

"You may say it, Robin. It won't grieve me."

" 'Twas teasing, Anne," he said, feeling a surge of anger over the memory. "Lads who should have known better. One lad in particular."

"Baldwin."

Robin gritted his teeth. "Father had pulled you into the house. I called to Baldwin, for I could not let his slurs go unavenged."

"Oh, Robin," she said softly. "I didn't know."

"Aye, well, there wasn't much to know. He thrashed me soundly for my cheek, then broke two of Nick's fingers as his reward for a challenge." He paused, then took another deep breath. "He left me wallowing in the mud."

Anne was silent. Robin waited for her to say something, but perhaps the shame of it was enough to make her wish she had wed elsewhere. He never should have told her—

"Is that all?"

Robin blinked. "Is that all?" he demanded.

He felt her lift her head. "Aye. Is that all?"

"He laughed at me!"

"Robin, he laughed at everyone," she said, sounding mightily confused.

"He humiliated me before every lad in the keep!"

"But," she asked, still sounding as if she simply could not fathom the depths of his shame, "what has that to do with your shunning me?"

"He humiliated me!"

"And you punished me for it?"

"Anne, damn you," Robin growled, "I wasn't going to see you laugh at me as well!"

He could see the faint outline of her face. She was shaking her head.

"I thought *I* had done something," she said softly.

"I didn't want to give you the chance to do anything," Robin said grimly.

"All this time, all these years wasted because of Baldwin. By the saints, Robin, we have made a great jumble of things."

"We?" he demanded. "I was the fool."

"I could have asked you what troubled you."

He gritted his teeth. "You did, Anne. More than once."

She smiled. He could hardly believe the sight, but there it was. "Very well," she said gently, "you were the fool.

I forgive you for it. Now you may apologize for staying away so long. I assume 'twas for much the same reason." Then he felt her stiffen. "I mean . . . well, what I meant to say was that you likely had a very good reason for being gone." She paused. "I doubt it included me."

Robin was tempted to ask her how she could think something so foolish, but he knew precisely where she had come by the notion. He'd given her ample reason over the years to believe just that. He stood up, then pulled her to her feet and wrapped his arms around her. He rested his cheek against her soft hair and closed his eyes.

And he came very close to weeping.

"Anne," he said, wincing at the crack in his voice. Saints, but she would think him a whimpering fool if he did not regain some control over himself. "Anne," he tried again, "there was not a day that passed that I did not think of you."

He felt her breath catch, then heard a sniffle. He could only hope that she wasn't weeping because the tidings were ill ones to her ears.

"I should have wed you the moment I won my spurs," he said quietly. "I should have come home, demanded the right from your father and wed you then. I've wasted five years and I've never been sorrier for anything in my life."

He paused, struck by an unwholesome thought.

"Unless," he said hesitantly, "unless you would have found that distasteful."

"Robin de Piaget, you are a fool."

She was weeping. Her arms were around him and she clung to him as if he were all that kept her upright.

Or as if he were very dear to her.

He chose to believe the latter. He gathered her even closer to him and wrapped his arms securely about her. He wanted to tell her that he loved her. He wanted with equal intensity to sweep her up into his arms and carry her to his bedchamber where he was almost certain they could come to an agreement on a few other things.

She was, after all, his wife.

There was a snort, a cough and a delicate stamping of feet. "Children, children," Joanna called, "where have you gone?"

"Damn her," Anne muttered.

Robin snorted. "I couldn't agree more." He cleared his throat purposefully. "We can see ourselves to bed, Grand-mère."

"Absolutely not," Joanna said. "Bring Anne back, Robin lad. She needs her rest. I'm sure you'll find some-where comfortable to sleep. Come out of there. 'Tis far too drafty for her."

Robin found himself obeying out of habit, then he dug his heels in a few paces from his grandmother. He looked at Anne to find that she was looking anywhere but at him.

"We *are* wed," Robin pointed out.

"Is she properly wooed?" Joanna demanded.

"Well—"

"I think not," Joanna said. She rose, took Anne by the hand and started toward the door. "I'll sleep with Anne tonight, just to keep her safe. Best practice your dancing a bit before you retire, love."

Anne looked back at Robin with wide eyes, but appar-ently she was unable to free herself. Robin scowled as he watched her be dragged off. The door was shut firmly.

Robin gritted his teeth.

He sat down with a curse, stretched out his legs and scowled. What were the penalties for separating one's love from one's grandmother using a blade?

He suspected that the list of his sins was long enough, so perhaps he would refrain. But this would be the last time his grandmother thwarted his plans. It looked as if the only way he would have Anne to himself would be to liberate her from his grandmother's vile clutches.

He stroked his chin and wondered if the weather might be tolerable enough for a small outing on the morrow.

37

Anne woke to a brisk knocking. She blinked, sat up and shook her head. Ah, nay, not that again.

And then she realized she was abed with Robin's grandmother, Robin had bedded down the saints only knew where, and her father and his were likely indulging in blissful slumber safely tucked away at Fenwyck. Could it be ruffians having overrun the keep? It certainly didn't sound like that sort of frantic pounding.

Anne yawned as the pounding continued. Lady Joanna slept like the dead and Anne would have had a fear for her had she not snored with such great enthusiasm. She rose quietly, pulled her cloak around her and went to the door.

"Aye?" she asked, pulling it open.

Robin stood there, looking purposeful. "Dress, lady. We've plans for the day."

She stifled a yawn. "We do?"

"Aye, and they do not include my grandmother, so endeavor not to wake her."

Anne felt a shiver go through her, and she suspected it wasn't fear. It was certainly enough to wake her fully. "Just us?"

Robin scowled. "Is that such an unappealing thought?"

"Oh, nay," she managed.

He grunted. "Then make haste, Anne. And dress warmly. I'll wait for you below."

He pulled the door shut quietly and Anne remained there, staring at it as if she hadn't seen it before. Robin of Artane had just told her he planned to have her to himself for the whole of the day.

Alone.

Unchaperoned.

Never mind that he was her husband. Never mind that he'd spent the past handful of days enduring numerous tortures in an effort to please her. That he wanted to be alone with her, with *her* mind you, was something she wasn't quite sure she could digest.

The door opened suddenly and Robin peered in.

"Don't hear you moving," he said.

And then he gave her the briefest of smiles before he shut the door again.

Anne wondered if she might manage to clothe herself before she fell over in a faint. Alone and facing his smiles at the same time?

By the saints, this was unexpected.

She shook her head to clear it, then went in search of clothes. With no idea of what Robin had in mind, she dressed as sensibly as she could. She could only hope his idea of a day of pleasure did not include a lengthy stay in the lists, though she wore her boots just in case.

Once she was dressed, she took a deep breath, put her shoulders back and opened the door. No sense in dawdling. Robin would come to fetch her otherwise.

Though she had to admit the thought of that wasn't unappealing either.

She shut the door behind her, then looked up and squeaked. Robin himself was leaning against the opposite wall with his arms folded over his chest and a frown on his face. Apparently the lists did not figure into his plans for the day, for she could see no mail on him. He pushed away from the wall and straightened. Anne looked up at him and felt somehow very small and fragile. She tried a smile.

"Will this suit?" she asked, holding up a bit of her gown for his inspection.

"Aye," he said, taking her hand. "Perfectly." He lifted her hand to his lips, then stopped and scowled. "Do I kiss?" he asked, sounding rather irritated, "or do I not? I vow my grandmother's peacocks have left me positively bewildered."

Well, there was no point in beginning to bite her tongue now. She'd spent the whole of her life sharpening it on the man before her, so she'd best continue as she'd begun. He might begin to worry if she didn't speak her mind.

"Kiss," she stated.

"Think you?"

"Definitely."

And so he did,

Anne felt tingles start on the back of her hand and work their way down her arm and up the back of her scalp. She shivered.

And he smiled.

"Think what those silly lads at court are missing," he said.

"As well as their ladies."

"Though I would kill anyone who took such a liberty with you," he added.

"You are barbaric, my lord."

"But do I suit?" he asked.

"Perfectly," she answered, without hesitation.

Robin stared at her for a moment or two in silence, looked over her head at the door behind her, then scowled.

"Damn her anyway," he grumbled.

And with that, he took Anne's hand and pulled her down the passageway with him. She hardly dared speculate on why he was having such unkind feelings toward his grandmother, but it seemed to have something to do with her inhabiting his bedchamber.

Or perhaps 'twas that she was inhabiting his bed.

That was almost too lustful a thought to contemplate, even given her recently lustful state of mind. But since Robin was in truth her husband, and since she had more courage than any bruised and bloodied lout he'd ever fought with—his words and not hers, though she had found them very much to her liking—there was no sense in not being honest about her feelings toward him.

For indeed, his kiss had been exceptionally memorable.

As were his confessions of the night before. She could hardly believe that such a simple confrontation with Baldwin had been what had ruined so much of their lives. Looking back on it now, she could understand Robin's actions completely. From the time she'd known him, she'd known he wished to prove himself worthy of Rhys's affection. The possibility of failure, and the accompanying disgrace, had driven him far past where it should have in the lists.

And it wouldn't have made any difference to Robin if he had been just recently recovered from a fever. That he'd been humiliated before the other lads would have devastated him.

But to think 'twas her opinion that had mattered so much to him.

The witless oaf.

She sighed as she stepped down the last step behind him into the great hall. Much as she grieved for their loss, she grieved as well for the suffering it had caused him. And for what? To prove himself superior to Baldwin? That had never been in question. To prove his worthiness to Rhys? Never had a son been more beloved of a father. To prove himself to her?

Rather that he had not shunned her.

But that was behind them. He took her hand in his as they crossed the great hall and Anne felt as if the years gone before had never been, so great was her pleasure in the present moment. Robin was hers, she was his, and nothing else mattered.

She even suspected he and his father would again see eye-to-eye before the winter was out. She had no doubts Rhys had been angry with him, but she very much suspected Rhys had pushed Robin to the altar simply because he had known it was what Robin wanted deep in his heart.

Hadn't Robin said he should have wed her earlier during their conversings the night before?

And for her, there was no question where her heart lay. Nay, she would thank Rhys when next she saw him, and flick her husband smartly on the ear if he didn't do the same.

They left the great hall and Robin slowed his pace to match hers as they descended the steps to the courtyard. In spite of all her fine thoughts, she couldn't help but wonder if Robin regretted her limp. She looked up at him.

"I'm sorry," she said.

"For what?" he asked gravely.

She sighed. "For going so slowly."

He shook his head. "You've no need to apologize for it. It gives me ample time to enjoy the beauty before me."

"Well, your father's keep is marvelous."

"I spoke of you," he said, "though I must admit Artane is a fine place as well. But you," he said, looking at her intently, "aye, you are a pleasure to look on at length."

She could hardly believe the change in him, but she wasn't about to argue. She smiled up at him. "Robin de Piaget, are you wooing me?"

"Aye," he said cheerfully. "Do you like it?"

"Very much," she admitted.

He squeezed her hand, then led her across the courtyard to where a cluster of men waited. Robin stopped, looked at her, and frowned thoughtfully.

"I've wondered what would be more comfortable," he said slowly, "but I couldn't decide. Do you prefer your own mount, or shall you ride with me?"

"I could bear my own," she answered.

"And the other?"

"I could bear that as well, if you like," she said.

"I'll endeavor not to drop you," he added.

"My thanks, I'm sure."

"We'll bring your mount just in case." He nodded at his men. "They'll come too, of course."

"Of course." She looked at the men, but they were busying themselves seeing to their gear. They were men Anne had seen before with Robin, and she suspected by looking at them that they were a handful of the fiercest of the lads he had brought from France with him.

"'Twould be foolhardy to take you from the keep without some men to guard you."

"Though you would be enough," she said.

"Likely so, but I fear I may become distracted and not be able to give my surroundings my full attention."

Fortunately it was cold outside, so the crisp air saw to the fire in her cheeks, else she would have been tempted to fan herself.

"The lads will disappear," he continued. "You'll never know they're there."

She looked up at him and frowned. "They're accustomed to this sort of thing?"

"If by *this sort of thing*, you mean secret trysts with lovers, then nay," he said, returning her frown. "I daresay they're more accustomed to scouting out the enemy. It would hardly serve them to show themselves before they've discovered anything, now would it?"

She made a solemn, silent vow never again to presuppose anything about her husband. She suspected that her guesses would never be close to the mark anyway. She sighed.

"Forgive me. I have misjudged you."

"'Tis never wise to believe rumor."

"I can see that now."

He leaned closer to her. "I have far less experience than I've been credited with," he whispered.

She looked up at him in surprise. "In truth?"

"In truth."

"But . . ."

"You've little experience with women at court if you think all their boasts are truthful. What else are they to say when I come to my bed, find them there waiting and boot them out with not so much as a kiss for their trouble?"

"Except the fair-haired lasses, of course," she said, wondering if he would now clout her in the nose for repeating her father's words.

He looked at her narrowly. "Your cheek is astonishing."

"And how dull you would find it otherwise." She squeezed his hand. "Let us leave your lovers, however few they may be and whatever their hair color, in the past, my lord."

"Gladly," he muttered as he led her to his mount, then swung up into the saddle. It was a low saddle, however, and she could easily see where she might fit before him on his horse's withers. She could only hope it would not be as uncomfortable as it looked.

One of Robin's men lifted her up and he settled her sideways across his thighs. He took up his reins and clucked at his horse.

"Painful?" he asked.

"That depends on the length of the journey," she said.

"Will you last to the shore?" he asked.

"The shore?" She looked at him with surprise. "Truly?"

"I thought it might please you."

"You thought well," she said happily. "Aye, 'twill be a pleasure to walk there. I've missed it this year."

He was silent as they made their way down to the outer gates and away from the keep. Anne grew used to the motion of his horse and the feel of his arms around her. She even found herself leaning her head against his shoulder.

"You know," he said slowly, "I have no other keep so close to the sea. Well, save one in France and 'tis unfit for habitation."

She thought on that for a bit, wondering what it was he was telling her. "And?"

"Well, I suppose my sire won't cast us outside the gates, but we may have to spend time in other places not so near the sea. Will that grieve you?"

She looked at him. "Does it matter?"

"Of course," he said, looking puzzled. "I don't wish for you to be unhappy."

"Robin, I daresay the place doesn't matter so much as the company."

He grunted thoughtfully, but said nothing more. Anne watched the land before her fall away to the sea and marveled not only at the beauty of it, but the delight of watching the like from the shelter of her husband's arms. Her husband. She could scarce accustom herself to the idea of calling him that, yet it seemed as if it always should have been so.

Once they had reached the shore, Robin bid his mount stop, then he swung down. The beast was perfectly still until Robin had held up his arms and pulled Anne into them. She looked around and was surprised to see none of his men.

"They're still here?" she asked.

He nodded. "Aye. Scouting and such. 'Tis what they're most adept at, and it pleases them as well."

"And that matters to you?"

He smiled dryly. "Though many would say a mere command should be enough to sway a man, I've found that such commands serve me better if given to men whose talents already lie with what they're required to do. I've the luxury of my own guard and the means with which to pay them very well. I chose men who suited my purposes and whom my purposes suited."

"And they are fond of you, I suppose," she said.

He shrugged. "I doubt they lie awake at night thinking on it, but I suppose they are fond enough." He straightened her cloak over her shoulders, then took her hand. "Their purpose, however, is to be forgotten today, so let us do so. I brought you here to have you to myself."

She shook her head and smiled as he took her hand. "I don't know that I'll ever accustom myself to hearing such things from you."

He sighed. "I suppose another apology—"

"Nay," she said with a laugh, "no more of those. I vow I'm not recovered from the ones I've already received."

He paused. "Perhaps, my lady, we should begin again."

"How mean you that?" she asked.

"Mayhap it would serve us to begin afresh, as if we had never met and had nothing of our past burdening us."

"Is that possible?" she mused.

"Is it worth the time to try?"

If such a thing were truly possible, she couldn't see how it could hurt. So she nodded. "Aye, I daresay it is."

He looked at her thoughtfully for a moment or two, then released her hand and shooed her away. "Go walk."

"I beg your pardon?"

"Go walk," he repeated. "Down the strand."

"By myself?"

"You'll be perfectly safe, if that's your worry. Besides, you never know who you'll encounter on a lonely strand in the north."

She hesitated. "The sand is not the easiest thing to walk on."

He frowned immediately. "Will it pain you?"

"It will shame me."

He rolled his eyes so forcefully, she feared they might stick up in his head.

"By the saints, Anne," he said, sounding mightily annoyed, "it matters not to me. Is there nothing I can do to convince you of that?"

She smiled. "I vow you just did." She took a pace backward and gave him a little wave. "I'm off to encounter handsome, dangerous strangers."

He grunted and folded his arms over his chest. Anne turned and began to walk north. The sand here was smooth and fine. If it hadn't been so bitterly cold from the sea air, she would have taken off her boots. A pity there was no sun, else the sand might have been warm. She looked up into the gray sky, heavy with clouds and wondered if she might get a soaking before the day was through.

She heard the thunder of horses' hooves and turned to see Robin coming toward her with her mount trailing behind him. He gave her a wide berth, then swung his beasts around, stopped them and dropped to the ground. He strode toward her and stopped a pace or two away.

And Anne wondered what she would have done had she not known him. Likely dropped to the sand in a swoon.

The wind blew his dark hair away from his face, leaving his rugged features fully revealed. His eyes were the color of the clouds. She was certain she had never seen a more handsome man, and she had certainly seen an enormous number of men over the course of her years.

And then he smiled gravely and made her a low bow.

"Fairest lady, I saw you walking along the shore and I trow my heart stopped within me, my mind seized upon your loveliness as if upon an elusive dream and I could do nothing but stop and plead for your name that I might ever carry it in my heart."

He blinked, then a look of complete consternation came over his features, as if he could scarce believe the words had come from his mouth. "By the saints," he said in amazement, "I've been corrupted by peacocks!"

Anne laughed before she could stop herself.

He scowled. "Ah, a saucy wench, I see. Mayhap you do not realize who you are laughing at."

"Doubtless I don't," she said, managing to reduce her mirth to a mere smile. "Though you look passing fierce."

"And you look passing fair," he returned. He looked her over, then frowned. "You've a hitch in your step, I see."

She didn't let her smile falter, though it was not easily done. "Aye."

"An old battle wound?"

"You could call it that."

He grunted. "Have them myself. Perhaps later we'll compare them. For now, I think I should acquaint you with my own sweet self, so you can see if I'm to your liking."

She listened to him dismiss her leg, and wondered if it might be just as easy for her to do the like herself. And why not? There was little she could do to change it.

Or to change the past, she realized with a start.

Perhaps Robin had matters aright. Could they not leave the painful things behind and begin afresh? If he could overlook her flaw, could she not overlook his foolishness?

She suspected she could.

She slipped her hands up the opposite sleeves of her cloak and waited patiently for Robin to begin his game.

"Robin de Piaget at your service," he said with a little bow. "Handy with a blade, not handy with the lute and perfectly incapable of rendering a decent rhyme."

She laughed softly. "Indeed."

"And I don't dance. Well," he amended, "not very well."

"Is that so?"

"Aye," he said. "But I've several good points you might be interested in."

"Then, by all means, trot them out and let me have a look at them."

"Well," he said, stroking his chin thoughtfully, "I've a pair of lovely gray eyes."

"You do indeed."

"I'm reasonable—"

"Are you?"

"Tolerant," he continued archly, "kind to a fault and ever pleasant to all."

"That is quite a list of virtues," she remarked.

"I've only begun. Let me know if the list grows too long for you and I'll fetch you a seat."

"How thoughtful of you."

"Add that to my list."

She looked up at him and smiled as he continued to enumerate in great detail all the things he was. And as she listened to him extol his virtues as if he were a stallion someone intended to sell, she realized that he did indeed have many fine characteristics. Had he been presented to her as a potential suitor, would she not have dropped to her knees and kissed her father's feet in gratitude?

She suspected she would have indeed.

"But," he said, "I've neglected to tell you the most important thing about myself, the thing I've carried in my heart the longest and the secret that few know." He looked down at her solemnly.

"And what would that great secret be, my lord?"

He paused. He looked at her for a moment or two in silence, then he held out his hands for hers. She pulled her hands free of her cloak and put her hands in his. His palms were callused, his fingers rough from work. But all she noticed truly was that his hands were warm and that they held hers gently. She looked up and found that his expression was a very tender one.

For Robin, that is.

"It is that I love you," he said quietly.

"Oh," she said, blinking. She cast about for something to say, but all she could do was stare up at him in complete surprise. She had expected him to reveal that he loved children, or had a soft place in his heart for hounds.

He waited.

And then he began to scowl.

"Well?" he demanded.

"I'm still recovering from that, my lord. Pray tell me you've no more revelations of that kind."

"It would be passing kind of you to reveal something of yourself! Something of that ilk!" he said heatedly.

She looked at him in surprise. "Well, of course I love you, you great oaf."

He spluttered for a moment, then glared at her. "Prettily spoken."

"Oh, Robin," she said, with a laugh. She went into his arms and hugged him tightly. "Surely you've always known it."

He shook his head. "Nay, Anne. I hoped it. And I told myself what a goodly life I would have, had I but your love in it."

She looked up at him. "And now that you have it?"

He smiled. "Today, my lady, knowing that you care for me only leads me to believe I could do anything you willed of me."

"You've already done that."

"What?" he asked. "Brought you to the shore and given you my heart?"

"Aye," she said, "that."

"And taken yours in return?"

She pulled her head back to look up at him. "That as well."

One of his eyebrows went up. "Is there aught else you would demand of me whilst I am baring my soul?"

"A kiss?"

"A fine idea."

"I thought so as well."

"If my lady will permit?"

"I suspect I will begin to demand if you don't cease with your babbling."

He smiled, then gathered her closer. "As my lady wishes," he said, lowering his head to hers.

And at that precise moment, it began to rain.

And it wasn't a pleasant, gentle rain.

The heavens opened and a torrent descended.

Robin clapped his hand to his head. "We are doomed!" he exclaimed.

And then the winds began to blow.

"Complain later," she said, holding her hands over her head. "Find us shelter now!"

He cursed. "Can you ride?"

"Gladly!"

He put her up into her saddle, then swung up into his

own. "To the forest, then," he called over the wind. "Follow me!"

It was only then that Anne realized he had shortened her stirrups for her. And to her great surprise, it was far easier to ride with her knees bent so far than it was with them scarce bent at all. She had little trouble keeping Robin's pace and each time he looked over his shoulder to see how she fared, she urged him on until they were flying across the ground. Laughter tore from her; she was powerless to stop it.

She saw Robin's guard keeping pace with them, a short distance away, of course, and just the sight of it relieved her. Not that she had any reason to fear, but it never hurt to have extra men about.

The forest was a goodly distance from the shore, and perhaps that was too lofty a title for it. There were trees, true, but 'twas nothing as tall as she'd seen near Fenwyck, nor as dense as she'd heard tell of in the north. But it would provide them at least a little relief from the storm and for that she was grateful. Once they were under the shelter of the trees, Robin swung down off his horse and held up his hands for her. She was out of breath from the exhilaration of riding so swiftly, and from her laughter.

He pulled her under a tree, then Anne found herself backed up against it with Robin in her arms.

"By the saints," he said breathlessly, "you are beautiful." His eyes were bright, his hair was blown all about and he was staring at her so intensely, Anne wondered if she might begin to melt. "I can hardly believe," he whispered, "that you are mine."

And then he bent his head to kiss her.

Anne was powerfully glad she had something to lean against. She closed her eyes as he buried his hands in her hair and tilted her face up. And when his mouth came down on hers, she couldn't stop a shiver, or the abrupt loss of her breath.

And then her surroundings faded until all she could feel

was Robin's mouth on hers and his strong arms about her. She gave herself up completely to his kiss.

And then she completely lost her sense of time passing. All she knew was that she simply could not have enough of Robin's mouth on hers.

And she wasn't at all sure that kissing was going to satisfy the longing he was stirring inside her. That wasn't a bad thing. He was, after all, her husband.

Slowly, she became aware of her surroundings. The rain continued to fall, pattering on the last autumn leaves above them. The wind continued to blow, wiping her hair and his. And then she noticed that Robin was dripping on her.

He tore his mouth away, then leaned his forehead against her, drawing in ragged breaths.

"Are you unwell?" she asked, her own breathing equally ragged.

"Ask me in an hour or so, when I've recovered."

She saw the twinkle in his eye and frowned at him. "Are you jesting at my expense?" she asked, wiping the rain from her face.

"Nay, my love," he whispered, kissing her again softly. "I'm giving you an honest answer. The saints be praised we have somewhere dry to sit here, for I doubt I have the strength to walk." He looked about him, then smiled at her. "Will you have something to eat?"

She smiled dryly. Robin's concern for the filling of his belly was nothing if not predictable. Perhaps he had suffered from too many polite meals at his grandmother's table. "As you will, Robin."

"Then sit you there on that log and I'll fetch my saddlebags. My grandmother's cook was persuaded to pack us something tasty."

"Using your gentle influence again, my lord?"

He snorted. "A drawn sword, rather. He was most unwilling to rise when asked."

She shuddered. "Then let us pray 'tis edible."

"Oh, it is," he said, coming to sit next to her. "I know

this, for I watched him sample everything before he packed it away. There should be no mystery as to his size."

Anne watched him as they ate, and found herself surprised by his ready smiles and hearty laughter. It had been years since she'd seen the like and she realized then how much she had missed it. Robin looked as if he'd shed a handful of years and a heavy load of care.

He looked up from his consumption of a tart and smiled at her. "What is it?"

She shook her head, smiling as well. "Nothing, really."

He hesitated. "Did I eat too much?"

She put her arm around his neck and leaned over to kiss him softly. "Nay, Robin. I was just looking at you."

"And finding me to your liking, apparently."

"Apparently," she agreed.

He reached up and held her hand that rested on his shoulder. "You know, Anne, my grandmother could find somewhere else to sleep."

"She could indeed."

He paused. "Should she?"

"What do you think?"

"I already know what I think," he said. "What I'm interested in are your thoughts."

She chewed on her lip for a moment or two, then cast aside any semblance of reticence. There was no point in it. "I think," she said slowly, "that she would be passing comfortable any number of other places."

Robin was on his feet before she had finished her words. "Then let us be off," he said. "Best see her settled early, so she has no complaints." He pulled her to her feet, then released her to go fetch his saddlebag. Anne watched, then noticed something on the ground near where they'd sat. She walked over and picked it up.

"This must have fallen out," she said, handing the scrap of parchment to him. "Words of love from Cook?"

"Wooing ideas from my grandmother, no doubt," Robin

said with a snort. He unfolded the paper, then went perfectly still.

The sight of the change in him from lover to warrior set Anne's hair on end.

She didn't think she wanted to know what had caused it.

38

Robin stood in the shelter of the trees and considered. He'd passed a marvelous day up to that point. Anne had seemingly found the contents of his heart bearable and his kiss tolerable. The rain had been a less than pleasant occurrence, but it had been remedied easily enough. He had looked forward to returning to the keep and passing the rest of his day closeted in his father's bedchamber with his wife, consummating their marriage. He had thought it an afternoon to relish.

He suspected that this new development, though, just might be enough to ruin that.

Robin looked down at the note and suppressed a shudder at the words written there.

> *I know where you sleep and you'll die there. I'll not rest until the keep is mine.*

Anne ripped the note from his hands before he could stop her. He watched her still completely as she read the words. Then she looked up at him in horror.

"It isn't over."

"Nay, my love. Apparently not."

She threw herself into his arms and he gathered her close. He gritted his teeth in frustration. Perhaps thinking Maude had been behind the attacks had been naive. But if not Maude, then who? Who would want Artane badly enough to kill for it?

He latched onto one name with strength borne of certainty.

Baldwin of Sedgwick.

He whistled out a bird call and within moments, his guard was surrounding them. Robin read them the note, but said nothing else. He wouldn't need to. They would understand that their duty was to look after Anne, for he'd spoken to them of it more than once in the past.

He looked back at his lady. "Can you ride?"

She nodded without hesitation.

He put her up into his saddle, then swung up behind her.

"Are we going home?" she asked.

"Briefly."

"Robin, what will we do?"

"Kill the bastard," Robin growled. He reached for the reins and kicked his horse into a gallop.

Half an hour later, he thundered into the inner bailey and dropped to the ground. He held up his arms for his lady, then set her on her feet. He bellowed for the acting captain of his father's guard.

"Sedgwick?" Robin demanded.

"Haven't seen him since yesterday, my lord," the man said, looking at him with wide eyes.

That brought Robin up short. If Baldwin had been gone a pair of days now, how could he have placed the note in their saddlebag?

He cursed, then pulled Anne along with him up the steps to the great hall. He found his grandmother loitering near the fire and collected her on his way up the stairs. Perhaps if they reasoned together, they might identify who had done this.

He looked at Anne as she followed him, with his guards trailing hard on her heels. He smiled grimly.

"How fare you?"

She shook her head. "I cannot possibly spend the rest of my life this way. We will lose our minds."

He nodded, agreeing completely.

He went into his father's bedchamber with sword drawn and a guard with a torch going before him. He searched the chamber thoroughly, then ushered Anne and his grandmother in. Once he'd started a fire and seated them to his liking, he handed his grandmother the note.

"What do you think?" he asked.

His grandmother peered at it, then pursed her lips. "An annoyance," she said dismissively.

"Whilst such a thing is indeed true, it is not so easily ignored," Robin said.

"Anne told me a bit of the happenings before my arrival," Joanna conceded. "I thought, however, that such troubles ended in the chapel."

Anne shivered. "Aye, so thought we as well." She looked at Robin. "Think you 'tis but a jest?"

Robin sat, rubbed his hands over his face and sighed deeply. "As much as I would like to believe thusly, I cannot risk my fate or yours on such a hope."

"But it could have been a servant," Joanna protested.

Robin scowled. "One who speaks French instead of peasant's English?"

"Mine do," Joanna said, then she blinked. "Think you it could have been—"

Robin shook his head. "These attacks began long before you arrived."

"But those were directed at me," Anne said. "Surely this isn't the same person."

"Perhaps," he said slowly, "they thought to strike at me through you."

"But what sense does that make?" she protested.

"How is it best to wound a man?" he asked with a grim smile. "Strike first at what he loves best."

"Oh," Anne said softly. "I see."

Joanna clapped her hands. "The saints be praised," she said happily. " 'Twas obviously all that civilizing, grandson, which has brought you to such a realization."

Robin glared at his grandmother. "The note," he said. "Let us think on that more, for 'tis our best clue. Now, I agree it couldn't be a servant—"

"Maude was a servant," Anne interrupted.

Robin turned his glare on her. "Meaning there could be another lord's daughter hiding in the kitchen with my death on her mind?"

" 'Tis possible," she offered.

He grunted. "Any other suggestions?"

"A scribe," Joanna said. "A priest. Another nobleman. Someone who can fashion his letters without mistakes."

"Well, I suppose that eliminates Sedgwick," Robin said with a snort.

"It could be those Lowlanders," Anne offered. "The border shifts so often and your sire always finds himself in the midst of whatever skirmish is happening. He has ever had troubles with them."

"Aye," Robin agreed, nodding slowly, "but what use would they have for the keep? Steal one of Father's daughters, aye, but his hall? They would find themselves routed within days."

"It could have been anyone, Robin," Anne said helplessly. "Men come and go through your sire's gates in droves. It could have been anyone who resented you."

"But how many of those men want Artane?"

"How many don't?" she returned with a half smile. "Robin, this is a marvelous hall."

"Maybe 'tis someone you offended dispensing justice," Joanna said suddenly. "How many souls did you anger that day, my love?"

Robin pursed his lips. "I dealt as fairly as I knew how, Grandmère."

She shrugged her shoulders. "Men are complicated creatures. I would look to my rolls were I you. And while you are about your business, Anne and I will remain here cozily. Send up the minstrels when you go, love."

Robin had no intentions of being dismissed so easily. He stood, pulled his grandmother up and embraced her heartily. "I love you, Grandmère," he said, kissing both her cheeks, "and I appreciate all you've done for my sorry self. I'm quite certain Anne will benefit the rest of her life from the courtly skills your lads have endeavored to teach me. But you're in my marriage bed and I want you out of it."

"But—"

" 'Tis best you pack up your lads and head home."

"But—"

" 'Twill be much safer. Anne and I will come for a visit once this is all sorted out."

"Nay," Joanna said, shaking her head. "I am of no value to any assailant, my lad. I'll just keep myself tucked up nicely in your sire's chamber."

"And if someone enters?" Robin demanded. "What then?"

His grandmother smiled, but it wasn't a very pleasant smile.

"Do you actually think," she said, leaning forward and looking at him intently, "that I've lived this long, survived as many kings and fended off as many undesirable suitors as I have without having learned a bit of this and that?"

"Well . . ."

"Think you my lads are for ornament only?"

"Aye, Grandmère. That is what I think."

"Then you haven't looked very closely at them." She sat back and smiled indulgently. "See to yourself, Robin, and leave me to my little comforts. I'll be safe enough here."

Robin considered. And he watched his grandmother consider as well, though he suspected the older woman was fairly sure of the outcome. After all, she was the one acquainted with her lads' skills. Finally, Robin sighed.

"Very well, Grandmère. The victory is yours."

"I'll think on a plan whilst I'm enduring my confinement," she said, tapping her finger against the arm of her chair. "We'll root out this fiend soon enough."

"May you have better luck than I've had," Robin said, inclining his head." He looked at Anne. "We had best pack, then, my lady."

"We're leaving?" Anne asked.

"For the moment. I'll not be a prisoner in my own hall."

"But where will we go?" she asked.

"Where I am most accustomed to sleeping."

"In a tent?" Joanna asked, aghast.

"Aye," Robin said, satisfied by the prospect. "Anne loves the shore, and I am very fond of my life. We'll stay out in the open, well beyond the range of any bows, and see if our assailant has the spine to come against us in a fair fight."

Joanna sighed. "I would say it isn't safe, but if anyone has the skill to protect Anne, it would be you, love." She patted his cheek. "Off with you, then. Unless," she said, with a calculating look, "unless you would like me to prepare the marriage bed—"

"Nay," Robin exclaimed, only to realize Anne had done the same thing. He wondered if he was as red in the face as his wife had suddenly become.

Joanna pursed her lips. "Robin, should you not send for your sire?"

He shook his head. "I want him and the children safely out of the way. This is a personal attack on me, not him. I'll see to it." He paused and looked at her. "Be careful, Grandmère."

"I always am."

"And you, my lady," Robin said, turning to Anne and pulling her to her feet, "will remain with me and I apologize in advance for the tedium you will endure."

"I'll be with you. How tedious could that possibly be?"

He only smiled grimly and hoped she wouldn't do him bodily harm when she realized the truth of the matter.

•   •   •

It was barely past noon when Robin found himself standing in the courtyard, watching his gear be packed into a wagon. He looked at the men doing it. They were all sworn to his service, those lads, and there wasn't a one of them he wouldn't trust with his life.

I know where you sleep.

He couldn't stop thinking about the note. He could scarce believe what he'd read, but as he still held the blighted scrap of paper in his hand, he couldn't deny that it was true.

And to think he'd believed Maude behind it all.

What a fool he'd been.

He gave more thought to what he'd just discussed with his grandmother. Was it possible it could have been one of her servants? He couldn't believe that. This all had begun long before they'd arrived.

I know where you'll sleep, and you'll die there.

All the more reason not to retreat to the safety of the keep. 'Twas obvious that someone inside had his death on his mind. All the more reason not to bolt himself inside his chamber and remain there. What would that serve him? To remain a virtual prisoner there?

Nay, he would sit idle. And he would not spend another day looking over his shoulder as he walked down a passageway.

I'll not rest until the keep is mine.

Not if he could help it. He had no choice but to draw out the fiend, face him on his own terms, then slay him.

For he would not give up anything that was his, not Anne, not the keep, nor his own life.

Which was why he was watching his gear be loaded into a wagon. He had given the matter quick, hard thought, and come to a decision. He would take Anne far from the keep, surround her with his men and see if their assailant had the bollocks to come against them.

For Robin was itching for a fight.

And his lads were equally as eager.

He looked about him and wondered if Baldwin had

returned. Was it possible his cousin was behind this? No doubt Baldwin wouldn't scorn Artane were it offered to him. But to obtain it by murder?

He seriously doubted his cousin had the imagination for such a thing. Nay, Baldwin's means of obtaining anything would be to lower his head and charge Robin. A note would likely be beyond the lout's capabilities.

But if not Baldwin, then who?

Robin shook his head. He wasn't sure how well he could investigate inside the keep if he were out of it, but he couldn't see any other option. The safest place for Anne was outside the keep. Perhaps then he could scrutinize whoever tried to come near them.

He dragged his hand through his hair. Someone wanted the keep. Someone wanted him dead. He could scarce believe it.

At least the latter was something he was accustomed to, for he certainly had made his share of enemies over the years. But he was wary and deft with a blade, so the ending of his life never concerned him much. Now, he had begun to feel differently. He had souls depending on him.

One soul, he corrected himself. He looked behind him to see her standing at the top of the steps up to the great hall. She'd come and gone a time or two, always accompanied by a pair of his lads, of course. He was relieved to see her coming outside again.

The weak autumn sunlight fell down upon her pale hair and upon the deep green of her cloak. Robin shook his head in wonder. Was it possible that she had grown more beautiful because he loved her, or had his love made her more beautiful? He surely didn't know.

With any luck he'd have a lifetime in which to come to a conclusion about it.

He turned back to supervising his packing.

39

Anne stood in the courtyard, heartily regretting her rash words about being happy with Robin wherever he was and whatever he was doing. The task of packing up enough gear and seeing to the keep in his absence, albeit a not very distant absence, was chafing to say the very least. Packing themselves up hadn't taken very long, but then had come preparations for meals, the gathering of documents for Robin to study and the grilling of each of his men. He took none but his own lads, and they were apparently accustomed to moving on in a hurry.

He had left his father's steward in charge and Anne watched the man carefully as Robin laid out for him what his duties would be. And when he'd warned the man that there was trouble afoot in the keep, he hadn't blinked. A glance at his scribblings left her in no doubt that this was not the assassin.

Even the priest had not escaped Robin's scrutiny. His hand was passing fair, but not the neat, precise characters in the note. Anne had begun to wonder if it might not be a woman's hand they were looking at. Though few women of her acquaintance could write, she certainly could, as could all Gwen's family.

And what of Gwen's ladies?

But that thought was so ridiculous, she immediately pushed it aside. She'd never sat in the same solar with anyone who would have wanted Artane for their own. Even Edith couldn't possibly be interested. Edith would likely rather wed with Robin than slay him.

Wouldn't she?

Anne shook her head as she stood waiting for Robin in the courtyard. Perhaps it was a passing nobleman whom Robin had recently offended. That was entirely possible. Perhaps, given the time, they would find out who it was.

Then they could retreat to a warm bedchamber, for much as Anne loved the sea, she suspected it would be a bloody cold fortnight spent there.

It was late afternoon before Robin's great tent was pitched. A fire had been lit before it and Anne found herself huddled next to it, shivering. They had already eaten, which should have warmed her, but the bitter wind from the north had stolen all her heat. She looked up as Robin threw himself down next to her.

"By the saints," he said with a scowl, "you wouldn't think a simple removal half a league from the hall would be this much trouble, would you?"

She shook her head with a smile. "I fear I've never done the like, so I've nothing to compare it to."

"Trust me," he said grimly, " 'tis usually far simpler than this. But at least we'll be safe." He looked at her. "Your lips are blue, lady."

"I'm nigh onto freezing."

He frowned. "I vow, Anne, I hadn't thought on that overmuch. I fear I was far too worried that we have a safe place to sleep."

"I'll manage," she said. "I would rather wake numb from cold, than numb from lack of life."

He reached for her hand and laced his fingers with hers.

"I'm sorry," he said simply. "Truly this wasn't how I would have had any of this proceed."

"And how would you have had it proceed, my lord?" she asked with a smile. "In a commonplace fashion with no death, destruction or keep-snatching hanging over us?"

"It would have been passing pleasant to have a quiet little Mass said over our heads, then retire to our quiet little bedchamber for a pair of weeks where meals could have been delivered to us without us worrying about dying from ingesting them."

She shrugged. "Dull."

"Pleasant," Robin insisted.

"I suppose we'll have to make do with what we have, then," she said, "since the other is not an option."

"I promise, my lady, that there will come a time when our lives are quite peaceful."

Anne only hoped they both lived that long. She looked at Robin and found him staring thoughtfully out at the sea. She followed suit, and it wasn't long before the ceaseless roar of the waves coming into shore had lulled her into a half sleep. It was not without alarm that she came to herself. Would Robin's men be just as soothed, and neglect what they were supposed to be seeing to?

And then another gust of arctic wind blew across the sand and Anne blinked. Perhaps they would be safe, as long as the wind blew. For all she knew, their assailant wouldn't have the courage to venture out in such weather.

A pity they themselves had been driven to the like.

"Anne?"

She looked at him and smiled reflexively at the sight. She suspected she would be hard-pressed to ever accustom herself to the fact that Robin was hers. Even harder still would be to realize that he was hers and apparently was content with that fact.

"I have something for you," he said, reaching inside his cloak and pulling forth a box.

His box.

Anne recognized it immediately and prayed she would

have the skill for a goodly bit of subterfuge. It wouldn't do for Robin to think she had ransacked his things while he'd been about his business.

She watched him lift the lid, then shield the contents from the wind. But she didn't miss the ribbons he carefully held onto, as if he treasured them in truth. He dug about for a moment or two, then pulled forth something wrapped in a bit of cloth.

And Anne forced herself not to decide beforehand what it all might mean.

Robin replaced his ribbons, shut the lid and tucked the box inside the tent. Then he carefully unwrapped the ring and held it to the firelight. Anne bit her lip. 'Twas still the same ring she had seen before and wondered about its purpose.

Robin buffed it for a moment with the cloth, then looked at her and smiled gravely.

"I wanted to give this to you in the chapel, but I would have had to cross swords with my father for the chance to fetch it from my chamber." He looked at the ring and his smile turned wistful. "Hard as it might be to believe, I've had this almost five years."

"As a token for some fair maid?" she asked before she could bite her tongue.

He looked at her, amused. " 'Tis your wedding ring, Anne, and it was ever meant to be such. Why else would the stone match your eyes, or the gold match your hair?"

"Oh," she said, but very little sound came out.

"You remember I told you about that first little skirmish in Spain?"

She didn't dare answer nay, so she nodded.

"I walked Nick through one of the worst rainstorms I've ever seen simply because I'd heard tell of a goldsmith whose skill was unsurpassed living near Madrid. The gem he had as well, though I would have searched for that had he not had something to suit."

"Indeed," she managed.

"It may be too large," he said, frowning down at it. "I

vow I could not remember what size might suit you, so I used my smallest finger for a model, then had the man decrease the size even more." He looked up at her and smiled. "Will you have it?"

Her hand was shaking as she held it out. Ah, how she had misjudged him. She watched as he took her hand and tried the ring on several fingers. The only place with which it met any success was on her thumb. Robin frowned.

"That won't do," he said, looking at her hand as if he could will her fingers to plumpen.

Anne curled her fingers into her palm. "It will suit for the moment."

"I could bind a bit of cloth to it, to make it fit elsewhere."

Anne hesitated to let him have it back, but she supposed he wasn't going to change his mind about giving it to her. After all, he'd had it fashioned with her in mind.

As amazing a thing as that was.

She heard a rip and groaned silently as she watched him continue to take his dagger to the hem of his tunic. He looked up at her from under his eyebrows and smiled.

"Sorry," he said. "I vow I'll mend it myself."

She pursed her lips. "That I doubt."

"I'm capable."

"You're also wed," she said dryly.

He laughed. "You would think you'd just sentenced yourself to a lifetime of mending my clothing."

"I have."

"I'll be more careful."

She'd seen Robin's clothing and she suspected a little more care wouldn't be enough to save her from hours of mending. But somehow, when he'd adjusted her ring to his liking, a bit of mending didn't sound like such an onerous task when she would have his ring on her finger to look at as she did the like.

He slipped his ring onto her finger, then took her hand in his and ran his finger over her ring.

And then he looked at her.

And she wondered if it was the fire to have warmed her so suddenly.

"There is," he said slowly, "other business we might see to as well this night."

"By the saints, Robin," she said with half a laugh, "you make it sound as if you're preparing for a clandestine conflict with some band of mercenaries."

He scowled at her. "I've never had a wife before. I'm not exactly certain how one goes about this . . . um—"

"Business?" she supplied.

He shut his mouth and scowled a bit more.

"Deflowering?" she offered.

He pursed his lips. "You've passed too much time with my sister, I can see that."

She only smiled. "If my father could see us now, he might think again about his assumptions."

Robin shook his head with a short laugh. "Saints, Anne, but our lives have been a tangle thus far."

She watched him rub his thumb over the back of her hand and smiled at the sight. It was all the more miraculous because she wore his ring. "How would you have had it go, my lord? If you had had the ordering of the day's events?"

"First," he said, looking at her with a dry smile, "I wouldn't have found myself in your bed before I wed you. A maid should never be subjected to a man's snores before she's already wed with him and 'tis too late to change her mind."

"I doubt I would have done that," she said.

"I was, frankly, astonished you came to the chapel at all," he continued. "Given the circumstances."

"It wasn't fully under my own sails," she admitted.

"And it should have been you and I there with the only sword bared mine as I laid it at your feet and pledged to protect you with my name and my body," he said, his smile turning grave. "I would change it if I could, my lady."

"But you cannot, so do not try. But you can entertain me with how things could have proceeded from there."

"A fine meal," he said, taking her hand in both his own. "A bit of dancing, perhaps."

"Which you are remarkably skilled at," she said with a smile.

"For a warrior with cloddish feet," he agreed. "And such compliments would have been met with ones of my own in which I praised your beauty and your own skill with the steps. And whilst all the rest of our family danced and made merry, we would have escaped to a tent made ready by the sea, surrounded by my guards that we might have had a great amount of privacy to be about our—"

"Business," she finished.

"Of course."

She looked behind them. "The tent is here, I see. And such a sturdy one."

He smiled. "I had it fetched once I arrived here. I had left much gear behind at Nick's hall in France, but subsequently saw that I might have a need for it."

"Then you planned to stay," she said softly.

"How could I leave?" he asked. "You were here."

She could only look at him, silently. He returned her look, but a corner of his mouth twitched.

"We have our tent," he said, with a little nod in its direction.

"So we do."

"It might be warmer inside," he offered. "Buried under blankets and furs and such."

She could hardly argue with that. Besides, the thought of being warm distracted her from the thought that she was surely on the verge of becoming Robin's wife in truth and that was a thought she had so often denied herself, it was almost painful to allow herself to entertain it.

Robin produced a candle, lit it in the fire, then entered the tent, pulling her inside with him. He set the candle on a stool, then straightened and looked at her.

"Does it suit?"

" 'Tis passing large, this tent of yours," she said, looking around her in surprise. "Luxurious, even."

"You didn't think I would shelter you in anything less, did you?"

She reached out and fingered one of the heavy cloth walls. "Substantial."

He smiled. "No one will see inside, my lady. We have our privacy."

"And our furs and blankets as well," she said. She looked at him and wondered just what she was supposed to do next. And then she looked at Robin and saw him truly. The gentleness in his expression was almost her undoing. She reached up and touched his cheek. "I can scarce believe I am here with you," she whispered. "That you have wed me."

"And who else could I have wed?" he asked, just as softly. He reached out and touched her cheek in return. "I loved you the moment I first clapped eyes on you—"

"When you put a worm down my gown—"

"And every moment since," he finished with a smile.

"Even when you didn't?" she asked gently.

"Every moment since," he repeated. "Especially during the moments in which I tried to convince myself I didn't. But I knew in my heart that my life would only be sweet if I had but one thing."

"One thing?"

He nodded. "If I had you." He tucked her hair behind her ears. "Not a day passed that you didn't consume my thoughts, neither did a night pass in which you did not haunt my dreams."

"I wish I had known," she said wistfully.

"Well, you know now," he said, "and if you'll give me time, I'll remind you every day from this moment on."

"And how will you do that, my lord?" she asked.

He took her hands and put them up around his neck, then drew her closer to him. "I'll tell you," he said, bending his head to kiss her. "I'll tell you a thousand ways every day, with every look, every word and every touch."

"When you're not grumbling at me," she breathed.

"Well," he said with a smile, "I have a reputation to maintain. Wouldn't want the lads to think I'd gone soft. But," he said, raising one eyebrow, "that will only be during the daytime."

"Is there any other time?"

"There is the night, my love. And during the nights, I will show you that I love you."

"Will you?" she managed.

"Perhaps not a thousand ways each night," he conceded, "but certainly enough that there will be no doubt in your heart that it could have been no one but you for me." He kissed her softly. "No one but you, Anne."

She looked up at him.

"Show me," she said simply.

"I will."

And he did.

40

Robin opened his eyes and came fully awake. It took him a moment or two, however, to understand why he was so warm and why he felt sand beneath his back instead of a finely stuffed goose-feather mattress.

He was warm because his wife was sprawled over him like a blanket and his back was paining him because he was sleeping on the shore.

He did have to admit, though, that there were a pair of positive details that came immediately to mind. One, he was still alive, which meant he had survived the night. Two was that he was deliciously warm despite his and his lady's lack of any clothing whatsoever.

There was, he decided, something to be said for life in a tent.

His candle had burned down to its final hour, but the light was enough that he could see Anne's eyelids flutter and open. She smiled a sleepy smile at him.

"Oh," she said with a yawn, "it's you."

He laughed in spite of himself. "Aye, my lady, 'tis me. The lout you fell asleep with last night."

"Did we sleep?" she asked pleasantly. "I surely don't remember much of that."

Nor did he, and he was certain that they hadn't slept all that long. He reached out and brushed his lady's hair back from her face and wondered if he slept still. Surely that she was his was naught but the stuff of dreams.

"You know," he said with a start, "I think I might make a poet yet."

"Think you?"

"I'm thinking very poetic thoughts about you, my love."

"A pity I've no paper and ink, else I would take them down. Geoffrey the lutenist would be most impressed."

He blinked, then looked at her in surprise. "He told you?" Then another thought occurred to him and he felt his eyes narrow. "You were in the alcove."

"I stand so accused."

"Anne!"

She only smiled and leaned closer to kiss him. "It was a marvelous gift, that morning," she said. "And I think you a perfectly fine bard. Too much gushing sours the song, don't you think?"

"What I think, my lady," he said, "is that you've insulted my fine minstrelsy skills. I have no choice but to demand reparation and satisfaction of you."

"Oh, please do," she said with a lazy smile. "Demand all you like."

He started to do just that, then hesitated. "Perhaps I am too bold," he said softly. He had worried, at first, that he might not only crush his lady, but injure her leg. He had been exceedingly careful, though he had to admit that his enthusiasm had overcome him a time or two.

She only smiled and shook her head. "I am well. Truly."

"Truly?"

"Aye. Be about your work, my lord. I would think we had yet a bit of night left and I vow I am still unconvinced completely that you love me."

He paused and looked at her. "You aren't truly, are you? Unconvinced?"

She smiled and pulled his head down to hers. "Leave your thoughts behind, Robin, and love me. 'Tis what you promised me. Remember?"

He could scarce forget. And so he loved her and as he did so, he could hardly contain his joy. By the saints, he had been blessed more than he deserved, for in Anne he had certain found his match, not only in wits but in spirit.

And then he found he could not think at all.

It was a great while later that he finally forced himself to lift up the bottom of the tent the slightest bit to determine if it were indeed daylight outside. He looked at his lady.

"I suppose we should rise," he said reluctantly.

"You still look very tired," she said. "You'll likely need a small rest after supper."

"Think you?"

"I'm almost certain of it."

He pulled away, then paused and looked at her. "Did I please you?"

"Which time?" she asked politely.

"Well," he grumbled, "we won't discuss the first time."

"Passing unpleasant," she agreed.

"It has improved since then, hasn't it?"

"Greatly."

"Then I did please you?"

"I'll tell you once I've discovered if I can walk again," she said, sitting up with a groan.

"Ah, Anne," he said, dragging his hand through his hair. "I feared you would suffer because of it."

"Robin," she said, flicking him smartly on the ear, "I meant it in jest. As a compliment," she added.

He blinked at her and wondered why he had ever thought Anne of Fenwyck to be shy and reticent.

"What?" she asked with a smile. "Do I offend you?"

"Saints, nay," he said, with feeling. "I prize your honesty."

"You may regret that someday."

He pursed his lips. "You've bludgeoned me with sharp

words regularly over the course of my life, my love. I daresay I would suffer from the lack of it if you ceased. Please, speak your mind freely."

She laughed. "Are these the words of love I can look forward to during daylight?"

"Those and more," he grunted. Then he looked at her appraisingly. " 'Tis barely dawn. Are you prepared for words, or would more deeds suit you better?"

She wasted no time returning to the comfort of warm coverings. "Deeds," she said. "Especially if they can be wrought under cover."

Robin blew out the candle. Anne of Fenwyck, lately of Artane, was his and he would miss no opportunity to show her that he was grateful for the like.

The dawn could wait a bit longer.

It was well past first light before he emerged from his tent, drawing his lady out behind him. He bid her wait for him whilst he looked about them and determined that all his guards were still at their posts. He called to his captain, who with Jason had pitched what would serve as a mess tent and garrison hall a goodly distance away. Jason emerged, rubbing his eyes, but looking none the worse for the wear. Robin beckoned to him. Jason looked about him, then dashed for their tent.

"Well?" Robin asked. "Any movement?"

"None, my lord," Jason said. "The men have been taking watches all night and nothing unusual occurred."

"And all are still accounted for?"

"Aye, my lord." Jason made Anne a bow. "My lady."

"My lord Ayre," she said in return.

Jason looked at Robin and smiled hesitantly. "You passed the night well, my lord?"

Robin snorted, put his hand on the back of Jason's neck and shook him. " 'Tis no affair of yours, my lad, but aye, we survived."

"The lady Anne looks lovely this morn," Jason said.

Robin looked at her and tried to frown. Her hair, which was ever tidy, looked as if she'd rolled from her bed without thought of comb or braid. Perhaps that came from his burying his hands in it too often.

And then there was her mouth, which looked as if it had been kissed thoroughly—and more than just once, at that.

Indeed, if Robin had to tell the tale true, it looked as if the woman had been thoroughly bedded the night before and had just risen to stretch before returning for more of the same.

And that was enough to make him seriously consider a small nap. After all, 'twas his duty to see his marriage well consummated.

"—justice rolls?"

"Eh?" Robin asked, realizing that Jason was talking to him. "What was that?"

"The justice rolls," Jason said again, looking at Robin with wide eyes. "Do you want them, my lord?"

He could think of several things he wanted much more than scribblings from his day of dispensing justice, but perhaps 'twas best he be about his business whilst he had the wits to concentrate on it. Besides, the sooner he managed to unravel the mystery of the note, the sooner he could pack up his gear and return to his father's bedchamber and his father's soft, comfortable goose-feather mattress.

And that left him looking at Anne purposefully.

"The rolls, my lord?" Jason said pointedly.

Damn the boy. Robin glared at his squire. "Fetch them," he growled. "I'll look them over right away."

Jason bolted and Anne laughed. Robin turned his glare on her. "Something amuses you?"

"You look at me as if I'm a tasty leg of mutton you've a mind to gnaw on."

" 'Tis a compliment," he said archly.

She smiled up at him. "I know. And I would kiss you for it, but your squire returns."

"So?"

"You've a reputation to maintain, my lord."

"It is but my squire."

"There is that," she agreed.

"Now, were it my captain, or another nobleman," he said slowly, "*then* I would no doubt be forced to forgo such sweet attentions until a more appropriate time."

"But it is just Jason," she said.

"He can be intimidated." He lifted one eyebrow. "Well?"

She wrapped her arms around his neck, stood on her toes and kissed him full on the mouth. Robin made a grab for her before she could pull away, and clutched her to him. And then he wondered at his own stupidity, for though it might have just been his squire gaping at him, there was his own distraction to worry about.

"No more," he gasped, when she pulled away. "By the saints, my mind is mush."

Anne only smiled serenely. "Poor lad. Shall I sit by you and aid you?"

"The saints preserve me," he said with feeling. "Jason, I hope you brought wine. Cold wine. Cold something. Quickly."

Anne laughed and Robin smiled at the sound. He stole a look at his lady and couldn't help the lightening of his heart either. She was beautiful and content and he could scarce believe he'd been fool enough to have let so long pass before he wed her.

At least he was a fool no longer.

He could only hope he would live long enough to enjoy that.

And it was with that thought that he set to work pouring through the scribe's notes, looking for something amiss. Jason fed the fire and Anne read over his shoulder. And he thought he might expire from the tedium of it all. He simply could not believe that disputes over livestock and water could anger a man enough to drive him to murder of his liege-lord.

Though he supposed he'd seen men murdered for less.

Indeed, he'd fought for men who had less reason for war than that. It was entirely possible that he had angered someone during his day of sitting in his father's chair. But he couldn't believe he could have inspired murder.

Though he'd certainly inspired the like in Maude of Canfield.

He shuddered and pushed himself to his feet. He needed to pace and whilst he could not go far, he could at least roam about the fire for a bit and see if that didn't provide him better answers than sitting idle.

Maude had wanted Anne dead, and he could almost understand that. Even when he'd looked on Maude with a bit of favor, he'd wondered if there was something amiss in her mind. He'd feared she would call their marriage banns herself after the first time he'd shared a trencher with her. But for her to ensconce herself in Artane as a servant for the sole purpose of harming Anne?

Unlikely.

It had to be someone else, someone with enough wits to plan a murder. Robin began to wonder if Maude had been but a pawn in the fiend's scheme. But that would mean that the true murderer had known of his association with Maude.

Which meant it had to be someone who had at least visited Canfield.

Or someone who had overheard gossip at Artane.

Robin paused and looked down at his lady. She sat near the fire with her lame leg stretched out before her and the other knee bent so she could rest her chin atop it. Her hair glinted in the sunlight as it lay spread about her shoulders. The light also caressed her fair skin, coloring its paleness with a golden hue. Robin felt his heart clench within him. He couldn't lose her. There was a part of him that almost wished he'd never had her, either in his bed or in his heart. He certainly could have spared himself grief that way.

Ah, but what he would have missed. He walked over to her, then knelt before her. He looked into her pale green eyes and couldn't stop himself from leaning forward and kissing her softly.

"I love you," he whispered. "By the saints, Anne, I vow I do."

She reached up and touched his cheek, her eyes full of tears. "I love you as well," she said quietly. "So much, it almost pains me to look at you."

"Then we are both in sorry shape, lady, for those are my thoughts exactly."

"Then what shall we do?" she asked wistfully.

"We shall live," he said. "Very long lives."

"I hope so," she said. "I hope so."

Robin looked at her a moment longer, memorizing her smile and the love he saw in her eyes. Then he rose and looked for his squire. The sooner he was about his work, the sooner he would solve his mystery.

But when he saw Jason and who accompanied him, he began to wonder if the solving might come sooner than later.

"Who," Robin said curtly as Jason came to a halt before him, "is this with you?"

"Reynaud of Agin," the man said with a low bow. "Lately of Segrave, thanks to the lady Joanna's generosity."

One of his grandmother's peacocks. Perfect. And Robin suspected he was the one who had been in charge of the pointy-toed shoes. It was hard to tell one from another, but Robin had seen more of this dolt than he'd cared to.

"I bring word from said lady," Reynaud said, with another bow. "Here."

A scroll was presented with a flourish. Robin read it quickly, scowled and looked up into the sky. He noted that it was blue, which was odd for the time of year. Usually the coast was wreathed in fog, but he wasn't ungrateful for a bit of sunshine.

Fog could, of course, easily hide an assassin.

Robin made a decision. He shoved the scroll at Reynaud.

"Tell her I agree," he said shortly.

"As you will, my lord," the man said with an expansive bow that almost caused him to impale an eye on his own ridiculous footgear. "I'll return immediately."

"Do that," Robin suggested. He watched until the man had summited the last rise of sand before he turned and went to sit next to his wife.

"Well?" she asked.

"My grandmother has a plan."

"Of course she does."

"It includes dancing."

Anne laughed. "Of course it does."

He scowled at her. "I'm not certain I like it."

"I could expect nothing less from you."

"She thinks to invite the surrounding nobles to a celebration in our honor."

"And will she interrogate them at the hall door, or invite them to the dungeon where she may use the hot irons?" Anne asked politely.

Robin grunted. "The saints preserve us."

"It might work."

"It might end both our lives."

"Teach me to use a knife," Anne suggested.

He looked at her and wondered if he could possibly do such a thing. Sweet Anne with a knife in her hand? He shook his head. Now, his sister was very handy with several lengths of blade and he had no trouble envisioning her plunging any number of said blades into any number of assailants. But Amanda had a steely side to her he could not credit Anne with.

"I can do it," she added.

Robin looked at her a bit longer and considered. Perhaps he misjudged her. She certainly looked determined enough. And he could see the advantages of her at least knowing enough to protect herself.

"Could you kill?" he asked softly.

She returned his look unflinchingly. "If it meant protecting you. Or a child. Aye, I could."

"You could not hesitate," he warned. "Hesitate and you would be lost."

"Teach me."

"I don't want to."

"But you need to."

He moved as close to her as he possibly could, then put his arm around her shoulders. It wasn't enough. He carefully lifted her into his lap and wrapped both arms around her. He closed his eyes and buried his face in her hair.

"Ah, Anne," he whispered. "I don't know how—"

"You'll manage," she said. "I'll help you."

He held her until the harshness of the idea trickled out of his soul. The waves rolled in one after another and the sound of it soothed him until he almost managed to think about it without wincing. And when he thought he could speak again, he sighed.

"Very well," he said wearily.

Anne pulled back and smiled at him. "You sound tired, my lord."

He managed a half smile. "Think you I could do with a rest?"

"A true rest, Robin," she said gently. "Put your head in my lap and sleep for a bit. I'll keep watch."

"I'll not lose you, Anne. I vow I won't."

"Rest, Robin."

"For a moment or two," he conceded.

He made her comfortable, then stretched out and put his head in her lap. His drawn sword lay by his side under his hand. He closed his eyes and sighed. He wouldn't sleep, but he would rest. He smiled faintly.

"A rest will likely serve me," he said quietly.

"Will it?"

"With any luck, my labors during the night will again be very heavy."

"Taxing," she agreed. "Surely."

He opened one eye. "Think you?"

She closed his eye with her hand, but not before he saw

her dry smile. "I think a great many things about your labors, my lord, but some of them I'll save for later. You would not sleep did I tell you of them now."

"I pleased you."

"Aye, Robin. You did."

He took her hand and held it between both his own.

And he counted the hours until he could again use something besides mere words to tell his lady wife just how deeply he loved her.

And perhaps whilst he was about his work, he would remind himself just how far he was willing to go to keep her safe.

He pitied the fool who had raised a sword against them.

41

Anne stood with her back to the hearth and forced herself to keep her hands down by her sides. That in itself was something of a battle. There was, of course, the pleasure of actually warming her hands against a blaze that had the might to restore some bit of warmth to her fingers. Though she certainly had not lacked for heat during the nights of the past se'nnight, the days had taken their toll.

Then there was the matter of the blade strapped to her forearm, under her sleeve where no one would mark it.

She felt decidedly, and uncomfortably, like a mercenary.

And a very unskilled one at that.

There was some comfort, though, in having Robin standing immediately at her left. He had told her repeatedly that he would not leave her side and should they be attacked, he could readily defend them both. She knew she should have taken comfort in that. After all, he was a swordsman without peer.

But even Robin couldn't see a crossbow bolt coming at them from across the hall.

She closed her eyes and prayed briefly for safety. Perhaps St. Christopher had been attending her devotions at his feet all those years and Robin would survive the eve intact. And once everyone retreated to their beds, she and Robin would retreat to the priest's chamber. The man hadn't been overly enthusiastic about the idea, but Robin had ignored his hesitancy. Robin had been adamant they would not find themselves trapped inside his sire's chamber.

"Anne, you remember Lord MacTavish, do you not?" Robin said pleasantly. "Arrived just this moment from his hall in the north."

One of Rhys's most troublesome neighbors, Anne noted as she smiled and nodded.

"A pleasure, my lord."

MacTavish grunted. "Best get a babe soon," he said curtly. "Artane's an old man."

And with that, he stomped off, bellowing for drink.

"Well," Robin said under his breath, "we can remove him from our list of suspects."

"Too obvious?"

"Too gluttonous. He already had sauce on his shirt. I doubt he'd interrupt his supper long enough for murder."

Anne smiled and shifted. As she did so, the weight of the blade against her arm caught her attention and sobered her instantly. By the saints, this was no matter for jesting. She had little doubt that the murderer would come, to prove his prowess if nothing else. How could she possibly expect to protect herself with a knife stuck up her sleeve? She could scarce draw it without trembling. Perhaps Robin had it aright; she likely couldn't kill. She would hesitate, and then all would be lost.

As if he knew her thoughts, Robin put his arm around her and gave her a firm squeeze. He looked down at her gravely, but said no word. Anne took a deep breath, put her shoulders back and nodded.

She would do what she had to if the time came.

Robin leaned over and put his mouth next to her ear. "I've plans for you."

"Do you?" she murmured.

"Later. We'll stuff a bit of cloth in the priest's ears. No sense in upsetting the man."

That he believed there would indeed be a later was reassuring. And even though she knew he was making light to ease her, she couldn't help a pang of sorrow over what she stood to lose.

To have Robin for so short a time, then have him taken from her?

And should they survive this, she would never survive it if he went off to war again.

"Stop thinking," Robin whispered. " 'Tis deafening."

"As you will, my lord."

"We've frillies about, my lady, listening and remembering. There are guards aplenty. Even my grandmother carries a very sharp needle or two and the saints only know what else. All will be well."

She looked up at him and tried to smile. "You'll not leave my side?"

"Not for a moment," he promised.

"I would be hard-pressed to guard your back otherwise."

He gave her a half smile, but she saw in his eyes that he was relieved at her words. There was love there too, in his glance, and she promised herself a goodly amount of time to contemplate that mystery once the assassin was caught and dealt with.

Joanna crossed the floor of the great hall, several of her lads in tow. She kissed Anne, then looked up at Robin.

"It would seem that all our guests have arrived, grandson. Shall we begin the celebration?"

"With some bit of talk?" Robin asked grimly.

"Of course. The lord must welcome his guests."

Robin looked as if he'd been commanded to clean the cesspit single-handedly. He sighed deeply, took Anne's hand and led her to the lord's table. Anne forced herself not to look behind them anxiously. Robin's captain and two other of his guardsmen were there, as well as Jason. Indeed, the entire great hall was ringed by either Robin's men or Joanna's, though the latter were certainly more recognizable in their brightly colored clothing.

"Honored guests," Robin said loudly, raising his cup in salute, "I bid you welcome to the celebration of my wedding. Eat your fill, drink until you're sated, and enjoy the fine minstrels who wish nothing more than to please your ears."

Anne watched him and realized that he hadn't tasted his wine. Perhaps others might have believed it, for he brought the cup to his lips, but he did not drink.

And then Robin began to talk to those around him. Indeed, he talked so much, he had no time to eat. Anne watched him cast a bit of everything placed before them to the dogs. When none fell to the floor in a fit, she reached for some supper.

Robin caught her hand and held it in both his own, continuing to speak to the lord next to him.

Perhaps he feared a slow poison.

She wondered if she would survive the night without something to eat.

"Bread," Joanna said from her right. "Perfectly delicious and beneficial."

Anne looked at her gratefully. "Nothing added?"

"None. My cook confirms it."

She didn't need to hear more. It was a poor meal when compared to the feast before them, but at least she wouldn't die from the enjoyment of it.

She sincerely hoped she could say the same for the dancing.

The minstrels performed throughout the meal, but when they truly began to play with enthusiasm, Anne knew the time had come for her and Robin to present themselves to the guests. Joanna had informed them that 'twas their duty to perform one dance by themselves for the company.

Men moved to the exits from the hall as Robin led her around the high table. The other tables had been pushed aside to allow room enough for movement. Robin looked

at her once as the music began and she knew he shared
her thoughts.

Let this not be our last.

Robin did not falter in his steps and she admired that
absently, storing up the memory to praise him for later.
Even with that, she sensed that his mind was elsewhere
and she decided that that too should be praised at her
earliest opportunity.

But no one moved.

No twang of a bowstring was heard above the lute.

No body launched itself over a table with blade bared.

Anne almost wondered if perhaps they had made a mistake. Could the missive have been a poor jest? She looked
about her. There was no one there from Canfield come to
avenge Maude's death. Not even Baldwin had returned to
torment them.

It was almost unsettling.

And then the dancing began in earnest.

Robin remained by her side despite the number of requests for his presence with some other nobleman's wife
or daughter. He demurred, he stalled and he pointedly
refused. Anne hoped he didn't offend half the countryside,
but she wasn't about to relinquish him so he could flatter
someone else.

The music stopped and she found herself facing her
lord. He took her hands and looked down at her solemnly.

"Safe so far," he said.

"Aye," she agreed. "Perhaps 'twas all a—"

And at that moment, 'twas as if the gates of Hell themselves had loosed a foul commotion.

There was a melee at the door to the great hall. Anne
lost count of the men who became embroiled in it. All
she knew was when the sea of bodies parted, three souls
stumbled out into the midst of the great hall and collapsed.

Nicholas, Amanda and Miles.

Robin grasped her hand and pulled. She stumbled several times as she struggled to keep up with his furious
strides. He knelt down next to his siblings.

"What befell you?" he demanded.

Amanda was crying so desperately, she couldn't speak. Neither Nicholas or Miles looked to be capable of answers either. They looked as if they'd just escaped a war. All three were covered with blood and it looked as if a good deal of that blood was their own.

"Robin," Anne said, tugging on Robin's sleeve, "they need care. I'll take them to Master Erneis."

He hesitated, then nodded. "I'll send my guard." He frowned deeply. "I should likely see to the settling of our guests."

"Aye," she said, "you should. Perhaps someone will reveal something in the confusion."

He took her hand and kissed it in his usual fashion. "I'll follow you as quickly as I can."

"I will be well. Watch your own back."

He nodded, then motioned to his men. Anne soon found herself surrounded again by his fierce lads and she felt a measure of relief in that.

It took a goodly amount of time to gather up the three wounded ones and herd them out to the healer's quarters. Anne saw them inside, leaving Robin's men without. There was no room for them and she suspected they might serve her better if they kept watch outside.

Nicholas's wounds were the gravest and Anne winced as she aided in stitching them closed. Amanda's sobs had subsided to mere trembling and sniffles. She sat at Nicholas's head, alternately wringing her hands and dragging her sleeve across her face.

"Just a scratch," Nicholas croaked.

Anne looked at Amanda. "What befell you?"

Amanda shook her head. "I cannot speak of it yet. See to Nicholas and tend him well."

Anne looked at Master Erneis and prayed he would manage the feat. She couldn't deny his skill, but she couldn't help either wishing for a bit of Berengaria's special potions that had ever worked so well. But Erneis was clever enough and 'twas a certainty he was used to wounds from a skirmish, so Anne felt somewhat relieved by that.

Then again, Sir Montgomery had been felled by a lesser wound than any of the ones Nicholas bore.

Anne pushed that thought aside.

She looked at Miles, who lay on a pallet, awaiting his turn patiently. Anne began to cut his tunic from him.

"Can you speak?" she asked.

"Always," he said with a weak smile.

"Then give me the tale. What happened?"

"Ruffians," he said with a cough. "They set upon us from the trees."

"What possessed you to leave the keep anyway?" Anne asked in surprise. "I thought you'd gone for a lengthy stay. And where were Nicky's guards?"

Miles groaned as she pulled cloth from under his back. "We rode ahead, leaving the men behind to bring our gear. And all was because of the missive you sent."

"We sent?" Anne asked.

"We assumed Robin had been in his cups when he wrote it," Amanda put in hollowly. "The scrawl was almost illegible."

"Many words . . . mis . . . spelled," Miles said, through gritted teeth.

"We sent no missive," Anne said in surprise.

Amanda looked at her and blinked for several moments in silence. "But," she said finally, "it said you needed us immediately."

"It was a lie," Anne said, feeling a chill go down her spine. "We never . . ."

She felt a breeze blow over the back of her neck.

As if someone had entered Master Erneis's inner chamber.

Anne jumped to her feet and spun around.

Edith of Sedgwick stood there, come from nowhere.

"I thought you would need aid," Edith said calmly.

But Anne saw much more than that in the woman's

eyes. Indeed, the coldness there sent shivers through her that she suspected no fire could warm.

She knew, she *knew* she was looking in the eyes of death.

Anne's mouth was completely dry. She tried to swallow, but 'twas futile.

"We could have used aid a handful of hours ago," Amanda said wearily.

Anne wanted to bid Amanda be silent, but she could form no words. All she could do was stare into Edith's eyes and see her own life extinguished there.

"Ruffians abound," Edith said, in that quiet, composed voice that made Anne want to scream. "Travel is very dangerous."

Miles snorted. "Deadly, I'd say."

"Deadly, then," Edith conceded with a shrug.

And then she slipped her hand inside her cloak. Anne watched in horror and realized that now was the time she should be reaching for her own dagger.

But she found, to her dismay, that she couldn't.

All she could do was stare death in the face and wait, powerless and terrified.

The door behind Edith opened and slammed shut. Booted feet stomped several times and a rubbing of hands followed.

"Bloody *frigid* place," Robin groused. "Excuse me, Edith. I should see how the little ones have fared."

Anne watched Edith remove her hand from under her cloak. Edith looked at Robin and smiled, a friendly smile that anyone would have been happy to receive.

"Your guards were kind enough to let me pass," Edith said. "I thought to be of some use, but apparently all is well here."

"My thanks," Robin said, patting her briefly on the shoulder. "You'll likely want to return to the hall. Take one of my men for your protection."

Anne wanted to blurt out that the man would be putting

his life in jeopardy, but all she could do was gape at Edith. Speech was beyond her.

Robin turned away to look over his siblings. Anne found herself facing Edith once more.

Edith smiled.

It was the most terrible thing Anne had ever seen.

"My lady," Edith whispered, then she turned and left the chamber.

Anne stood there and shook.

But once the door was closed, she turned and threw herself at Robin. He staggered in surprise, then regained his balance and pulled her close.

"What?" he asked, looking baffled. "What is it?"

"It's her," Anne hissed. She pointed back at the door. *"Her!"*

"Who?" he asked, blinking stupidly.

"Edith, you fool!"

He looked at her as if he'd never seen her before. "What are you babbling about, Anne?"

"Edith!" Anne whispered frantically. "She's the murderer!"

Robin's jaw slid down. "Surely you jest."

"I do nothing of the sort!"

"Anne, it's *Edith*," he said, as if her very name guaranteed her purity and goodness.

"She's behind it!"

He groaned and pulled her close, wrapping his arms around her. "Anne, I believe that you believe such a thing," he said quietly. "I believe you've had a hellish fortnight—"

"Which have no doubt seemed like a hellish pair of years with you as company—" Amanda put in.

Anne held onto her husband before he could pull away and retaliate.

"A hellish *fortnight*," he stressed, "and perhaps that has you overwrought."

"I am not overwrought."

He pulled back and looked down at her gravely. "Anne, what has Edith to gain by hurting me?"

"Maybe she just wants me dead so she can have you," Anne said, starting to shake.

"Why she'd want him is a mystery," Amanda muttered.

Robin looked heavenward and blew out his breath. And in that small gesture that he had made countless times over the course of his life, Anne found comfort. Robin was obviously digging deep inside himself for the patience to endure his sister's barbs. At least there was something still the same in a world where everything had just changed. It was almost enough to lead her to believe there might be hope for the righting of their lives. But that wouldn't come truly until Robin saw the truth she had seen.

"You're wrong," she said bluntly to him.

He scowled at her. Slowly, though, his scowl turned into a thoughtful frown. "What will you have me do?"

"Tell your guards not to let her in again."

He looked at her for a moment in silence, then nodded. "As you will, my lady. But I still cannot believe such evil of her."

"Time will tell," Anne said grimly.

Robin hugged her briefly. "Aye, it will. Now, let us unravel this tangle here." He kept his arm around her and turned to face his siblings. "The tale, if you please."

Anne soon found herself sitting on a stool while Robin paced and listened. But she could hardly concentrate. No matter what Robin thought, she knew what she had seen.

And she had seen her own failing in the face of that. She'd had a weapon, yet been powerless to use it. Perhaps 'twas time she enlisted Amanda's aid in the like. She suspected by the condition of her foster sister's clothes that defending herself with a blade or two had not been beyond her abilities. Anne herself could attest to Amanda's ready tongue and flat of hand, for Amanda had defended her honor many a time against pages who were cheeky enough to voice their insults.

"Where is the missive?" Robin asked.

Amanda produced a crumpled, bloody bit of paper and handed it to Robin. Robin smoothed it out and stared at it.

"I did not send this."

Miles laughed a half laugh. "I told Amanda you spelled with more skill than that, but she was convinced."

Robin scowled at his sister, then looked at his brother. "Who delivered it?"

"No one we knew."

"Then why did you believe it?"

Miles pointed to the back of the letter. "Your seal, brother."

Robin flashed a look at Anne, then looked back at his siblings. "Who set upon you?"

"Hired ruffians," Miles said promptly. "But a goodly amount of them. Perhaps a dozen."

"How many slain?"

"Eight, perhaps. Fortunately for us, Nick's guard arrived as we were almost overcome. The rest of our assailants fled as they heard the men approach." Miles smiled at Amanda. "Our sister was most fierce. I daresay they believed to find a swooning maid when they realized that her hose and tunic were a ruse. Instead they found themselves facing a mightily wielded dagger."

"Dispatch any?" Robin asked his sister.

She looked at him bleakly. "Aye. One."

Robin was silent a moment or two, then he crossed the chamber, bent down and put his arms around his sister.

"I'm sorry," he said quietly. "That never comes without a price."

Amanda looked as if she might burst into tears. Anne watched her take a deep breath and then let it out raggedly.

"Aye," she agreed. "It didn't."

Robin kissed her forehead, then rose and looked down at her. "You seem to have earned your share of marks."

Amanda managed a tremulous smile. "Apparently I

need more practice with a blade, for words certainly didn't defend me as well as they usually do."

Anne watched as Master Erneis turned his attentions to Amanda and realized that her fierceness had indeed not come without cost. Though her wounds were not grave, she did have a hurt or two that would require needle and thread. Perhaps skill with a blade came more dearly than Anne had counted.

"To continue our sorry tale," Miles said, taking a deep drink of the healer's draught, "after the rest fled, we gathered ourselves and the guard up and rode hard for the keep. 'Twas all we could do to get past your men." He looked at Robin. "I assume you've had further troubles?"

Robin produced his own note and handed it to his brother.

"What's it say?" Nicholas asked weakly.

"Someone has Rob's death on their minds," Miles said mildly. He looked at Nicholas and shrugged. "The usual."

Anne reached for Robin's hand, a single name burning in her mind.

"Anne, my love," he said, "Edith doesn't want me."

"You don't know that—"

"Her sire has suitors for her," Robin insisted.

"But you didn't see her—"

"She was likely as disturbed by these events as we are."

"I am unconvinced."

He sighed. "I will keep watch for her."

"And for Sedgwick as well," Miles put in. "He surely has no love for you."

"There are many who have no love for me," Robin said grimly. "And we've little to fear from Baldwin, as he hadn't deigned to grace us with his august presence of late."

Anne felt the entire chamber still. Even the healer ceased with his ministrations and looked up at Robin. They remained thusly for several moments, no one moving, no one scarce breathing.

"You don't think . . ." Miles whispered.

"It couldn't be," Amanda said, shaking her head.

"Well," Nicholas croaked, "the spelling of the note . . . was indeed dreadful."

Anne looked up at Robin in surprise. "Think you 'tis possible?"

"I think," he said slowly, "that any decision we make right now will be the wrong one. We've all suffered too many hurts of late to reason clearly." He looked at his siblings and managed something of a smile. "Rest this night and we'll think on the tangle tomorrow. I've no doubt things will look much clearer in the light of day."

"I doubt it," Miles said quietly. "But I could do with some rest. Unless you'd have me stand guard?"

"My guards are without. Nick's can be sent for. We'll be perfectly safe here."

"But what of your grandmother?" Anne asked. "And Jason? He was left inside to keep watch over her."

Robin hesitated. "She is not incautious."

"But she might not be looking in the right direction."

He sighed. "Very well. I'll have word sent to her."

"Better that you lock Edith in the dungeon," Anne said with a shiver.

"And then how are we to know if she's behind it?" Robin asked with a smile.

"The attacks would cease."

"Better that they continue," he said, suddenly looking very intent. "Aye, there is great sense in that. Perhaps we have been going about this in the wrong manner."

"How?" she asked. "By protecting ourselves?"

"Exactly," he said. "Perhaps I would do better to make myself an easy mark and see who comes to take me."

"You cannot be serious," she said.

"He is," Miles said. "Look at that fiendish light that has entered his eyes." He shook his head. "It never bodes well."

Anne looked up at her husband and saw that Miles had it aright. And she very much suspected that there would be absolutely nothing she could do to dissuade him from whatever witless plan he was brewing up in his head.

And if he intended to find himself dead on the morrow, there was naught she could do but hold on to him well that night. She pushed him toward the door.

"Send your grandmother's message," she commanded.

He blinked, then went to the door to do just that. Anne turned to her foster brothers and sister.

"You three rest."

There were three nods of varying degrees to answer her. Then she turned to Master Erneis.

"Have you a place Robin can rest in peace?" There were beds aplenty in the chamber they stood in, but there was no privacy to be had. And given that she had other things in mind for her husband besides sleep, those beds out in the open simply wouldn't do.

"Aye, my pallet in there," he said, pointing across the chamber. "You can draw the curtain if you wish to block out the light."

"You'll keep watch over my family?" Robin asked wearily. "Wake me if aught goes amiss."

"Aye to both, my lord."

Robin looked at him and shivered. "Forgive me, Master Erneis, but I've passed too much of my life in these chambers of yours. Know 'tis with great reluctance that I deprive you of your bed."

Anne pulled Robin along before he could think better of it.

Erneis's little chamber wasn't as luxuriously private as Robin's tent, but it would do. Anne pulled the curtain across and wrapped her arms around him. He looked down at her with a frown.

"No sleep?" he asked.

"Later."

He pulled her close to him and hugged her tightly. "All will be well, Anne. I vow it."

"But in case it isn't, come you here and endeavor not to make too much noise."

She felt him smile against her mouth.

"Ah, Anne, I do love you."

"Then show me," she said as she pulled him down to the pallet with her. " 'Tis the night, after all."

"And I do keep my promises."

"Then promise me you won't do anything foolish."

"I don't know if 'tis fair to wring a promise from a man whilst he is abed with his lady wife."

"Promise me, Robin," she said, pulling his head down to hers and kissing him thoroughly. "Promise me."

He only groaned in answer and she supposed that was assurance enough. She shuddered to think what he might have in mind, and she only hoped it wouldn't be foolhardy enough to end his life. For even though she couldn't have said who was behind the attack on Nicholas, Amanda and Miles, she had no doubts who had written the note Robin had found. But there was one thing she didn't understand, and it was the one thing that left doubt in her mind over her assumption.

Why would Edith want Artane?

And if she did want Artane, why would she want Robin dead?

"Anne, stop thinking," Robin whispered.

"I can't—"

"Aye, you can. Here, let me help you."

Well, she couldn't deny that he was persuasive and very distracting. And perhaps Robin had it aright and things would look clearer in the morning. There was no sense in not making best use of the night while she had it.

42

Five days later Robin stood on the steps leading up to the great hall and chafed at the sight greeting his eyes. It had taken him this long to politely invite all his guests to leave, and that had been accomplished only after several days of expensive entertainment and sustenance. He'd even gone so far as to have a private little bit of jousting for their enjoyment, knowing full well 'twas outlawed save for tournaments the king might call for his own sport.

He'd never had a more unpleasant day on the field.

He had come to realize that there was much more to being lord of a keep than he'd suspected before and it had mostly to do with endeavoring not to humiliate his potential allies in the lists. He had, of course, come away the victor in the end, for he would not fail just to appease someone else's pride, but it had been an exhausting bit of exercise, for he'd dragged each and every match he'd been party to out far longer than he would have liked.

And then there was having to continually keep half his attention focused on Anne and his grandmother in the stands.

Not to mention looking out for himself so he didn't find the addition of an arrow lodged between his ribs.

So it was with great enthusiasm and relief that he had watched the last of his neighbors depart through the front gates. If he could only move his grandmother and her entourage along with the same alacrity, he might be able to turn his attentions back to his original plan.

Becoming easy prey.

He felt a hand slip into his and he didn't even have to look to see who it was. He smiled in spite of himself. By the saints, what he had almost missed through his own stubbornness.

"I don't suppose it will serve me to tell you yet again that I do not like this."

He looked at his lady and felt his heart ache within. It seemed he couldn't look at her anymore without immediately wondering how it would be to lose her.

Or to lose himself and thereby never have her again.

"You can tell me," he said calmly, "but nay, it will not serve you."

"Bloody stubborn man."

He winced at the genuine worry in her eyes. "Anne, what else can I do?"

She sighed. "Nothing other than this."

"I will be careful."

She held up her arm and he could see the blade inside her sleeve. "I could guard your back."

"Let us pray you will have no need, but I would be glad of it just the same."

Though after having seen what killing a man, albeit in defense, had done to his sister, Robin wasn't at all sure he wanted Anne anywhere near a murderer. Amanda was still trembling almost a se'nnight later.

He stared out over the courtyard and wondered a great many things. Who could have put his seal on a missive without his having noticed it?

Unless it was his father's seal.

Robin turned that thought over in his head. He doubted his sire would have left such a thing behind, but 'twas possible. It was also possible it could have been removed from his sire's solar at any point over the last fortnight, by any number of people.

Baldwin, for instance.

But why would Baldwin want to hurt Robin's family? Before he could give that more thought, his own words came back to him with the force of a dozen fists.

How is it best to wound a man? Strike first at what he loves best.

He blew out his breath slowly. Perhaps Baldwin was behind the attack. Robin was beginning to believe it more all the time. Baldwin had, after all, been absent for over a fortnight, he would have had ample time to filch something from Rhys's solar and he certainly had no love for Nicholas or Miles. And 'twas also a certainty that Baldwin couldn't spell to spare his own life. Robin would have been surprised if the man could have signed his own name.

Why he would have wanted to injure Amanda was a mystery, but hadn't Miles said the ruffians had been surprised to find her there? Perhaps Baldwin had wanted to slay Robin's brothers and keep Amanda for himself.

Which certainly would have guaranteed him Artane in time.

Assuming Amanda wouldn't have murdered him in his own bed.

Aye, Robin thought with a nod, 'twas entirely possible that Baldwin was behind the entire thing. He could have had Robin's note written by someone else and slipped into the foodstuffs at precisely the right moment. He would have been away from the keep at the time, which would have removed suspicion from him.

The more Robin thought about it, the easier the thought rested with him. He could understand Baldwin's motives, indeed he could sympathize with him. It would have chafed Baldwin sorely to have had Robin as his liege-lord, and that only if Baldwin had survived his uncle and his uncle's infant son. And Sedgwick's liege-lord was precisely what Robin would become on his father's death. Not that Robin wanted Sedgwick, but it was his, after all. Baldwin had nothing. Why not seek for Artane itself if he were planning on a little murder?

The door opened behind him and Robin spun, his blade halfway from its sheath. His grandmother held up her hands in surrender.

"Only me, love, come to bid you farewell. If you're certain—"

"I am," Robin said quickly, replacing his sword. "Lovely to see you, Grandmère. Have a pleasant journey home."

Joanna pursed her lips and frowned at him, then turned to Anne. His wife at least received a sunny smile.

"I'm so pleased to see you so well settled, my love," she said, giving Anne a kiss. "I wish you good fortune of this one. A little more polish and he'll be quite presentable."

"Goodbye, Grandmère," Robin said pointedly.

Anne only laughed as Joanna flicked Robin smartly on the ear before she descended the steps. Her lads made her comfortable in a spacious wagon, then the company set off—not as quickly as Robin would have liked, but they did leave eventually. And once they were gone, Robin turned to Anne.

"I'm going to the lists."

"I'll come."

He hesitated. "I would rather see you safely guarded inside."

"I'm sure you would," she said, but she didn't move. "Anne . . ."

"Robin, I'm not leaving you alone." She looked up at him and there were tears welling up in her eyes. "Think you I could bear a single day without you?" she asked. "Have you thought of that?"

"Continually," he said, pulling her close and wrapping his arms around her. "Every moment of every day, that is the thought that haunts me and breaks my heart." He squeezed her gently, then pulled back far enough to look down at her seriously. "But I want an entire lifetime with you, Anne. We'll not have that unless I end this. Today."

"I'm coming with you."

He hesitated, then relented. "You'll sit by the wall. With my guards—"

"No guards."

He blinked. "But—"

"You said yourself it wouldn't serve you to have guards. I'll not need them either."

"But—"

"Robin, how else will anyone come against you?"

He knew she was right, but he could hardly stomach the thought of her sitting half a field away from him without anyone near her. As fond as she was of her little blade, he knew it would scarce serve her if someone came at her truly.

But surely Baldwin wouldn't have a go at Anne if Robin were there, standing mostly empty-handed. He had seriously considered leaving his sword behind as well. It would be just too tempting a target for Sedgwick to resist.

Robin took Anne's face in his hands, kissed her softly, then took her hand.

"Come along, then," he said. "Let us have this finished."

He slowed his pace down the steps to hers almost without thinking. But it was something else he could certainly repay Baldwin for, for it had been Baldwin to dare her to ride that stallion in her youth. Robin set his jaw. Baldwin would have no more power to work any more harm in their lives. Robin would see to that himself.

The short journey to the lists seemed to take nothing less than an eternity. With every step, Robin wondered if it would be the last he'd take with his love. By the time he had reached the inner bailey wall, he realized how useless such thoughts were to him. He would either survive or he wouldn't. Brooding about it wouldn't change anything.

Best, then, that he not fail.

He paused at a little bench set against the wall. He looked down at his lady, saw the weak sun glinting on her fair hair and her pale visage as she lifted it to him. He took her in his arms and kissed her with all the passion he had in him, so that she might never forget just how deeply he loved her.

"I will not fail us," he said hoarsely. "Anne, I vow it with my life."

She only shook her head and clutched him tightly to her. And then, just as suddenly, she stepped away from him.

"I'll be waiting for you," she said quietly.

Robin nodded and unbuckled his swordbelt.

"Robin," she gasped.

He drew the blade and handed it to her, then dropped the scabbard onto the bench. He smiled gamely.

"If I'm to be prey, may as well be easy prey."

"Robin, nay—"

"Think you I am only skilled with a blade?" he asked.

"You are skilled with many things, my lord," she said briskly, "but no doubt your sword might serve you?"

"I'll return for it." He sat her—and rather unwilling she was about it—on the bench, stepped back and made her a low bow. "Until later, my lady."

He took one last look at her, gingerly holding his sword over her knees with her hand on its hilt, and prayed he wasn't making the biggest mistake of his life, leaving her there alone. For himself, he couldn't think of anything more sensible. If Baldwin were truly behind all this, then seeing Robin in such a defenseless position would be too much temptation to resist.

And so Robin turned and walked out to the middle of the lists. He turned, faced the road that led between the inner and outer gates and folded his arms across his chest.

And he waited.

There was no movement and very little sound. Perhaps things seemed quiet after such commotion over the past few days. Robin had instructed the outer guards to let no one who did not belong to the keep to enter and no one at all to leave. That way if Baldwin did return, he would be let pass and would no doubt quickly come to the lists to take his pleasure.

And if it were someone from within the keep, they would be hard-pressed to bolt.

He continued to wait.

He looked over at Anne. She had taken his sword and propped it up against the bench. Perhaps she tired of the delay. He couldn't blame her. He was half tempted to sit down and have a little rest himself.

And then he saw movement near the gates.

Baldwin of Sedgwick.

Robin smiled. Perhaps this would go as he planned after all. He tapped his foot impatiently and watched his cousin hesitate. Robin held wide his arms to show he bore no weapon.

Baldwin, as expected, took the bait. He turned his horse and walked it across the lists. He came to a halt some thirty paces away. Robin didn't wait for him to speak.

"Finished with your labors at Wyckham?" Robin asked pleasantly.

Baldwin's jaw went slack and that told Robin immediately all he needed to know. Baldwin shut his mouth with a snap and scowled.

"I was on an errand—"

"To procure ruffians?" Robin smiled politely. "I understand my sister dispatched one of them quite handily. Best scout a little harder next time for mercenaries, cousin. Those don't look to have earned their gold."

Baldwin's mouth worked for several moments, but he seemed incapable of producing intelligent speech. Then he gathered his wits about him.

"You whoreson," he spat.

Robin only smiled. "My mother was not a whore, my lad. I wouldn't want to hazard a guess about yours, however."

Baldwin roared and spurred his horse forward. Robin sidestepped him and turned. Baldwin wheeled his mount around and looked at Robin, apparently weighing the benefits of making another pass. He made no move, however, so Robin could only assume he'd thought better of the impulse. Robin contemplated drawing the knife tucked in his belt. That might infuriate Baldwin enough to force him to act and who knew what sort of sport that might provide him with.

"My mother was a lady," Baldwin snarled. "And at least I know who my father was."

Robin blinked, then shrugged. It was obviously meant as an insult, but he couldn't for the life of him divine why he should be offended by it. He looked at his cousin who was currently drawing his sword with a great flourish, and wondered if he might have an answer or two before he dispatched the cretin.

"You wanted my siblings dead?" Robin asked.

"The lads," Baldwin said. "And you, of course."

"Of course. But my sister too? Passing unsporting of you, I'd say."

"I didn't want *her* dead," Baldwin said, sounding disgruntled. "Damned idiots didn't realize she was a she. I have other plans for her."

"You wouldn't survive the night in her bed," Robin assured him. "She's very handy with a blade."

"A woman can't wield a blade if she's been beaten enough," Baldwin said.

Robin couldn't even contemplate the like and he would be damned before he saw Amanda in the clutches of a wretch like the one facing him.

"Well," he said, "there's no need to worry about that, for you'll not get close enough to touch her, much less feel the bite of her blade." Robin cocked his head to one side and looked at Baldwin. "I am confused about one thing, though."

"More than that, I'd say," Baldwin snorted.

"Why Maude? Why Anne?"

"Maude was a sniveling twit," Baldwin said in disgust. "She was here to torment you until I could kill you."

"And she happened to dislike Anne?" Robin asked. "A little extra trouble for your trouble?"

"Aye," Baldwin said with a nod.

Robin was unsurprised. The only thing that did surprise him was the fact that he hadn't seen it from the start. The saints only knew where Baldwin had dredged Maude up from, but he could understand Baldwin's desire to make him miserable.

And damn him if it hadn't been quite effective.

But now it could be over and Robin could scarce wait to begin. He held open his arms. "Here I am, Baldwin. Do your worst and let's have this at an end."

Baldwin balked. "You have no sword."

"Don't need one."

Baldwin's expression darkened considerably. "I'll not fight you that way. There is no honor in it."

"Yet there is honor in poisoning a child," Robin said slowly. "And pushing a woman down the stairs."

"That was Maude's work. Mine is to kill you and I'll not do it unless you face me truly!"

Robin sighed. This was just his luck—to be fighting an imbecile with ideals. Robin wondered if it would be worth his time to return and fetch his sword, or if he should just take his knife and throw it through Baldwin's eye. Though it was tempting to do just that, he realized with a start that he found it just as unsporting as Baldwin likely would.

By the saints, he was losing his wits.

"Well," he said with a goodly bit of disappointment in his voice, "I had hoped you would find yourself with bollocks equal to taking me on, but if you've misplaced them—"

Baldwin charged. And as Robin flung himself out of Baldwin's way, he realized he'd found Baldwin's sore point. Apparently it wasn't his parentage, his sister or his honor. That it was what rested inside his hose shouldn't have come as much of a surprise.

Baldwin's horse seemingly had as little fondness for Robin as Baldwin did, for Robin found himself diving and rolling to avoid the slashing hooves. He heaved himself to his feet and flung his dagger before his own arrogance did him in.

His knife lodged in Baldwin's leg. Sedgwick leaned over to jerk it free at the precise moment his mount reared yet again. Baldwin went crashing to the ground. Robin stood there, sucking in air, and waited for his enemy to rise to his feet. Baldwin jerked Robin's knife free and threw it at him with all his strength. Robin heard the blade whistle past his ear and wondered if he might have given his cousin too little credit. He spotted his dagger and dove for it, feeling somewhat grateful he'd been cavalier enough to have left his mail behind, for the lack of it certainly aided him in quick movements.

He came up with his dagger in time to see Baldwin bearing down on him. Robin rolled aside as Baldwin's sword went ferociously point-down in the dirt.

"Nicely done," Robin said brightly. "Think you you'll ever manage to stick it in my flesh?"

Baldwin howled with fury and Robin barely made his feet before Baldwin was swinging his blade with mighty strokes. It was as Robin scarce avoided being decapitated that he began to contemplate the merits of perhaps returning to his lady for his blade. Baldwin dropped his sword suddenly and hunched over, gasping for breath.

"You aren't going to faint, are you?" Robin demanded.

Baldwin only waved him away.

Robin sighed. No sense in not taking advantage of Baldwin's generosity. He sighed and turned to retrieve his sword only to stop dead in his tracks.

It was at that precise moment that he realized he had made a terrible miscalculation.

Edith stood next to Anne some thirty paces behind him.

She had a knife to Anne's throat and Robin's sword in her other hand. Anne was so pale, Robin thought she might faint. She stood, still as stone. Edith glared at Baldwin.

"Finish him," she commanded.

"He doesn't have his sword," Baldwin wheezed. "I'll not do it unless I do it fairly."

And just when Robin thought things couldn't deteriorate any further, he looked behind Edith to see his siblings shuffling across the field. Perfect.

"Stop," he shouted. "Edith has a knife!"

The trio came to a teetering halt. Edith dragged Anne to the side so she could see both Robin and his siblings.

"Come no closer," she shouted. "I'll kill her if you do!" She looked at Robin and then threw his sword toward him. "There," she said. "Take your blade."

Robin looked at her, trying to judge her trustworthiness. As if having a blade across his love's neck wasn't indication enough of that! But he wasn't about to discount the aid his sword would provide him. He retrieved it carefully, then backed away slowly. He didn't dare look at Anne.

"Baldwin," Edith commanded. "Finish him."

Robin continued to back up until he had both Baldwin and Edith in his sights. Baldwin had apparently recovered his breath. He was scratching his head, scowling.

"I've been thinking," he began.

"The saints preserve us," Edith said with a sigh.

"What good will it do me to kill him?" he asked, pointing at Robin, "when Miles is Artane's son of the flesh? He's the one I should be doing in. Robin means nothing."

"Robin means everything!" Edith exclaimed. "Dispatch him, you half-wit!"

Baldwin continued to stare at her. "You really want me to kill him? I thought you wanted him for yourself."

"I want his keep," Edith said. "The grave can have him for all I care."

"I don't know why he matters anyway," Baldwin groused. "He's not Artane's son anyway."

"Baldwin, you imbecile," Edith said in disgust, "of *course* he's Artane's son. Have you not two good eyes in your head?" She pointed back at Robin's siblings. "Look you at Miles, then look at Robin. They could be demon twins for all they resemble each other! And look you at Nicholas. Artane's image, only with fair hair!"

Baldwin looked. Robin found himself looking as well. It was true Miles and Nicholas looked powerfully alike, save the color of the hair, but Robin had assumed it was because . . . well, he had no idea why. It had just been so.

"What are you saying?" Baldwin demanded. "That Robin is Rhys's son?"

Edith clapped her hand to her forehead. "Aye! Sired on Gwennelyn of Segrave. I overheard her speaking of it to Lord Rhys when first I came here."

Robin gaped at her and felt his sword slide down to rest point-down in the dirt. "You did?"

Edith glared at him, then slowly she began to smile. It was a very chilling smile. "Aye. Didn't you know? Ah, apparently not. Then allow me to share the truth. Rhys sired both you and Nicholas, apparently within hours of each other on the night before your mother wed with Alain of Ayre. Did you never wonder why Ayre wanted so little to do with you before his untimely demise? I daresay he couldn't stomach looking at you and seeing his enemy staring back at him through your eyes."

Robin could scarce believe it. He looked at Anne and found that even she was looking at him with compassion.

"You knew?" he asked hoarsely.

"I suspected."

Robin vowed three things in that moment. One, he would finish Baldwin. Two, he would rescue Anne and throw Edith in the dungeon. And three, when next he saw his sire, he would kill him.

With his dullest blade.

His sire. Robin snorted. The man deserved to be disemboweled in the most painful way possible.

He glared at Anne. "Think you *he* knows?"

"Doubtful," Anne managed. "Or it could be that he already thinks of you as his, so heredity doesn't mat—"

Edith pushed her blade against Anne's throat and she ceased speaking immediately.

"Enough," Edith snapped. "Baldwin, be about your business. Once he's dead, you've four more here to see to."

"I don't want to," Baldwin said. "Look you; he won't even raise his blade against me."

Robin wished for nothing more than ten minutes to stagger about the lists like a drunken man, reeling from the impact of what he'd just learned. Hadn't he always wondered why he and Nick looked so much alike? Hadn't he marveled that he and Miles resembled each other so greatly when they only shared a mother in common?

"Now!" Edith commanded.

Robin promised himself a good think later. For now, he had to finish Baldwin and free Anne, likely within the same moment. He suspected if he killed Baldwin and couldn't reach Anne within the same heartbeat, Edith would finish her with that blade across her beautiful white neck.

And the thought of that almost paralyzed him.

He turned to Baldwin. "Very well," he said, raising his blade. "I'll give you the fight you want."

"At least you'll die a man," Baldwin sneered.

"One could hope," Robin said with a sigh.

And then it was begun. Robin pushed aside thoughts of how much rested on what he did at present, of how many lives depended on his showing there. His sword hilt was slippery in his hands and his legs felt unsteady beneath him. And he had to admit that during the first few clashes of his blade against Baldwin's he thought he might not manage it. He found himself falling back and it wasn't a matter of strategy. His blade felt heavy and awkward. His mind was clouded with shock and dismay.

And his cousin was beginning to wear the look of contempt he'd worn during every encounter in Robin's youth.

And for a moment, Robin wondered if he would fail.

Their swords came together with a mighty clash, the blades slipped down until they were locked at the hilt. Baldwin's face was a hand's breadth from his. His breath almost knocked Robin over by itself.

"Pitiful whelp," Baldwin sneered. "Shall I leave you wallowing in the mud again?"

Robin felt the humiliation of that moment wash over him again as freshly as if it had just happened. He almost went down on his knees.

"Robin."

Anne's quiet voice carried across the field. Robin looked at her and saw the trust in her eyes. She was standing with a blade across her neck, her life resting on his performance, and still she could look at him as if she thought he couldn't fail.

Robin turned and looked at his cousin and as he did, he remembered who he was.

The best bloody swordsman on English soil.

After all, all that de Piaget blood was apparently flowing through his veins and his father was a bloody good swordsman himself.

Damn him to hell.

Robin shoved Baldwin away from him. "No mud for me today," Robin said simply. "As you can see, fool, the ground is dry. But I suppose I couldn't expect someone of your few wits to appreciate the difference."

Baldwin charged and Robin fended off his attack easily. Indeed, he wondered why he'd had so much trouble with Sedgwick in the first place. The man was nowhere near his equal.

"Make haste!" Edith exclaimed.

"I'm trying!" Baldwin bellowed, increasing the fury of his attack.

Robin clucked his tongue as he easily kept his cousin at bay. "I fear those clumsy strokes simply will not win the day for you. Perhaps if you had trained a bit harder in your youth."

"Finish him!" Edith shouted.

Baldwin turned and spat at his sister. Robin didn't waste any time with thoughts of a fair fight. Perhaps he could finish Baldwin quickly and that would cause Edith to at least drop her guard for a moment. That would be enough to rescue Anne. It would have to be enough.

He suspected it might be all he would have.

Robin stepped up behind Baldwin, ready to plunge his blade through Baldwin's heart when he turned.

Only Baldwin didn't turn.

Robin watched in amazement as Edith shoved Anne away from her and slapped her brother as hard as she could across his face. Then she jerked him around and pushed him toward Robin.

"Take him," she demanded.

Baldwin stumbled, thanks to another great push, then spun aside the moment before he would have skewered himself on Robin's uplifted blade.

Edith, however, was apparently not so graceful.

Robin watched in horror as she tripped and fell.

Full onto his sword.

It came thrusting out her back, through her dress, bloodred and glinting dully in the sunlight.

Robin released his sword before he knew that was what he intended. Edith lay facedown on the ground, unmoving. Robin knelt down next to her, then rolled her on her side. She looked up at him.

"I . . . wanted . . . Artane," she breathed.

Then her eyes stared at nothing.

"You bastard!" Baldwin roared.

Robin looked up in time to see Baldwin looming over him, his sword bared and raised. Robin realized with a sickening flash that he would not have time to pull his sword from Edith's body and wield it quickly enough to fend off Baldwin's attack, nor would his only other weapon—the pitiful dagger that found itself dropped somewhere behind him in the dirt—have been sufficient for the task.

And then Baldwin stopped. With his sword upraised, he turned in surprise. Robin leaped to his feet, looking about him frantically for his dagger.

But it was unnecessary.

Anne stood there, trembling but holding her ground. Baldwin looked at her, then his sword slipped from his hand. He slowly began to fall toward her. She jumped backward awkwardly in time to have him fall at her feet.

There was a blade buried to the hilt in his back.

Robin stepped over Edith's remains and dragged Anne a few paces away, then hauled her in his arms.

"Are you hurt?" he asked frantically.

She shook her head and clung to him, trembling.

"By the saints, a man could not ask for a finer woman to guard his back," Robin said, with feeling. "He would have killed me, else."

"M-my p-p-pleasure." Her teeth were chattering. "D-don't ask m-me to d-do it ag-gain."

He laughed in spite of himself. "Pray that we never have another need, lady, but 'twas very well done."

He stood there with his love in his arms and felt a great wave of relief wash over him. They were safe. He closed his eyes and rested his cheek atop Anne's head.

" 'Tis finished," he whispered.

Anne nodded. "Edith planned it, Robin. She told me as much."

"I should have listened to you."

"You should have listened to me about a great many things."

He pulled back and scowled down at her. "Did you truly know?"

"About your sire? Aye."

"And you didn't tell me?"

"Would you have listened?"

"Of course not," Robin said. He looked up as the rest of their little group shuffled over to them. He met Nicholas's gaze and received an answering look of irritation. "I'll kill him," Robin growled

"I'll help," Nicholas said. "Give me time to heal, so we may do a thorough job of it."

"Think you *he* knows?" Robin demanded of Anne. "And how is this possible?"

"The usual way, I suspect," Nicholas said dryly. "And if you don't know what that is, you're in more trouble than I thought."

"I know very well *how* 'twas accomplished," Robin snapped. "I just want to know for a certainty *when*."

"Hmmm," Nicholas said. "We might just discover that I am the eldest."

"Ha," Robin said, but the very thought of that pierced him to the quick. He looked at Nicholas. "Think you?"

"That would be a question for your father," Anne said. She was smiling, damn her. "Why don't you ask him?"

"I fully intend to," Robin growled.

She waited. "Well, go ahead."

He cursed her, but she only continued to smile.

"Go on," she said, pointing behind him. "There he is."

Robin turned around to see none other than Rhys de Piaget, the bloody bastard, standing behind him, looking rather green. Robin decided words could be had later in abundance, as well as questions as to why Rhys found himself at that very moment standing in Artane's bailey. Now was the time for action. He launched himself at his sire, determined to throttle the life from the man.

"You knew!" Robin bellowed, taking his father down to the dirt. "You *knew* and you never said anything!"

"Robin!" his mother exclaimed. "Release him!"

Robin clutched his sire about the throat and pounded his head against the dirt a time or two for good measure. "Damn you!" he shouted.

And then, quite suddenly, he found himself on his back with Rhys's substantial self pinning him there. Robin

snarled out a curse or two, but realized that his father—
damn him to hell a thousand times—was still every bit
his equal in size and strength.

And no wonder.

What with him being his sire and all.

Robin glared at his mother. "You knew as well!"

And damn *her* if she didn't look just as sheepish as her
husband.

"Why didn't you tell me!" Robin demanded. "Damn
you both!"

He had to curse, for he realized, with a start, that if he
didn't continue to snarl and bellow, he quite likely would
break down and sob. All the years he had spent cursing
the fact that he was Alain of Ayre's son and not Rhys de
Piaget's. All the times he had turned himself inside out
to prove he was worthy of being Rhys's adopted heir. All
that time and energy and effort. And for what?

Well, he had to concede that it had served him well,
but he'd be damned if he'd admit it.

Rhys rolled off him and hauled Robin to his feet. He
frowned.

"I wasn't sure—"

"*Merde*," Robin snarled.

"Very well," Rhys returned hotly, "I wanted it desperately and then by the time I was quite sure and I dared
discuss the matter with your mother, you were already my
heir anyway and what purpose would it have served?"

"I would have known I was yours!" Robin bellowed,
then he realized he sounded like a child of five summers.
He glared at his sire. "It would have been nice to have
known."

"It makes no difference," Rhys insisted.

"It makes a difference to me!"

"It makes you a bastard!" Rhys exclaimed, then he shut
his mouth with a snap and glared at Robin.

Robin felt his jaw slide down. And then he heard someone begin to laugh. He looked over at Nicholas and

watched as his brother shuffled over and flung his arm around Robin's shoulders.

"Ah," he said with a last weak chuckle, "what a special kinship we have, Rob. Bastards both."

"I should thrash the both of you for your cheek," Rhys said sternly. "This is hardly talk for the field."

Robin could only stare at first his sire—his true sire, no less—then at his mother.

"I am having the most difficult time taking this in," he said finally. He looked for his wife. "And you?"

Anne smiled as she came and stood at his other side and put her arm around his waist.

"I love you whatever and whoever you are."

Robin grunted, then looked at his mother. "You could have told me. And how was this accomplished? Do you not think I deserve to know?"

"We could discuss it inside," Rhys said pointedly.

"Nay," Robin said. "I was married with a corpse at my heels, I may as well learn my parentage with a pair of them cooling behind me. Please, give me the tale."

Rhys looked at Gwen. "Well, wife. Go ahead. Give him the tale."

"Coward," she said fondly.

He grunted, then put his arm around her. "I wed her in my heart the night before she was forced to marry Alain of Ayre."

"Are you certain he's the elder?" Nicholas asked pleasantly.

Robin elbowed his brother in the ribs. "Continue, if you please."

"Aye, I'm quite certain," Rhys said, glaring at Nicholas, "for unlike you two randy stallions, I was a virgin before I took my lady to my bed."

Robin gaped at his sire. "You weren't."

"I certainly was."

"How did you manage that?" Nicholas asked, in admiration.

"I loved Gwen from my youth and vowed if I could

not have her, I would have no one." He looked at Robin. "And so I made her mine. And then those bloody Fitzgeralds filled me full of drink and when next I woke, your mother was wed to another and I was abed with," he looked at Nicholas, "um, well, your dam. And I knew nothing more of her until she died and we found you."

"Well," Robin said, blinking.

"Aye," Nicholas said, sounding just as surprised.

"And I don't regret either," Rhys growled, "and if you care to face me over blades to satisfy yourselves, I'll be happy to oblige you."

"You could have told us," Nicholas pointed out. "I already knew I was a bastard."

Rhys shook his head. "I could not have loved you more, even if I had not sired either of you. I saw no point."

"And now we know?" Robin asked.

"Will you have the entire isle know you're a bastard?"

"That depends," Miles put in. "Do I inherit all now?"

Robin gaped at his brother until he realized Miles was not in earnest. Rhys only glared at his other son, then looked at Amanda. He sobered.

"I fear, daughter, that I have no such startling revelations for you."

Nicholas put his arm around Amanda and pulled her over to lean on her. "It looks as if you and I are the only ones unrelated, sister dear."

"The saints have looked on me kindly then," she said, scowling up at him.

Nicholas only laughed and kissed her forehead. "You love me and you know it well." He looked at his sire. "Well, if you've no more interesting tidbits for us, I'm returning to bed." He made Robin a shaky bow. "My gratitude, brother, for ridding the keep of our foul murderers. I'll hear the entire tale when I'm more myself. Amanda, let me lean on you and help me back to the healer's house. Too much excitement in one day has completely sapped my strength."

Robin watched his brother, his very real brother mind

you, slowly and painfully make his way back to the inner bailey. He looked at his mother to find her looking at him with something akin to compassion.

"Are you so very angry?" she asked quietly.

He sighed. "I'll survive it."

"We didn't think it would serve you."

Robin looked at his sire. "And you? What's your excuse?"

"I don't need an excuse. I'm your father and I can still thrash you on any field."

Robin found himself pulled suddenly into his sire's arms and crushed in an embrace from which he wasn't sure he would emerge intact.

"I'm proud you're mine," Rhys said hoarsely. "No matter how the deed came about in the beginning."

Robin slapped his father's back several times, then pulled away. "Then I may still stretch forth my greedy hands for all your lands and gold when you die?"

Rhys looked at Gwen. "This is your fault, this greed of his. I never had such lust for land."

"Ha," Gwen said, poking him firmly in the chest with her finger. " 'Tis a flaw that runs entirely in *your* family."

"Why are you home?" Robin interrupted.

"Thugs tried to slay me on a little outing," Rhys said. "I caught one, beat Sedgwick's name from him and we returned home as quickly as we could. Would have been here sooner if we hadn't been swarmed by your grandmother's bloody artistes."

"I didn't need aid," Robin said stiffly.

"Never thought you would," Rhys returned. "I just didn't want to miss out on a chance to watch you thrash Baldwin. If ever anyone deserved it, 'twas him."

"But Edith," Gwen said, with a shake of her head. "Tragic, truly."

"Not if you'd been here the past month," Robin said grimly. He looked at his sire. "Well, since you're here, Anne and I will be off."

"We will?" Anne asked.

"Aye," Robin said shortly. "To the shore."

"We're not staying," Rhys said.

"We aren't?" Gwen asked, sounding very unenthusiastic about another journey.

"Your mother requires our presence," Rhys said, sounding equally as unenthusiastic about another journey—especially if it seemed to include Segrave as a destination. "Once she learns of what we've just discussed—and I've no doubt she'll hear of it before we've a chance to tell her—I will never have another decent meal at her table. Besides," he said, reaching out to clap Robin on the shoulder, "my son is perfectly capable of seeing to my hall." He smiled at Gwen. "Think you?"

"Damn," Miles muttered. "So much for my inheriting everything."

Robin made a few gruff noises to cover something he couldn't identify as either relief of joy, then he embraced his father, embraced his mother and looked at his wife.

"I'm still for the shore, lady. What say you?"

"As you will," she said, but she looked as if the prospect didn't displease her.

Robin smiled his sunniest smile at her, then realized that he had more to do than run off without another thought. He turned and looked at the fallen siblings behind him. He shook his head, then went to pull his sword from Edith's body. He laid her on her back and closed her eyes. A shadow fell over him and he looked to find his sire kneeling across from him.

"A troubled girl," Rhys said quietly.

"She wanted Artane," Robin said. "Nothing but Artane."

"Can you blame her?" Rhys asked with a faint smile.

"I don't know that I'd kill for it," Robin answered with just as faint a smile. " 'Tis but a pile of stones, after all."

"Home is a different place entirely," Rhys agreed.

Robin looked at Anne and suddenly felt everything in his world shift. It settled into a peaceful, serene place and he knew without a doubt that as long as he had her by his side, the place most certainly didn't matter.

But she did love the shore.

And Artane was right there on the coast.

Robin clapped his father on the shoulder. "I'll take your keep, Papa," he said.

"And my gold, no doubt," Rhys groused.

"I won't spend it all whilst you're away."

"We aren't leaving quite yet," Rhys said. "I've a mind to talk to my steward and see what havoc you've wreaked. I understand there was a fair gathering here the past se'nnight. Is there perchance aught left in my larder?"

Robin rose. "I'll see you about it tomorrow. I've other business to attend to this day."

"Don't mind this," Rhys said dryly, gesturing expansively before him. "I'll see to it."

"Consider it a wedding gift to me," Robin said.

"I already gave you a bloody wedding gift and as you remember it was almost everything I have!"

"Damn," Miles grumbled loudly.

Robin smiled at his brother, gathered up his lady and began to make his way across the lists.

"They look happy," came his father's voice.

"Are they happy?" his mother asked from behind them.

"Aye, and their 'happiness' has ruined my sleep for almost a se'nnight," Miles complained loudly. "Let us be grateful they're making for Robin's tent where they won't keep the rest of us awake tonight."

Robin looked at Anne and felt himself begin to blush. "Sorry," he whispered.

She only put her arm around his waist and hugged him. "They'll survive it." She looked up at him and smiled. "Are you happy?"

"Deliriously. Giddy, even, now that I have the peace to enjoy it. And for that I thank you kindly."

" 'Twas nothing."

"Nay, my love, 'twas a very great thing requiring much skill and courage."

"You would have done the same for me. Indeed, I'll wager you were trying."

Robin shivered once. "It was a passing close thing, Anne. I about fell over in a faint when I saw her standing with her blade across your throat." He looked at her. "You may tell me again that I was wrong, if you like."

She shook her head with a smile. "I'll just savor it in silence."

He snorted, but couldn't help a smile. "I love you," he said as they made their way to the stables.

"And I you."

Robin walked up the way to the inner bailey with his lady wife at his side and smiled to himself. He could scarce believe that not two months earlier he had come home expecting to bolt from it the first chance he got.

Now it looked as if he might never have to leave. And as he listened to the distant roar of the waves and smelled the tang of sea air trickling through the bailey, he couldn't imagine anything else. He had a marvelous hall to watch over and a beautiful, courageous woman who loved it as much as he did. And she loved him as well. He looked at his lady wife and smiled.

Life without her? Never.

Eternity with her?

Aye, and then some.

He shook his head with a smile and continued on his way.

Epilogue

The woman stood at the door of the healer's house and stared out over the courtyard, eyeing the dirt and flat-laid stone. Her mind spun with the things she had learned that morn of herbs and such. She had found a goodly work to do, and an unexpected one at that. But it behooved her to learn a bit of healing, given that she was at least for the moment looked to as Artane's lady. It had been a morn of many surprises.

For she had learned yet another thing that would surely change her life's course.

She was to bear a child come spring.

She looked at the distance separating her from the great hall and, judging the distance to be not unmanageable, released the doorframe and carefully descended the steps to the stone path that led to the great hall.

The weak autumn sunlight glinted off her pale hair and off the gold embroidery adorning her dark green cloak. The latter was a gift from her love, for green was one of his preferred colors.

"How fares the fairest flower in Artane's garden this morn?"

The voice from behind her startled her, and she turned

quickly to look at who spoke. And then she smiled.

"I doubt I am the fairest flower in the garden," she said, but the saying of it did not pain her.

"You are the fairest flower in *my* garden," her lord said, putting his arm about her shoulders and pulling her close. "Is not my opinion the one that matters the most?"

She had no argument for that, so she merely smiled in reply and walked with him to the great hall. He matched his mounting of the steps to her pace, then opened the door for her with a low bow.

"After you, my lady."

"How gallant you are, my lord."

"You'll avoid letting on about that to anyone else, of course."

"Of course. Your reputation is at stake."

He merely grunted and saw her inside the hall.

And once there, Anne of Artane looked about her and felt a joy sweep through her that she was certain would never dim. There, clustered by the hearth, were the souls she loved best. All Artane's children were there, laughing and talking about things that pleased them. Missing were Artane's lord and lady, but that was nothing unusual these days. They had taken to traveling about and Anne couldn't begrudge them their freedom for a bit. They could be called back readily enough for the welcoming of their first grandchild.

She realized, as she stood with her hand in her husband's, that the scene before her would not always be as it was now. Nicholas would wed, as would Amanda and Isabelle. Miles would seek his own way and she suspected that even the little lads would find things to pull them away from home.

Home. Even the very word made her heart swell within her breast and forced tears to her eyes. It was more than she ever could have hoped for.

But should everyone in the scene before her leave, it would not diminish her happiness, nor make her any less content with her life. For her home was not before her, nor was it in the stones that surrounded her.

Her home was standing beside her, holding her hand under his cloak and wearing a gruff expression that belied the caressing of her fingers. Whatever else happened, whatever souls came and went from the keep, if Robin was beside her, she would still have that still, quiet place she had longed for the whole of her life.

"You're weeping again." Robin looked down at her and frowned.

"I'm happy."

He shook his head and pursed his lips. "I vow, my love, that I will never understand joy of that ilk. But if you're happy, then I cannot complain."

She suspected that he would understand it very well indeed someday, but she kept that to herself. This was not the place for tender conversings. She would save that discourse for the privacy of their own chamber. And then she would give him the tidings of his coming child and see if that didn't give him reason to weep a tear or two of joy.

But for now, the joy was hers and she would nestle it close to her heart and savor it. She turned and slipped her arms around Robin's waist and laid her head on his chest. She closed her eyes and sighed.

Strong arms came around her and a cheek came to rest gently on her head.

"Does something ail you, my love?"

"Nay," she whispered.

"And the reason for your sweet arms about me?"

She sighed and smiled. "No reason. Other than happiness because I'm home."

"Home," he repeated, and his arms tightened around her. "Aye, my love. You are there indeed."

Anne smiled.

Aye, she was there, indeed.

ROMANTIC ROOTS

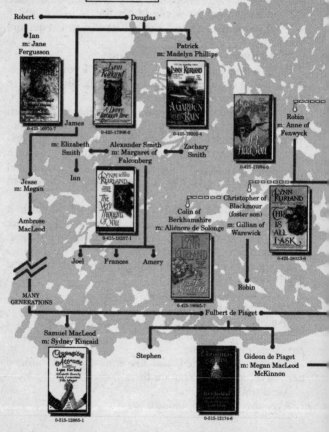

MACLEOD

Robert ● ──────────── Douglas

Ian
m: Jane Fergusson

Patrick
m: Madelyn Phillips

James

Robin
m: Anne of Fenwyck

m: Elizabeth Smith ── Alexander Smith
m: Margaret of Falconberg

Zachary Smith

Jesse
m: Megan

Ian

Christopher of Blackmour (foster son)
m: Gillian of Warewick

Colin of Berkhamshire
m: Aliénore de Solonge

Ambrose MacLeod

Joel   Frances   Amery

Robin

MANY GENERATIONS

Fulbert de Piaget ●

Samuel MacLeod
m: Sydney Kincaid

Stephen

Gideon de Piaget
m: Megan MacLeod McKinnon

0-425-16970-7
0-425-17906-0
0-425-19202-4
0-425-17094-0
0-425-18297-1
0-425-18033-6
0-425-19985-7
0-515-12865-1
0-515-12174-6

DE PIAGET

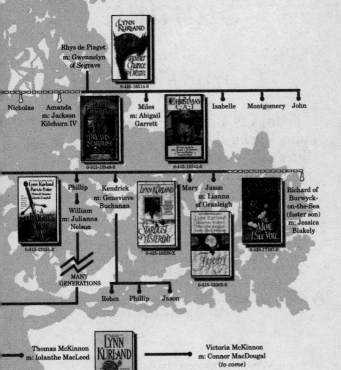

Rhys de Piaget
m: Gwennelyn
of Segrave

0-425-16514-0

| Nicholas | Amanda m: Jackson Kilchurn IV | | Miles m: Abigail Garrett | | Isabelle | Montgomery | John |

0-515-13948-3   0-425-16542-6

Phillip   Kendrick m: Genevieve Buchanan   Mary   Jason m: Lianna of Grasleigh   Richard of Burwyck-on-the-Sea (foster son) m: Jessica Blakely

William m: Julianna Nelson

0-515-13151-2   0-425-18238-X   0-515-13362-0   0-425-17107-8

MANY GENERATIONS

Robin   Phillip   Jason

Thomas McKinnon
m: Iolanthe MacLeod   Victoria McKinnon
m: Connor MacDougal
(to come)

0-425-18197-9